JUSTICE LEAGUE UNLIMITED

The Ties That Bind

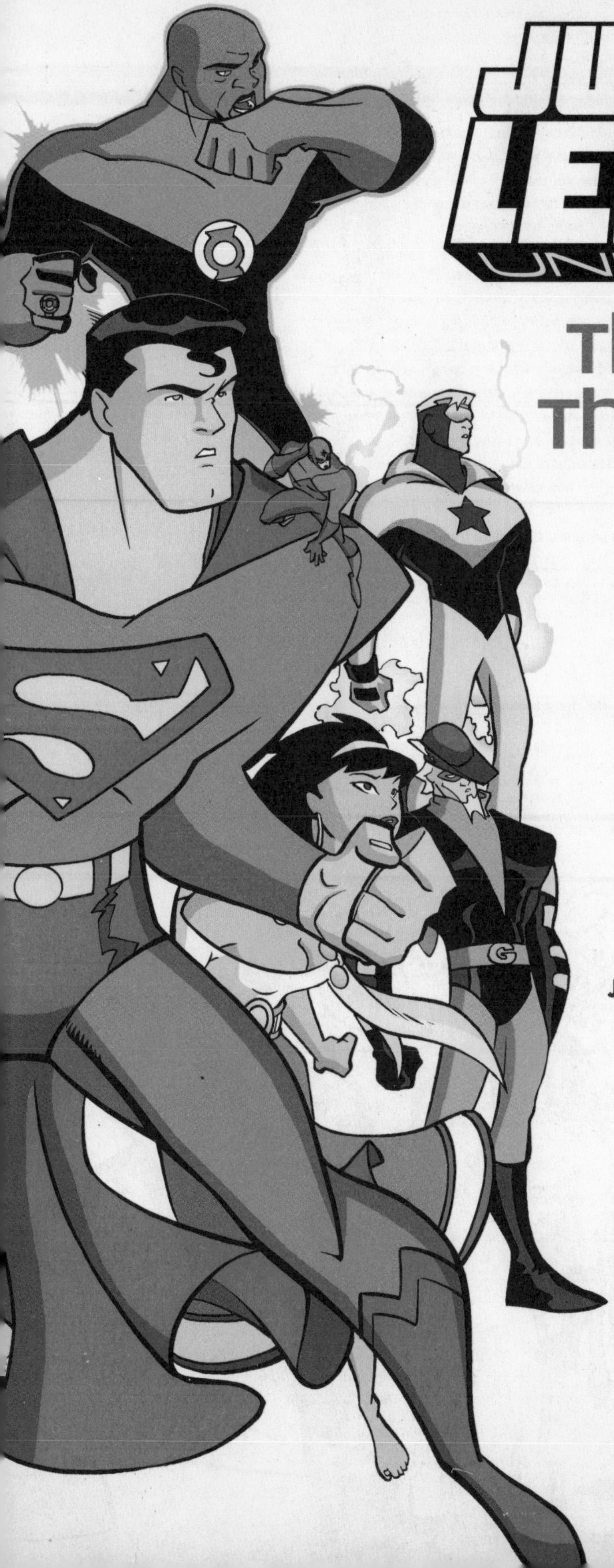

WRITTEN BY
ADAM BEECHEN
PAUL D. STORRIE

ILLUSTRATED BY
CARLO BARBERI
RICK BURCHETT
ETHEN BEAVERS
GORDON PURCELL
JIM ROYAL
LARY STUCKER
BOB PETRECCA
JESSE DELPERDANG

COLORED BY
HEROIC AGE

LETTERED BY
TRAVIS LANHAM
PHIL BALSMAN
ROB LEIGH

JUSTICE LEAGUE UNLIMITED: THE TIES THAT BIND

DC Comics
1700 Broadway, New York, NY 10019
A Warner Bros. Entertainment Company.
Printed in Canada. First Printing.

ISBN: 978-1-4012-1691-7

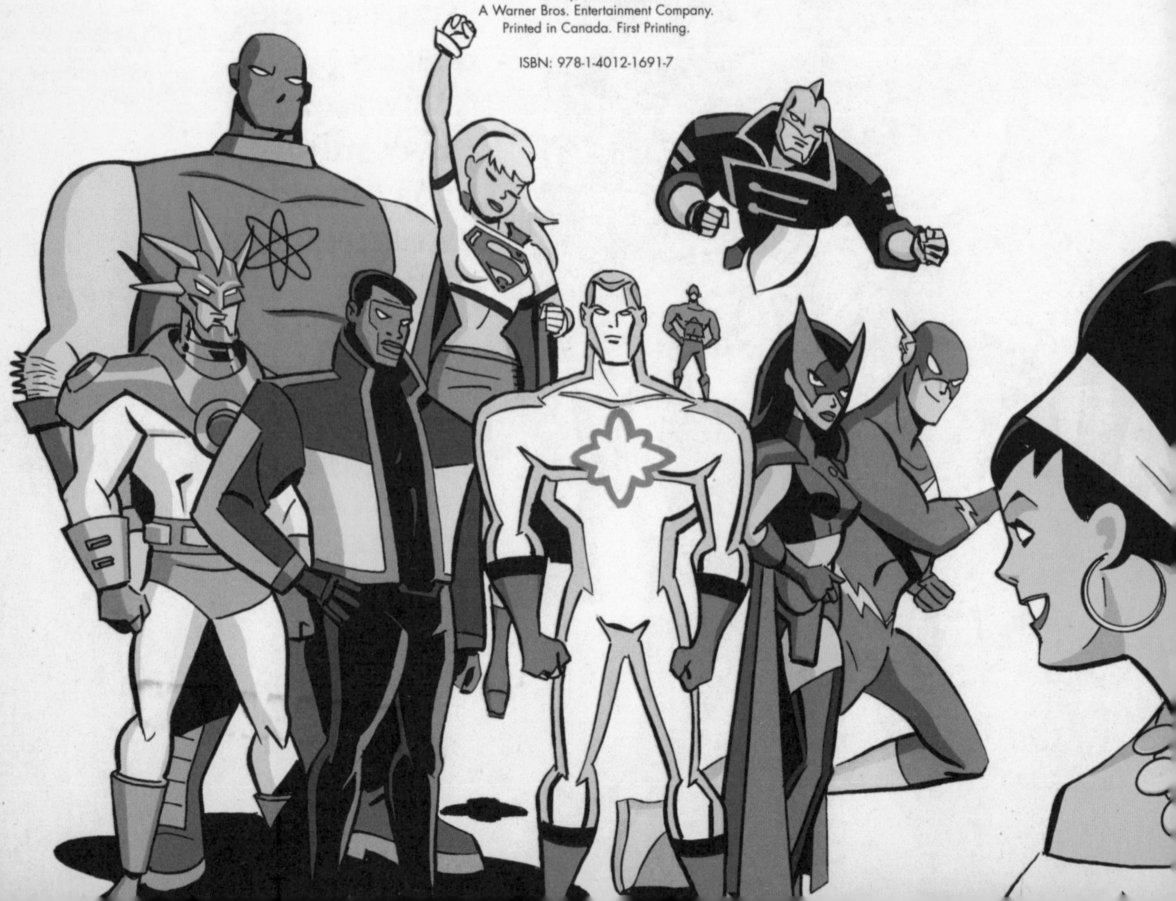

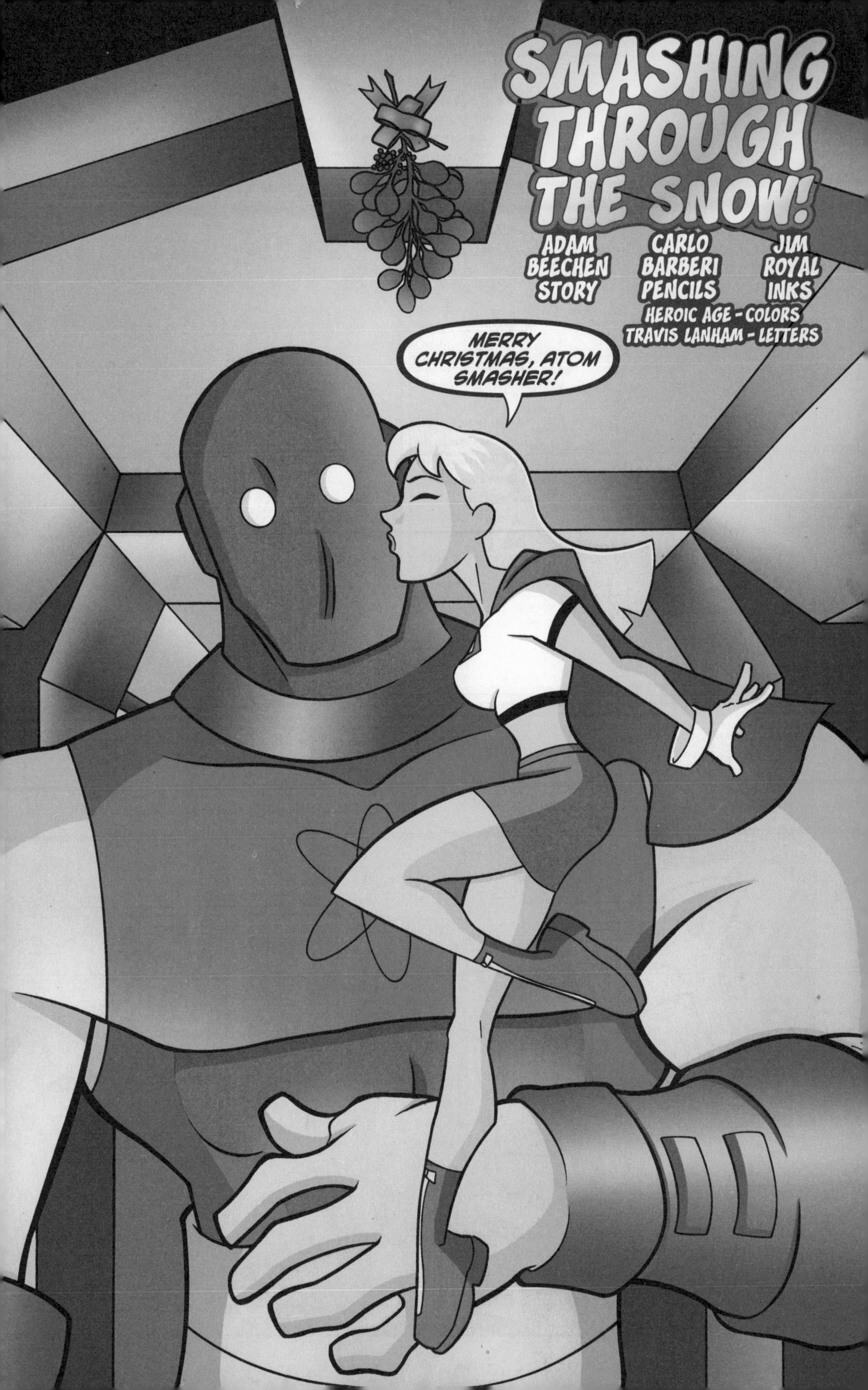

SMASHING THROUGH THE SNOW!
ADAM BEECHEN STORY
CARLO BARBERI PENCILS
JIM ROYAL INKS
HEROIC AGE - COLORS
TRAVIS LANHAM - LETTERS
MERRY CHRISTMAS, ATOM SMASHER!

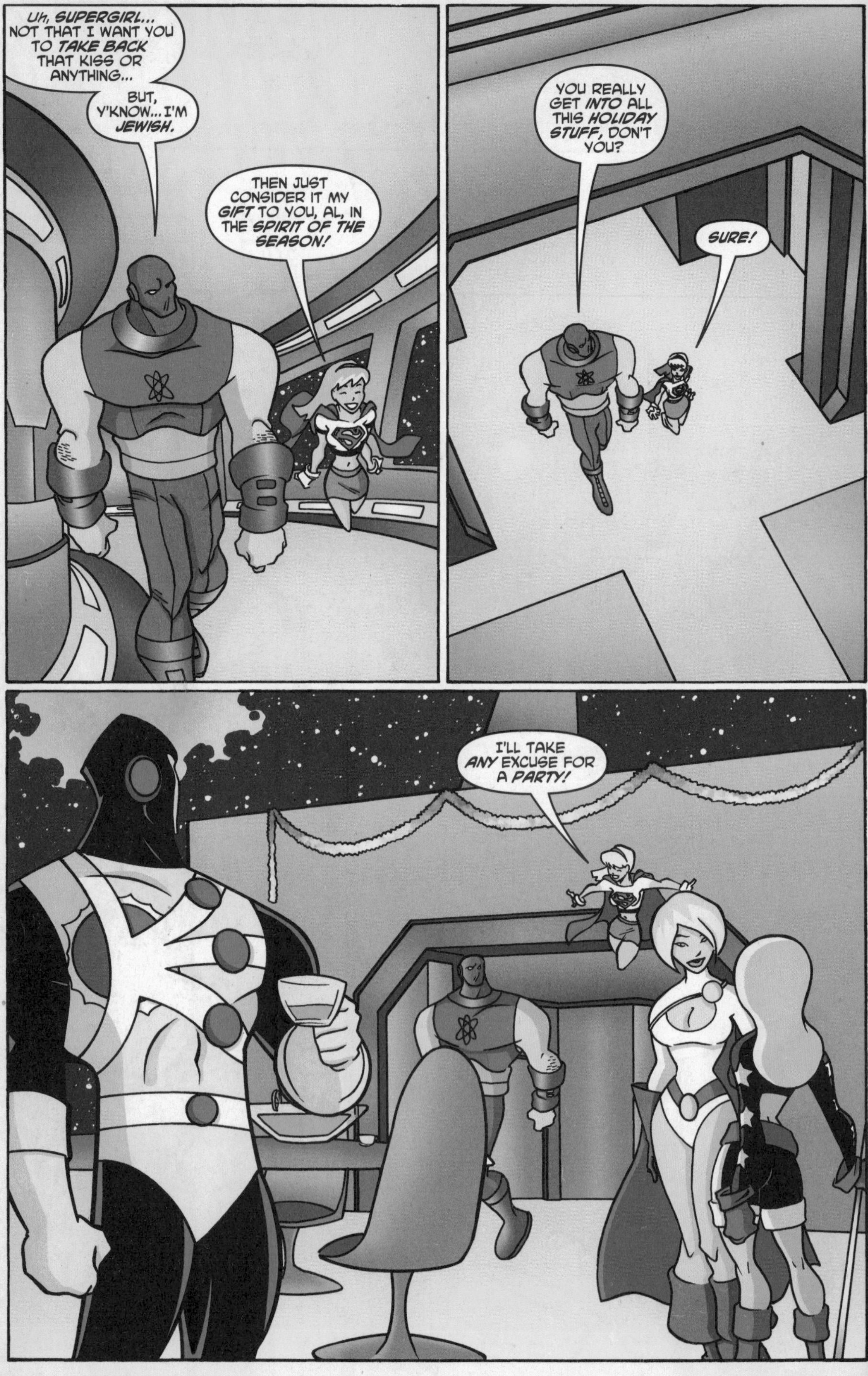
Uh, SUPERGIRL... NOT THAT I WANT YOU TO TAKE BACK THAT KISS OR ANYTHING...
BUT, Y'KNOW... I'M JEWISH.
THEN JUST CONSIDER IT MY GIFT TO YOU, AL, IN THE SPIRIT OF THE SEASON!
YOU REALLY GET INTO ALL THIS HOLIDAY STUFF, DON'T YOU?
SURE!
I'LL TAKE ANY EXCUSE FOR A PARTY!

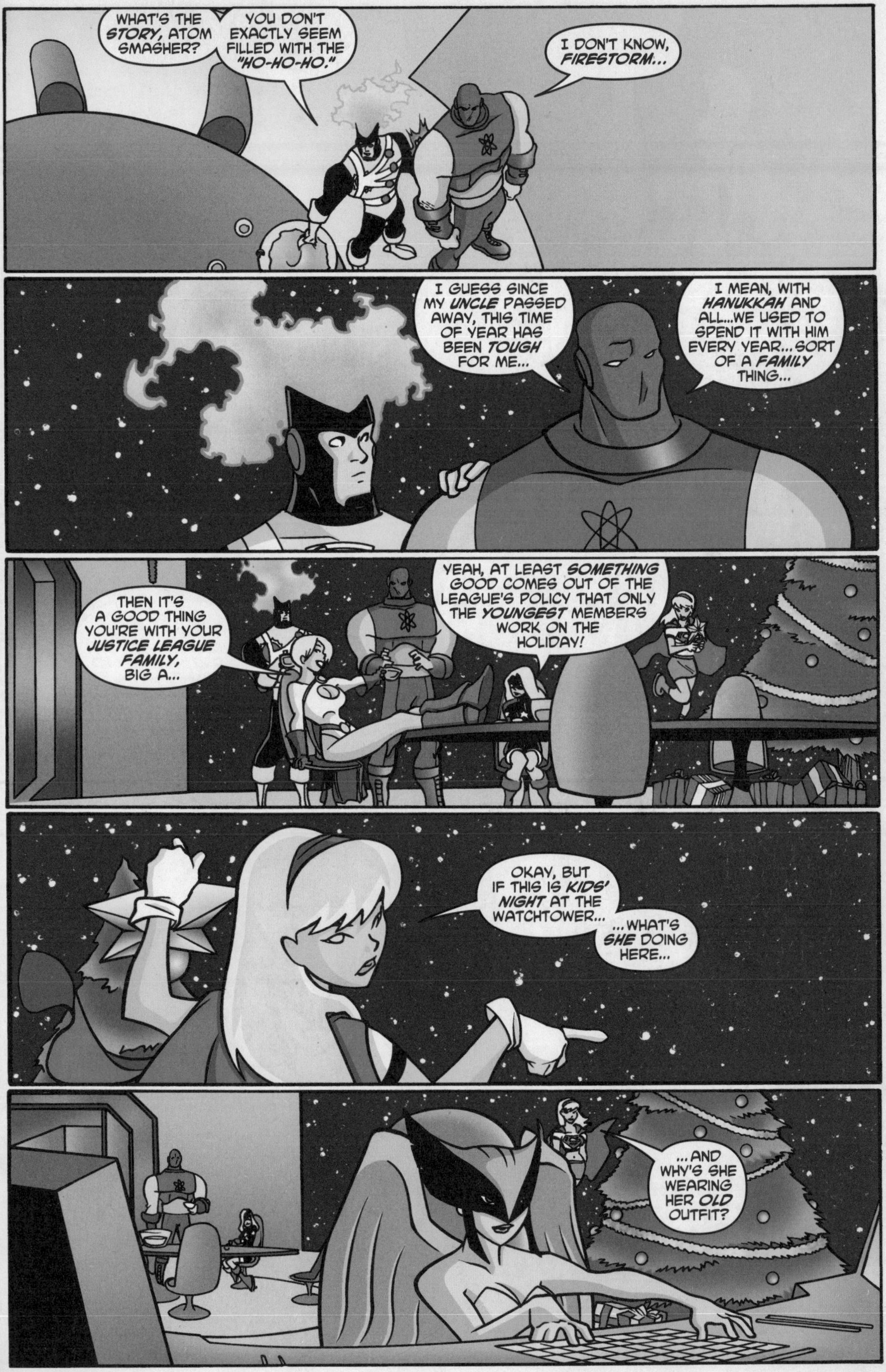
WHAT'S THE STORY, ATOM SMASHER?
YOU DON'T EXACTLY SEEM FILLED WITH THE "HO-HO-HO."
I DON'T KNOW, FIRESTORM...
I GUESS SINCE MY UNCLE PASSED AWAY, THIS TIME OF YEAR HAS BEEN TOUGH FOR ME...
I MEAN, WITH HANUKKAH AND ALL...WE USED TO SPEND IT WITH HIM EVERY YEAR...SORT OF A FAMILY THING...
THEN IT'S A GOOD THING YOU'RE WITH YOUR JUSTICE LEAGUE FAMILY, BIG A...
YEAH, AT LEAST SOMETHING GOOD COMES OUT OF THE LEAGUE'S POLICY THAT ONLY THE YOUNGEST MEMBERS WORK ON THE HOLIDAY!
OKAY, BUT IF THIS IS KIDS' NIGHT AT THE WATCHTOWER...
...WHAT'S SHE DOING HERE...
...AND WHY'S SHE WEARING HER OLD OUTFIT?

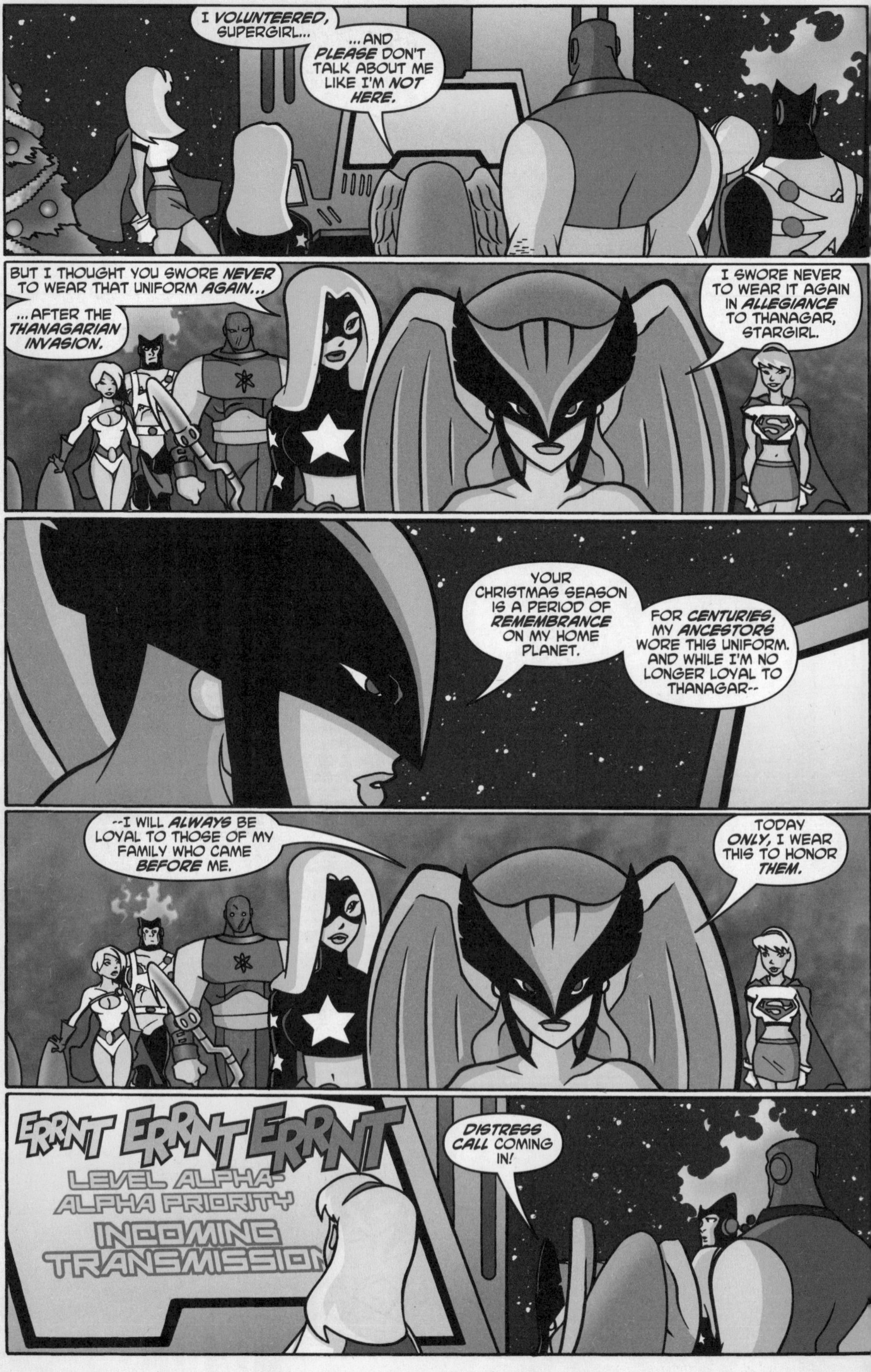
I VOLUNTEERED, SUPERGIRL...
...AND PLEASE DON'T TALK ABOUT ME LIKE I'M NOT HERE.
BUT I THOUGHT YOU SWORE NEVER TO WEAR THAT UNIFORM AGAIN...
...AFTER THE THANAGARIAN INVASION.
I SWORE NEVER TO WEAR IT AGAIN IN ALLEGIANCE TO THANAGAR, STARGIRL.
YOUR CHRISTMAS SEASON IS A PERIOD OF REMEMBRANCE ON MY HOME PLANET.
FOR CENTURIES, MY ANCESTORS WORE THIS UNIFORM. AND WHILE I'M NO LONGER LOYAL TO THANAGAR--
--I WILL ALWAYS BE LOYAL TO THOSE OF MY FAMILY WHO CAME BEFORE ME.
TODAY ONLY, I WEAR THIS TO HONOR THEM.
ERRNT ERRNT ERRNT
LEVEL ALPHA-ALPHA PRIORITY
INCOMING TRANSMISSION
DISTRESS CALL COMING IN!

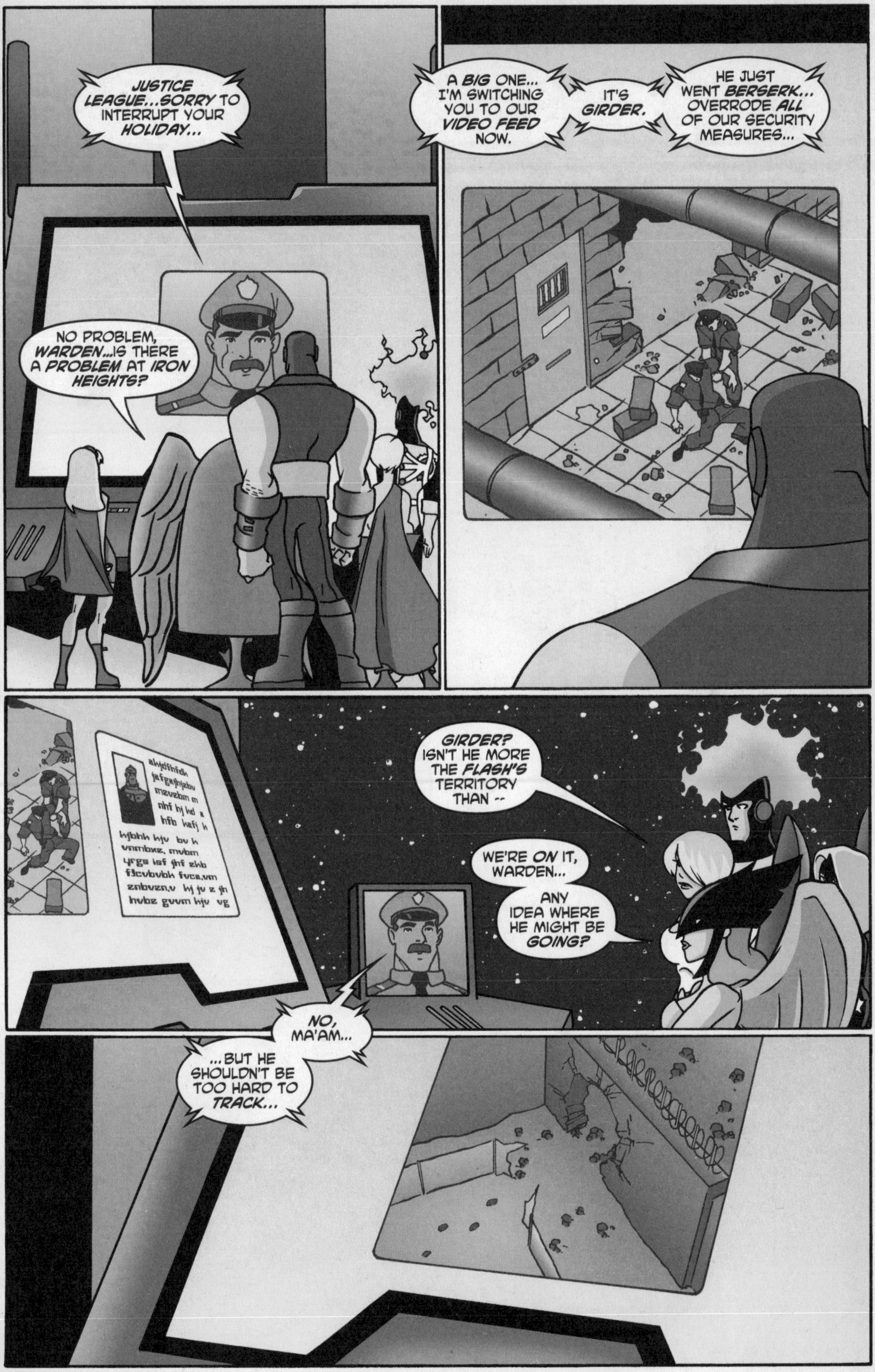
JUSTICE LEAGUE...SORRY TO INTERRUPT YOUR HOLIDAY...
NO PROBLEM, WARDEN...IS THERE A PROBLEM AT IRON HEIGHTS?
A BIG ONE... I'M SWITCHING YOU TO OUR VIDEO FEED NOW.
IT'S GIRDER.
HE JUST WENT BERSERK... OVERRODE ALL OF OUR SECURITY MEASURES...
GIRDER? ISN'T HE MORE THE FLASH'S TERRITORY THAN --
WE'RE ON IT, WARDEN...
ANY IDEA WHERE HE MIGHT BE GOING?
NO, MA'AM...
...BUT HE SHOULDN'T BE TOO HARD TO TRACK...

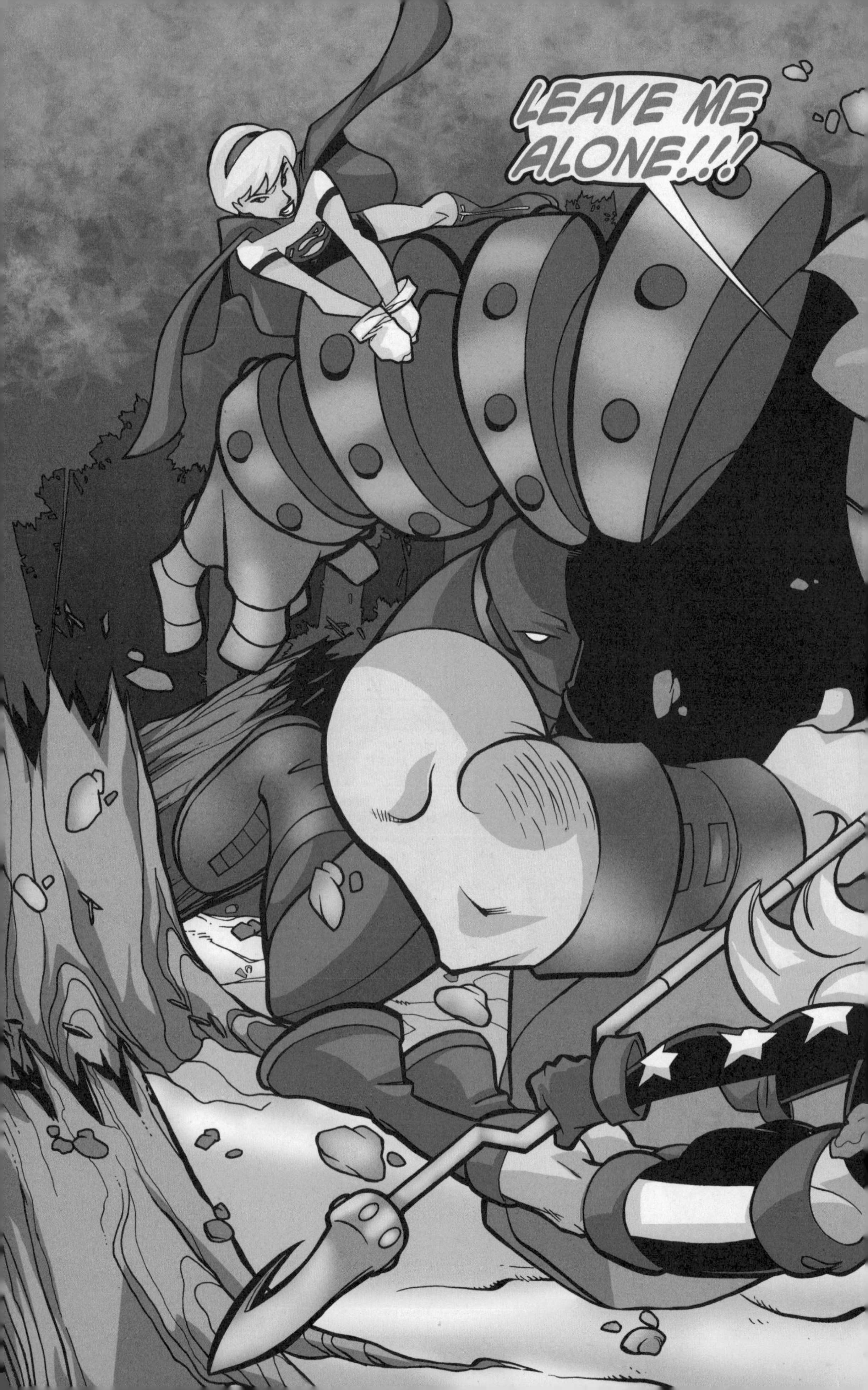
LEAVE ME ALONE!!!

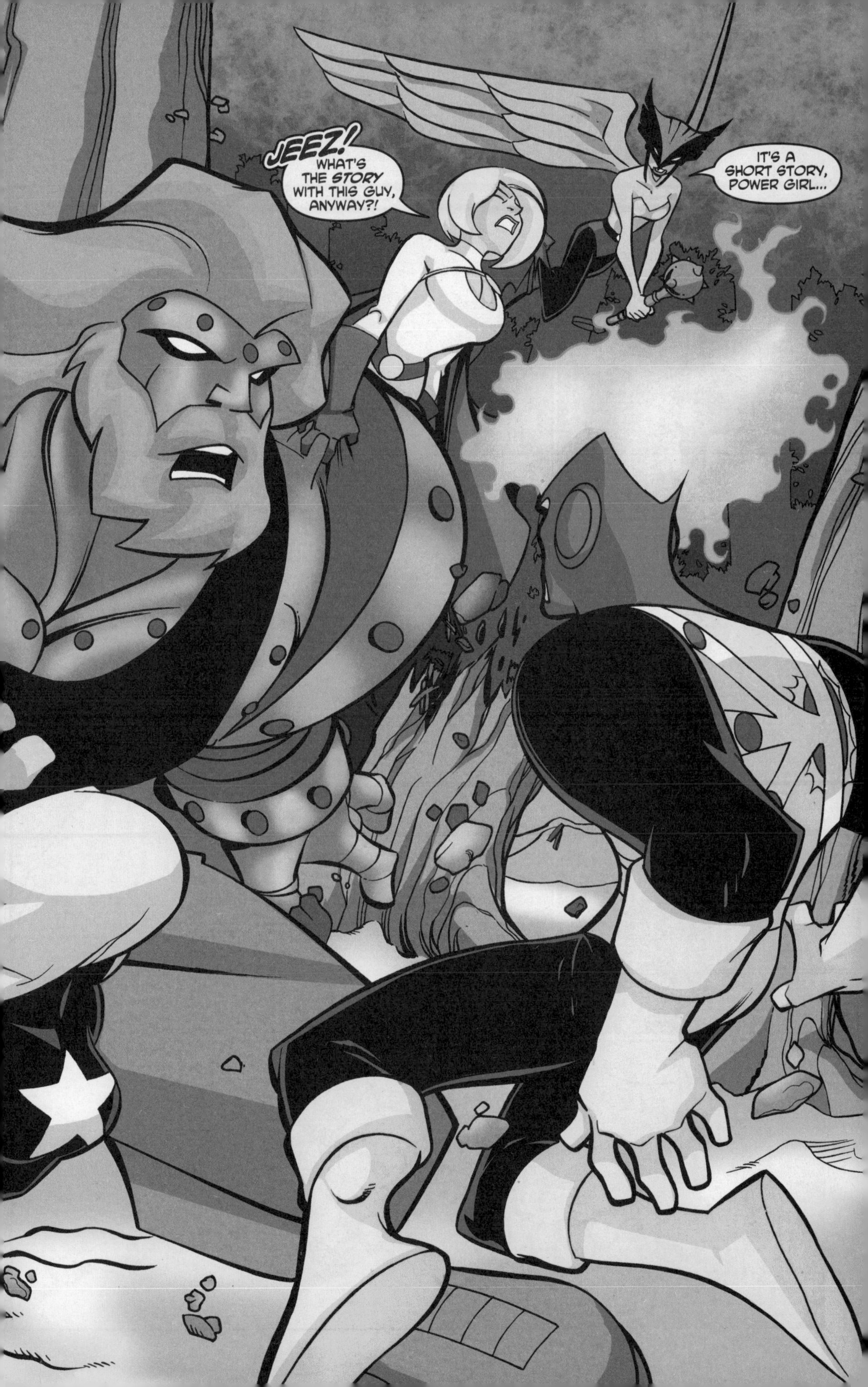
JEEZ!
WHAT'S THE STORY WITH THIS GUY, ANYWAY?!
IT'S A SHORT STORY, POWER GIRL...

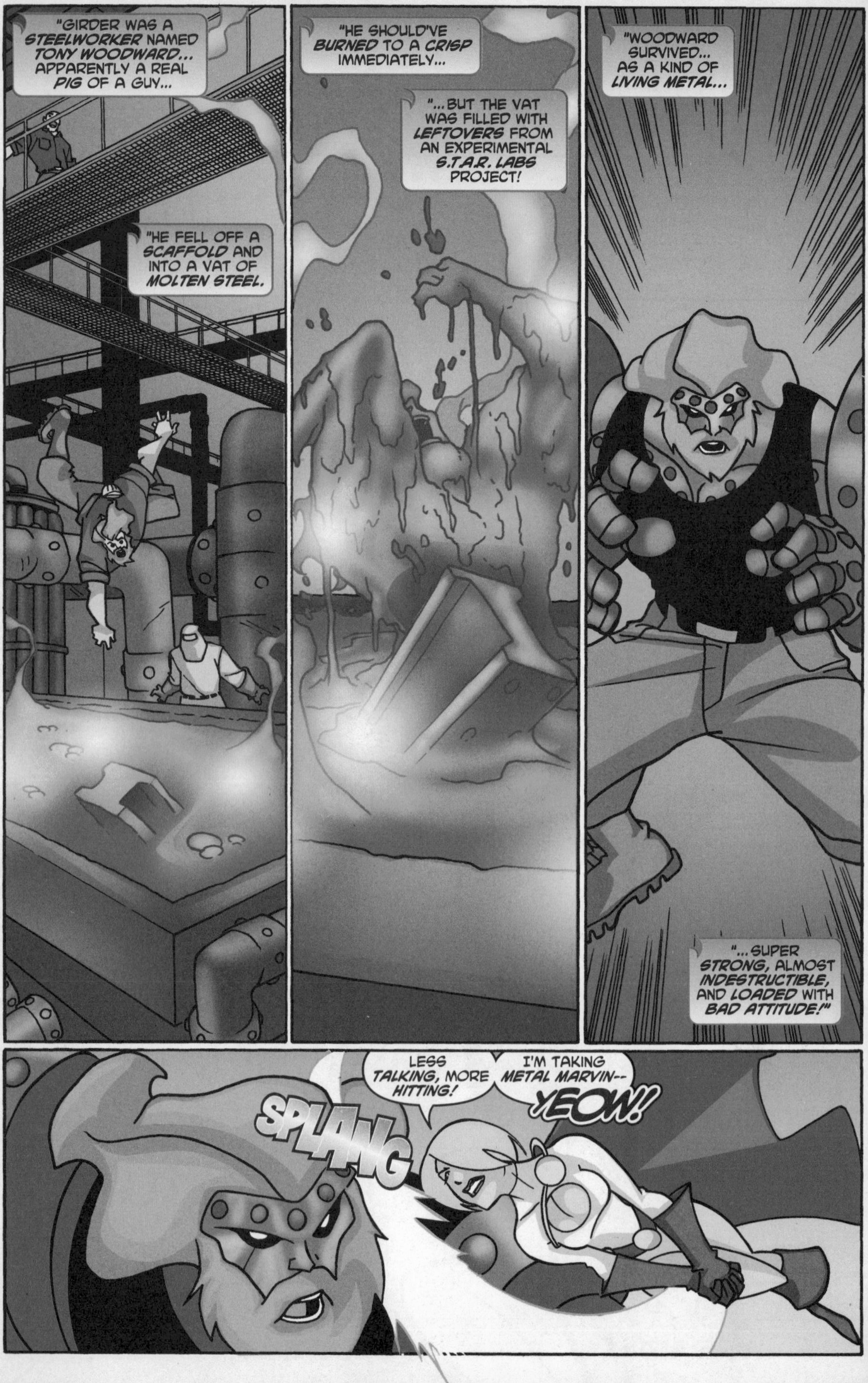
"GIRDER WAS A STEELWORKER NAMED TONY WOODWARD... APPARENTLY A REAL PIG OF A GUY...
"HE FELL OFF A SCAFFOLD AND INTO A VAT OF MOLTEN STEEL.
"HE SHOULD'VE BURNED TO A CRISP IMMEDIATELY...
"...BUT THE VAT WAS FILLED WITH LEFTOVERS FROM AN EXPERIMENTAL S.T.A.R. LABS PROJECT!
"WOODWARD SURVIVED... AS A KIND OF LIVING METAL...
"...SUPER STRONG, ALMOST INDESTRUCTIBLE, AND LOADED WITH BAD ATTITUDE!"
LESS TALKING, MORE HITTING!
I'M TAKING METAL MARVIN--
YEOW!
SPLANG

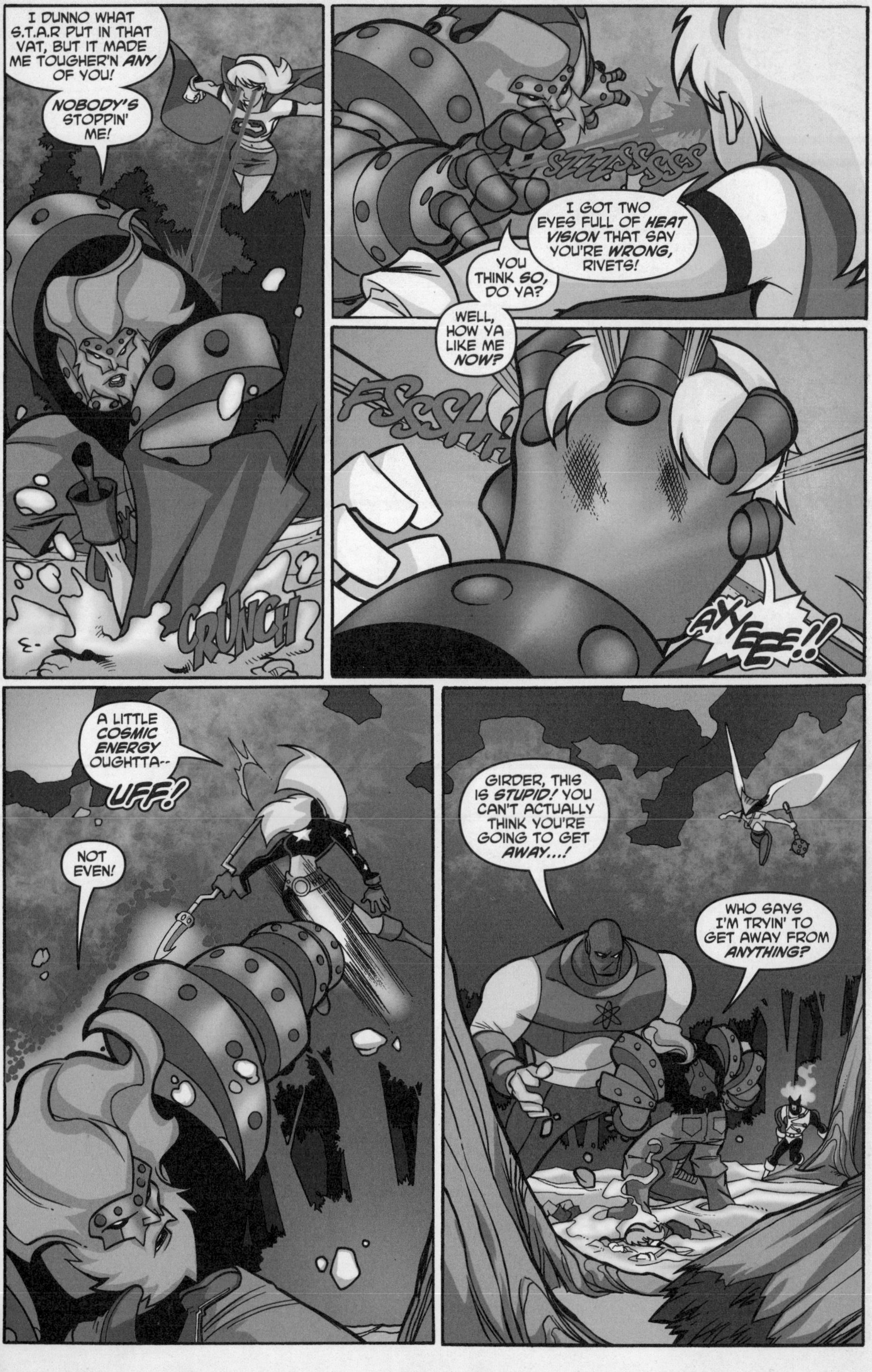

I DUNNO WHAT S.T.A.R PUT IN THAT VAT, BUT IT MADE ME TOUGHER'N ANY OF YOU!
NOBODY'S STOPPIN' ME!
CRUNCH
SZZZSSSSS
I GOT TWO EYES FULL OF HEAT VISION THAT SAY YOU'RE WRONG, RIVETS!
YOU THINK SO, DO YA?
WELL, HOW YA LIKE ME NOW?
FSSSHH
AYYEEEE!!
A LITTLE COSMIC ENERGY OUGHTTA--
UFF!
NOT EVEN!
GIRDER, THIS IS STUPID! YOU CAN'T ACTUALLY THINK YOU'RE GOING TO GET AWAY...!
WHO SAYS I'M TRYIN' TO GET AWAY FROM ANYTHING?

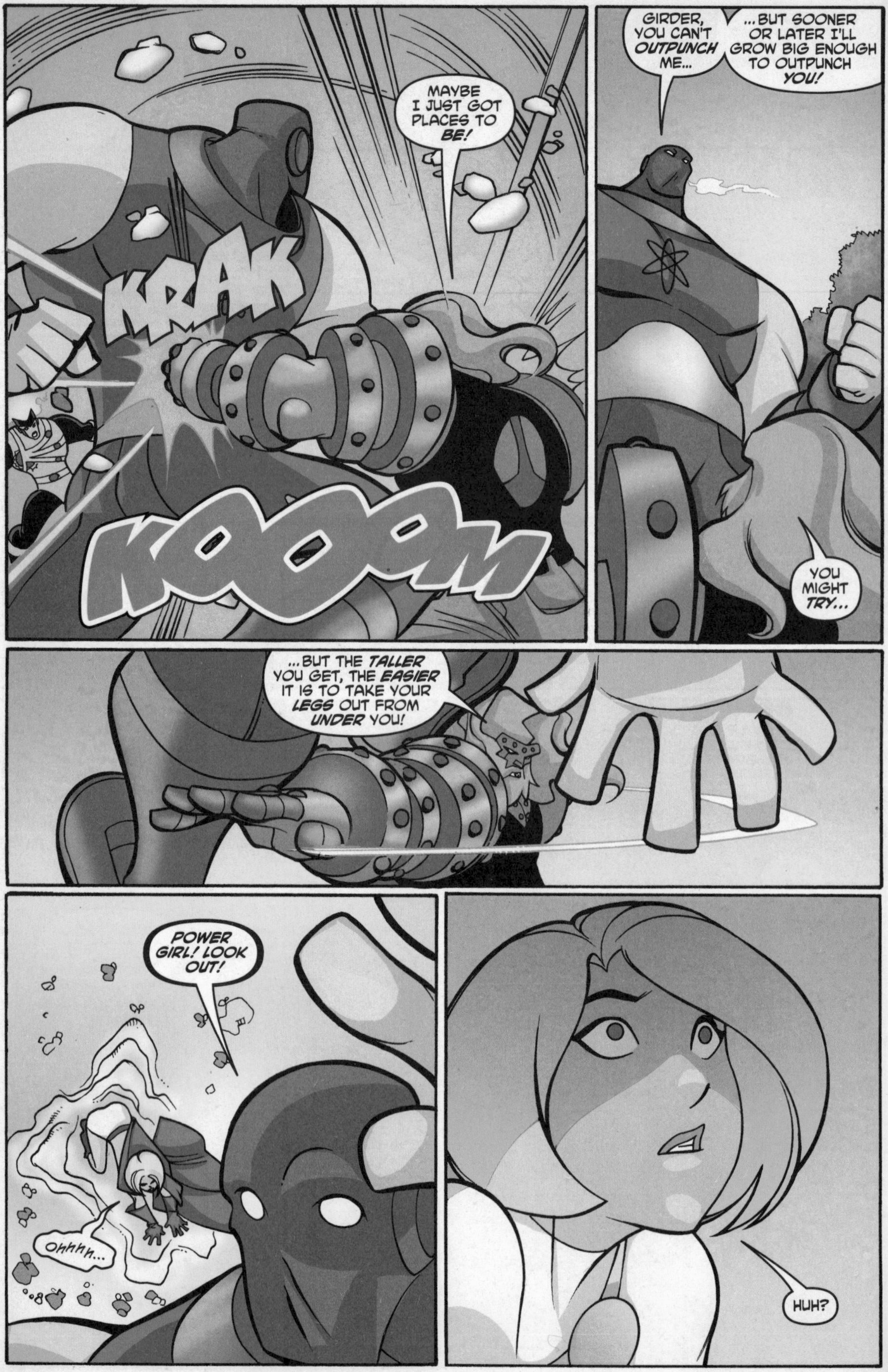
MAYBE I JUST GOT PLACES TO BE!
KRAK
KOOOM
GIRDER, YOU CAN'T OUTPUNCH ME...
...BUT SOONER OR LATER I'LL GROW BIG ENOUGH TO OUTPUNCH YOU!
YOU MIGHT TRY...
...BUT THE TALLER YOU GET, THE EASIER IT IS TO TAKE YOUR LEGS OUT FROM UNDER YOU!
POWER GIRL! LOOK OUT!
Ohhhh...
HUH?

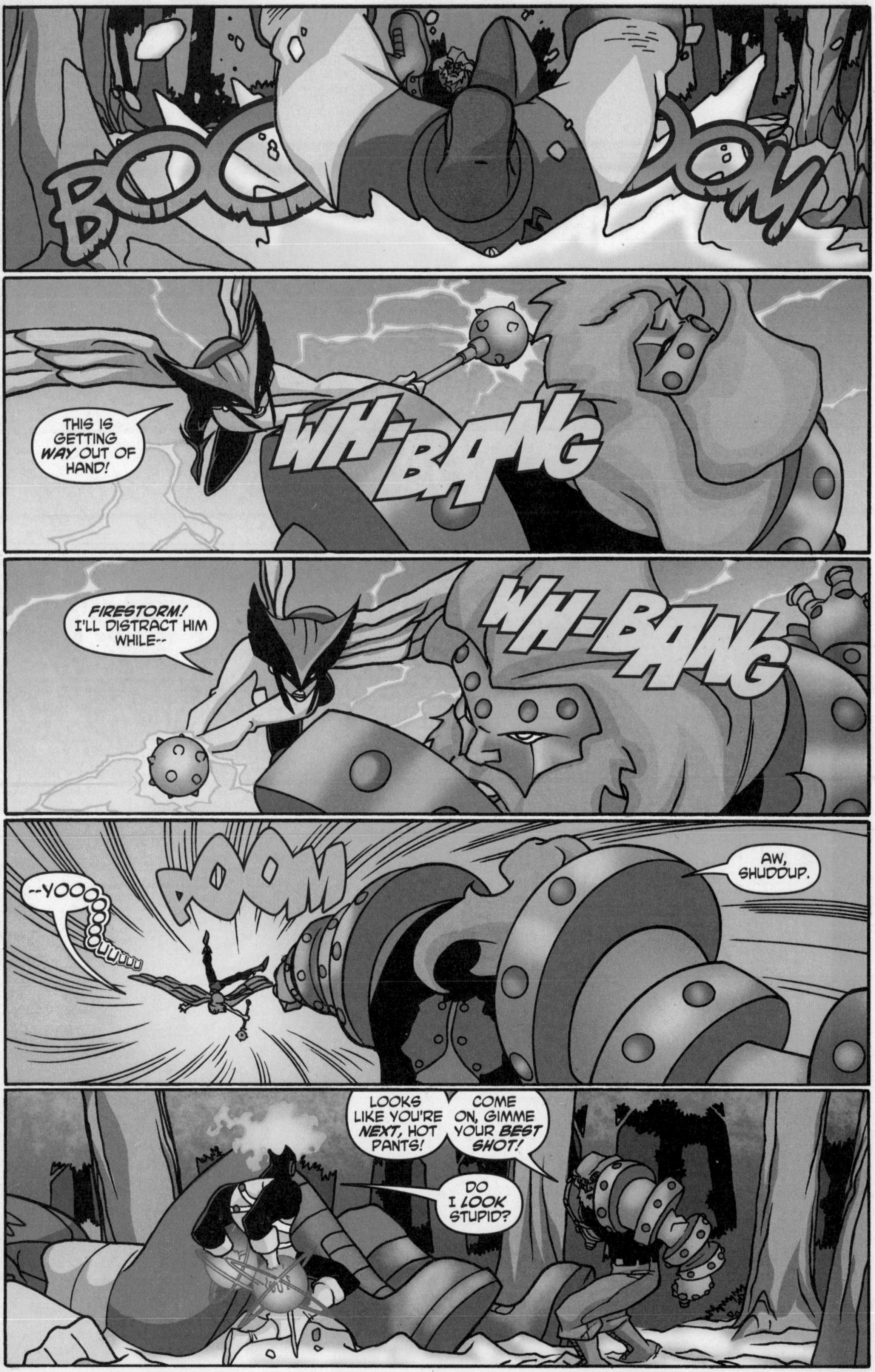
BOOOOM
THIS IS GETTING WAY OUT OF HAND!
WH-BANG
FIRESTORM! I'LL DISTRACT HIM WHILE--
WH-BANG
POOOM
--YOOOOOOOUUUUU
AW, SHUDDUP.
LOOKS LIKE YOU'RE NEXT, HOT PANTS!
COME ON, GIMME YOUR BEST SHOT!
DO I LOOK STUPID?

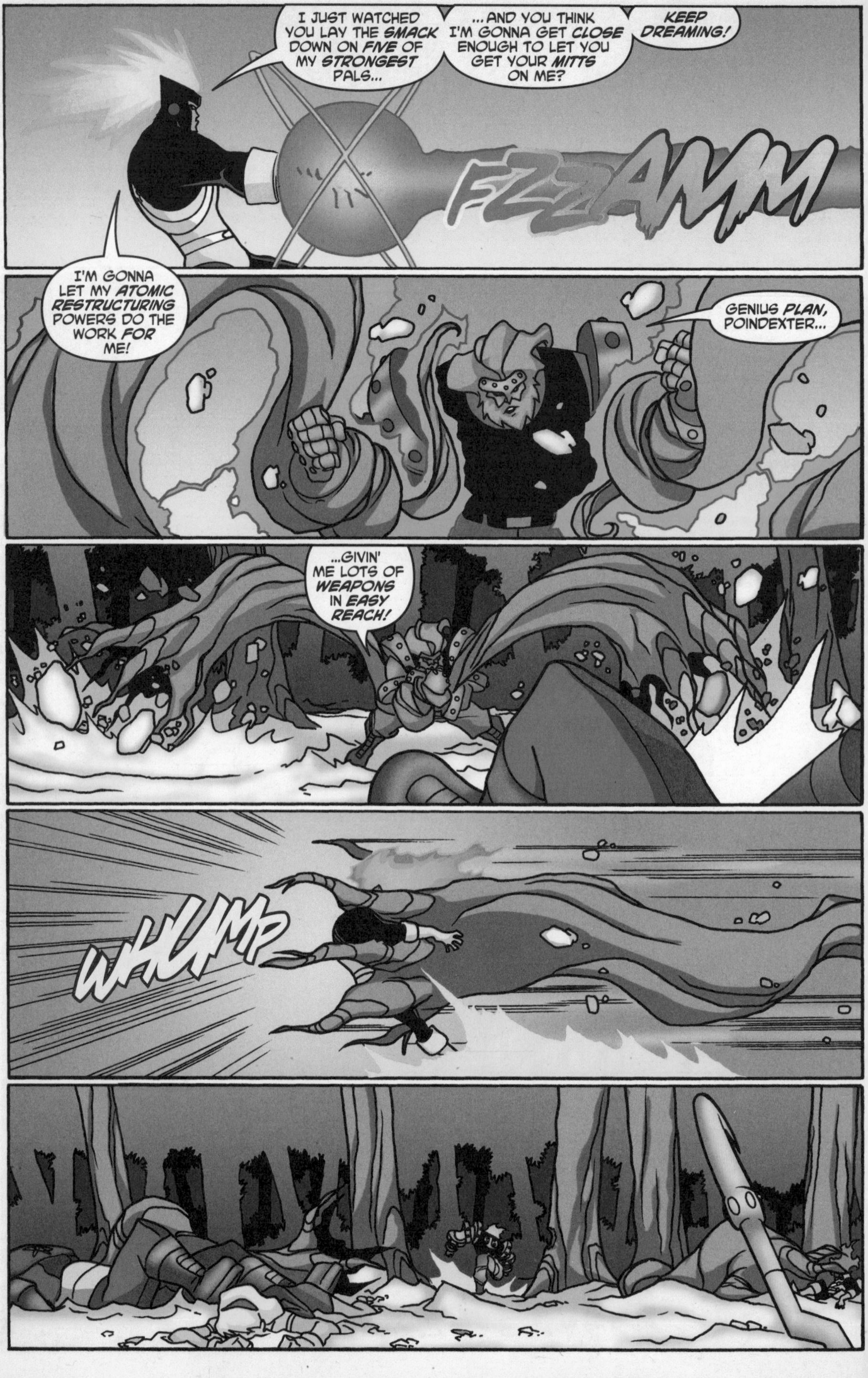
I JUST WATCHED YOU LAY THE SMACK DOWN ON FIVE OF MY STRONGEST PALS...
...AND YOU THINK I'M GONNA GET CLOSE ENOUGH TO LET YOU GET YOUR MITTS ON ME?
KEEP DREAMING!
FZZAMM
I'M GONNA LET MY ATOMIC RESTRUCTURING POWERS DO THE WORK FOR ME!
GENIUS PLAN, POINDEXTER...
...GIVIN' ME LOTS OF WEAPONS IN EASY REACH!
WHUMP

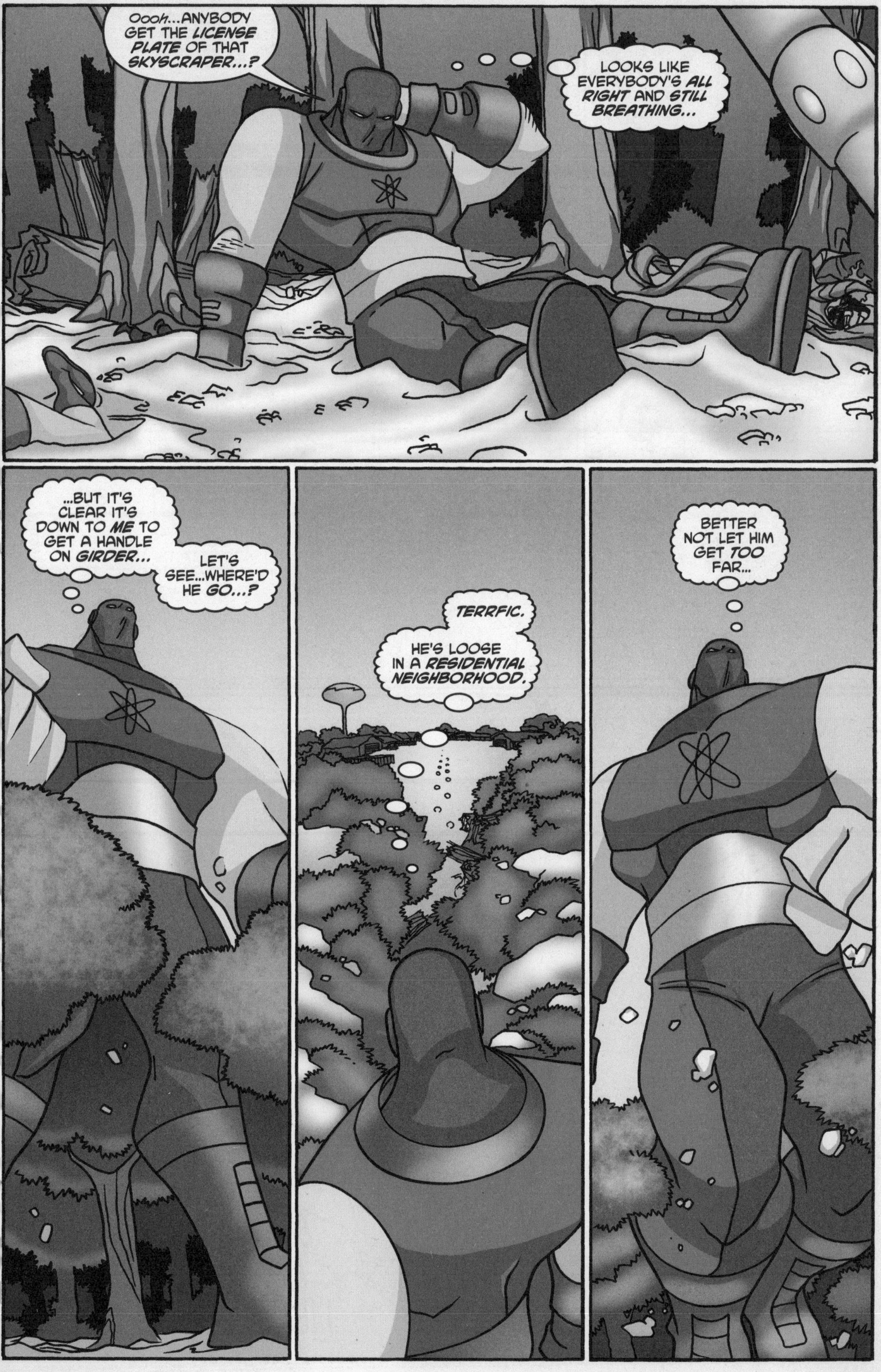
Oooh...ANYBODY GET THE LICENSE PLATE OF THAT SKYSCRAPER...?
LOOKS LIKE EVERYBODY'S ALL RIGHT AND STILL BREATHING...
...BUT IT'S CLEAR IT'S DOWN TO ME TO GET A HANDLE ON GIRDER...
LET'S SEE...WHERE'D HE GO...?
TERRFIC.
HE'S LOOSE IN A RESIDENTIAL NEIGHBORHOOD.
BETTER NOT LET HIM GET TOO FAR...

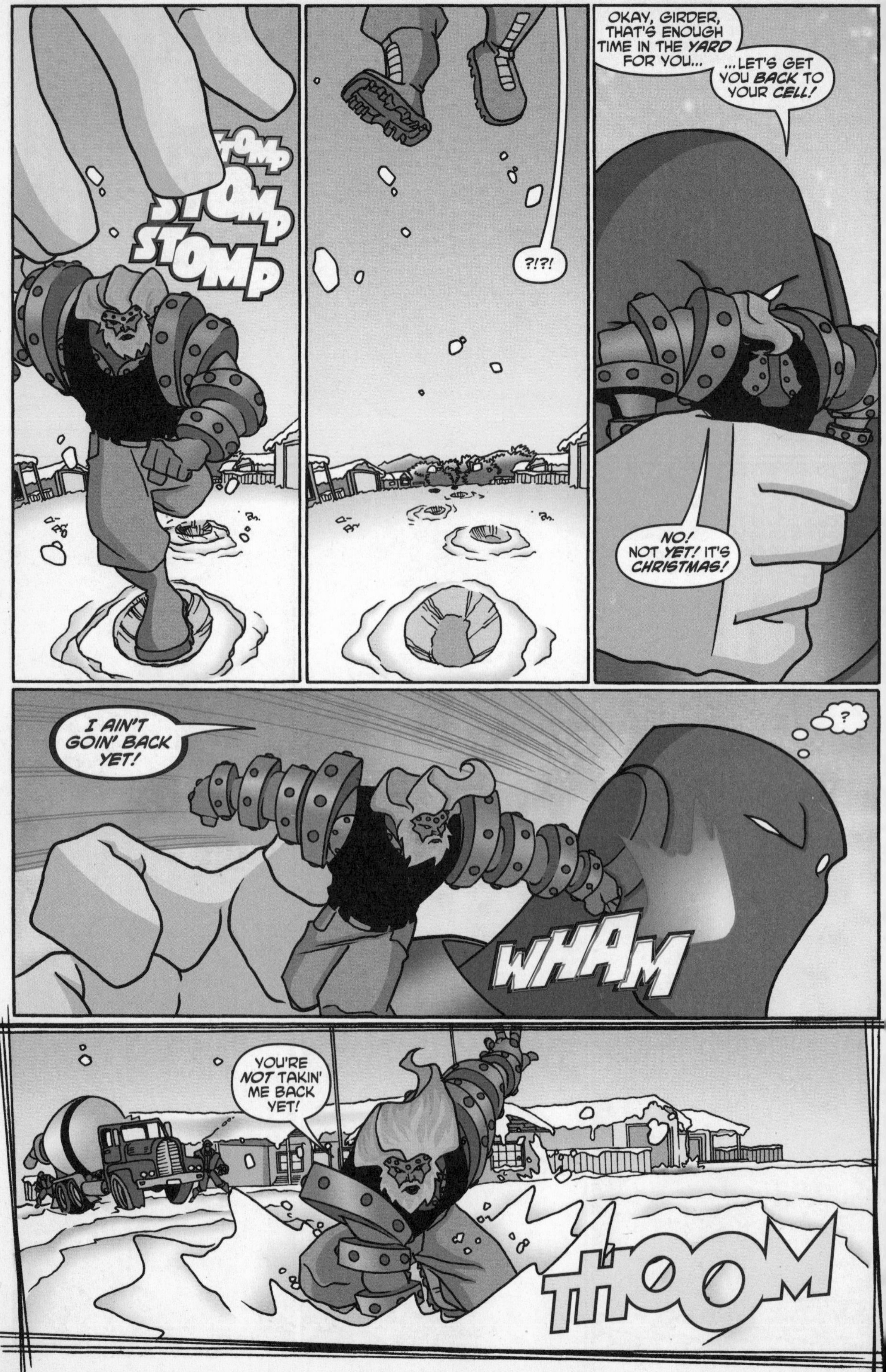
STOMP
STOMP
STOMP
?!?!
OKAY, GIRDER, THAT'S ENOUGH TIME IN THE YARD FOR YOU...
...LET'S GET YOU BACK TO YOUR CELL!
NO! NOT YET! IT'S CHRISTMAS!
I AIN'T GOIN' BACK YET!
?
WHAM
YOU'RE NOT TAKIN' ME BACK YET!
THOOM

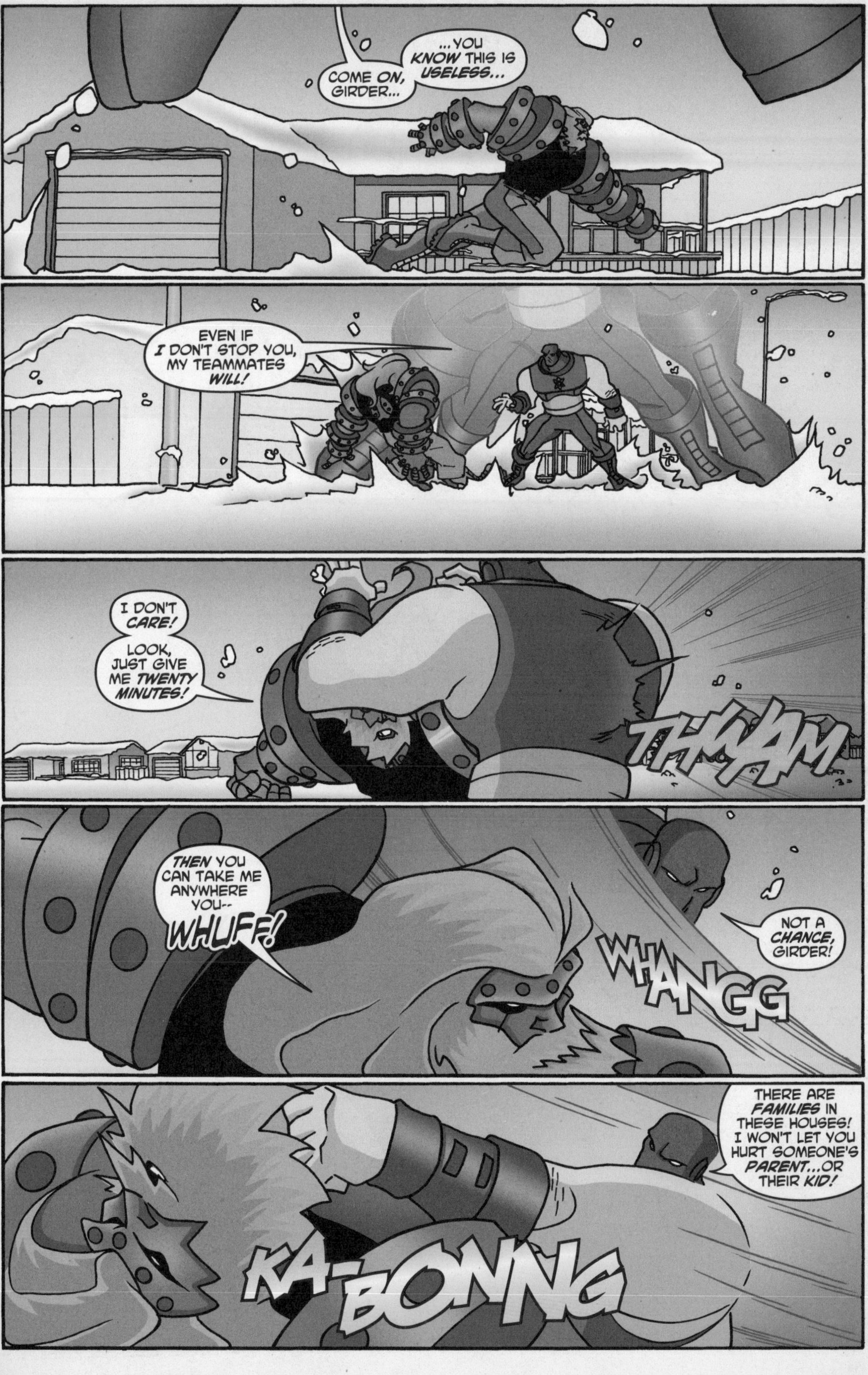
COME ON, GIRDER...
...YOU KNOW THIS IS USELESS...
EVEN IF I DON'T STOP YOU, MY TEAMMATES WILL!
I DON'T CARE!
LOOK, JUST GIVE ME TWENTY MINUTES!
THWAM
THEN YOU CAN TAKE ME ANYWHERE YOU-- WHUFF!
WHANGG
NOT A CHANCE, GIRDER!
THERE ARE FAMILIES IN THESE HOUSES! I WON'T LET YOU HURT SOMEONE'S PARENT...OR THEIR KID!
KA-BONNG

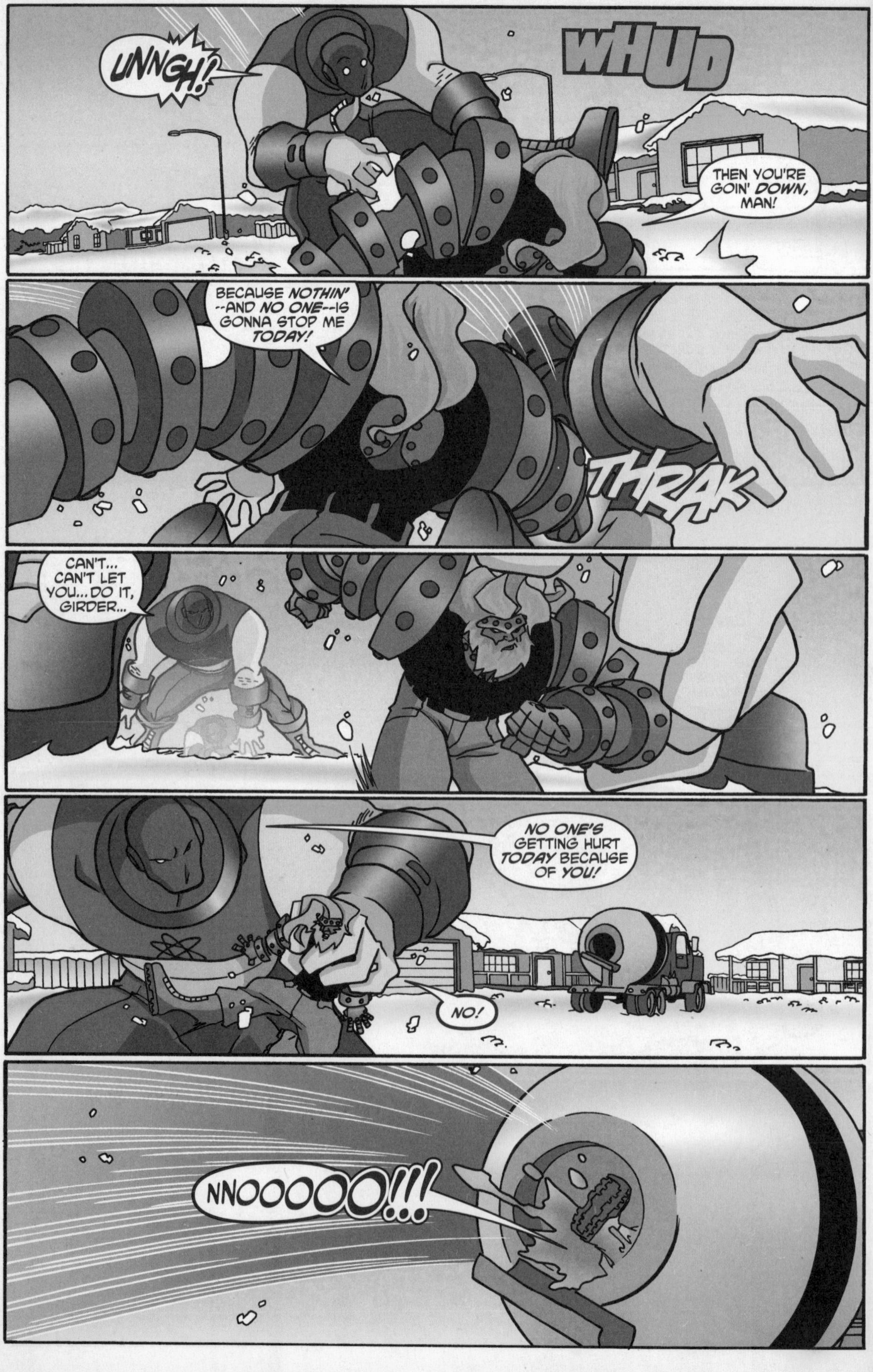
UNNGH!
wHUD
THEN YOU'RE GOIN' DOWN, MAN!
BECAUSE NOTHIN' --AND NO ONE--IS GONNA STOP ME TODAY!
THRAK
CAN'T... CAN'T LET YOU...DO IT, GIRDER...
NO ONE'S GETTING HURT TODAY BECAUSE OF YOU!
NO!
NNOOOOOO!!!

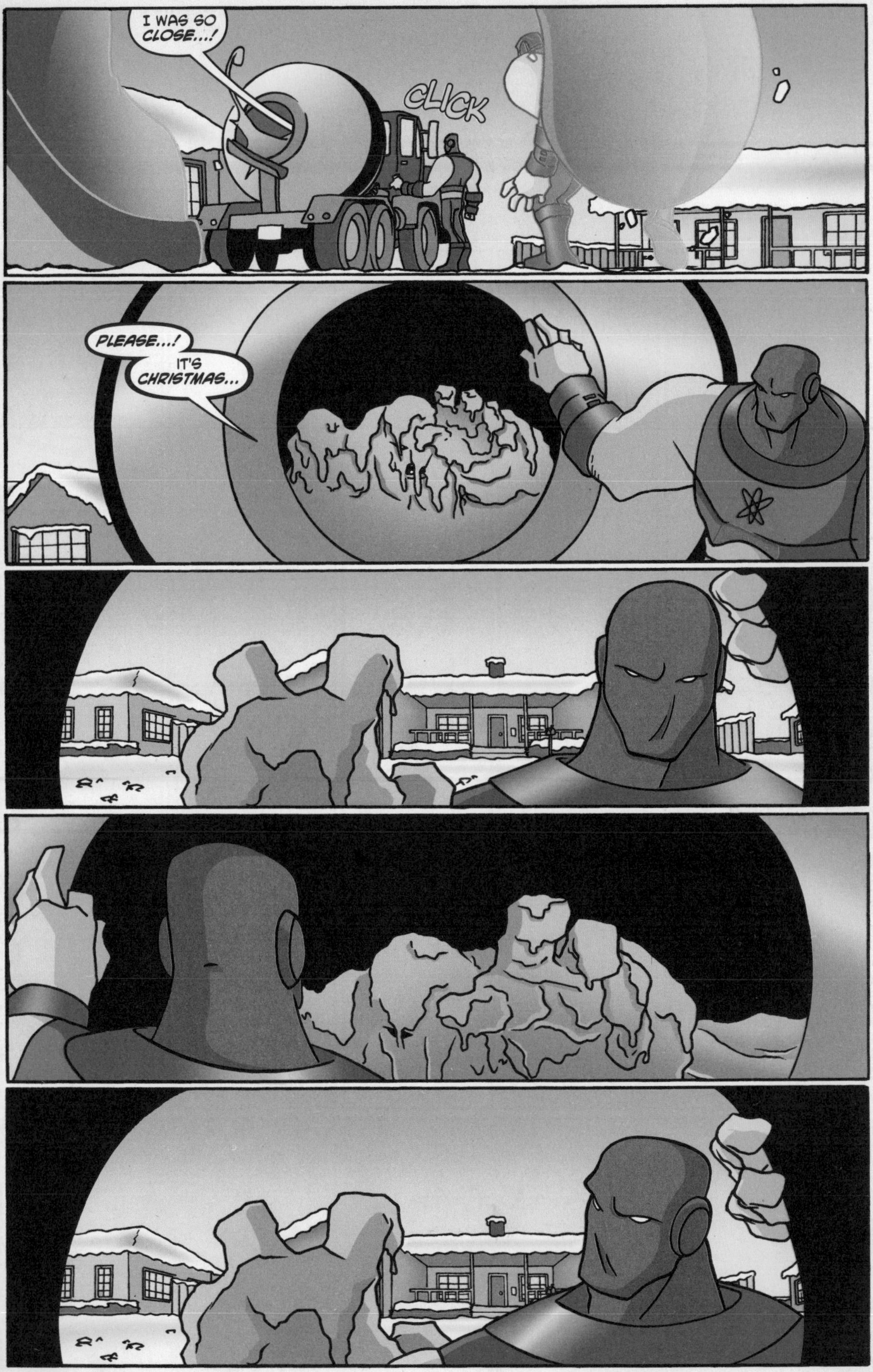
I WAS SO CLOSE...!
CLICK
PLEASE...! IT'S CHRISTMAS...

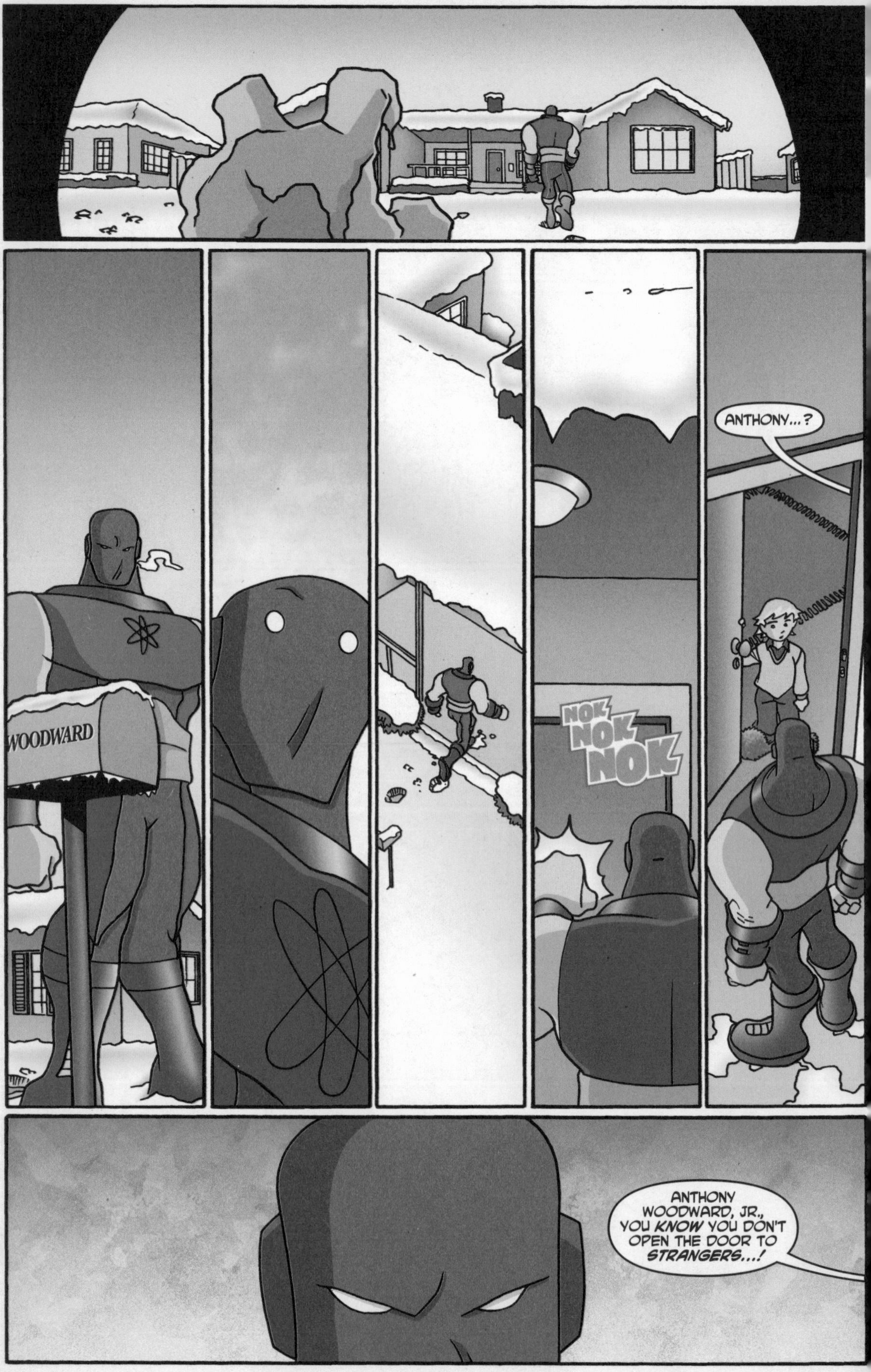
WOODWARD
NOK NOK NOK
ANTHONY...?
ANTHONY WOODWARD, JR., YOU *KNOW* YOU DON'T OPEN THE DOOR TO *STRANGERS...!*

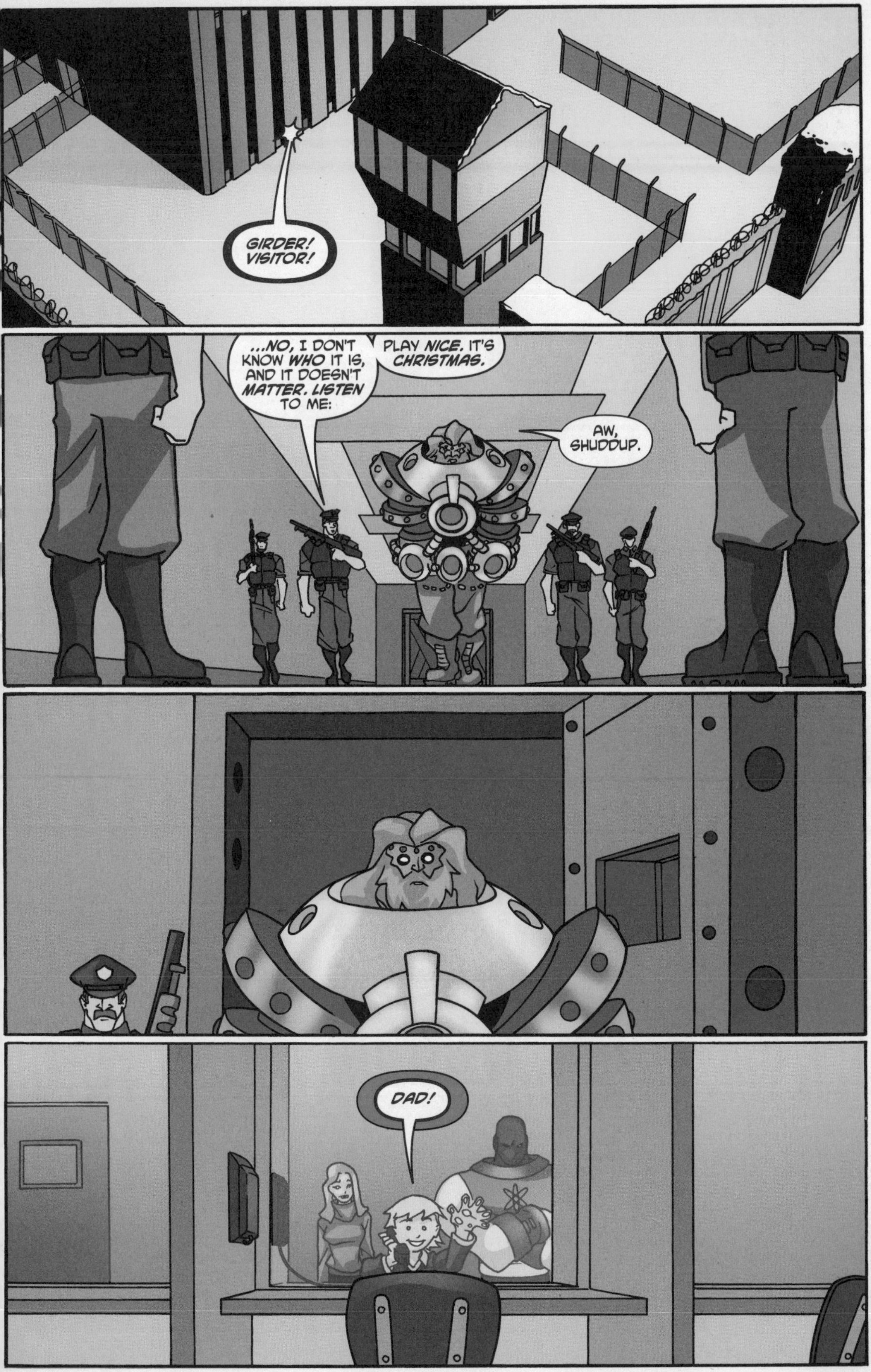
GIRDER! VISITOR!
...NO, I DON'T KNOW WHO IT IS, AND IT DOESN'T MATTER. LISTEN TO ME:
PLAY NICE. IT'S CHRISTMAS.
AW, SHUDDUP.
DAD!

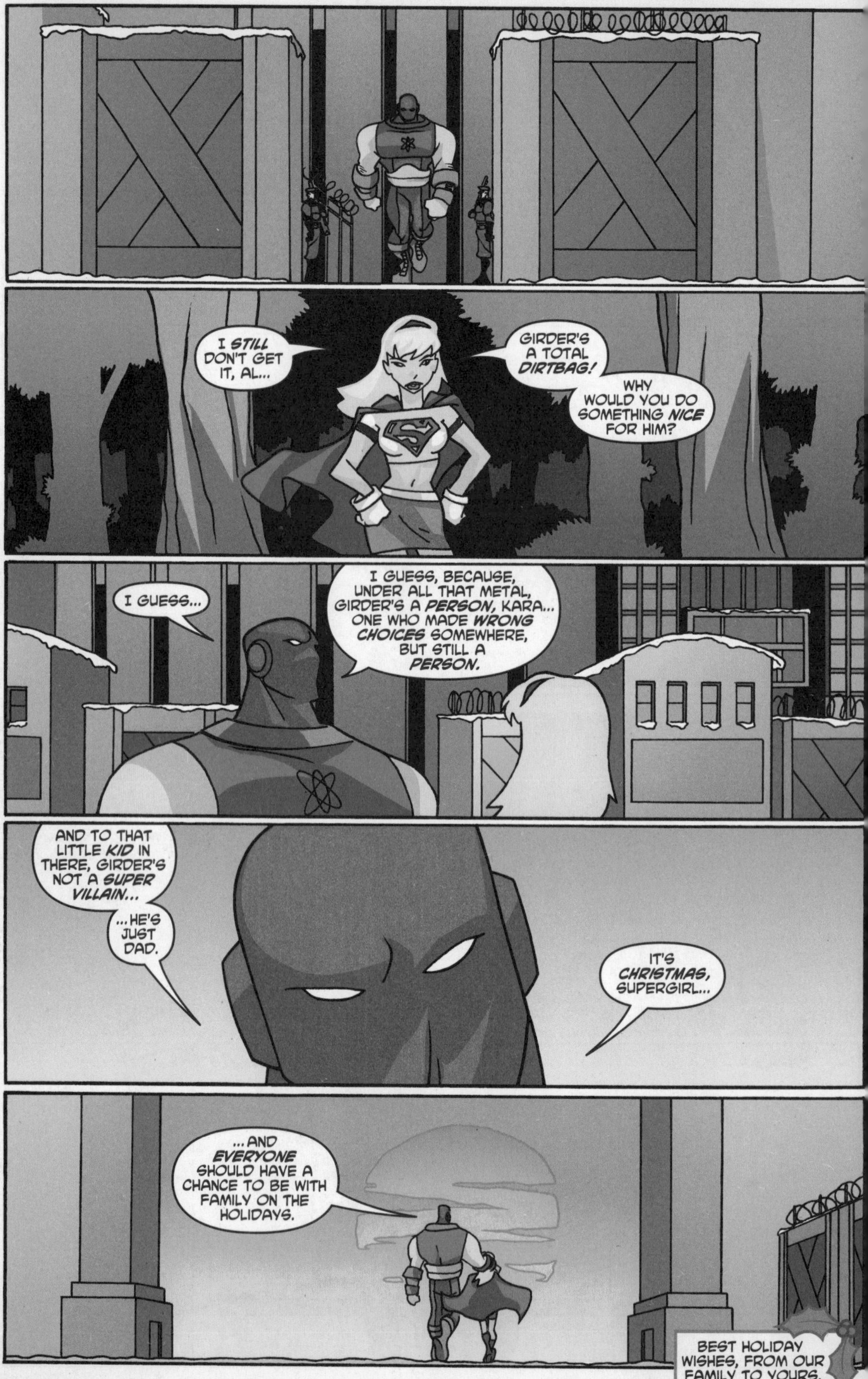
I STILL DON'T GET IT, AL...
GIRDER'S A TOTAL DIRTBAG!
WHY WOULD YOU DO SOMETHING NICE FOR HIM?
I GUESS...
I GUESS, BECAUSE, UNDER ALL THAT METAL, GIRDER'S A PERSON, KARA... ONE WHO MADE WRONG CHOICES SOMEWHERE, BUT STILL A PERSON.
AND TO THAT LITTLE KID IN THERE, GIRDER'S NOT A SUPER VILLAIN...
...HE'S JUST DAD.
IT'S CHRISTMAS, SUPERGIRL...
...AND EVERYONE SHOULD HAVE A CHANCE TO BE WITH FAMILY ON THE HOLIDAYS.
BEST HOLIDAY WISHES, FROM OUR FAMILY TO YOURS.

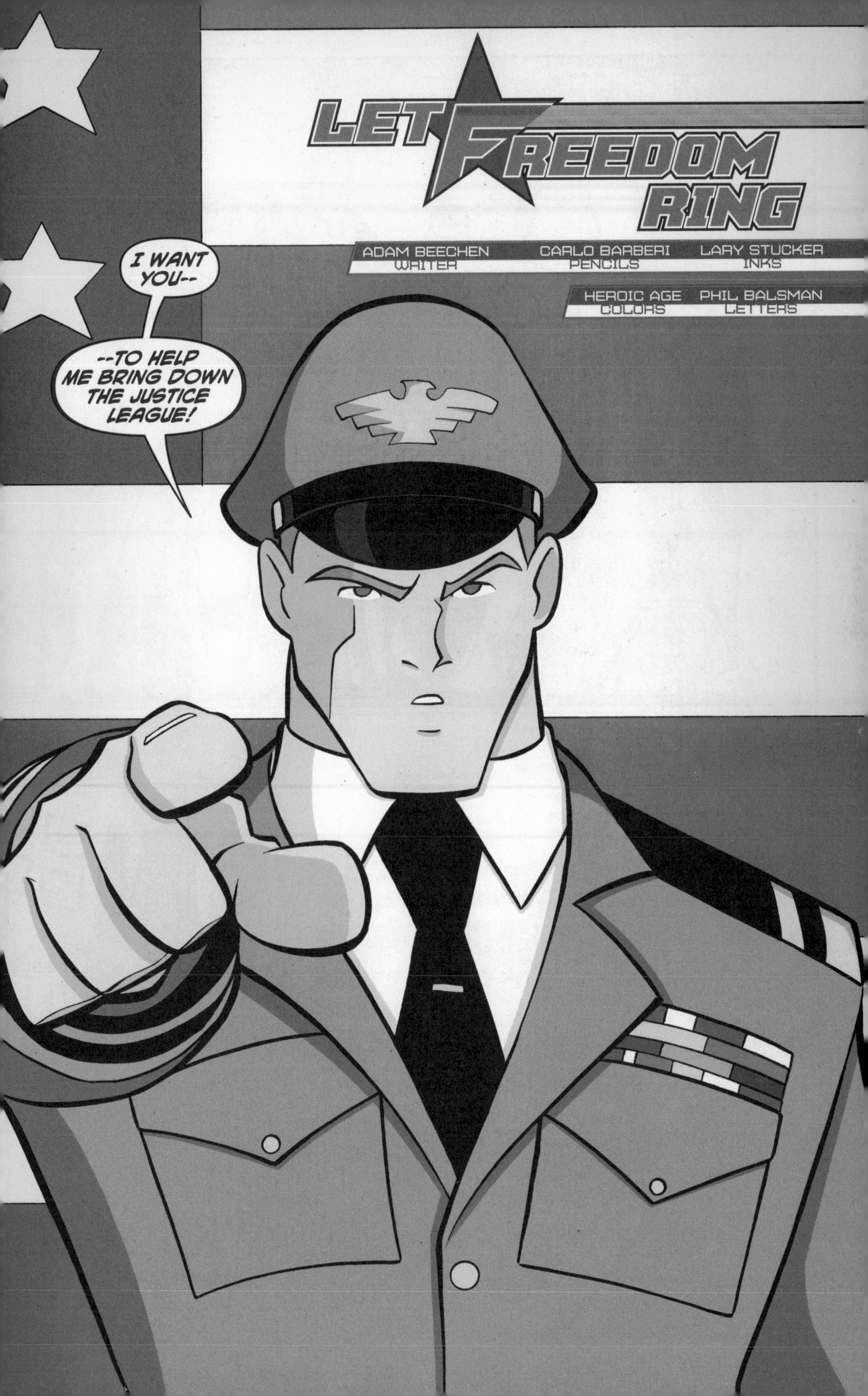
LET FREEDOM RING
ADAM BEECHEN WRITER
CARLO BARBERI PENCILS
LARY STUCKER INKS
HEROIC AGE COLORS
PHIL BALSMAN LETTERS
I WANT YOU--
--TO HELP ME BRING DOWN THE JUSTICE LEAGUE!

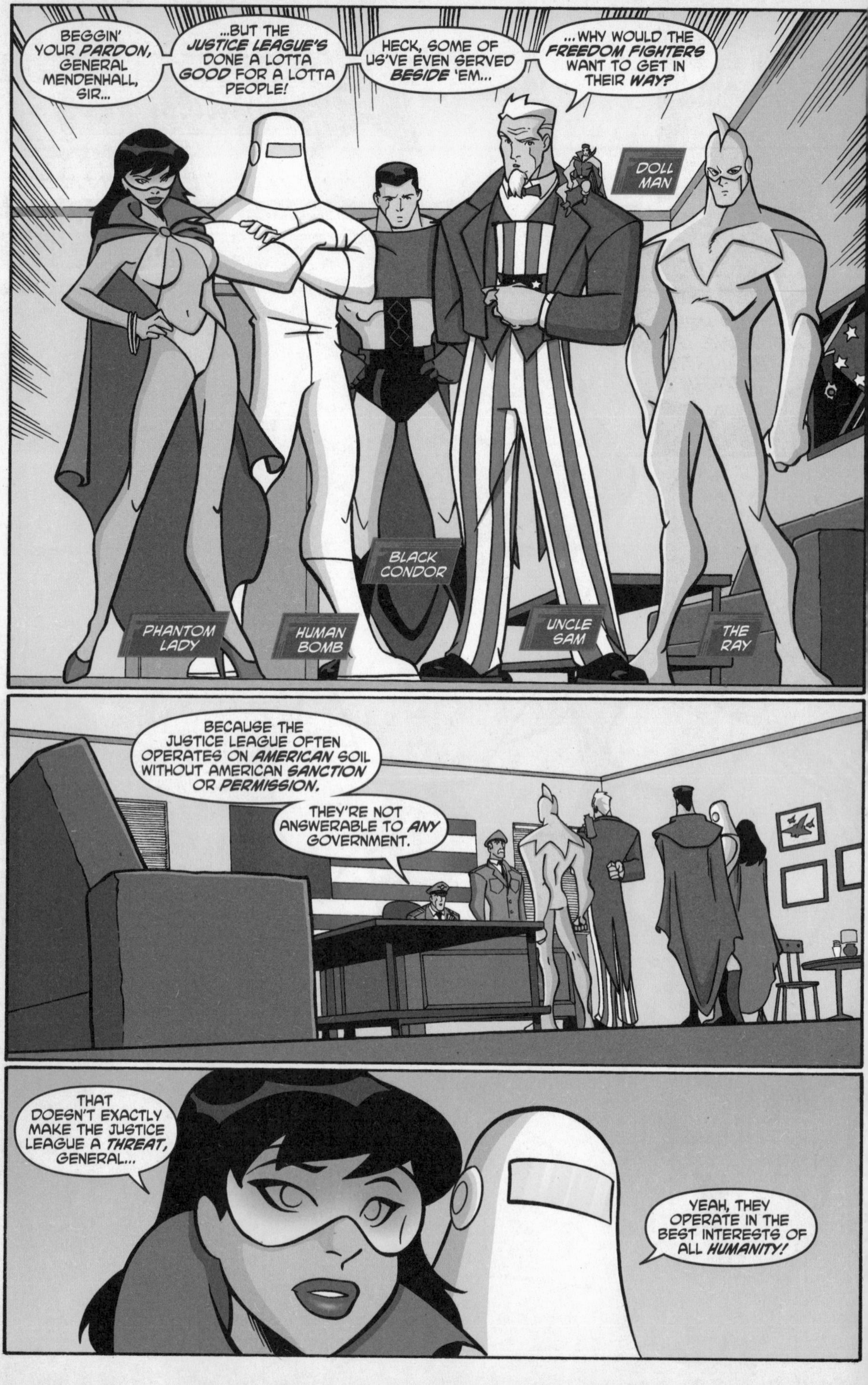
BEGGIN' YOUR PARDON, GENERAL MENDENHALL, SIR...
...BUT THE JUSTICE LEAGUE'S DONE A LOTTA GOOD FOR A LOTTA PEOPLE!
HECK, SOME OF US'VE EVEN SERVED BESIDE 'EM...
...WHY WOULD THE FREEDOM FIGHTERS WANT TO GET IN THEIR WAY?
DOLL MAN
BLACK CONDOR
PHANTOM LADY
HUMAN BOMB
UNCLE SAM
THE RAY
BECAUSE THE JUSTICE LEAGUE OFTEN OPERATES ON AMERICAN SOIL WITHOUT AMERICAN SANCTION OR PERMISSION.
THEY'RE NOT ANSWERABLE TO ANY GOVERNMENT.
THAT DOESN'T EXACTLY MAKE THE JUSTICE LEAGUE A THREAT, GENERAL...
YEAH, THEY OPERATE IN THE BEST INTERESTS OF ALL HUMANITY!

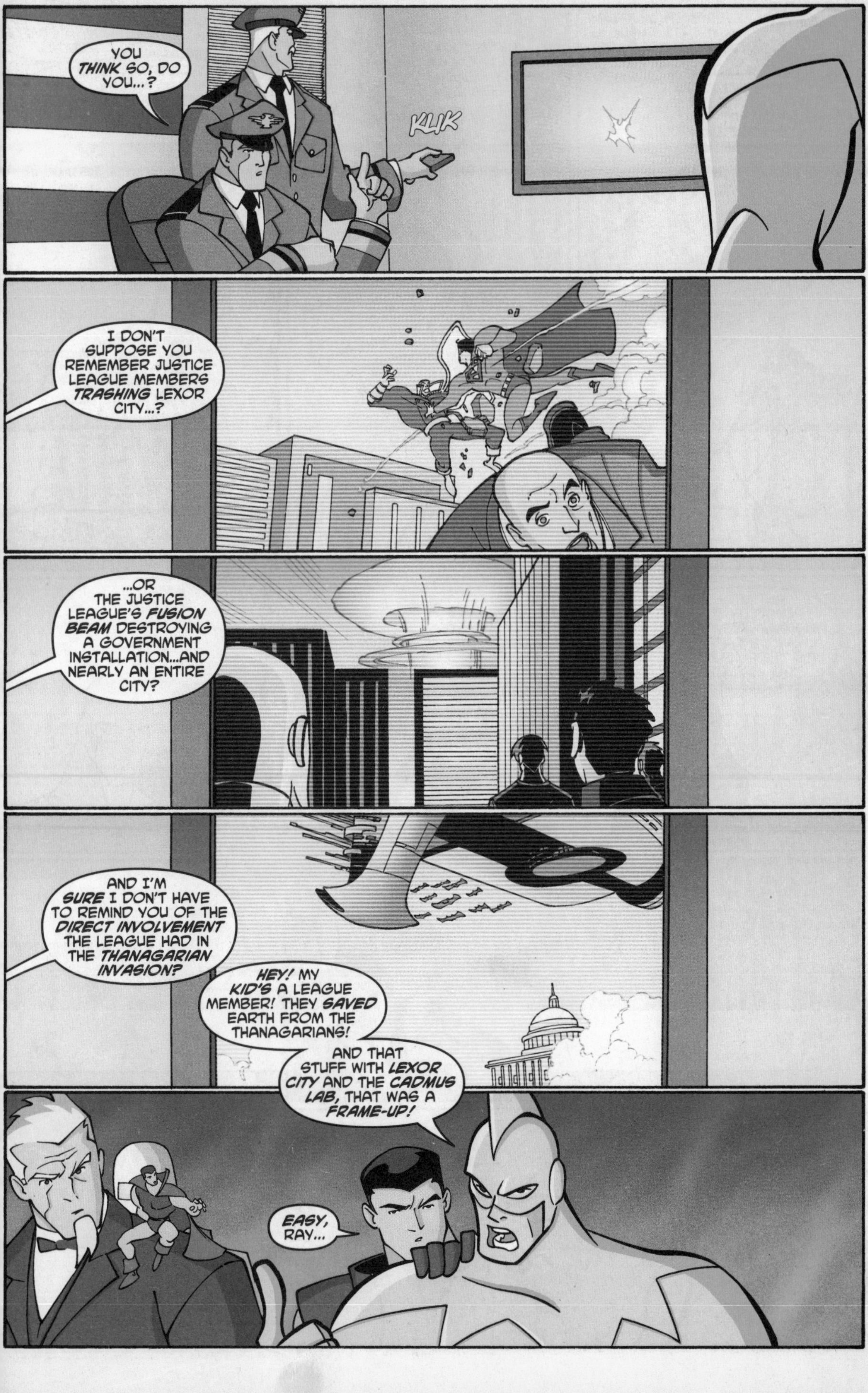
YOU THINK SO, DO YOU...?
KLIK
I DON'T SUPPOSE YOU REMEMBER JUSTICE LEAGUE MEMBERS TRASHING LEXOR CITY...?
...OR THE JUSTICE LEAGUE'S FUSION BEAM DESTROYING A GOVERNMENT INSTALLATION...AND NEARLY AN ENTIRE CITY?
AND I'M SURE I DON'T HAVE TO REMIND YOU OF THE DIRECT INVOLVEMENT THE LEAGUE HAD IN THE THANAGARIAN INVASION?
HEY! MY KID'S A LEAGUE MEMBER! THEY SAVED EARTH FROM THE THANAGARIANS!
AND THAT STUFF WITH LEXOR CITY AND THE CADMUS LAB, THAT WAS A FRAME-UP!
EASY, RAY...

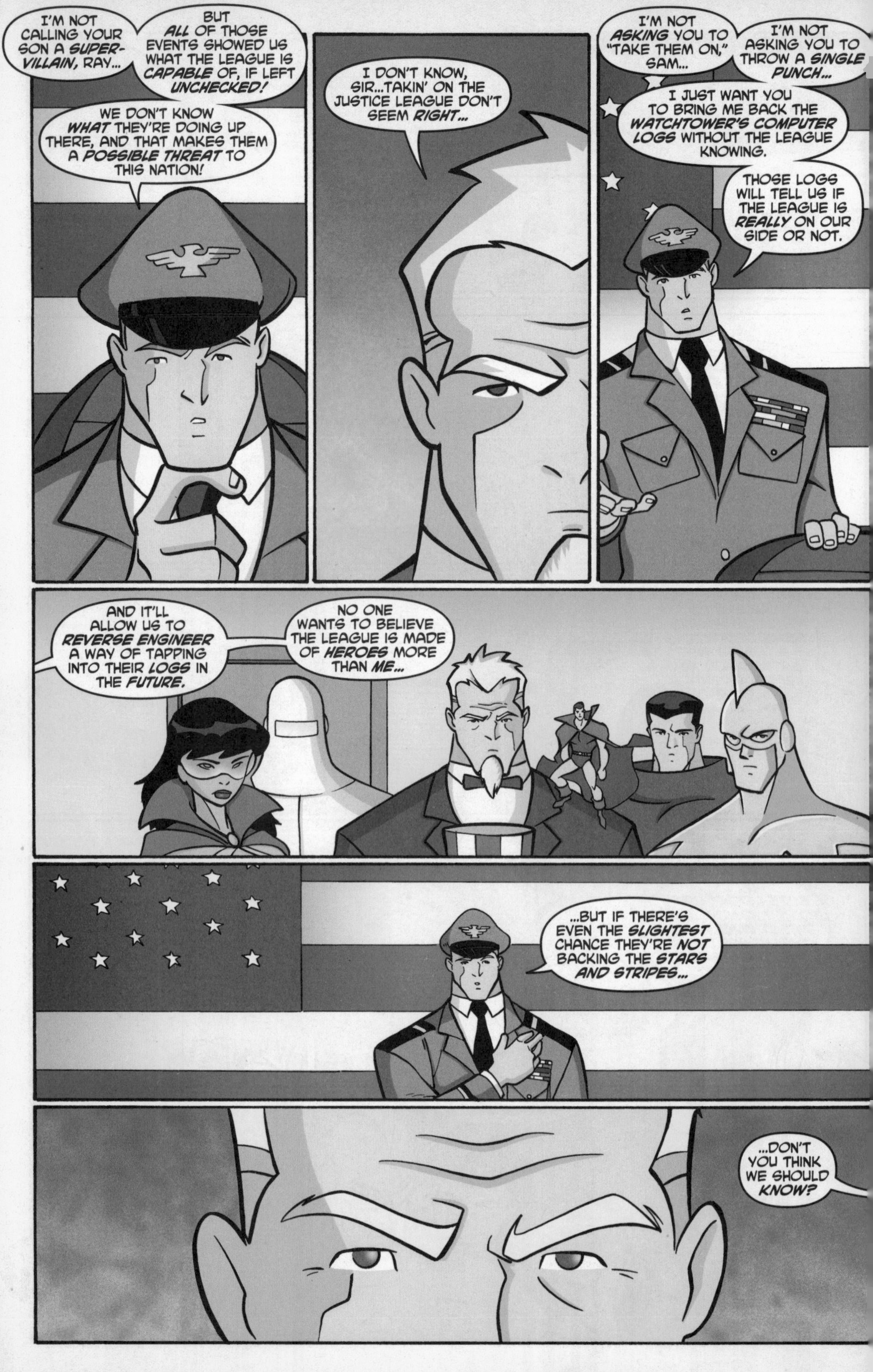
I'M NOT CALLING YOUR SON A SUPER-VILLAIN, RAY...
BUT ALL OF THOSE EVENTS SHOWED US WHAT THE LEAGUE IS CAPABLE OF, IF LEFT UNCHECKED!
WE DON'T KNOW WHAT THEY'RE DOING UP THERE, AND THAT MAKES THEM A POSSIBLE THREAT TO THIS NATION!
I DON'T KNOW, SIR...TAKIN' ON THE JUSTICE LEAGUE DON'T SEEM RIGHT...
I'M NOT ASKING YOU TO "TAKE THEM ON," SAM...
I'M NOT ASKING YOU TO THROW A SINGLE PUNCH...
I JUST WANT YOU TO BRING ME BACK THE WATCHTOWER'S COMPUTER LOGS WITHOUT THE LEAGUE KNOWING.
THOSE LOGS WILL TELL US IF THE LEAGUE IS REALLY ON OUR SIDE OR NOT.
AND IT'LL ALLOW US TO REVERSE ENGINEER A WAY OF TAPPING INTO THEIR LOGS IN THE FUTURE.
NO ONE WANTS TO BELIEVE THE LEAGUE IS MADE OF HEROES MORE THAN ME...
...BUT IF THERE'S EVEN THE SLIGHTEST CHANCE THEY'RE NOT BACKING THE STARS AND STRIPES...
...DON'T YOU THINK WE SHOULD KNOW?

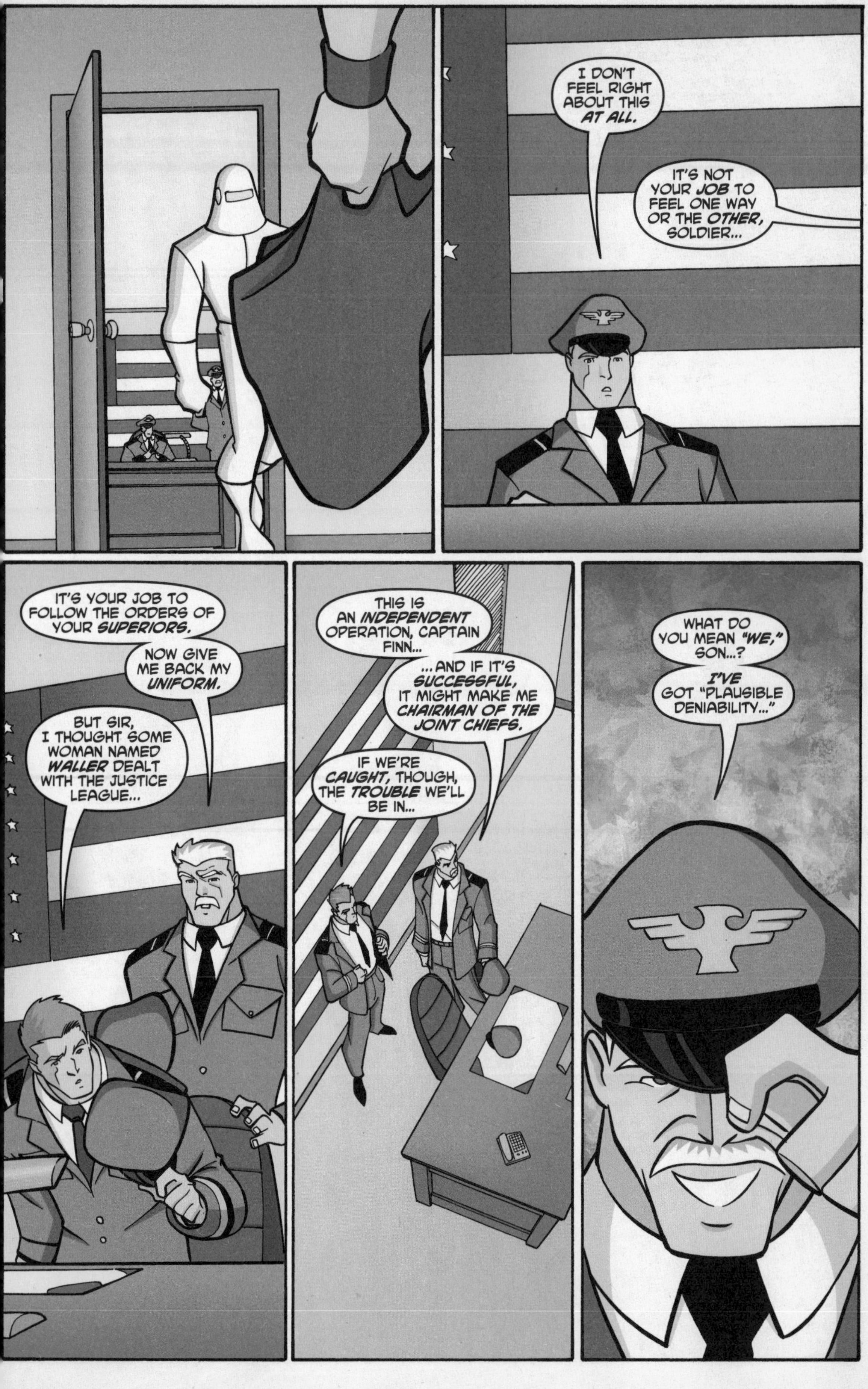
I DON'T FEEL RIGHT ABOUT THIS AT ALL.
IT'S NOT YOUR JOB TO FEEL ONE WAY OR THE OTHER, SOLDIER...
IT'S YOUR JOB TO FOLLOW THE ORDERS OF YOUR SUPERIORS.
NOW GIVE ME BACK MY UNIFORM.
BUT SIR, I THOUGHT SOME WOMAN NAMED WALLER DEALT WITH THE JUSTICE LEAGUE...
THIS IS AN INDEPENDENT OPERATION, CAPTAIN FINN...
...AND IF IT'S SUCCESSFUL, IT MIGHT MAKE ME CHAIRMAN OF THE JOINT CHIEFS.
IF WE'RE CAUGHT, THOUGH, THE TROUBLE WE'LL BE IN...
WHAT DO YOU MEAN "WE," SON...?
I'VE GOT "PLAUSIBLE DENIABILITY..."

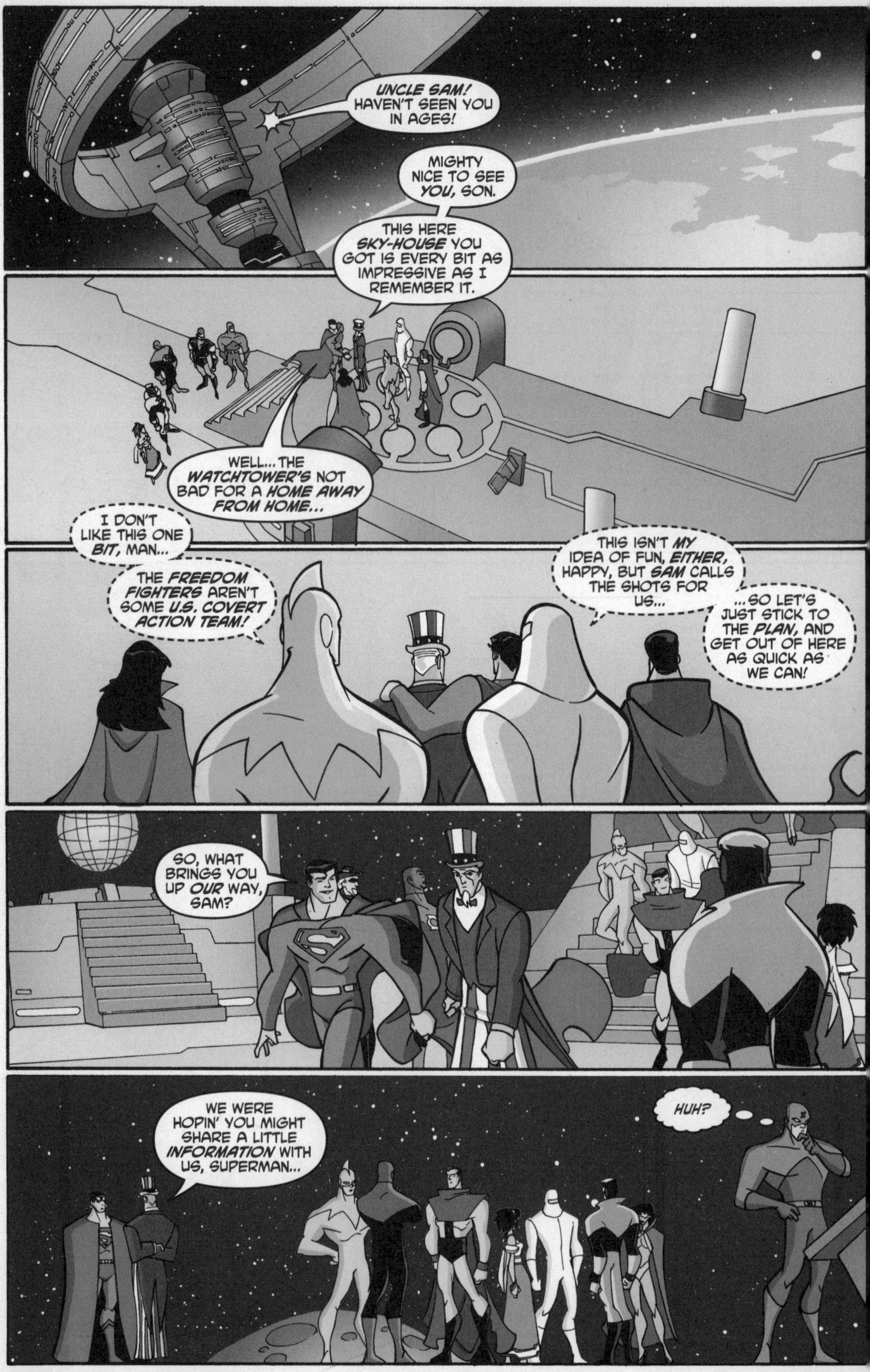

UNCLE SAM! HAVEN'T SEEN YOU IN AGES!
MIGHTY NICE TO SEE YOU, SON.
THIS HERE SKY-HOUSE YOU GOT IS EVERY BIT AS IMPRESSIVE AS I REMEMBER IT.
WELL... THE WATCHTOWER'S NOT BAD FOR A HOME AWAY FROM HOME...
I DON'T LIKE THIS ONE BIT, MAN...
THE FREEDOM FIGHTERS AREN'T SOME U.S. COVERT ACTION TEAM!
THIS ISN'T MY IDEA OF FUN, EITHER, HAPPY, BUT SAM CALLS THE SHOTS FOR US...
...SO LET'S JUST STICK TO THE PLAN, AND GET OUT OF HERE AS QUICK AS WE CAN!
SO, WHAT BRINGS YOU UP OUR WAY, SAM?
WE WERE HOPIN' YOU MIGHT SHARE A LITTLE INFORMATION WITH US, SUPERMAN...
HUH?

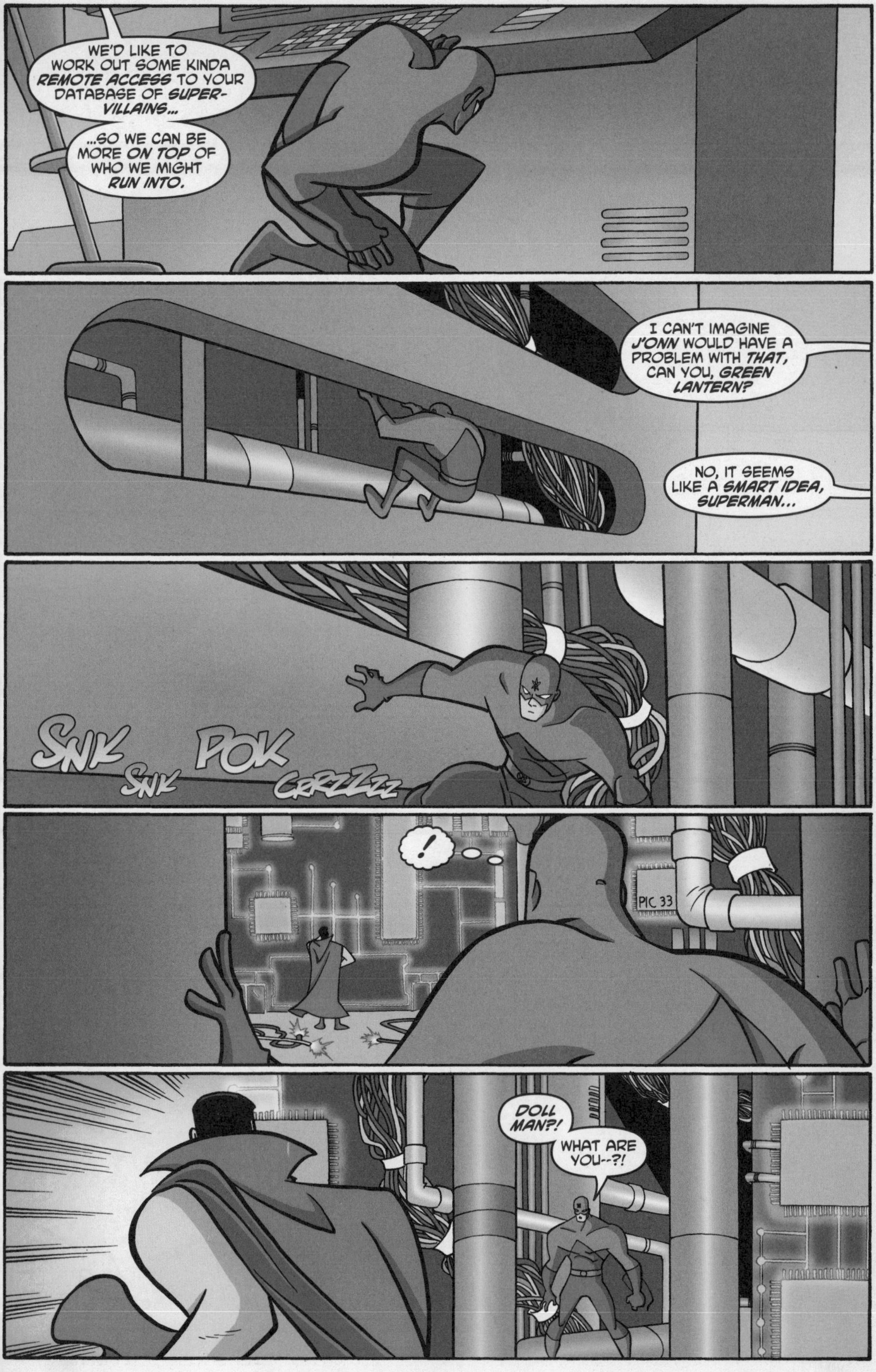
WE'D LIKE TO WORK OUT SOME KINDA REMOTE ACCESS TO YOUR DATABASE OF SUPER-VILLAINS...
...SO WE CAN BE MORE ON TOP OF WHO WE MIGHT RUN INTO.
I CAN'T IMAGINE J'ONN WOULD HAVE A PROBLEM WITH THAT, CAN YOU, GREEN LANTERN?
NO, IT SEEMS LIKE A SMART IDEA, SUPERMAN...
SNK SNK
POK
CRRZZZzz
!
PIC 33
DOLL MAN?!
WHAT ARE YOU--?!

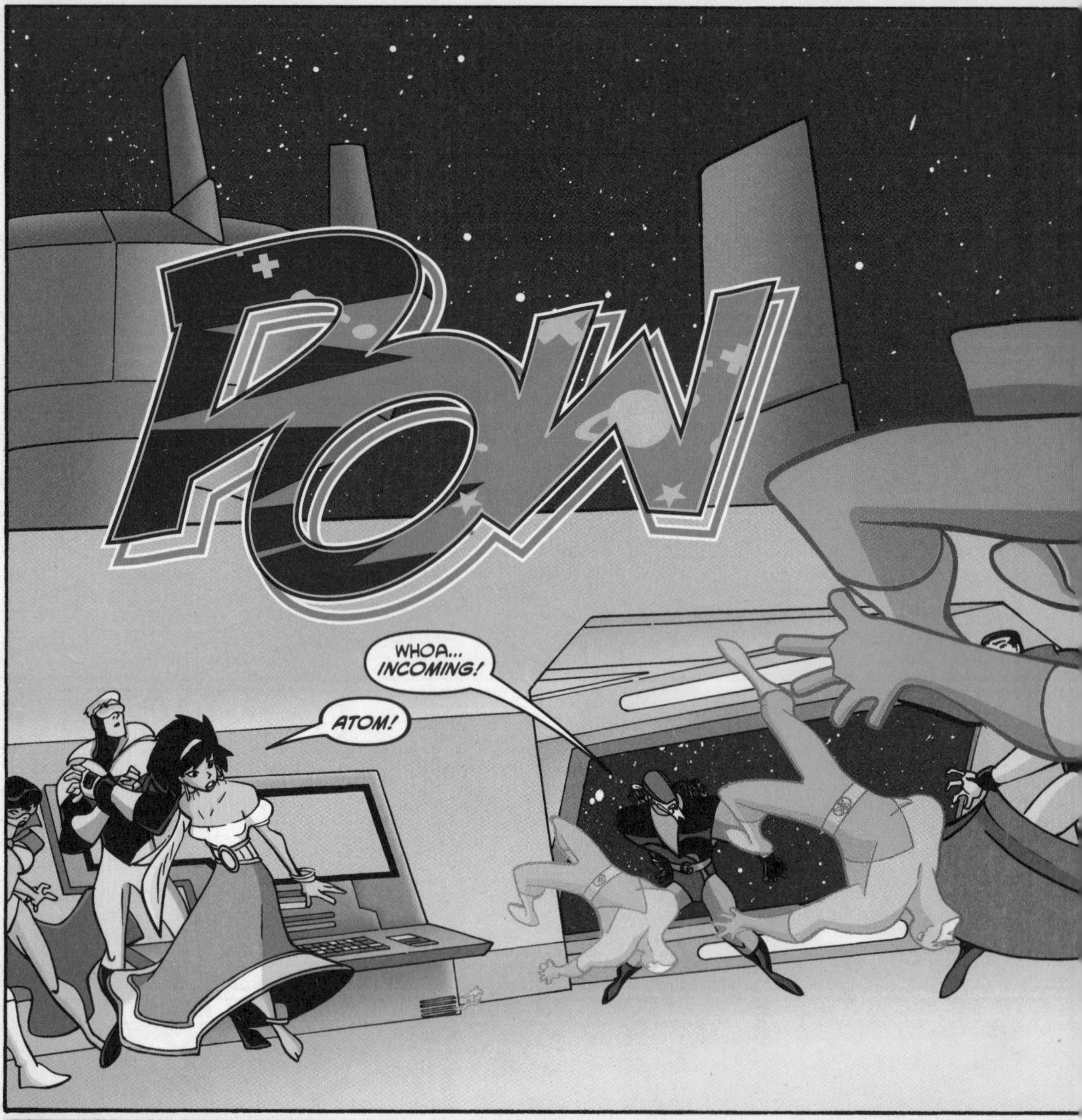
POW
WHOA... INCOMING!
ATOM!

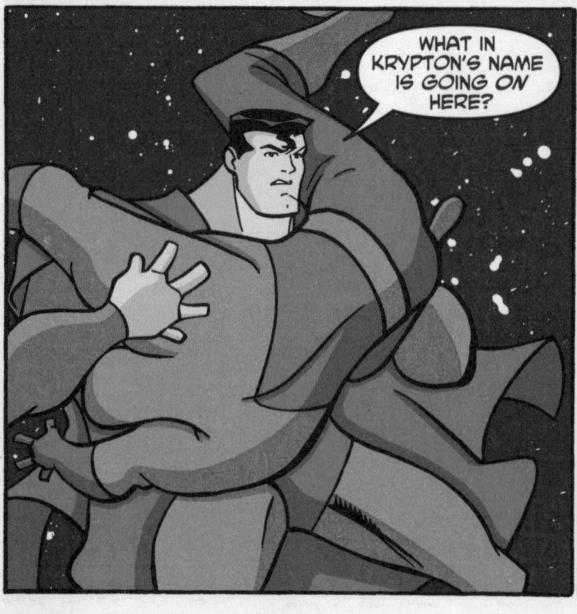
WHAT IN KRYPTON'S NAME IS GOING ON HERE?

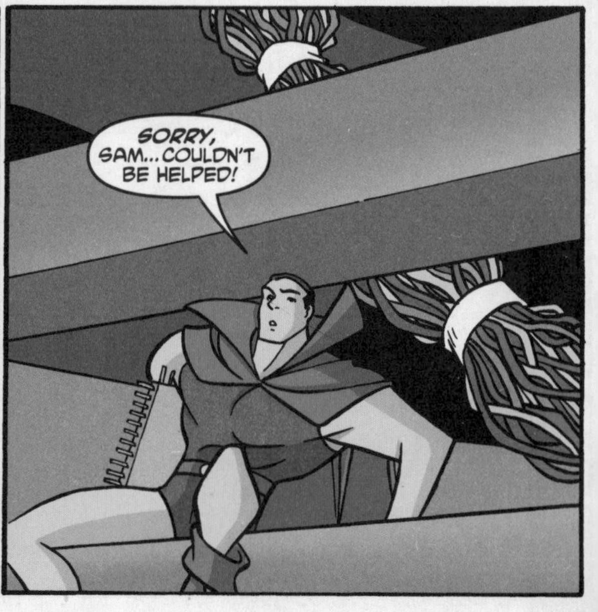
SORRY, SAM...COULDN'T BE HELPED!

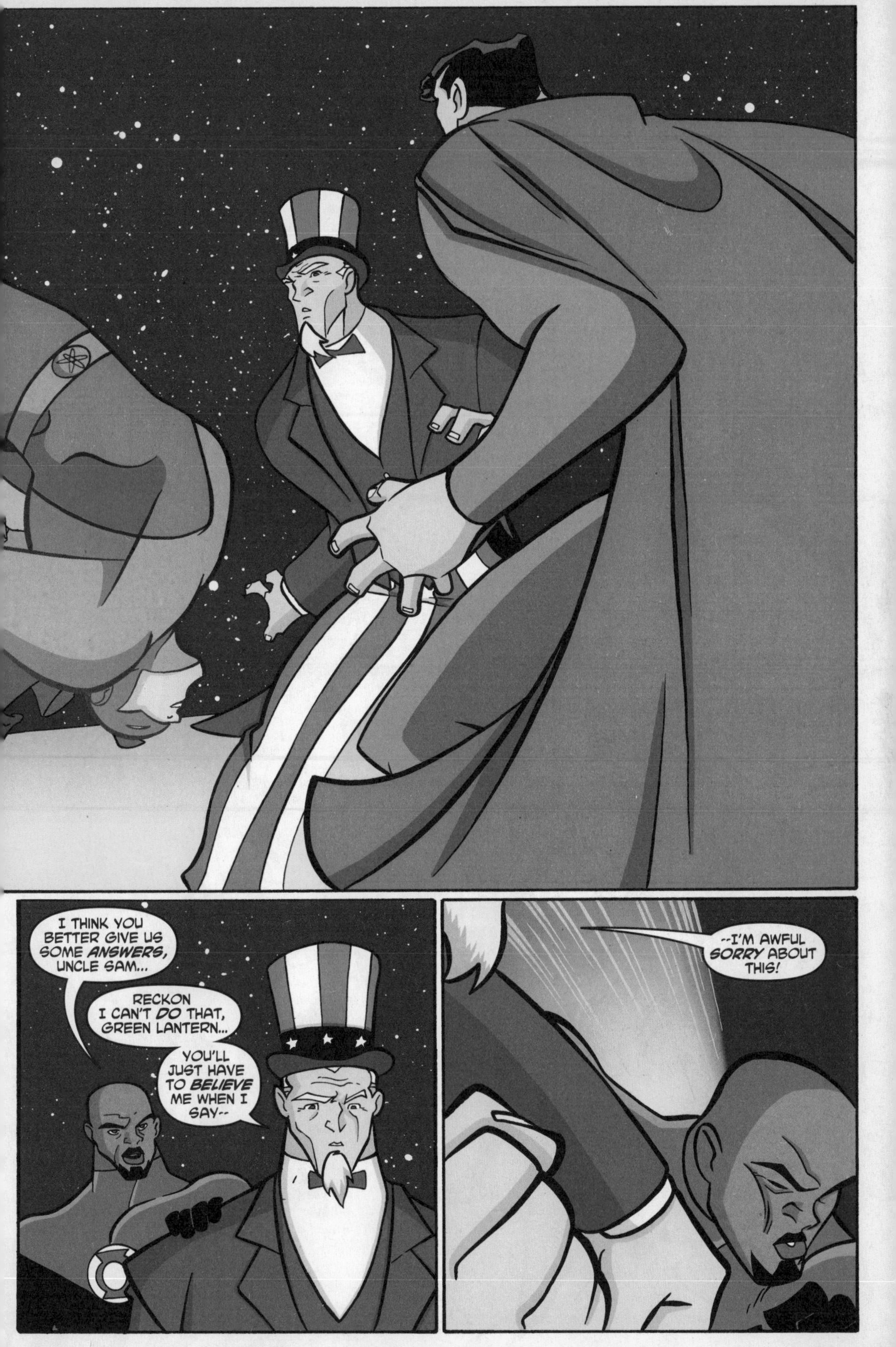
I THINK YOU BETTER GIVE US SOME ANSWERS, UNCLE SAM...
RECKON I CAN'T DO THAT, GREEN LANTERN...
YOU'LL JUST HAVE TO BELIEVE ME WHEN I SAY--
--I'M AWFUL SORRY ABOUT THIS!

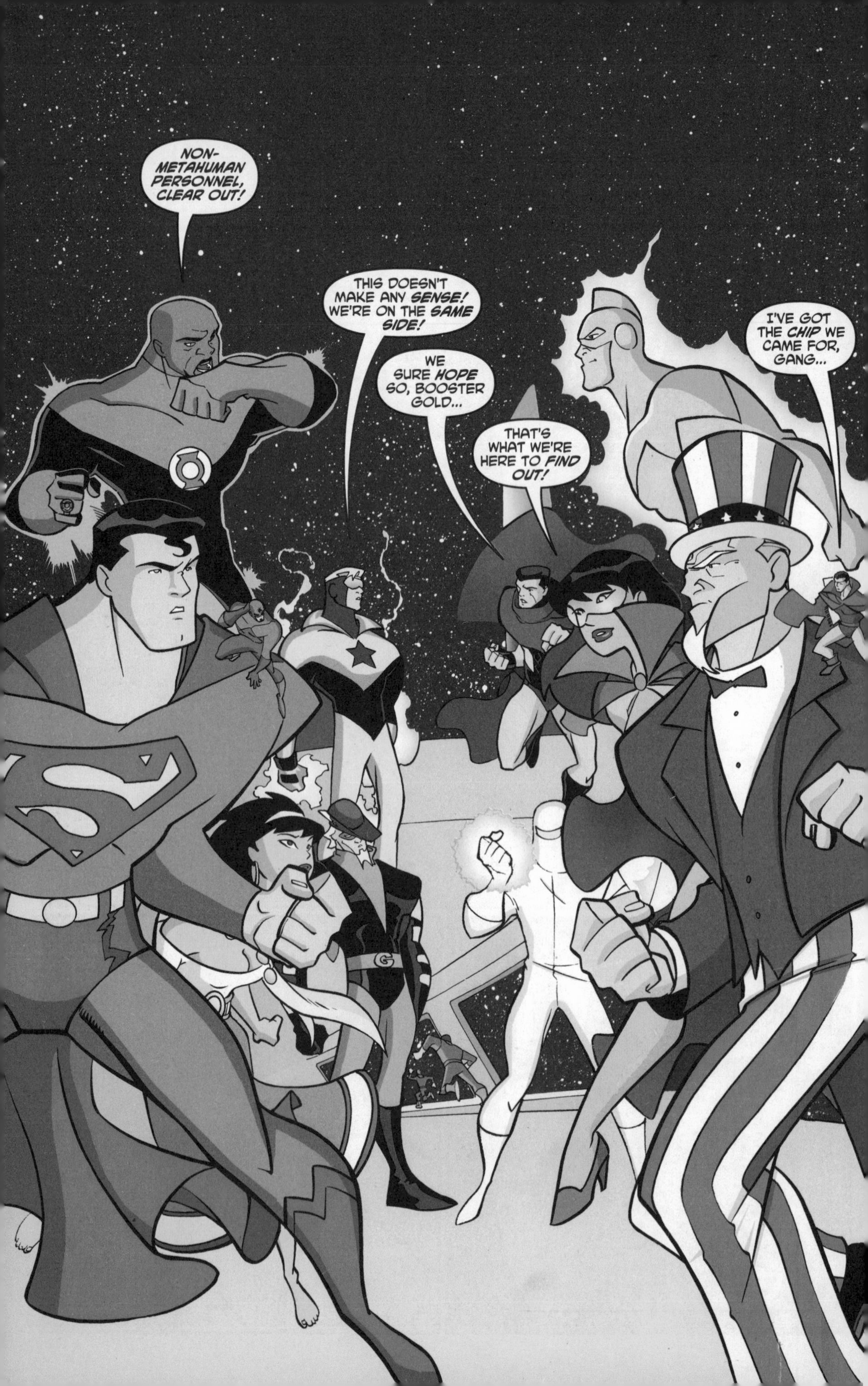
NON-METAHUMAN PERSONNEL, CLEAR OUT!
THIS DOESN'T MAKE ANY *SENSE!* WE'RE ON THE *SAME SIDE!*
WE SURE *HOPE* SO, BOOSTER GOLD...
THAT'S WHAT WE'RE HERE TO *FIND OUT!*
I'VE GOT THE *CHIP* WE CAME FOR, GANG...

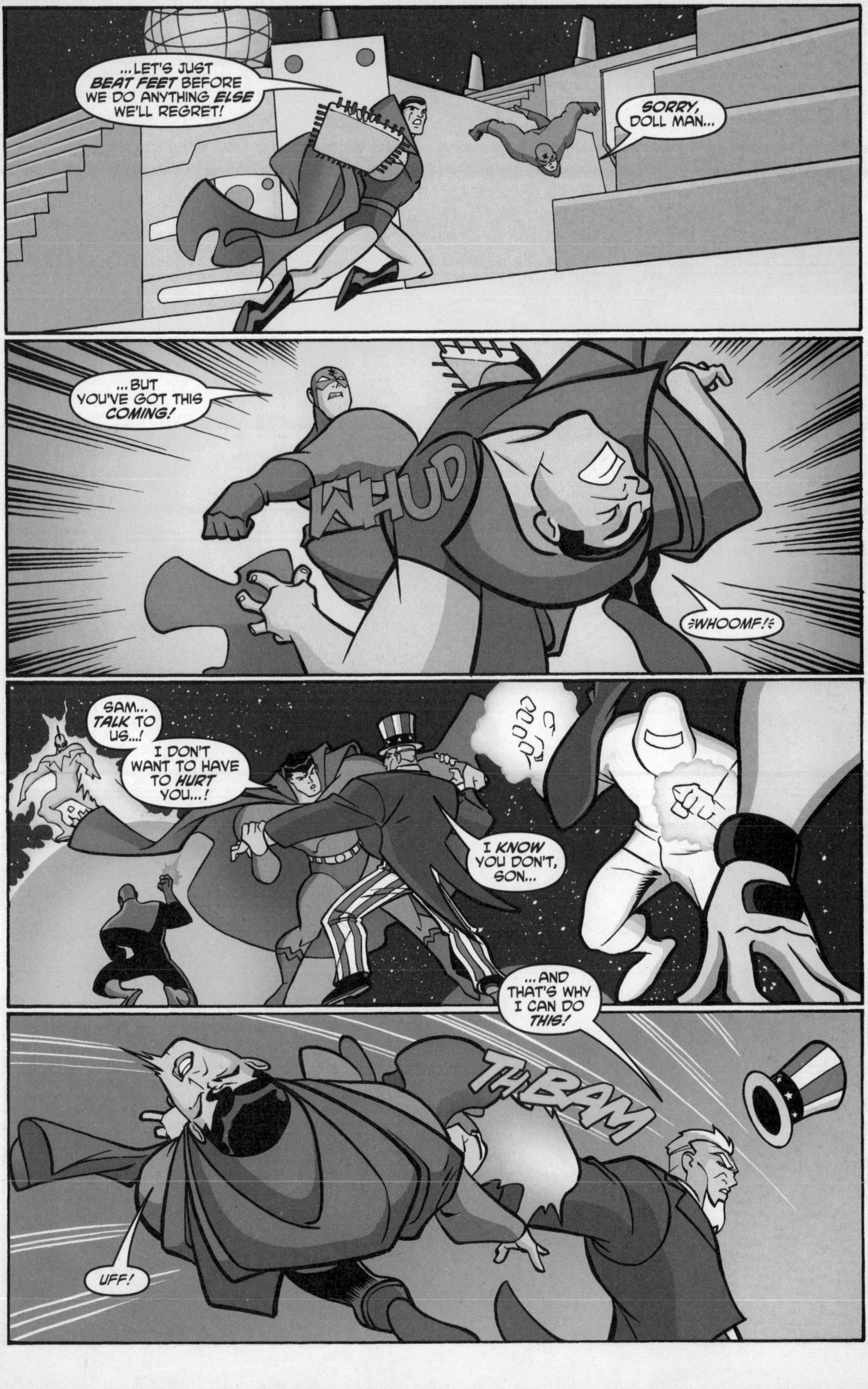
...LET'S JUST BEAT FEET BEFORE WE DO ANYTHING ELSE WE'LL REGRET!
SORRY, DOLL MAN...
...BUT YOU'VE GOT THIS COMING!
WHUD
WHOOMF!
SAM... TALK TO US...!
I DON'T WANT TO HAVE TO HURT YOU...!
I KNOW YOU DON'T, SON...
...AND THAT'S WHY I CAN DO THIS!
THBAM
UFF!

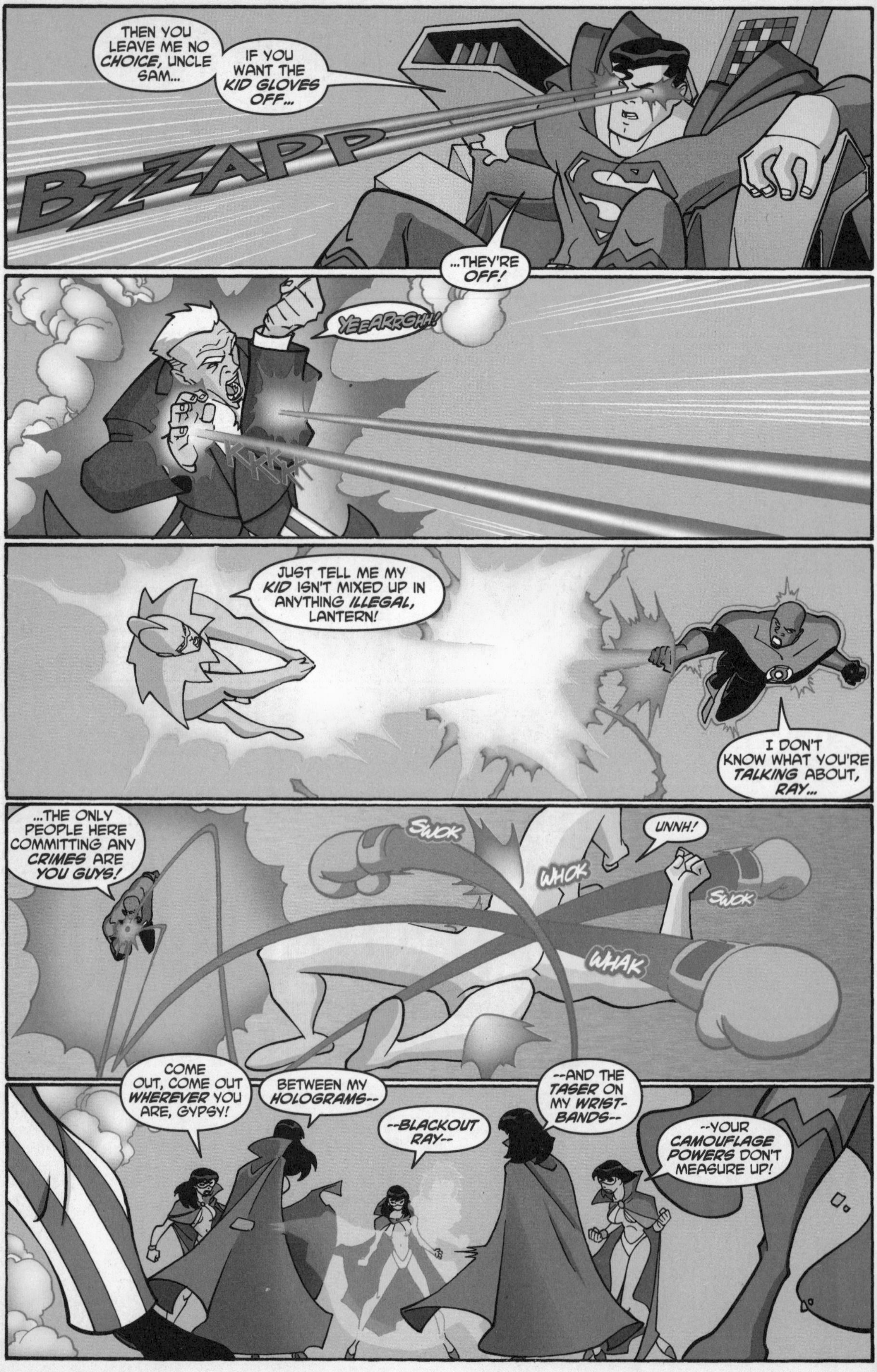
THEN YOU LEAVE ME NO CHOICE, UNCLE SAM...
IF YOU WANT THE KID GLOVES OFF...
BZZAPP
...THEY'RE OFF!
YEEARRGHH!
KKKK
JUST TELL ME MY KID ISN'T MIXED UP IN ANYTHING ILLEGAL, LANTERN!
I DON'T KNOW WHAT YOU'RE TALKING ABOUT, RAY...
...THE ONLY PEOPLE HERE COMMITTING ANY CRIMES ARE YOU GUYS!
SWOK
UNNH!
WHOK
SWOK
WHAK
COME OUT, COME OUT WHEREVER YOU ARE, GYPSY!
BETWEEN MY HOLOGRAMS--
--BLACKOUT RAY--
--AND THE TASER ON MY WRIST-BANDS--
--YOUR CAMOUFLAGE POWERS DON'T MEASURE UP!

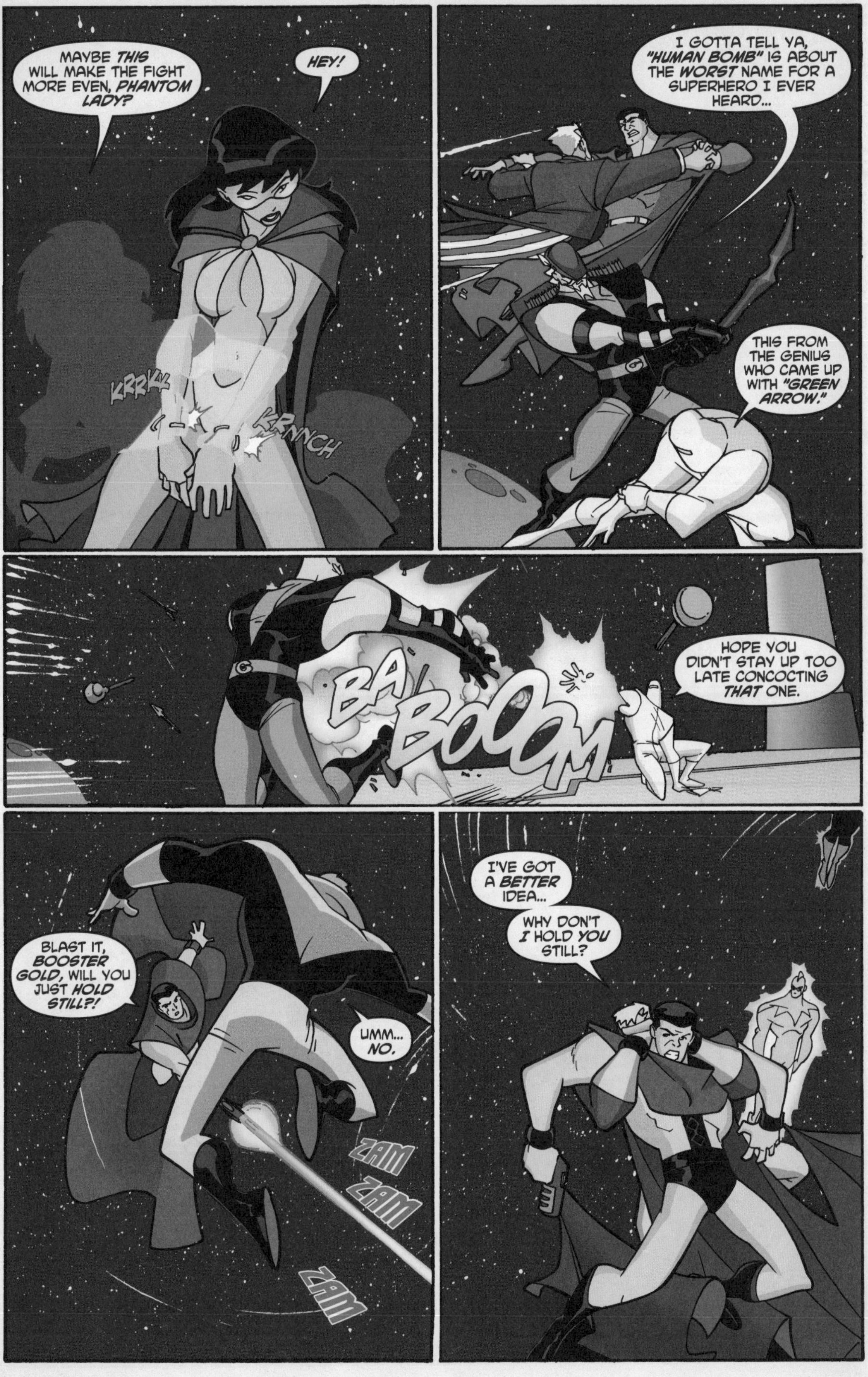

MAYBE THIS WILL MAKE THE FIGHT MORE EVEN, PHANTOM LADY?
HEY!
KRRKL
KRNNCH
I GOTTA TELL YA, "HUMAN BOMB" IS ABOUT THE WORST NAME FOR A SUPERHERO I EVER HEARD...
THIS FROM THE GENIUS WHO CAME UP WITH "GREEN ARROW."
BA BOOOM
HOPE YOU DIDN'T STAY UP TOO LATE CONCOCTING THAT ONE.
BLAST IT, BOOSTER GOLD, WILL YOU JUST HOLD STILL?!
UMM... NO.
ZAM
ZAM
ZAM
I'VE GOT A BETTER IDEA...
WHY DON'T I HOLD YOU STILL?

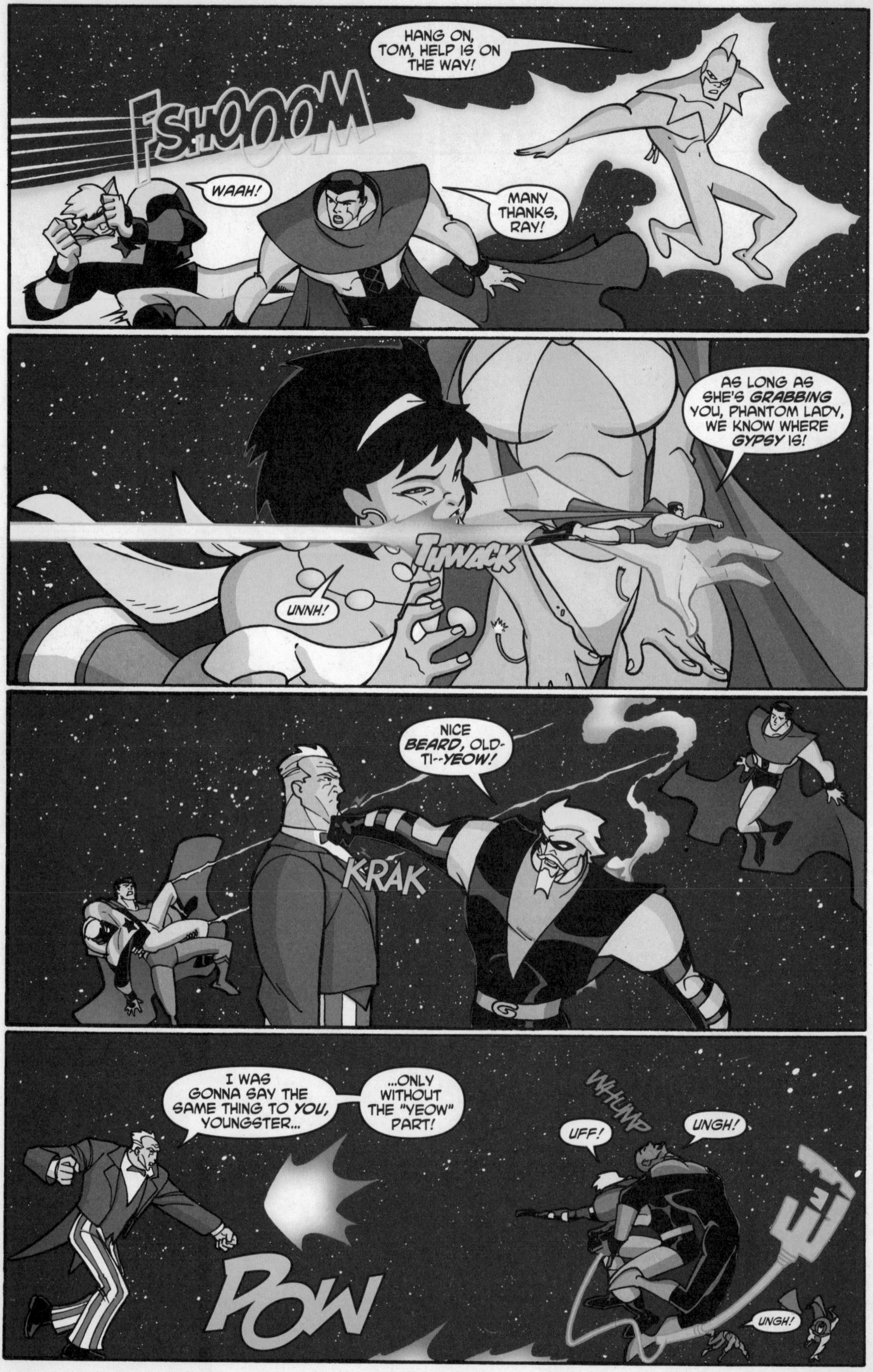
HANG ON, TOM, HELP IS ON THE WAY!
FSHOOOM
WAAH!
MANY THANKS, RAY!
AS LONG AS SHE'S *GRABBING* YOU, PHANTOM LADY, WE KNOW WHERE *GYPSY* IS!
THWACK
UNNH!
NICE *BEARD*, OLD-TI--*YEOW!*
KRAK
I WAS GONNA SAY THE SAME THING TO *YOU*, YOUNGSTER...
...ONLY WITHOUT THE "YEOW" PART!
WHUMP
UFF!
UNGH!
POW
UNGH!

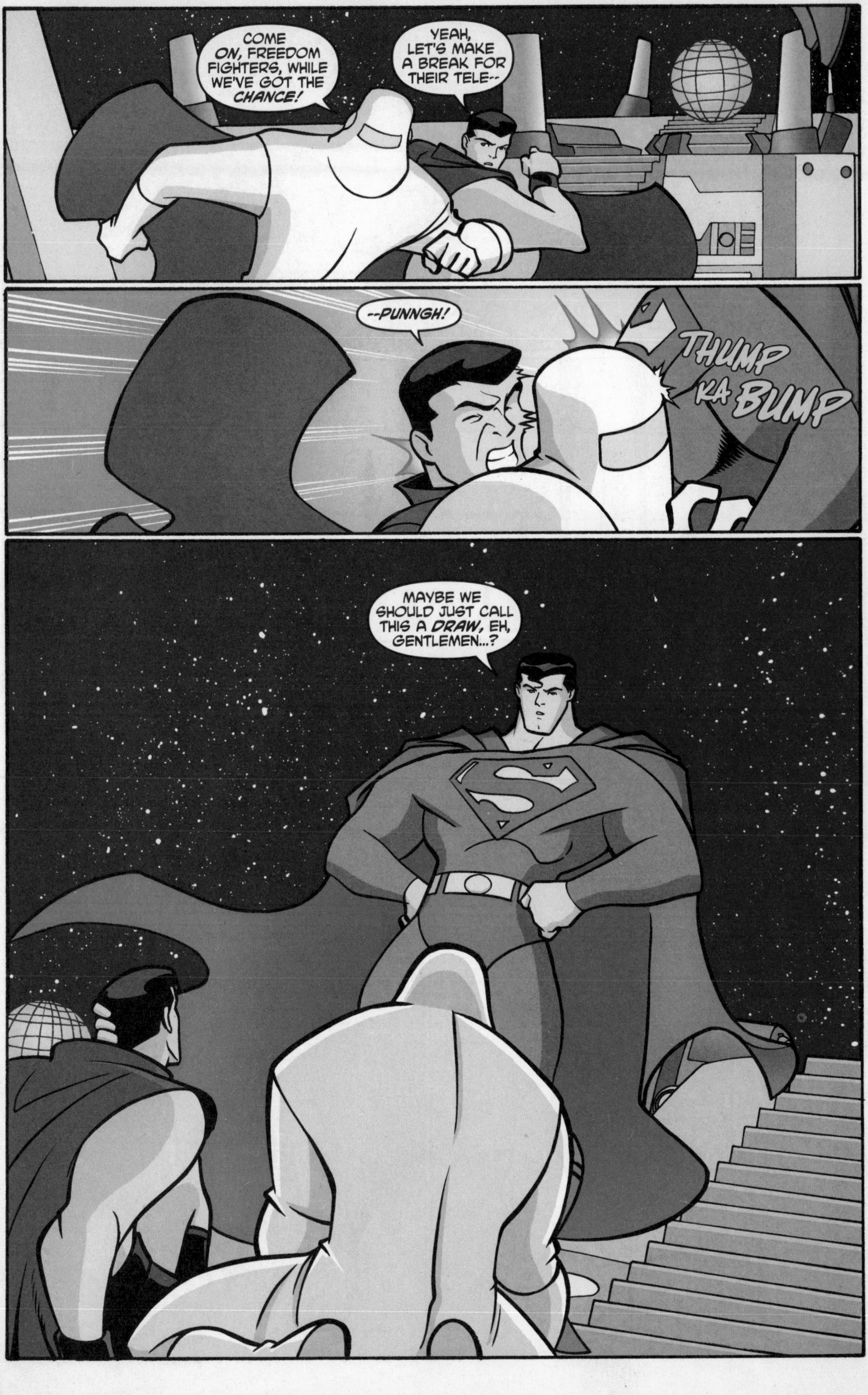
COME ON, FREEDOM FIGHTERS, WHILE WE'VE GOT THE CHANCE!
YEAH, LET'S MAKE A BREAK FOR THEIR TELE--
--PUNNGH!
THUMP KA BUMP
MAYBE WE SHOULD JUST CALL THIS A DRAW, EH, GENTLEMEN...?

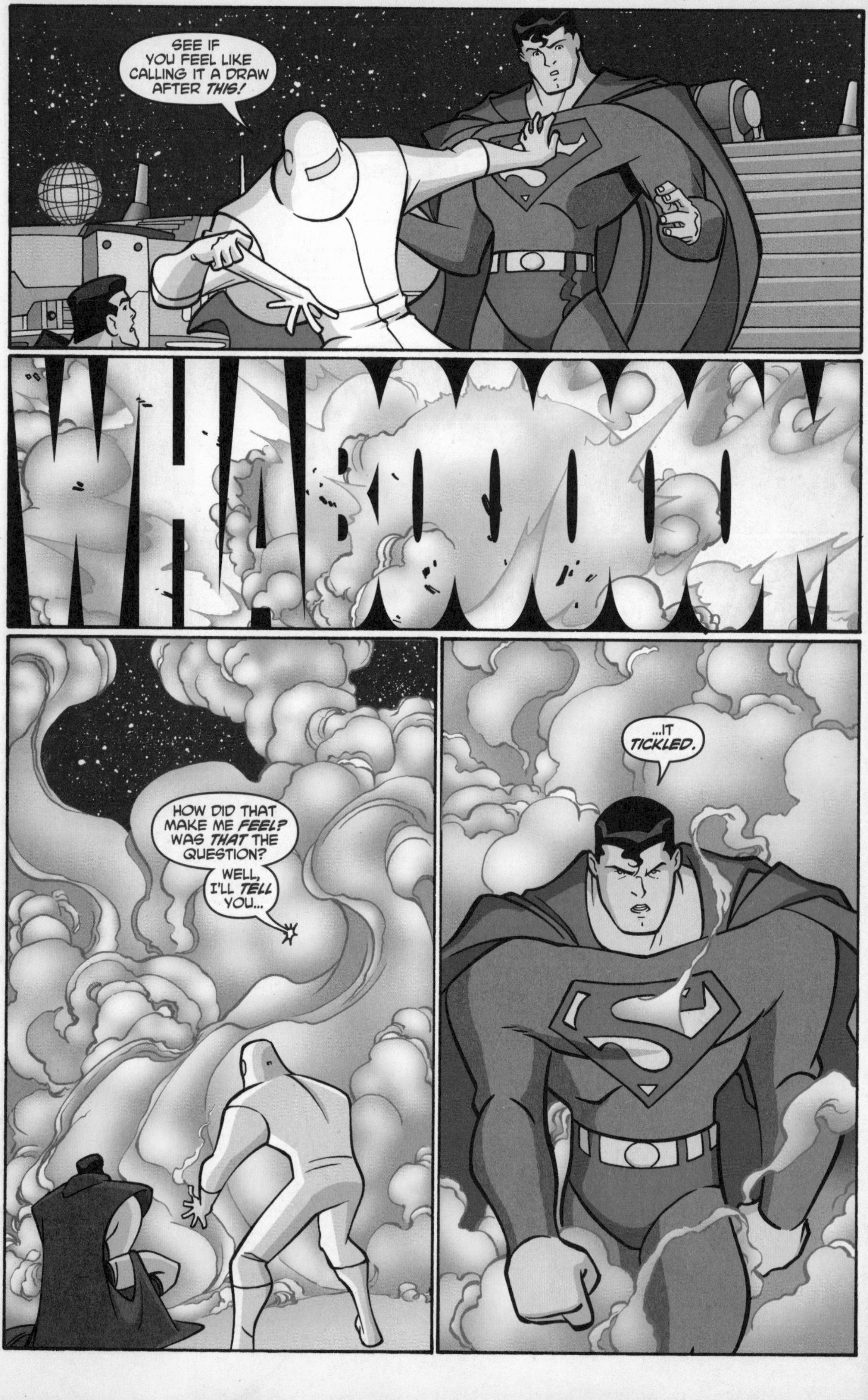
SEE IF YOU FEEL LIKE CALLING IT A DRAW AFTER *THIS!*
WHABOOOOM
HOW DID THAT MAKE ME *FEEL?* WAS *THAT* THE QUESTION?
WELL, I'LL *TELL* YOU...
...IT *TICKLED.*

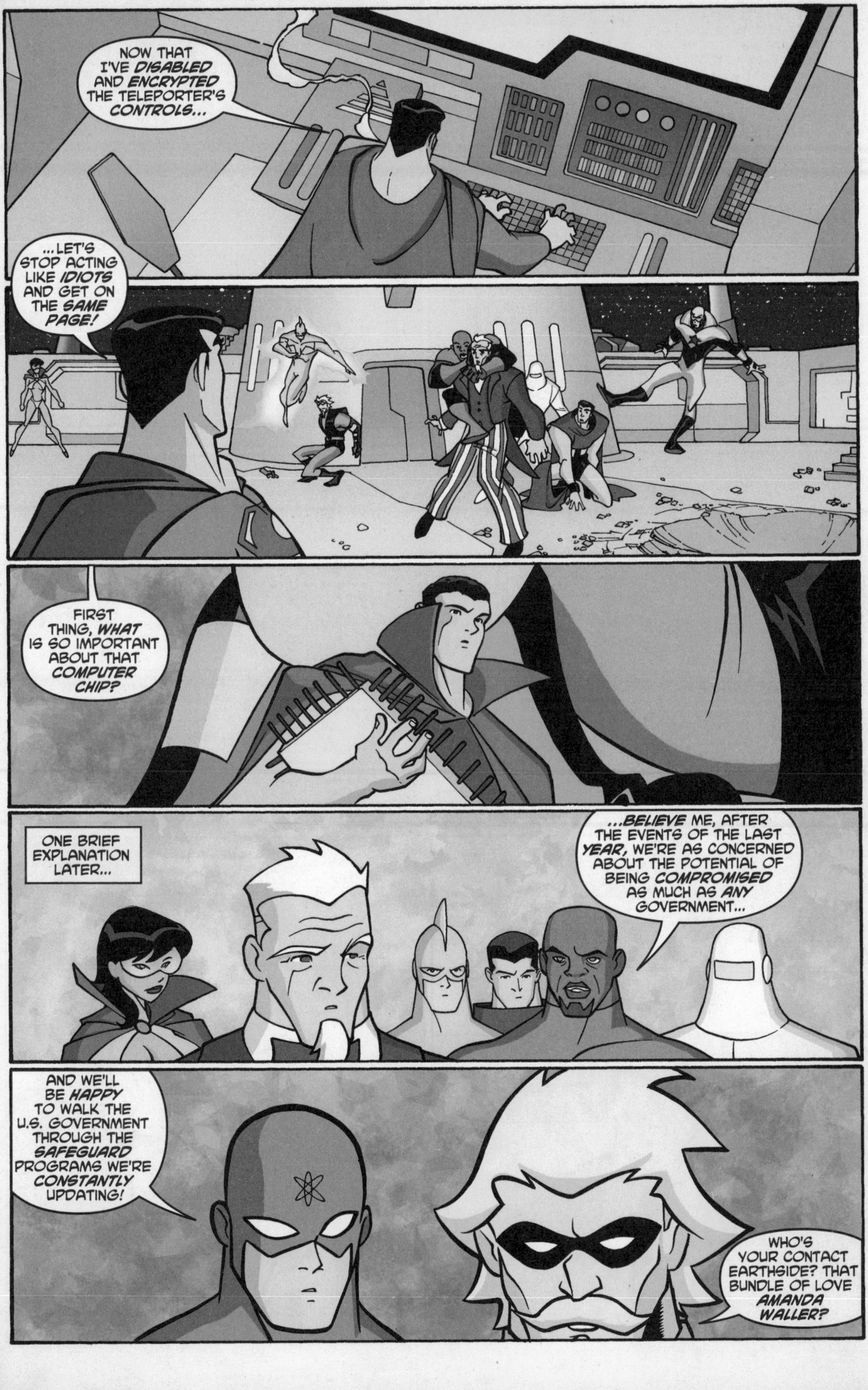
NOW THAT I'VE DISABLED AND ENCRYPTED THE TELEPORTER'S CONTROLS...
...LET'S STOP ACTING LIKE IDIOTS AND GET ON THE SAME PAGE!
FIRST THING, WHAT IS SO IMPORTANT ABOUT THAT COMPUTER CHIP?
ONE BRIEF EXPLANATION LATER...
...BELIEVE ME, AFTER THE EVENTS OF THE LAST YEAR, WE'RE AS CONCERNED ABOUT THE POTENTIAL OF BEING COMPROMISED AS MUCH AS ANY GOVERNMENT...
AND WE'LL BE HAPPY TO WALK THE U.S. GOVERNMENT THROUGH THE SAFEGUARD PROGRAMS WE'RE CONSTANTLY UPDATING!
WHO'S YOUR CONTACT EARTHSIDE? THAT BUNDLE OF LOVE AMANDA WALLER?

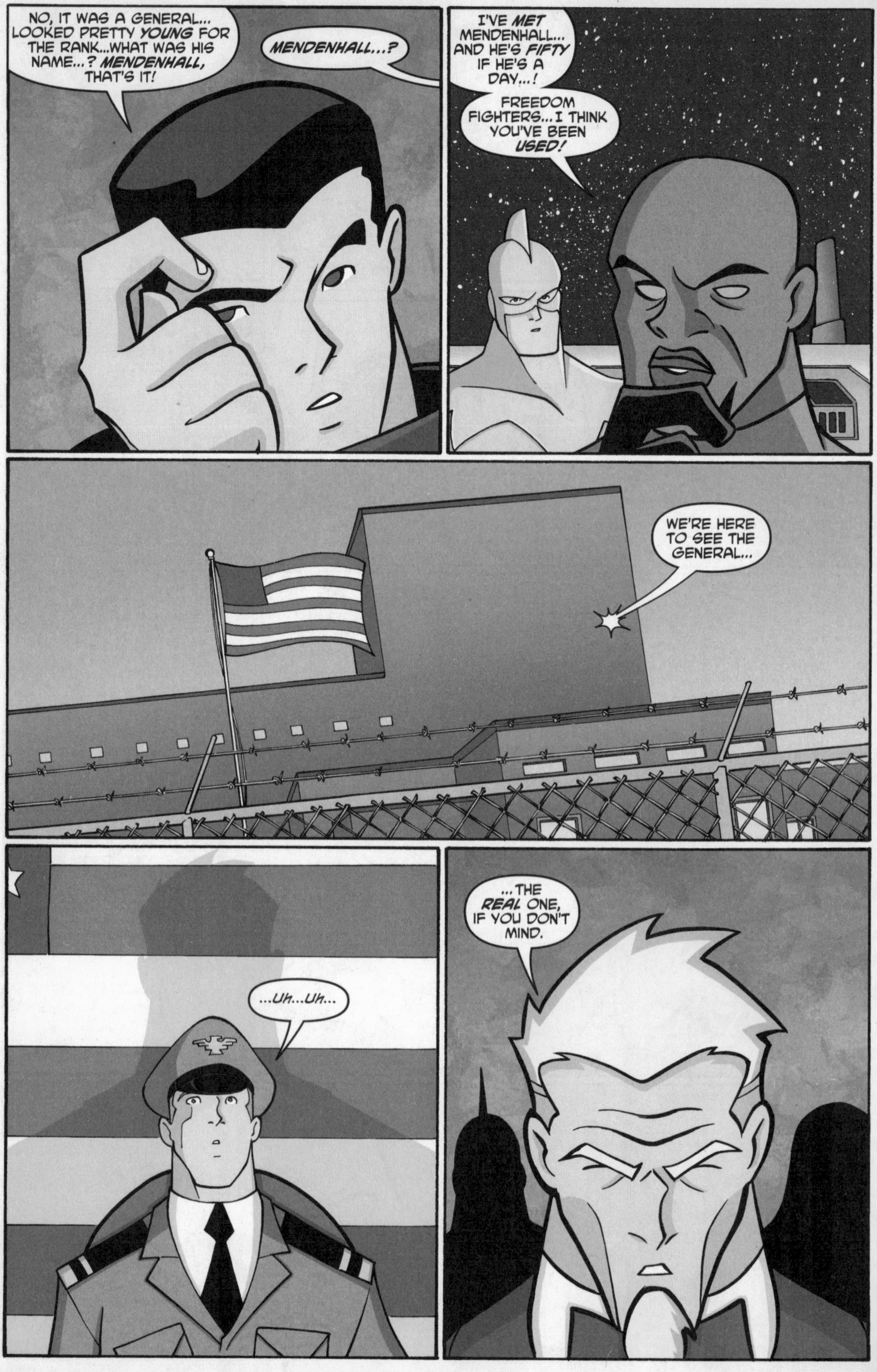
NO, IT WAS A GENERAL... LOOKED PRETTY YOUNG FOR THE RANK...WHAT WAS HIS NAME...? MENDENHALL, THAT'S IT!
MENDENHALL...?
I'VE MET MENDENHALL... AND HE'S FIFTY IF HE'S A DAY...!
FREEDOM FIGHTERS...I THINK YOU'VE BEEN USED!
WE'RE HERE TO SEE THE GENERAL...
...Uh...Uh...
...THE REAL ONE, IF YOU DON'T MIND.

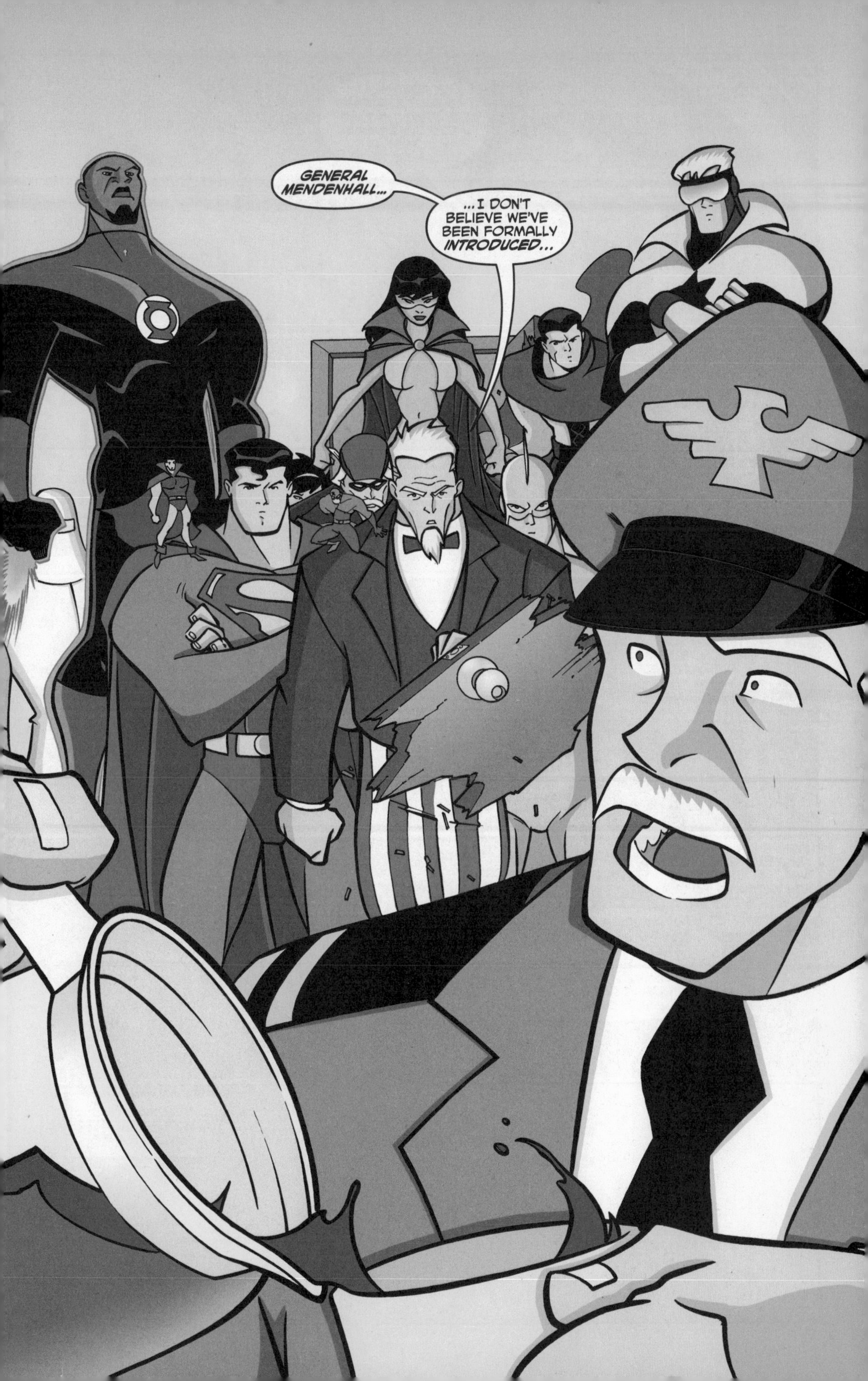
GENERAL MENDENHALL...
...I DON'T BELIEVE WE'VE BEEN FORMALLY *INTRODUCED*...

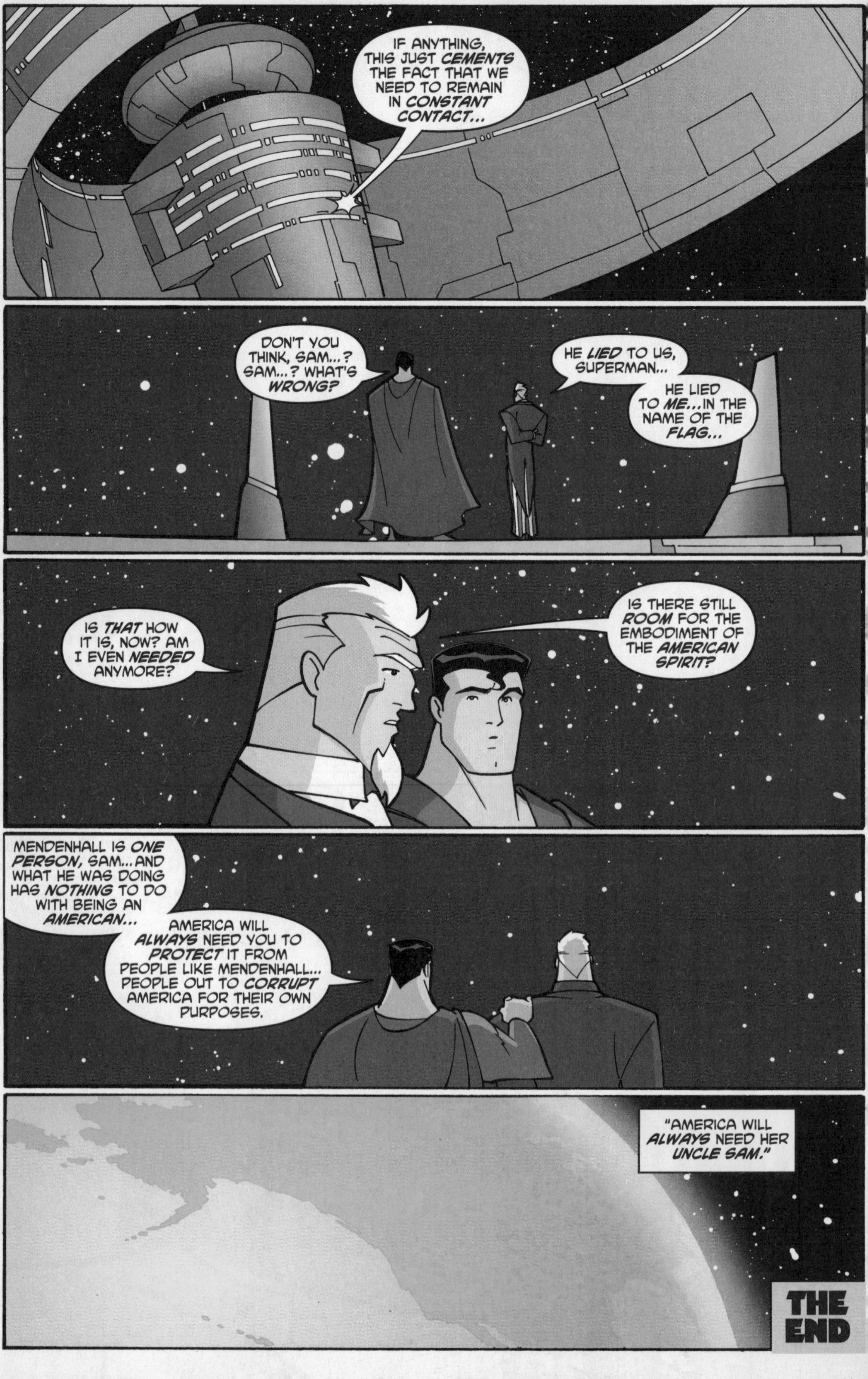
IF ANYTHING, THIS JUST CEMENTS THE FACT THAT WE NEED TO REMAIN IN CONSTANT CONTACT...
DON'T YOU THINK, SAM...? SAM...? WHAT'S WRONG?
HE LIED TO US, SUPERMAN...
HE LIED TO ME...IN THE NAME OF THE FLAG...
IS THAT HOW IT IS, NOW? AM I EVEN NEEDED ANYMORE?
IS THERE STILL ROOM FOR THE EMBODIMENT OF THE AMERICAN SPIRIT?
MENDENHALL IS ONE PERSON, SAM...AND WHAT HE WAS DOING HAS NOTHING TO DO WITH BEING AN AMERICAN...
AMERICA WILL ALWAYS NEED YOU TO PROTECT IT FROM PEOPLE LIKE MENDENHALL... PEOPLE OUT TO CORRUPT AMERICA FOR THEIR OWN PURPOSES.
"AMERICA WILL ALWAYS NEED HER UNCLE SAM."
THE END

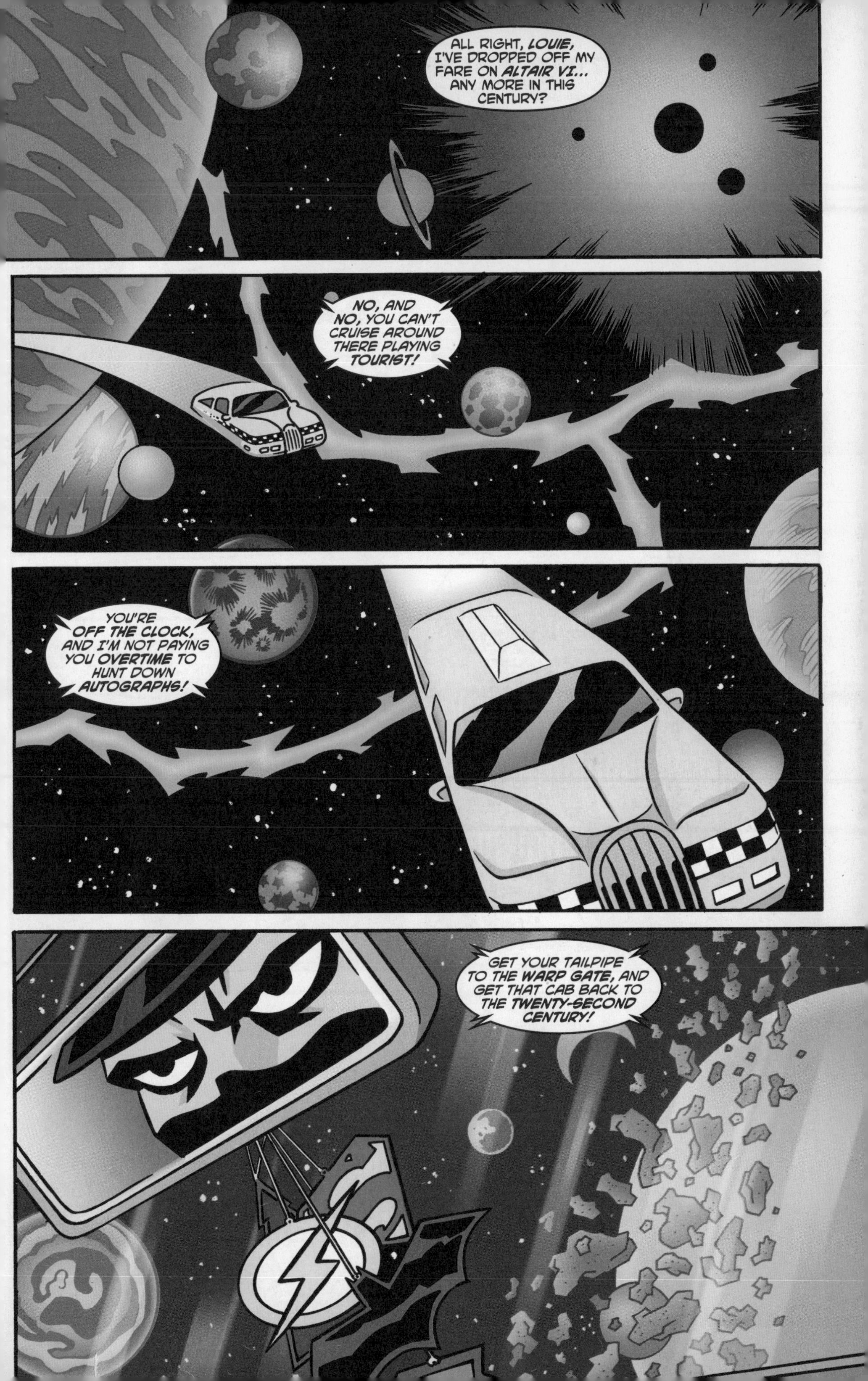
ALL RIGHT, LOUIE, I'VE DROPPED OFF MY FARE ON ALTAIR VI... ANY MORE IN THIS CENTURY?
NO, AND NO, YOU CAN'T CRUISE AROUND THERE PLAYING TOURIST!
YOU'RE OFF THE CLOCK, AND I'M NOT PAYING YOU OVERTIME TO HUNT DOWN AUTOGRAPHS!
GET YOUR TAILPIPE TO THE WARP GATE, AND GET THAT CAB BACK TO THE TWENTY-SECOND CENTURY!

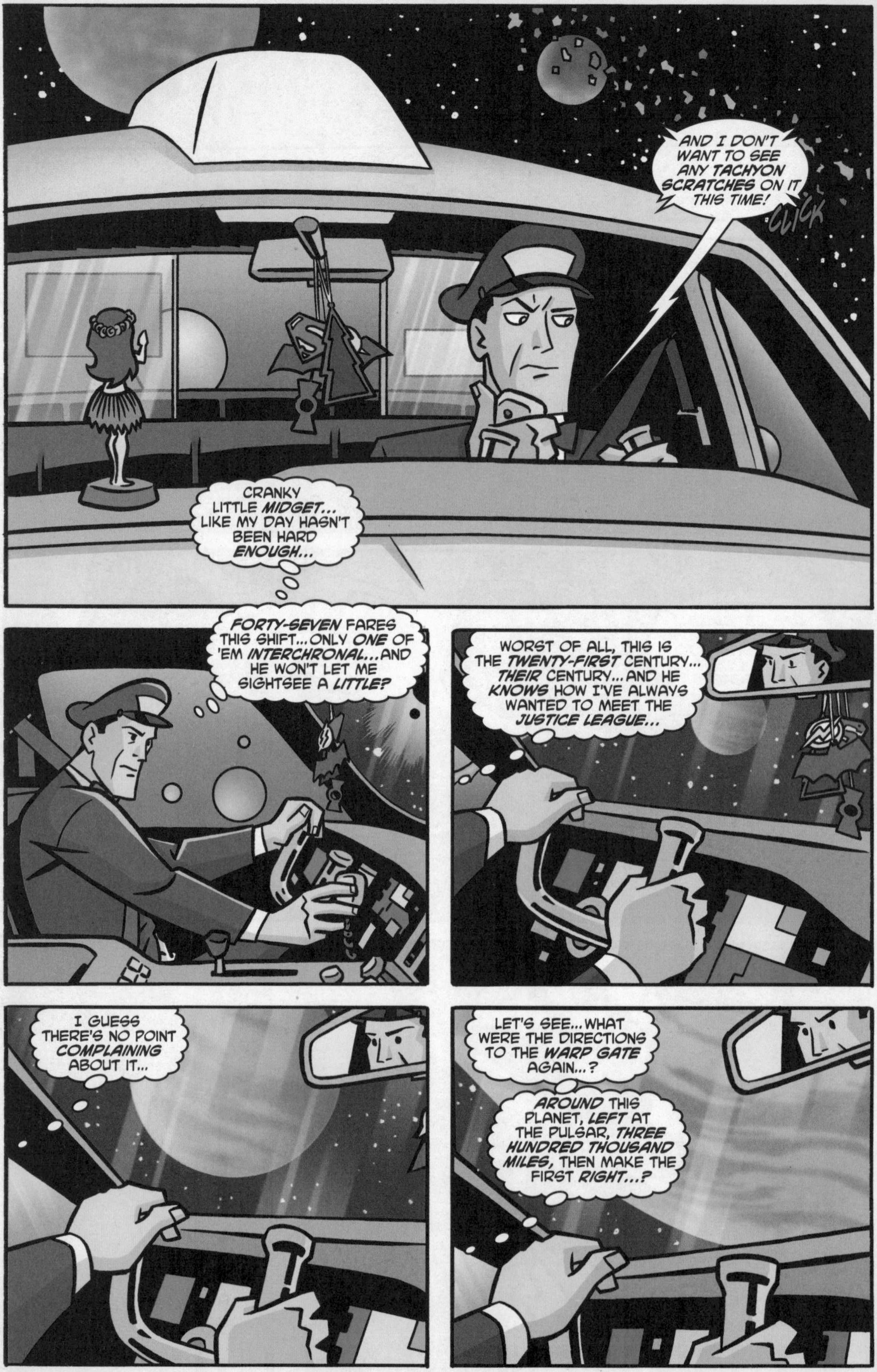
AND I DON'T WANT TO SEE ANY TACHYON SCRATCHES ON IT THIS TIME!
CLICK
CRANKY LITTLE MIDGET... LIKE MY DAY HASN'T BEEN HARD ENOUGH...
FORTY-SEVEN FARES THIS SHIFT...ONLY ONE OF 'EM INTERCHRONAL...AND HE WON'T LET ME SIGHTSEE A LITTLE?
WORST OF ALL, THIS IS THE TWENTY-FIRST CENTURY... THEIR CENTURY...AND HE KNOWS HOW I'VE ALWAYS WANTED TO MEET THE JUSTICE LEAGUE...
I GUESS THERE'S NO POINT COMPLAINING ABOUT IT...?
LET'S SEE...WHAT WERE THE DIRECTIONS TO THE WARP GATE AGAIN...?
AROUND THIS PLANET, LEFT AT THE PULSAR, THREE HUNDRED THOUSAND MILES, THEN MAKE THE FIRST RIGHT...?

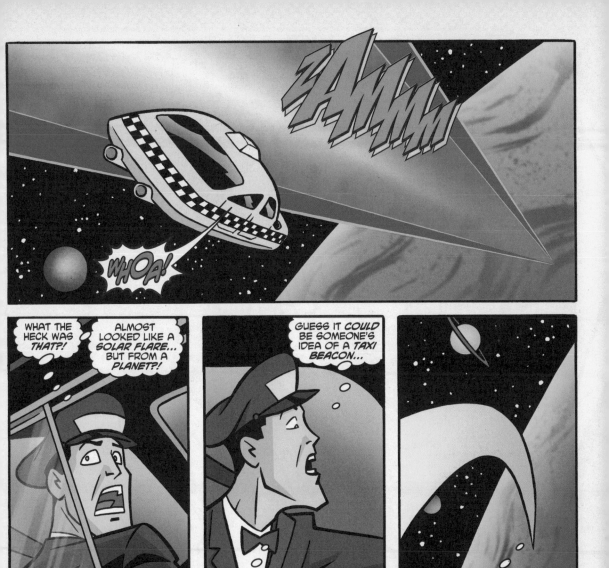

ZAMMM

WHOA!

WHAT THE HECK WAS *THAT?!* ALMOST LOOKED LIKE A *SOLAR FLARE...* BUT FROM A *PLANET?!*

GUESS IT *COULD* BE SOMEONE'S IDEA OF A *TAXI BEACON...*

PRETTY *STUPID* AND *DANGEROUS* IDEA, THOUGH...

OH, WELL... THIS *WAS* A *PRIMITIVE CENTURY,* I GUESS...

MIGHT AS WELL *CHECK IT OUT,* LONG AS I'M *HERE...*

IF IT *IS* A *FARE,* MAYBE IT'LL TAKE ME PAST *EARTH...*

...AND I CAN GET A *CLOSE-UP LOOK* AT THE *WATCHTOWER* AND--

FARE 48

ADAM BEECHEN - writer
ETHEN BEAVERS - artist
HEROIC AGE - colorist
ROB LEIGH - letterer

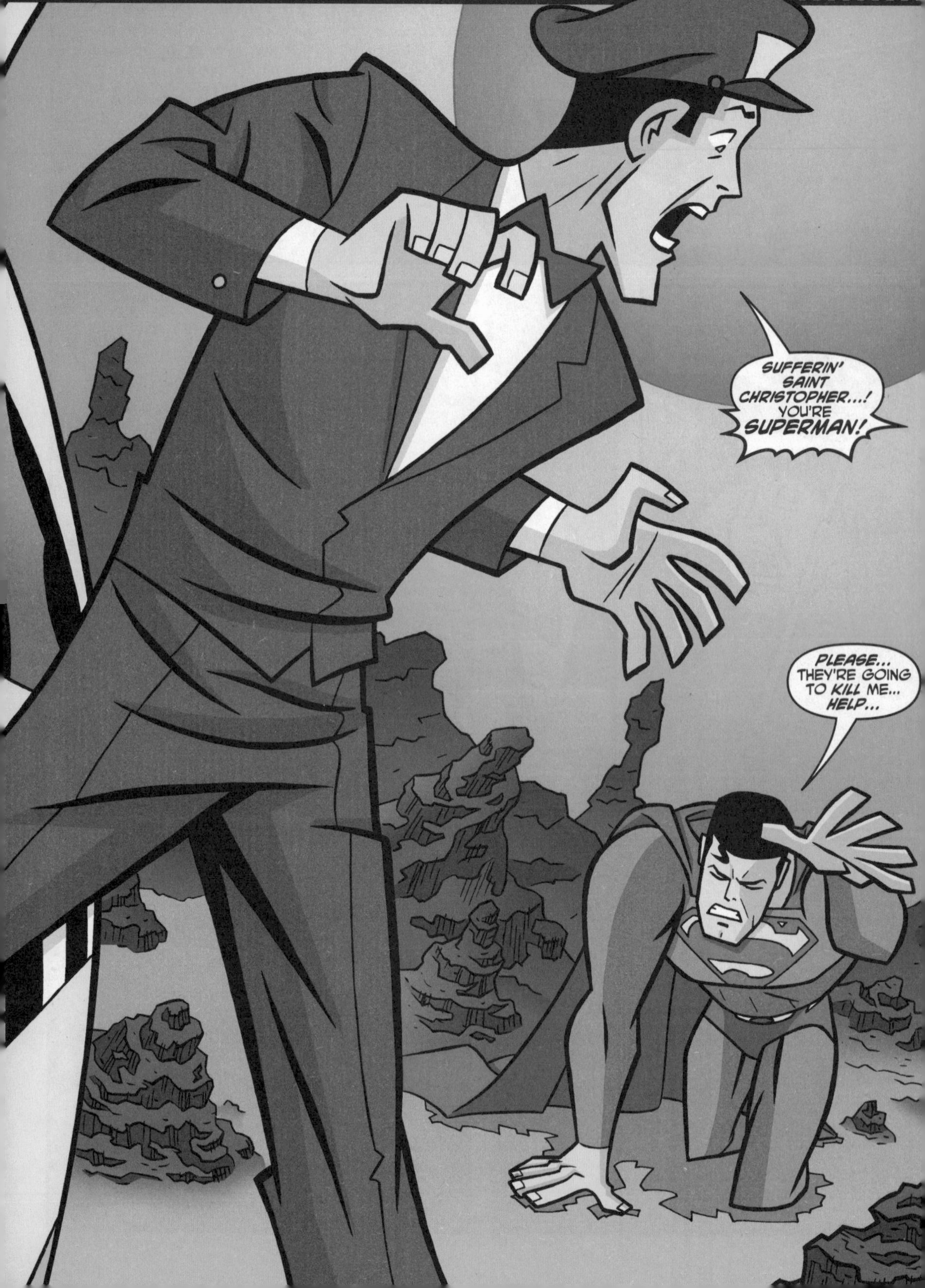

SUFFERIN' SAINT CHRISTOPHER...! YOU'RE SUPERMAN!
PLEASE... THEY'RE GOING TO KILL ME... HELP...

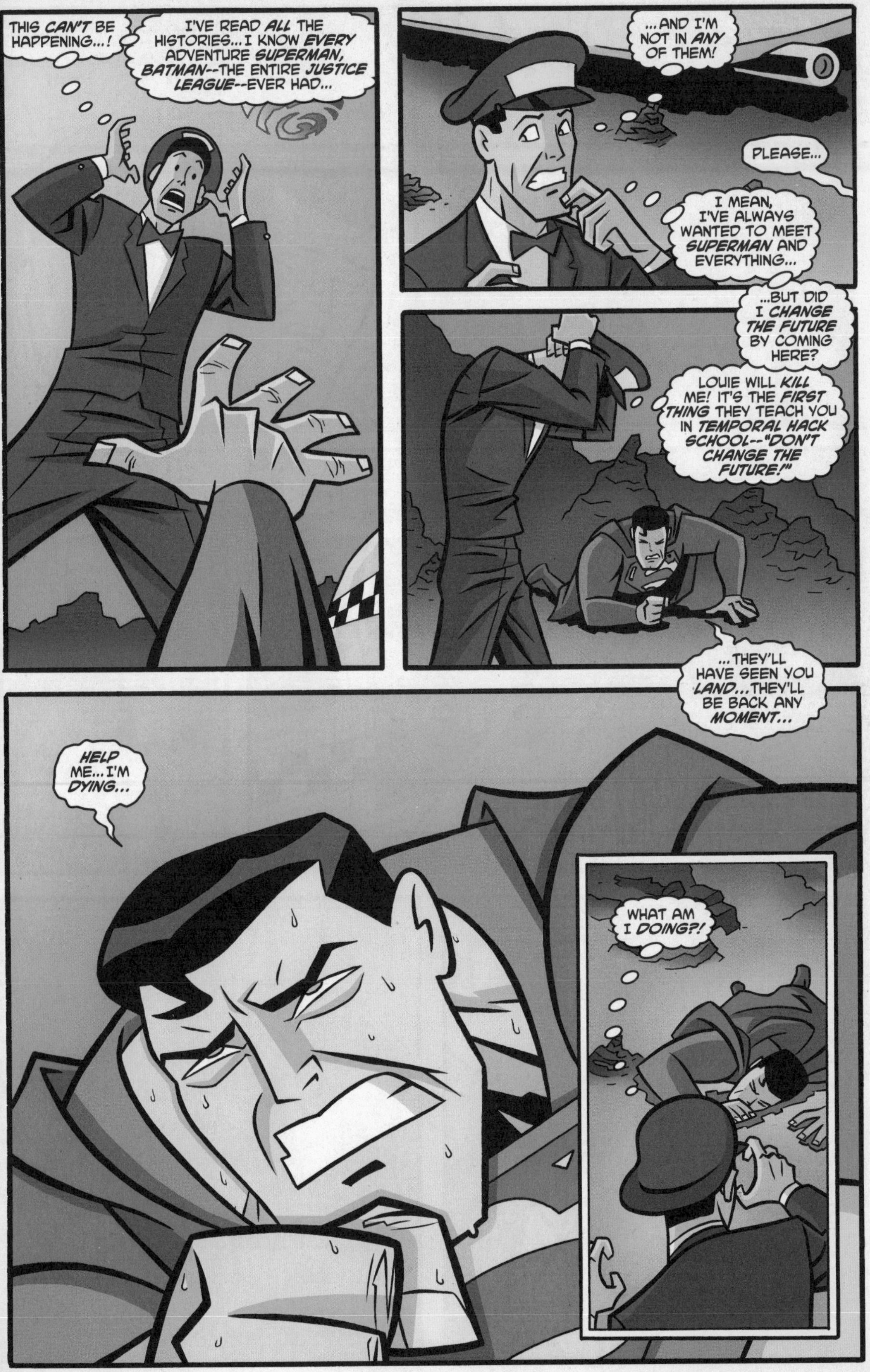

THIS CAN'T BE HAPPENING...!
I'VE READ ALL THE HISTORIES...I KNOW EVERY ADVENTURE SUPERMAN, BATMAN--THE ENTIRE JUSTICE LEAGUE--EVER HAD...
...AND I'M NOT IN ANY OF THEM!
PLEASE...
I MEAN, I'VE ALWAYS WANTED TO MEET SUPERMAN AND EVERYTHING...
...BUT DID I CHANGE THE FUTURE BY COMING HERE?
LOUIE WILL KILL ME! IT'S THE FIRST THING THEY TEACH YOU IN TEMPORAL HACK SCHOOL--"DON'T CHANGE THE FUTURE!"
...THEY'LL HAVE SEEN YOU LAND...THEY'LL BE BACK ANY MOMENT...
HELP ME...I'M DYING...
WHAT AM I DOING?!

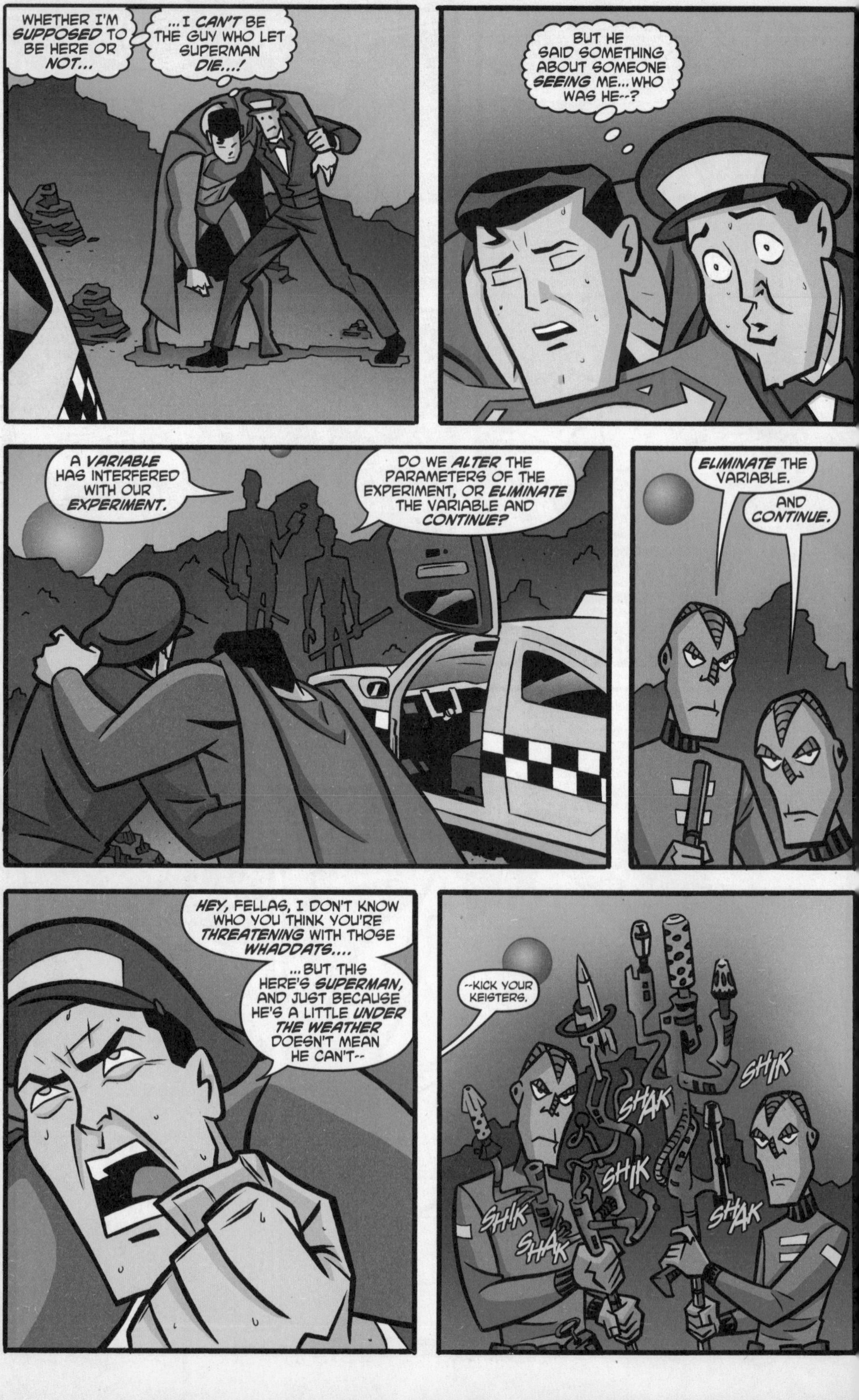
WHETHER I'M SUPPOSED TO BE HERE OR NOT...
...I CAN'T BE THE GUY WHO LET SUPERMAN DIE...!
BUT HE SAID SOMETHING ABOUT SOMEONE SEEING ME...WHO WAS HE--?
A VARIABLE HAS INTERFERED WITH OUR EXPERIMENT.
DO WE ALTER THE PARAMETERS OF THE EXPERIMENT, OR ELIMINATE THE VARIABLE AND CONTINUE?
ELIMINATE THE VARIABLE.
AND CONTINUE.
HEY, FELLAS, I DON'T KNOW WHO YOU THINK YOU'RE THREATENING WITH THOSE WHADDATS....
...BUT THIS HERE'S SUPERMAN, AND JUST BECAUSE HE'S A LITTLE UNDER THE WEATHER DOESN'T MEAN HE CAN'T--
--KICK YOUR KEISTERS.
SHIK
SHAK
SHIK
SHIK
SHAK
SHAK

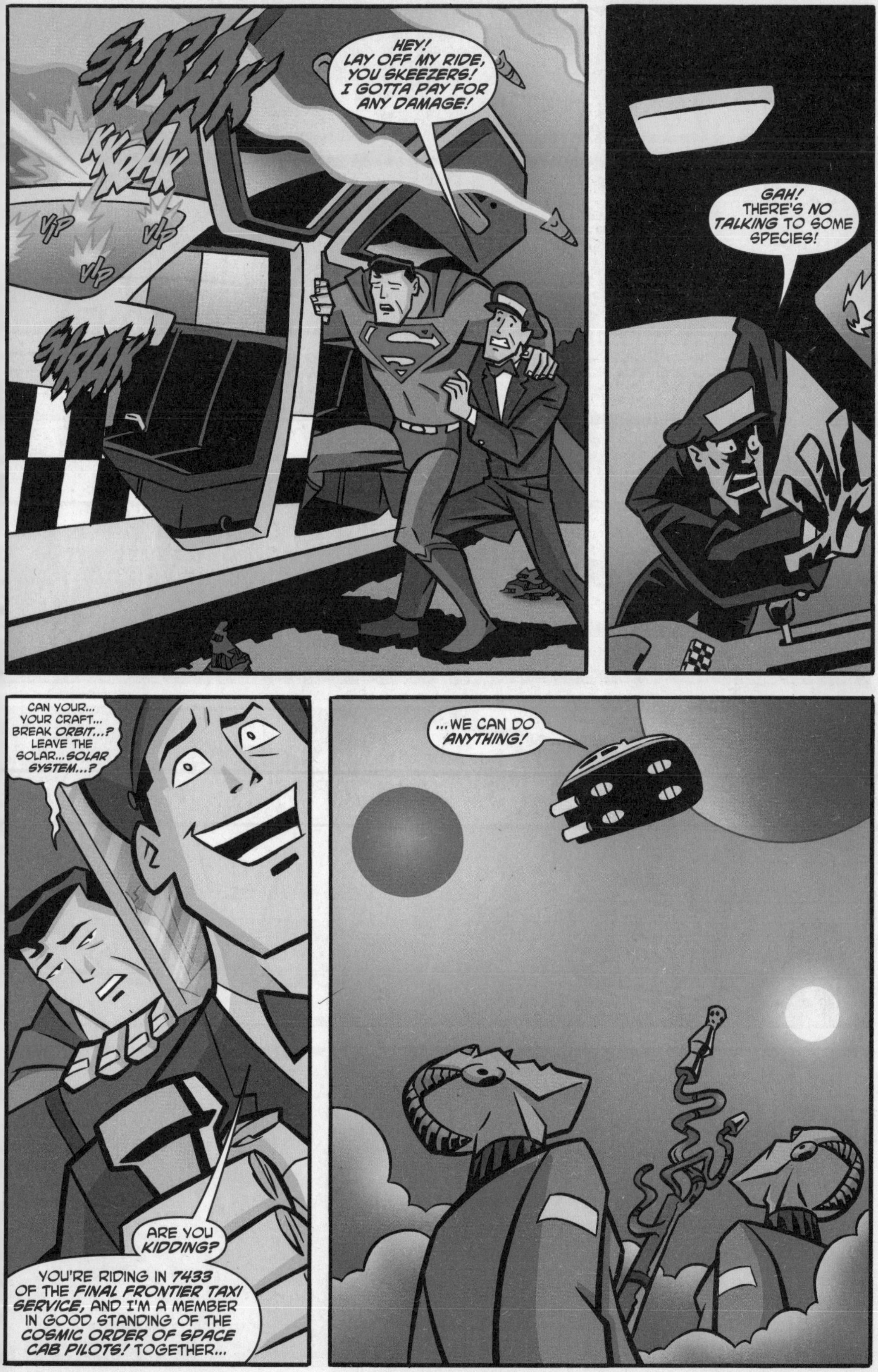
SHRAK
KKRAK
VIP
VIP
VIP
HEY! LAY OFF MY RIDE, YOU SKEEZERS! I GOTTA PAY FOR ANY DAMAGE!
SHRAK
GAH! THERE'S NO TALKING TO SOME SPECIES!
CAN YOUR... YOUR CRAFT... BREAK ORBIT...? LEAVE THE SOLAR...SOLAR SYSTEM...?
ARE YOU KIDDING?
YOU'RE RIDING IN 7433 OF THE FINAL FRONTIER TAXI SERVICE, AND I'M A MEMBER IN GOOD STANDING OF THE COSMIC ORDER OF SPACE CAB PILOTS! TOGETHER...
...WE CAN DO ANYTHING!

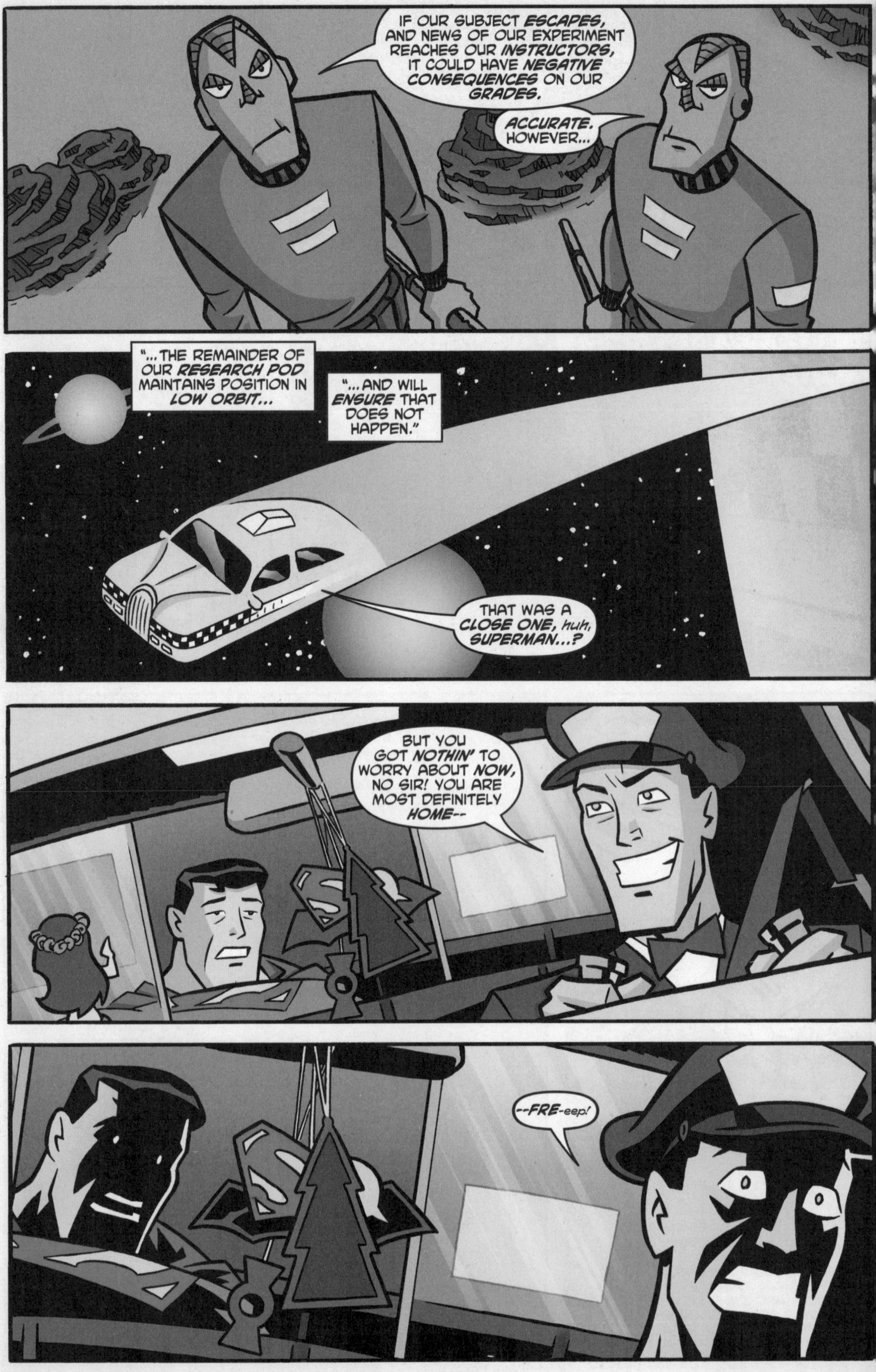
IF OUR SUBJECT ESCAPES, AND NEWS OF OUR EXPERIMENT REACHES OUR INSTRUCTORS, IT COULD HAVE NEGATIVE CONSEQUENCES ON OUR GRADES.
ACCURATE. HOWEVER...
"...THE REMAINDER OF OUR RESEARCH POD MAINTAINS POSITION IN LOW ORBIT...
"...AND WILL ENSURE THAT DOES NOT HAPPEN."
THAT WAS A CLOSE ONE, huh, SUPERMAN...?
BUT YOU GOT NOTHIN' TO WORRY ABOUT NOW, NO SIR! YOU ARE MOST DEFINITELY HOME--
--FRE-eep!

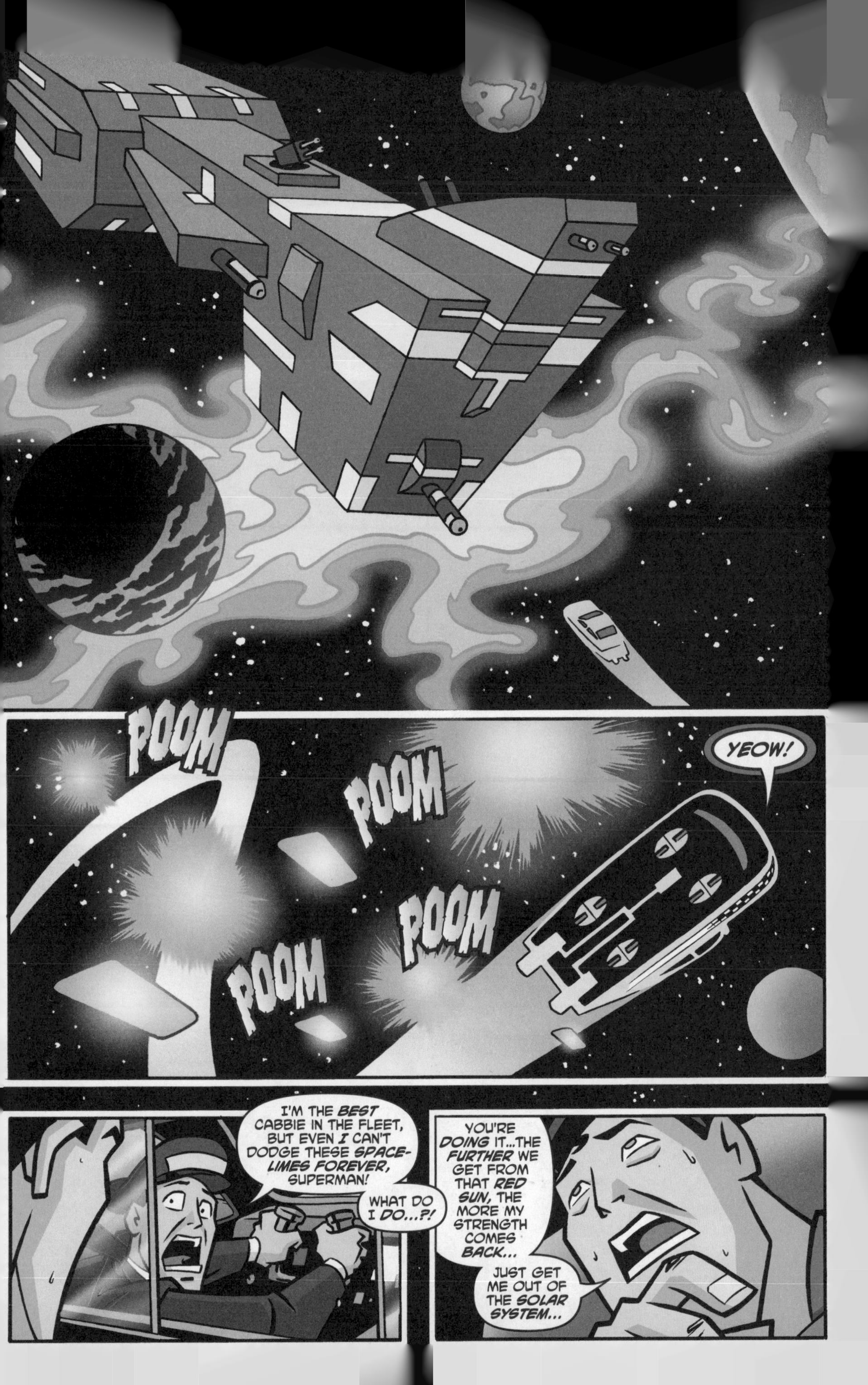
POOM
POOM
POOM
POOM
YEOW!
I'M THE BEST CABBIE IN THE FLEET, BUT EVEN I CAN'T DODGE THESE SPACE-LIMES FOREVER, SUPERMAN!
WHAT DO I DO...?!
YOU'RE DOING IT...THE FURTHER WE GET FROM THAT RED SUN, THE MORE MY STRENGTH COMES BACK...
JUST GET ME OUT OF THE SOLAR SYSTEM...

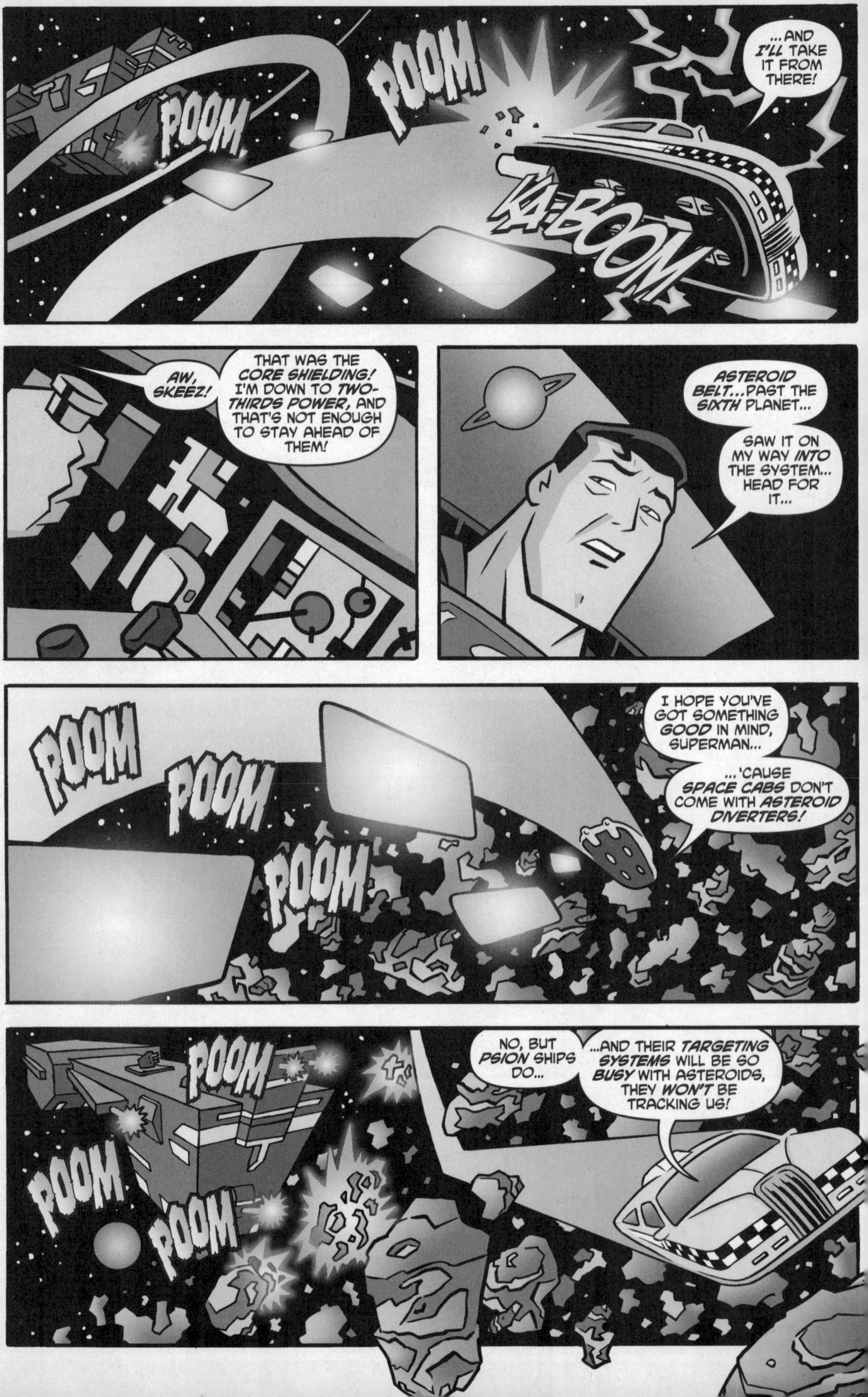
POOM
POOM
...AND I'LL TAKE IT FROM THERE!
KA-BOOM
AW, SKEEZ!
THAT WAS THE CORE SHIELDING! I'M DOWN TO TWO-THIRDS POWER, AND THAT'S NOT ENOUGH TO STAY AHEAD OF THEM!
ASTEROID BELT...PAST THE SIXTH PLANET...
SAW IT ON MY WAY INTO THE SYSTEM... HEAD FOR IT...
POOM
POOM
POOM
I HOPE YOU'VE GOT SOMETHING GOOD IN MIND, SUPERMAN...
...'CAUSE SPACE CABS DON'T COME WITH ASTEROID DIVERTERS!
POOM
POOM
POOM
NO, BUT PSION SHIPS DO...
...AND THEIR TARGETING SYSTEMS WILL BE SO BUSY WITH ASTEROIDS, THEY WON'T BE TRACKING US!

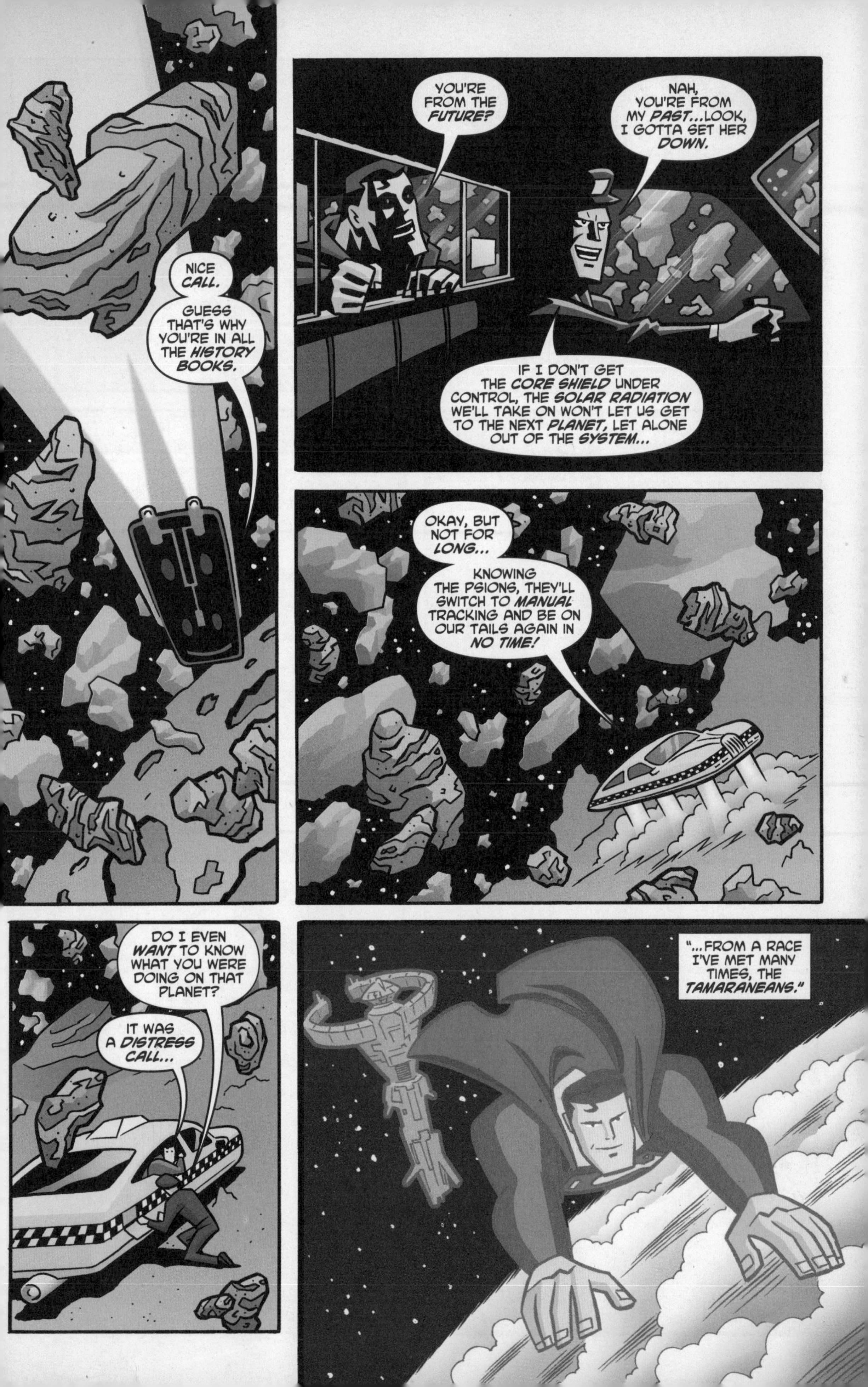
NICE CALL.
GUESS THAT'S WHY YOU'RE IN ALL THE HISTORY BOOKS.
YOU'RE FROM THE FUTURE?
NAH, YOU'RE FROM MY PAST...LOOK, I GOTTA SET HER DOWN.
IF I DON'T GET THE CORE SHIELD UNDER CONTROL, THE SOLAR RADIATION WE'LL TAKE ON WON'T LET US GET TO THE NEXT PLANET, LET ALONE OUT OF THE SYSTEM...
OKAY, BUT NOT FOR LONG...
KNOWING THE PSIONS, THEY'LL SWITCH TO MANUAL TRACKING AND BE ON OUR TAILS AGAIN IN NO TIME!
DO I EVEN WANT TO KNOW WHAT YOU WERE DOING ON THAT PLANET?
IT WAS A DISTRESS CALL...
"...FROM A RACE I'VE MET MANY TIMES, THE TAMARANEANS."

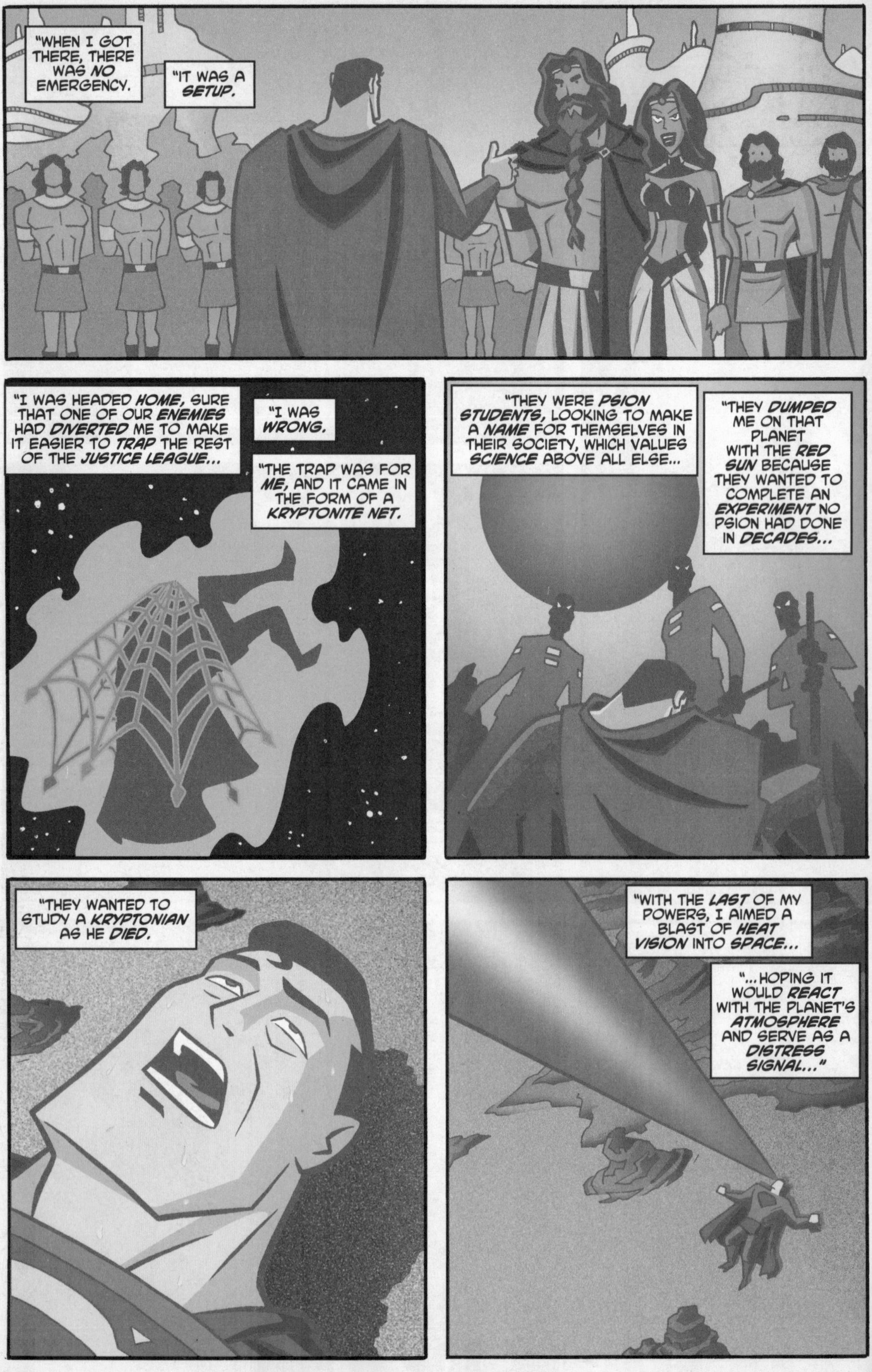
"WHEN I GOT THERE, THERE WAS NO EMERGENCY.
"IT WAS A SETUP.
"I WAS HEADED HOME, SURE THAT ONE OF OUR ENEMIES HAD DIVERTED ME TO MAKE IT EASIER TO TRAP THE REST OF THE JUSTICE LEAGUE...
"I WAS WRONG.
"THE TRAP WAS FOR ME, AND IT CAME IN THE FORM OF A KRYPTONITE NET.
"THEY WERE PSION STUDENTS, LOOKING TO MAKE A NAME FOR THEMSELVES IN THEIR SOCIETY, WHICH VALUES SCIENCE ABOVE ALL ELSE...
"THEY DUMPED ME ON THAT PLANET WITH THE RED SUN BECAUSE THEY WANTED TO COMPLETE AN EXPERIMENT NO PSION HAD DONE IN DECADES...
"THEY WANTED TO STUDY A KRYPTONIAN AS HE DIED.
"WITH THE LAST OF MY POWERS, I AIMED A BLAST OF HEAT VISION INTO SPACE...
"...HOPING IT WOULD REACT WITH THE PLANET'S ATMOSPHERE AND SERVE AS A DISTRESS SIGNAL..."

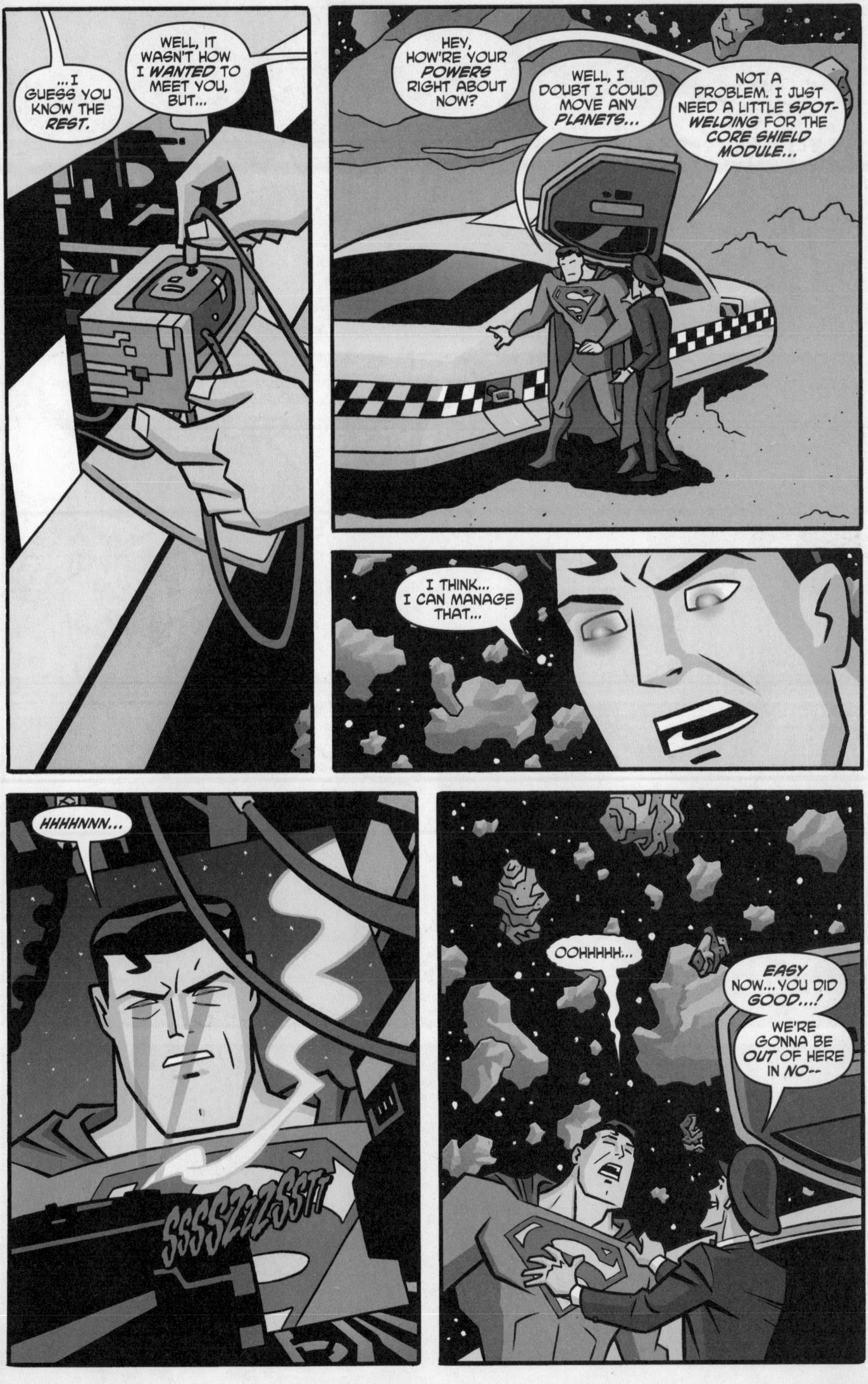
...I GUESS YOU KNOW THE REST.
WELL, IT WASN'T HOW I WANTED TO MEET YOU, BUT...
HEY, HOW'RE YOUR POWERS RIGHT ABOUT NOW?
WELL, I DOUBT I COULD MOVE ANY PLANETS...
NOT A PROBLEM. I JUST NEED A LITTLE SPOT-WELDING FOR THE CORE SHIELD MODULE...
I THINK... I CAN MANAGE THAT...
HHHHNNN...
SSSSZZZSSTT
OOHHHHH...
EASY NOW...YOU DID GOOD...!
WE'RE GONNA BE OUT OF HERE IN NO--

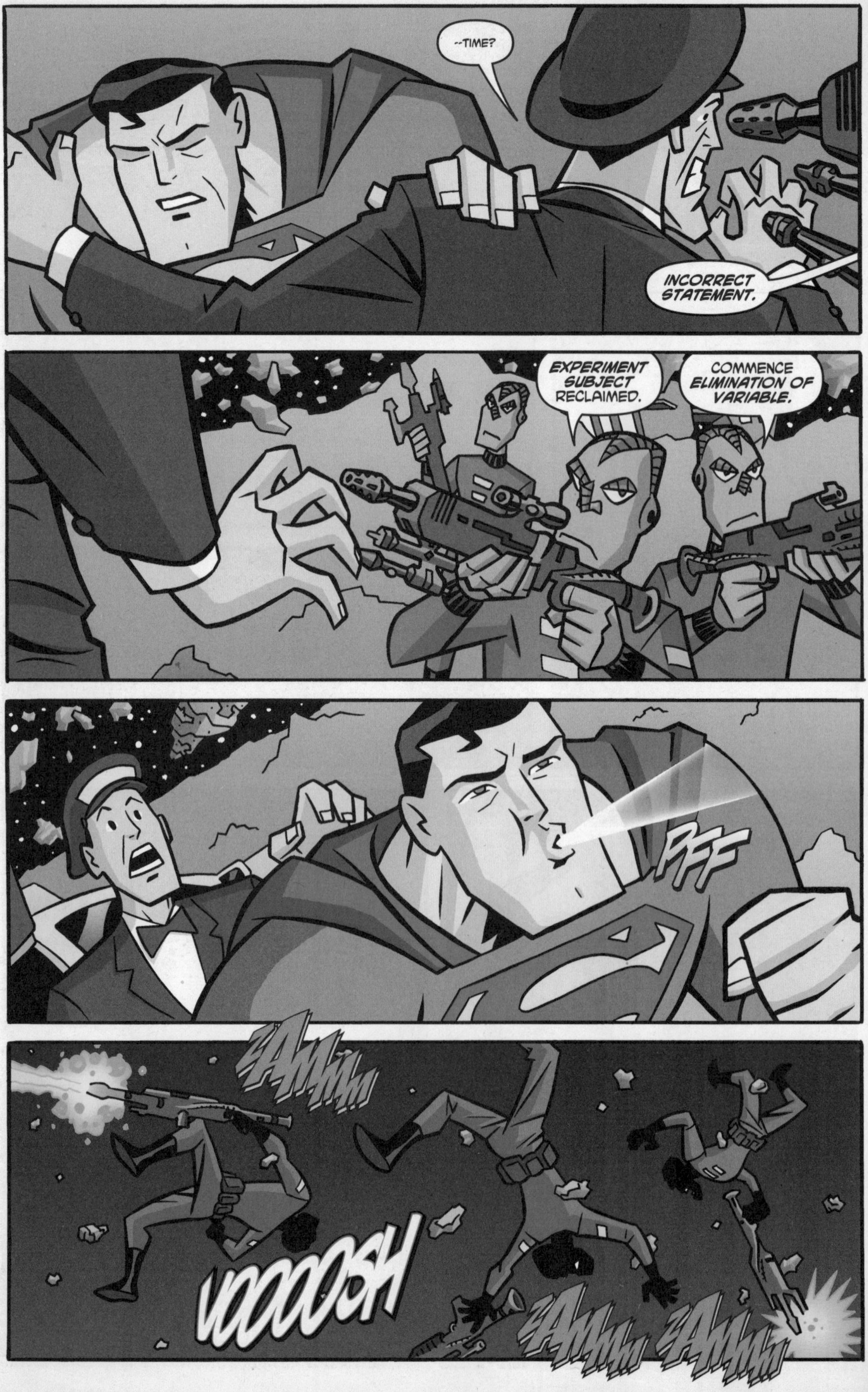
--TIME?
INCORRECT STATEMENT.
EXPERIMENT SUBJECT RECLAIMED.
COMMENCE ELIMINATION OF VARIABLE.
PFF
ZAMMM
VOOOOSH
ZAMMM
ZAMMM

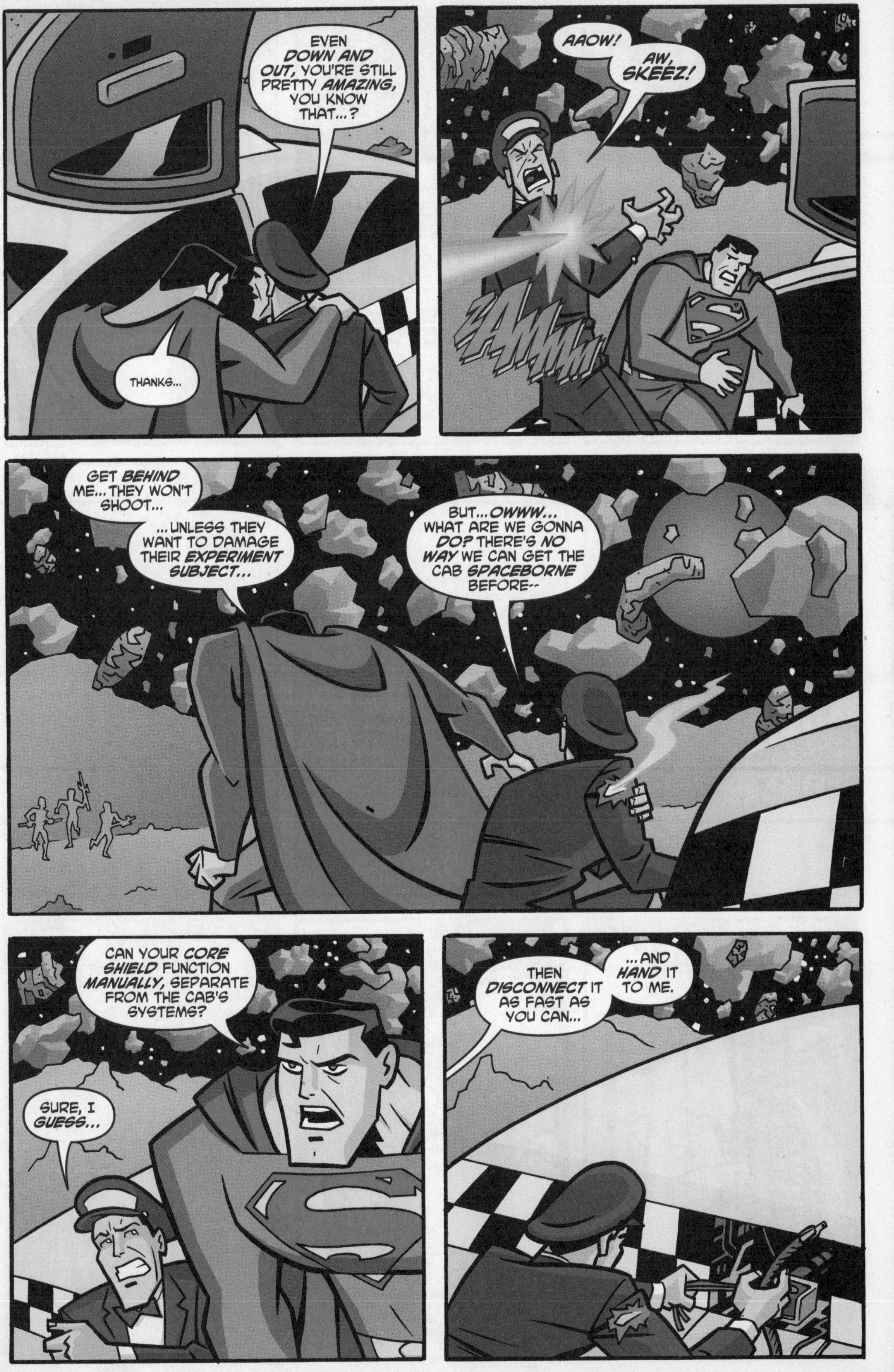
EVEN DOWN AND OUT, YOU'RE STILL PRETTY AMAZING, YOU KNOW THAT...?
THANKS...
AAOW!
AW, SKEEZ!
ZAMMM
GET BEHIND ME... THEY WON'T SHOOT...
...UNLESS THEY WANT TO DAMAGE THEIR EXPERIMENT SUBJECT...
BUT... OWWW... WHAT ARE WE GONNA DO? THERE'S NO WAY WE CAN GET THE CAB SPACEBORNE BEFORE--
CAN YOUR CORE SHIELD FUNCTION MANUALLY, SEPARATE FROM THE CAB'S SYSTEMS?
SURE, I GUESS...
THEN DISCONNECT IT AS FAST AS YOU CAN...
...AND HAND IT TO ME.

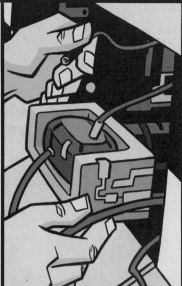

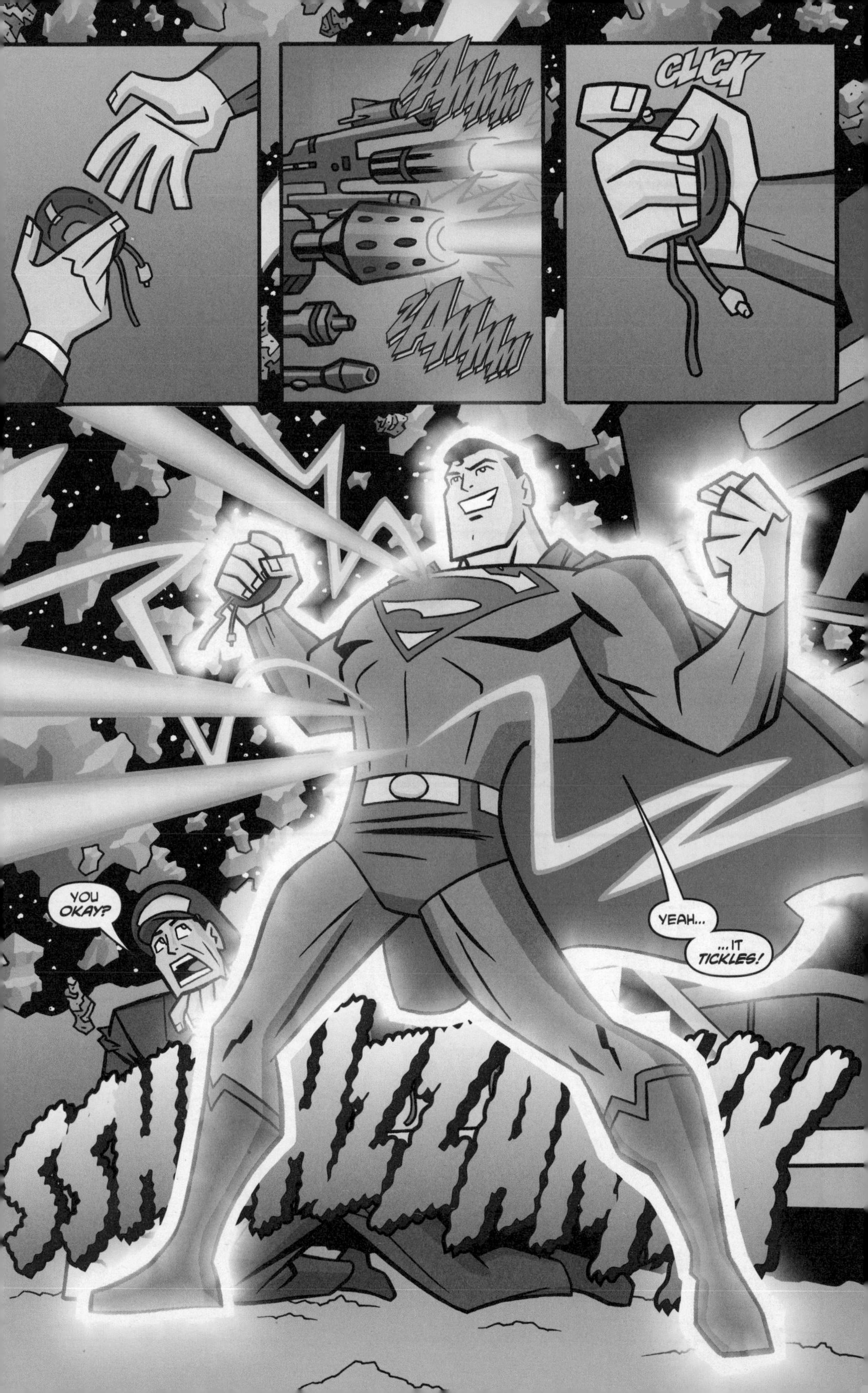
ZAMMM
ZAMMM
CLICK
YOU OKAY?
YEAH...
...IT TICKLES!

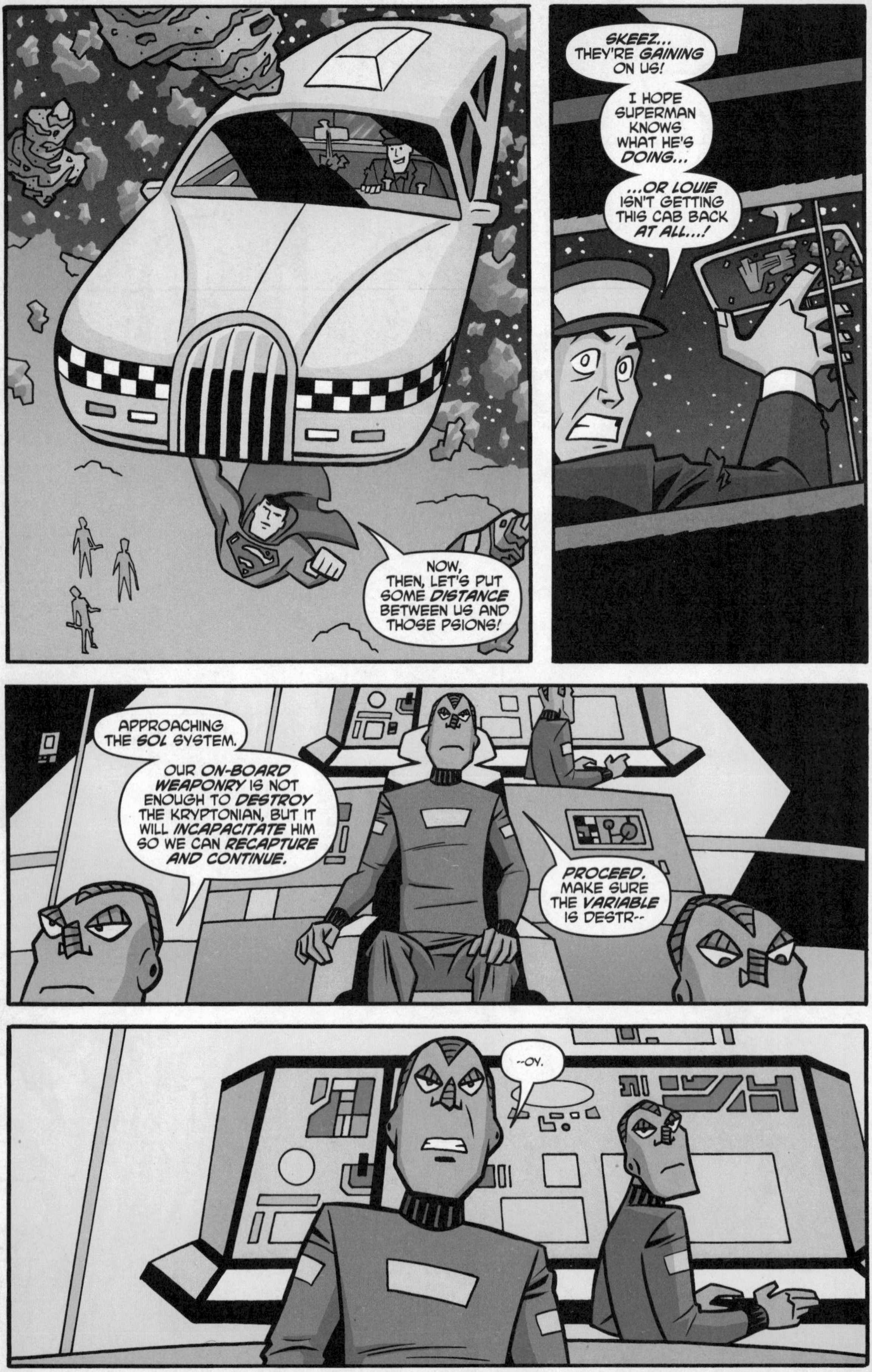
NOW, THEN, LET'S PUT SOME DISTANCE BETWEEN US AND THOSE PSIONS!
SKEEZ... THEY'RE GAINING ON US!
I HOPE SUPERMAN KNOWS WHAT HE'S DOING...
...OR LOUIE ISN'T GETTING THIS CAB BACK AT ALL...!
APPROACHING THE SOL SYSTEM.
OUR ON-BOARD WEAPONRY IS NOT ENOUGH TO DESTROY THE KRYPTONIAN, BUT IT WILL INCAPACITATE HIM SO WE CAN RECAPTURE AND CONTINUE.
PROCEED. MAKE SURE THE VARIABLE IS DESTR--
--OY.

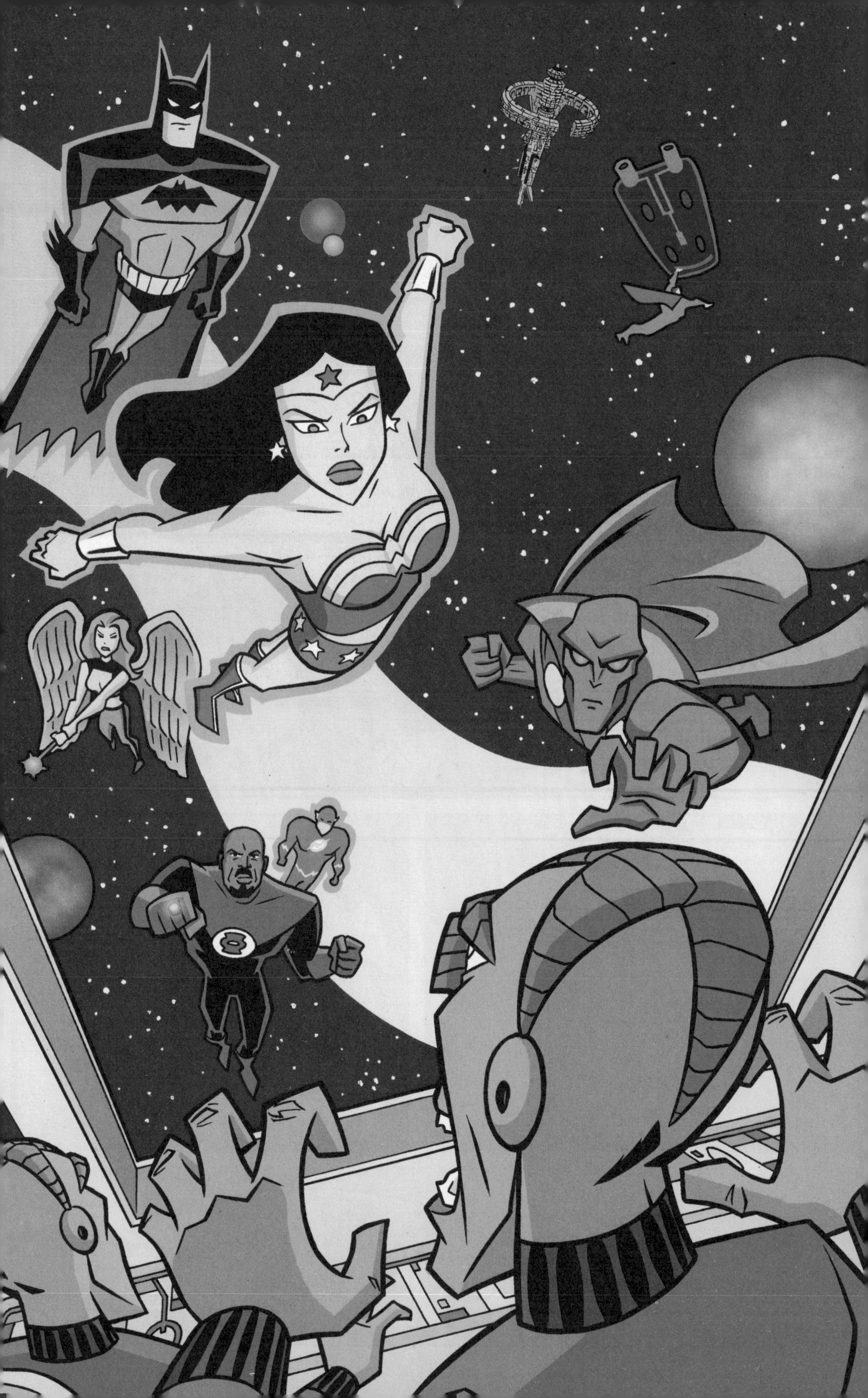

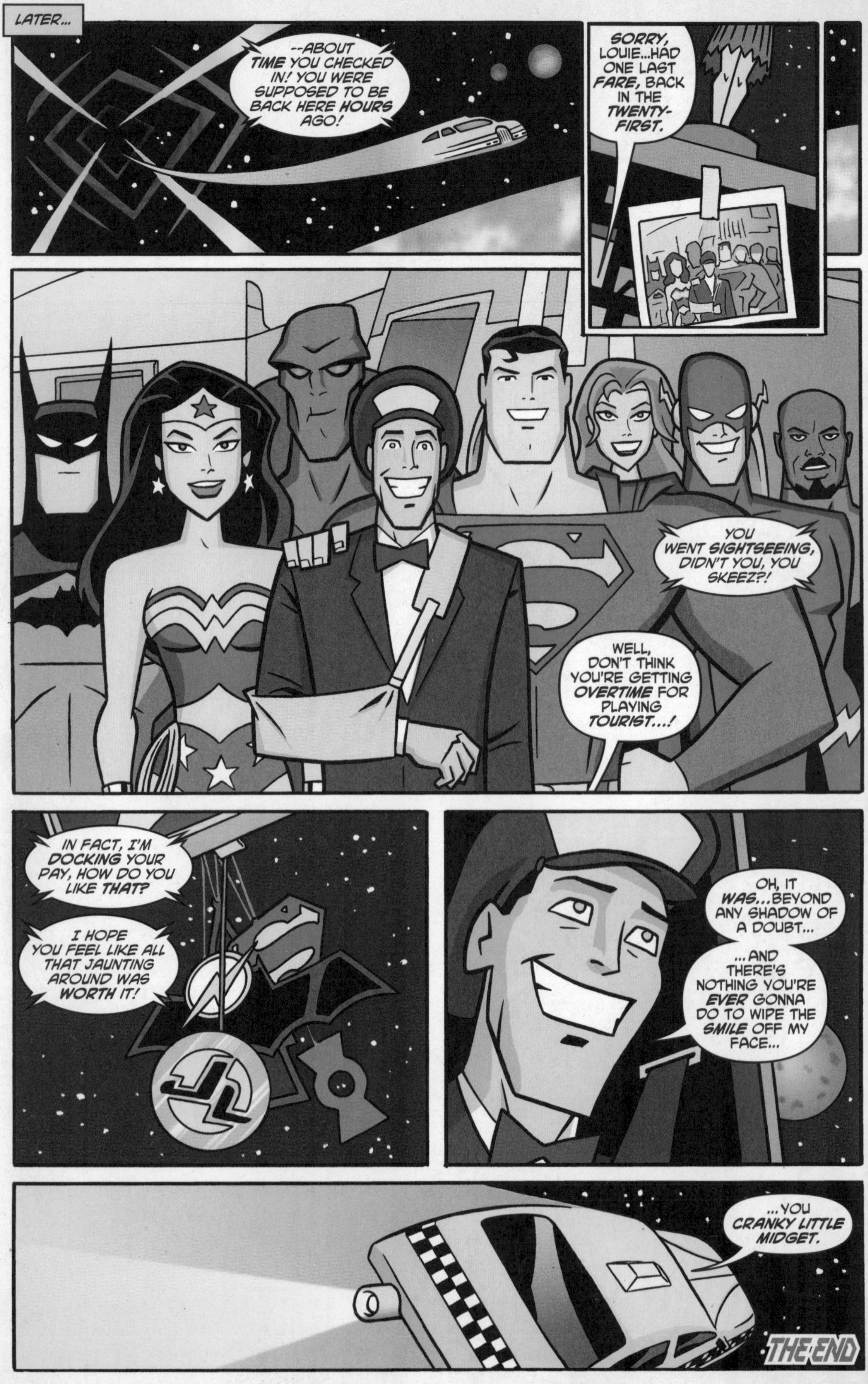
LATER...
--ABOUT TIME YOU CHECKED IN! YOU WERE SUPPOSED TO BE BACK HERE HOURS AGO!
SORRY, LOUIE...HAD ONE LAST FARE, BACK IN THE TWENTY-FIRST.
YOU WENT SIGHTSEEING, DIDN'T YOU, YOU SKEEZ?!
WELL, DON'T THINK YOU'RE GETTING OVERTIME FOR PLAYING TOURIST...!
IN FACT, I'M DOCKING YOUR PAY, HOW DO YOU LIKE THAT?
I HOPE YOU FEEL LIKE ALL THAT JAUNTING AROUND WAS WORTH IT!
OH, IT WAS...BEYOND ANY SHADOW OF A DOUBT...
...AND THERE'S NOTHING YOU'RE EVER GONNA DO TO WIPE THE SMILE OFF MY FACE...
...YOU CRANKY LITTLE MIDGET.
THE END

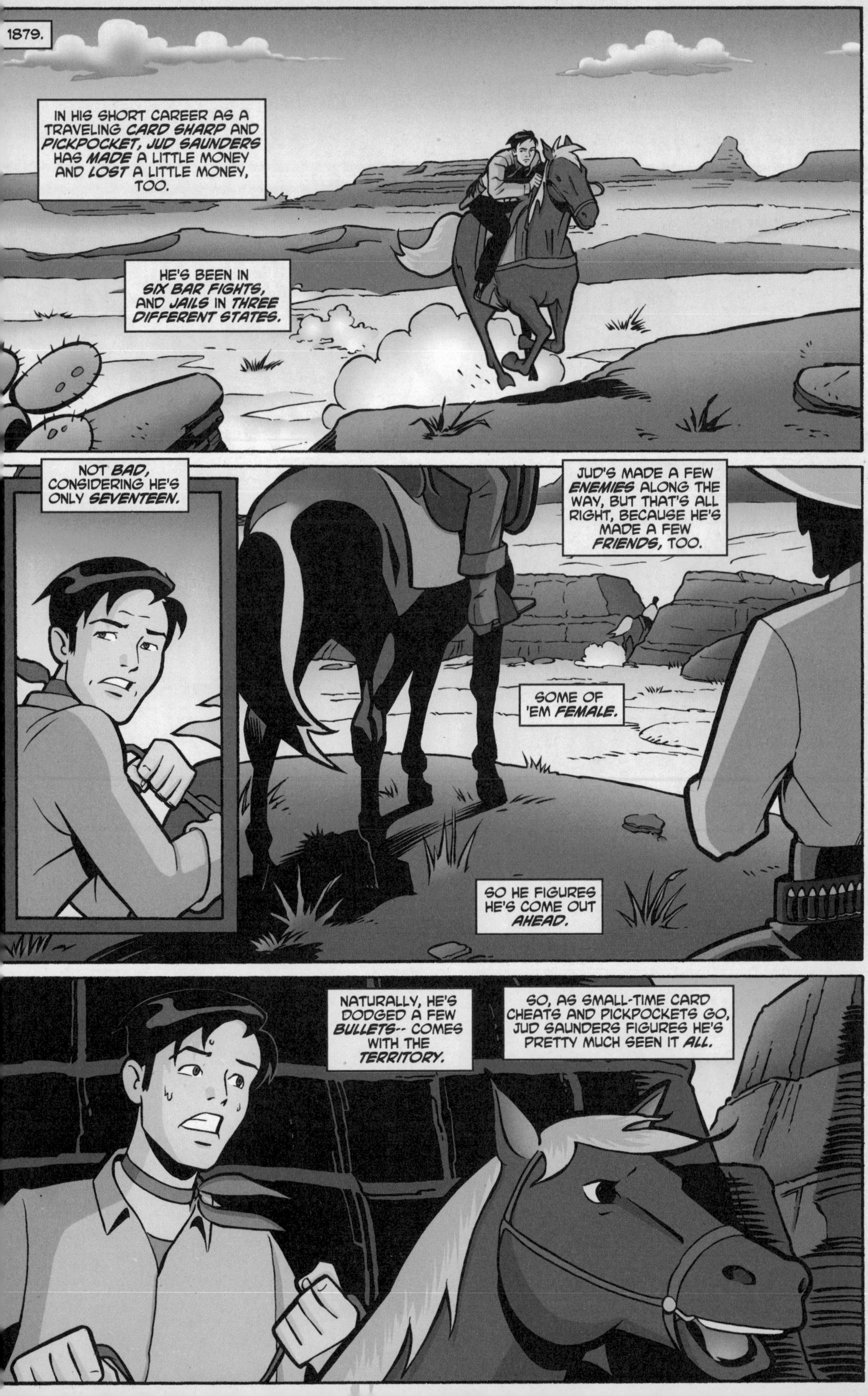
1879.
IN HIS SHORT CAREER AS A TRAVELING CARD SHARP AND PICKPOCKET, JUD SAUNDERS HAS MADE A LITTLE MONEY AND LOST A LITTLE MONEY, TOO.
HE'S BEEN IN SIX BAR FIGHTS, AND JAILS IN THREE DIFFERENT STATES.
NOT BAD, CONSIDERING HE'S ONLY SEVENTEEN.
JUD'S MADE A FEW ENEMIES ALONG THE WAY, BUT THAT'S ALL RIGHT, BECAUSE HE'S MADE A FEW FRIENDS, TOO.
SOME OF 'EM FEMALE.
SO HE FIGURES HE'S COME OUT AHEAD.
NATURALLY, HE'S DODGED A FEW BULLETS-- COMES WITH THE TERRITORY.
SO, AS SMALL-TIME CARD CHEATS AND PICKPOCKETS GO, JUD SAUNDERS FIGURES HE'S PRETTY MUCH SEEN IT ALL.

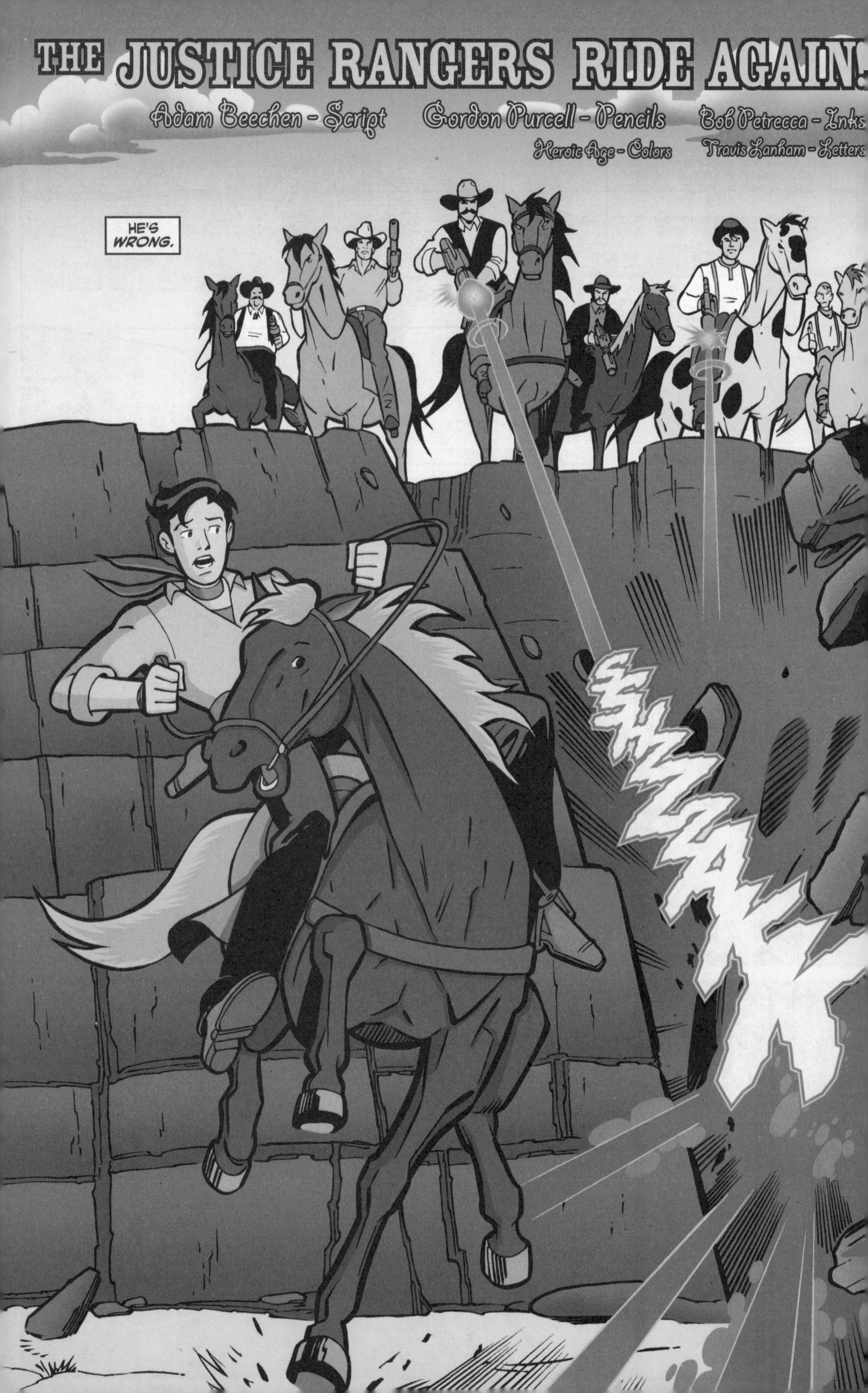
THE JUSTICE RANGERS RIDE AGAIN!
Adam Beechen - Script
Gordon Purcell - Pencils
Bob Petrecca - Inks
Heroic Age - Colors
Travis Lanham - Letters
HE'S WRONG.
SSHHZZAAKK

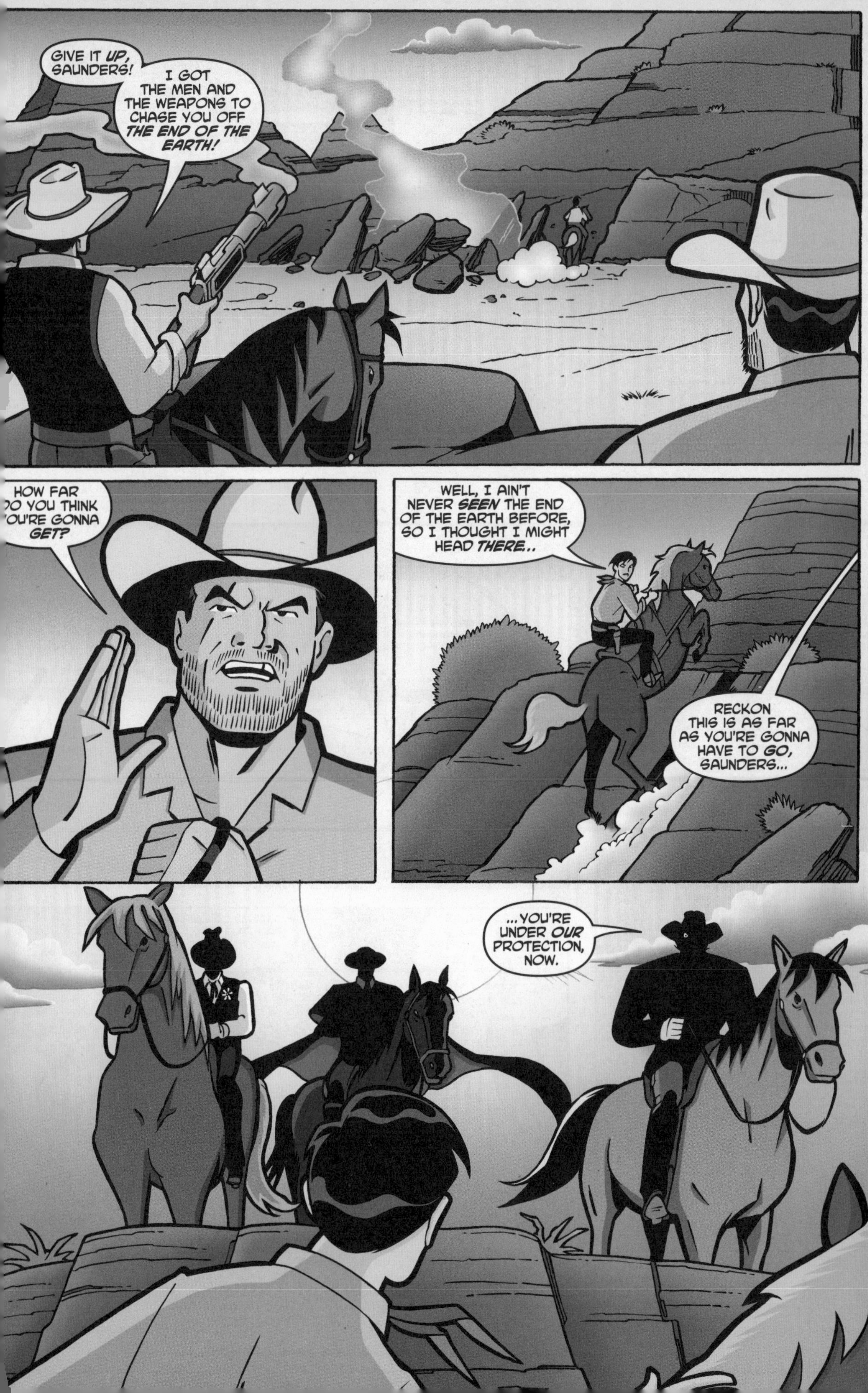

GIVE IT UP, SAUNDERS!
I GOT THE MEN AND THE WEAPONS TO CHASE YOU OFF THE END OF THE EARTH!
HOW FAR O YOU THINK OU'RE GONNA GET?
WELL, I AIN'T NEVER SEEN THE END OF THE EARTH BEFORE, SO I THOUGHT I MIGHT HEAD THERE...
RECKON THIS IS AS FAR AS YOU'RE GONNA HAVE TO GO, SAUNDERS...
...YOU'RE UNDER OUR PROTECTION, NOW.

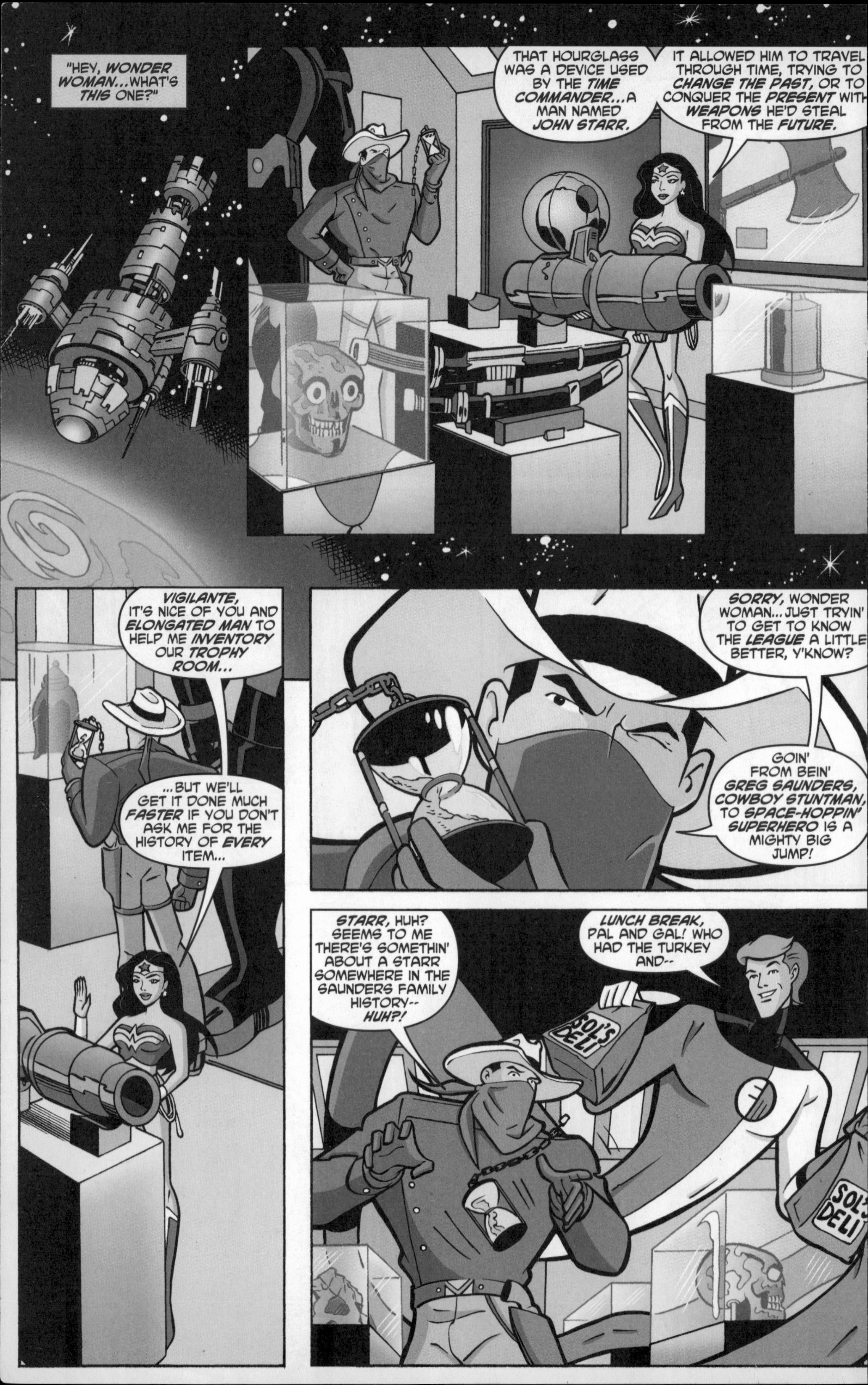
"HEY, WONDER WOMAN...WHAT'S THIS ONE?"
THAT HOURGLASS WAS A DEVICE USED BY THE TIME COMMANDER...A MAN NAMED JOHN STARR.
IT ALLOWED HIM TO TRAVEL THROUGH TIME, TRYING TO CHANGE THE PAST, OR TO CONQUER THE PRESENT WITH WEAPONS HE'D STEAL FROM THE FUTURE.
VIGILANTE, IT'S NICE OF YOU AND ELONGATED MAN TO HELP ME INVENTORY OUR TROPHY ROOM...
...BUT WE'LL GET IT DONE MUCH FASTER IF YOU DON'T ASK ME FOR THE HISTORY OF EVERY ITEM...
SORRY, WONDER WOMAN... JUST TRYIN' TO GET TO KNOW THE LEAGUE A LITTLE BETTER, Y'KNOW?
GOIN' FROM BEIN' GREG SAUNDERS, COWBOY STUNTMAN, TO SPACE-HOPPIN' SUPERHERO IS A MIGHTY BIG JUMP!
STARR, HUH? SEEMS TO ME THERE'S SOMETHIN' ABOUT A STARR SOMEWHERE IN THE SAUNDERS FAMILY HISTORY-- HUH?!
LUNCH BREAK, PAL AND GAL! WHO HAD THE TURKEY AND--
SOL'S DELI
SOL'S DELI

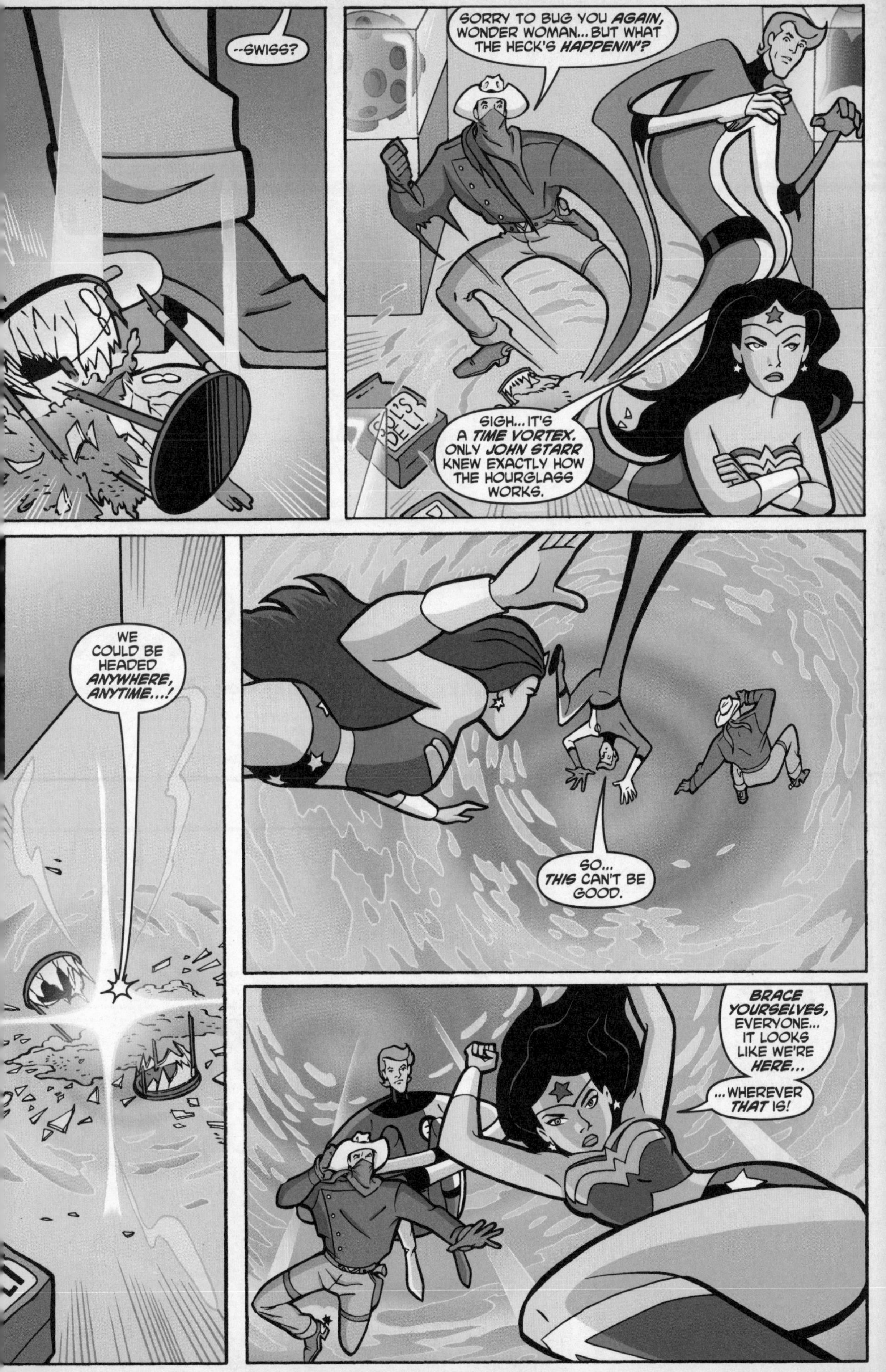
--SWISS?
SORRY TO BUG YOU AGAIN, WONDER WOMAN... BUT WHAT THE HECK'S HAPPENIN'?
SOL'S DELI
SIGH... IT'S A TIME VORTEX. ONLY JOHN STARR KNEW EXACTLY HOW THE HOURGLASS WORKS.
WE COULD BE HEADED ANYWHERE, ANYTIME...!
SO... THIS CAN'T BE GOOD.
BRACE YOURSELVES, EVERYONE... IT LOOKS LIKE WE'RE HERE...
...WHEREVER THAT IS!

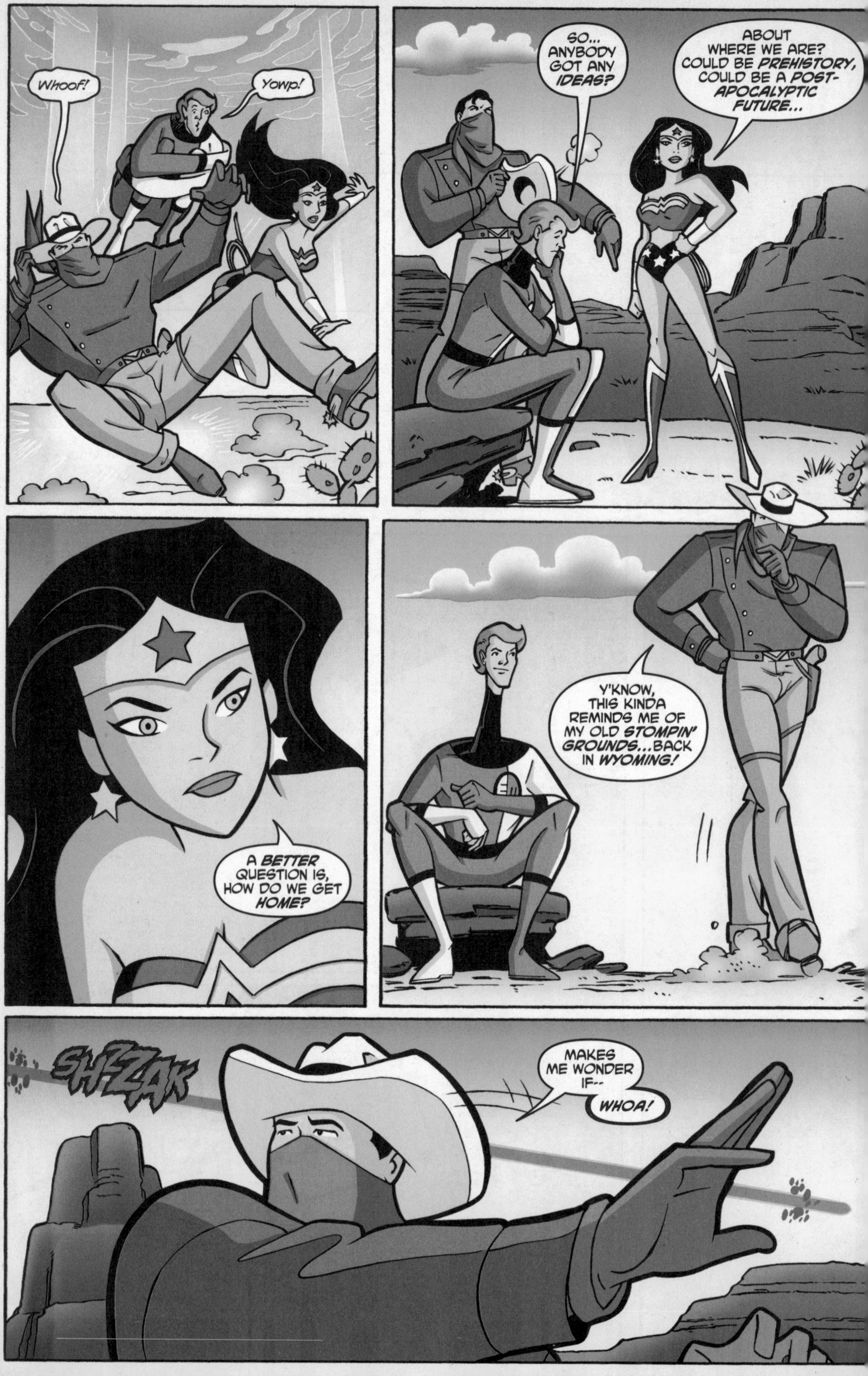
Whoof!
Yowp!
SO... ANYBODY GOT ANY IDEAS?
ABOUT WHERE WE ARE? COULD BE PREHISTORY, COULD BE A POST-APOCALYPTIC FUTURE...
A BETTER QUESTION IS, HOW DO WE GET HOME?
Y'KNOW, THIS KINDA REMINDS ME OF MY OLD STOMPIN' GROUNDS...BACK IN WYOMING!
SHZZAK
MAKES ME WONDER IF--
WHOA!

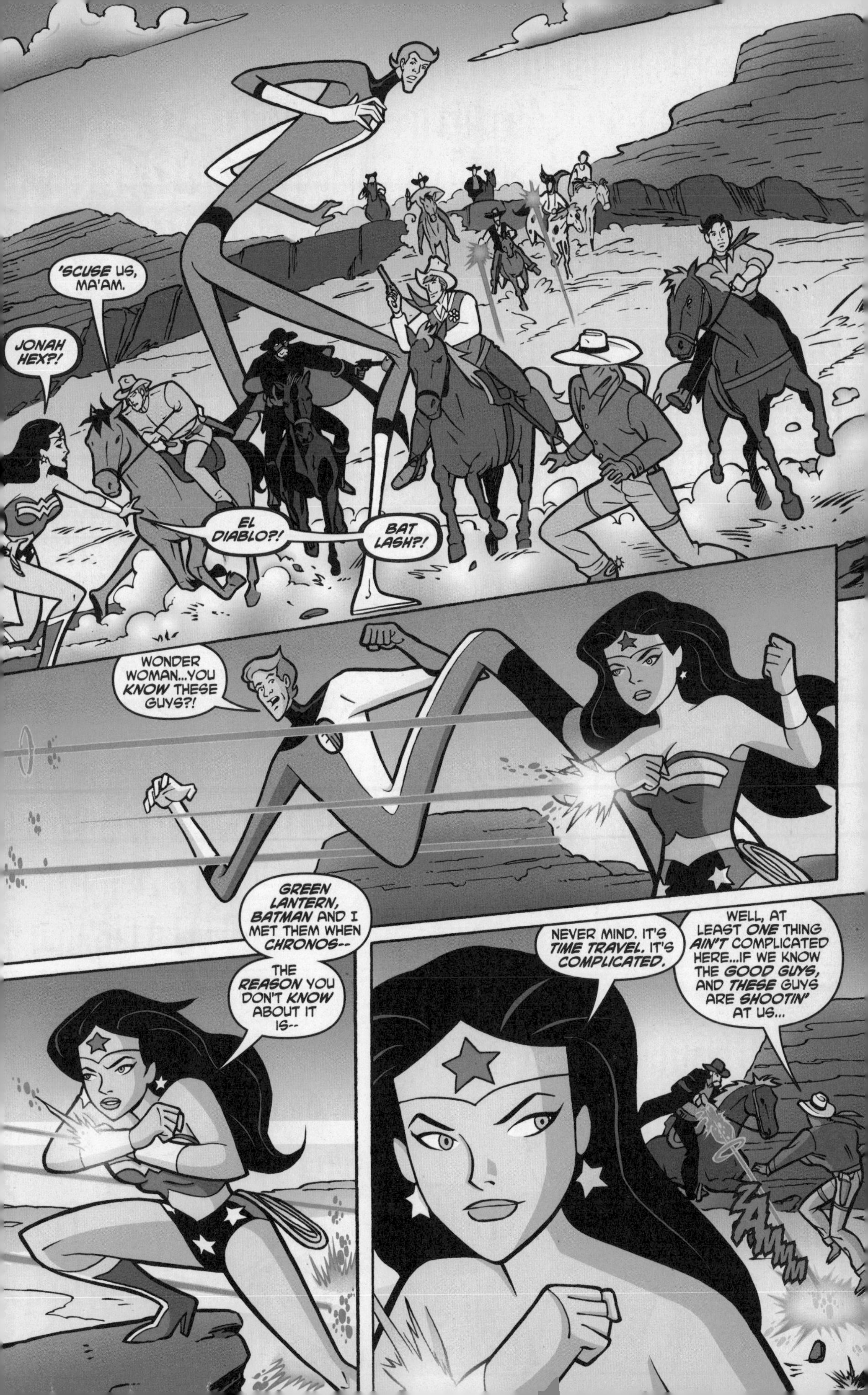
'SCUSE US, MA'AM.
JONAH HEX?!
EL DIABLO?!
BAT LASH?!
WONDER WOMAN...YOU KNOW THESE GUYS?!
GREEN LANTERN, BATMAN AND I MET THEM WHEN CHRONOS--
THE REASON YOU DON'T KNOW ABOUT IT IS--
NEVER MIND. IT'S TIME TRAVEL. IT'S COMPLICATED.
WELL, AT LEAST ONE THING AIN'T COMPLICATED HERE...IF WE KNOW THE GOOD GUYS, AND THESE GUYS ARE SHOOTIN' AT US...
ZANNNG

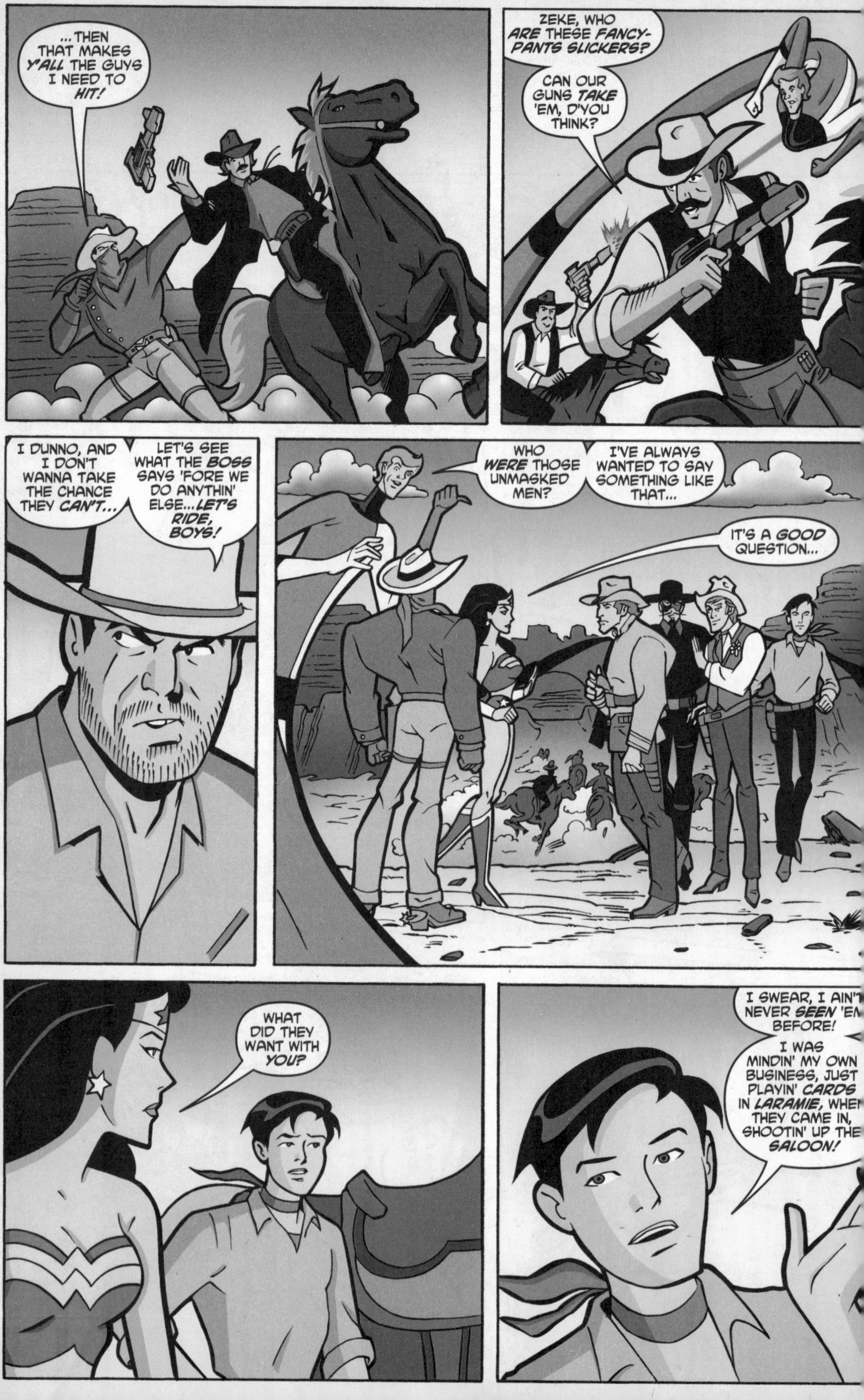

...THEN THAT MAKES Y'ALL THE GUYS I NEED TO HIT!
ZEKE, WHO ARE THESE FANCY-PANTS SLICKERS?
CAN OUR GUNS TAKE 'EM, D'YOU THINK?
I DUNNO, AND I DON'T WANNA TAKE THE CHANCE THEY CAN'T...
LET'S SEE WHAT THE BOSS SAYS 'FORE WE DO ANYTHIN' ELSE...LET'S RIDE, BOYS!
WHO WERE THOSE UNMASKED MEN?
I'VE ALWAYS WANTED TO SAY SOMETHING LIKE THAT...
IT'S A GOOD QUESTION...
WHAT DID THEY WANT WITH YOU?
I SWEAR, I AIN'T NEVER SEEN 'EM BEFORE!
I WAS MINDIN' MY OWN BUSINESS, JUST PLAYIN' CARDS IN LARAMIE, WHEN THEY CAME IN, SHOOTIN' UP THE SALOON!

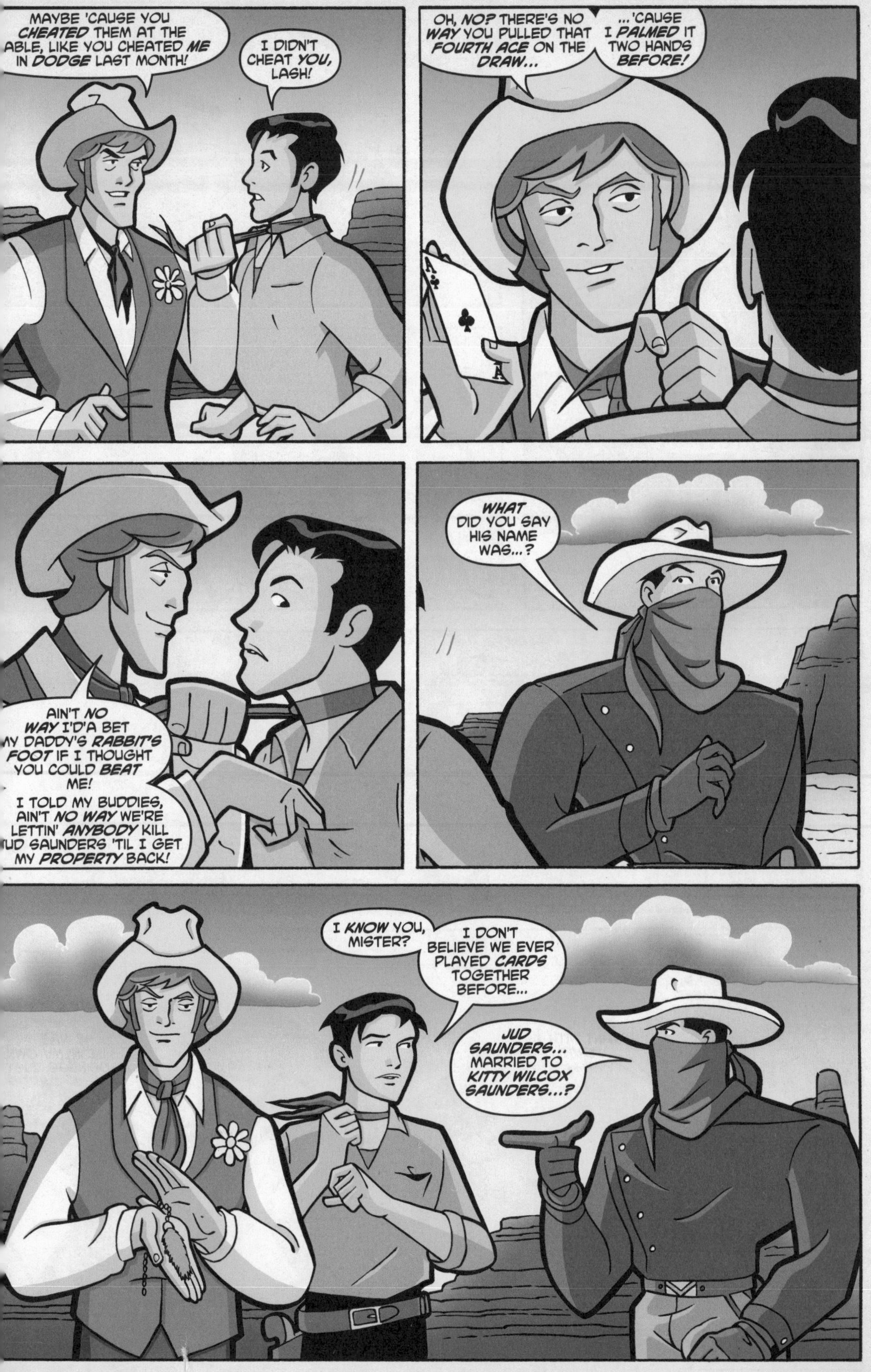
MAYBE 'CAUSE YOU CHEATED THEM AT THE ABLE, LIKE YOU CHEATED ME IN DODGE LAST MONTH!
I DIDN'T CHEAT YOU, LASH!
OH, NO? THERE'S NO WAY YOU PULLED THAT FOURTH ACE ON THE DRAW...
...'CAUSE I PALMED IT TWO HANDS BEFORE!
AIN'T NO WAY I'D'A BET MY DADDY'S RABBIT'S FOOT IF I THOUGHT YOU COULD BEAT ME!
I TOLD MY BUDDIES, AIN'T NO WAY WE'RE LETTIN' ANYBODY KILL JUD SAUNDERS 'TIL I GET MY PROPERTY BACK!
WHAT DID YOU SAY HIS NAME WAS...?
I KNOW YOU, MISTER?
I DON'T BELIEVE WE EVER PLAYED CARDS TOGETHER BEFORE...
JUD SAUNDERS... MARRIED TO KITTY WILCOX SAUNDERS...?

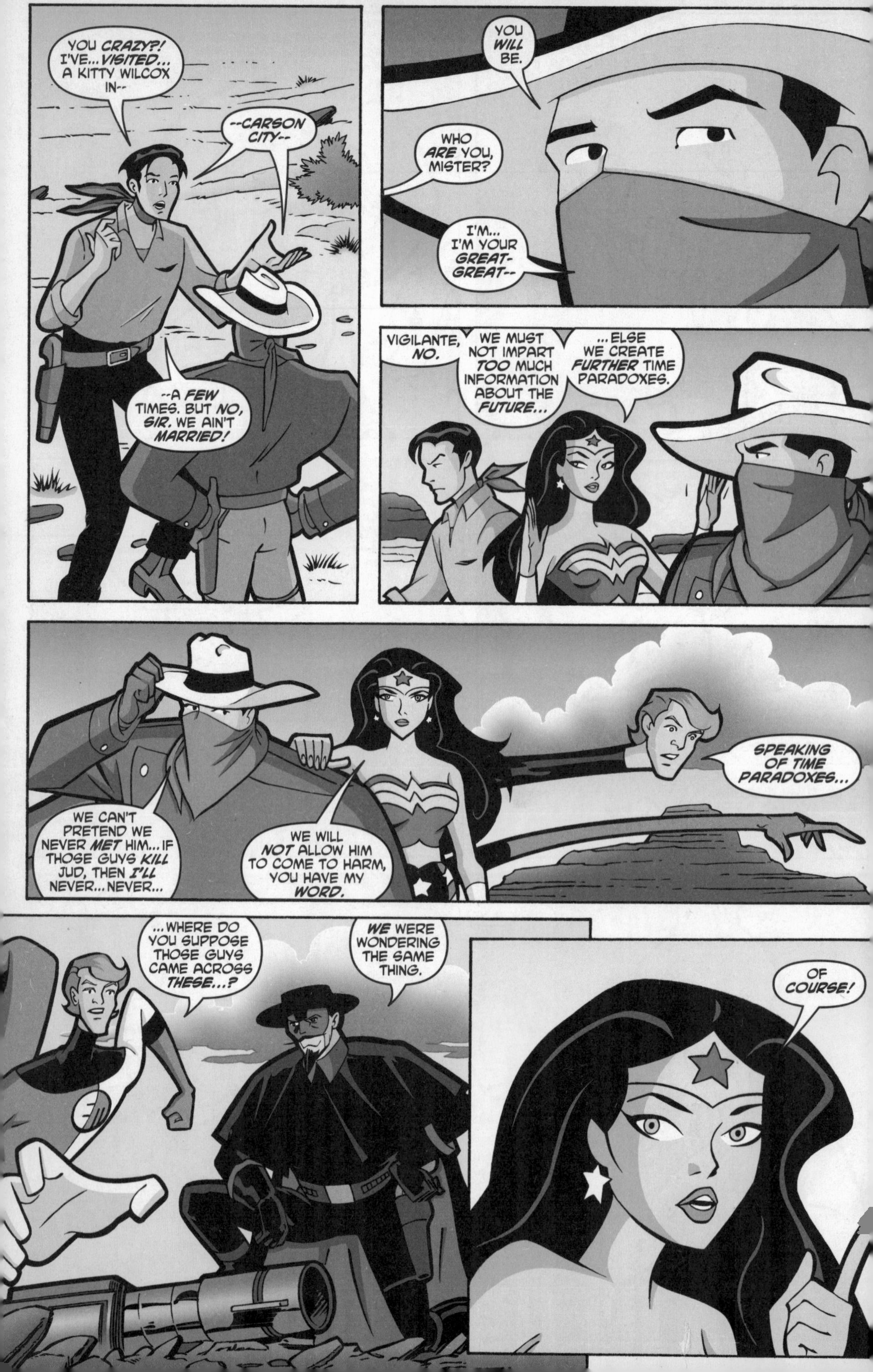
YOU CRAZY?! I'VE...VISITED... A KITTY WILCOX IN--
--CARSON CITY--
--A FEW TIMES. BUT NO, SIR. WE AIN'T MARRIED!
YOU WILL BE.
WHO ARE YOU, MISTER?
I'M... I'M YOUR GREAT-GREAT--
VIGILANTE, NO.
WE MUST NOT IMPART TOO MUCH INFORMATION ABOUT THE FUTURE...
...ELSE WE CREATE FURTHER TIME PARADOXES.
WE CAN'T PRETEND WE NEVER MET HIM...IF THOSE GUYS KILL JUD, THEN I'LL NEVER...NEVER...
WE WILL NOT ALLOW HIM TO COME TO HARM, YOU HAVE MY WORD.
SPEAKING OF TIME PARADOXES...
...WHERE DO YOU SUPPOSE THOSE GUYS CAME ACROSS THESE...?
WE WERE WONDERING THE SAME THING.
OF COURSE!

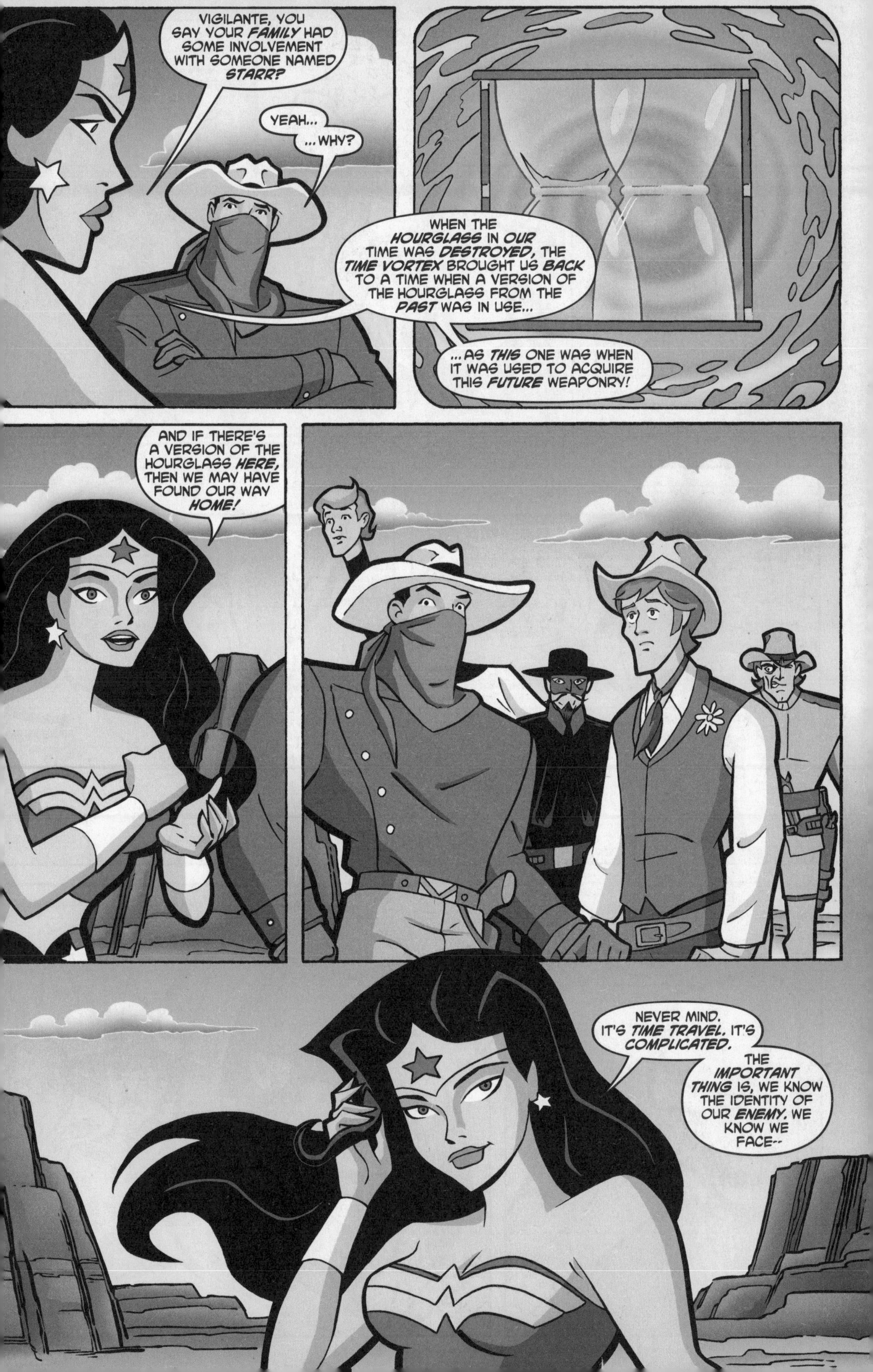
VIGILANTE, YOU SAY YOUR FAMILY HAD SOME INVOLVEMENT WITH SOMEONE NAMED STARR?
YEAH...
...WHY?
WHEN THE HOURGLASS IN OUR TIME WAS DESTROYED, THE TIME VORTEX BROUGHT US BACK TO A TIME WHEN A VERSION OF THE HOURGLASS FROM THE PAST WAS IN USE...
...AS THIS ONE WAS WHEN IT WAS USED TO ACQUIRE THIS FUTURE WEAPONRY!
AND IF THERE'S A VERSION OF THE HOURGLASS HERE, THEN WE MAY HAVE FOUND OUR WAY HOME!
NEVER MIND. IT'S TIME TRAVEL. IT'S COMPLICATED.
THE IMPORTANT THING IS, WE KNOW THE IDENTITY OF OUR ENEMY. WE KNOW WE FACE--

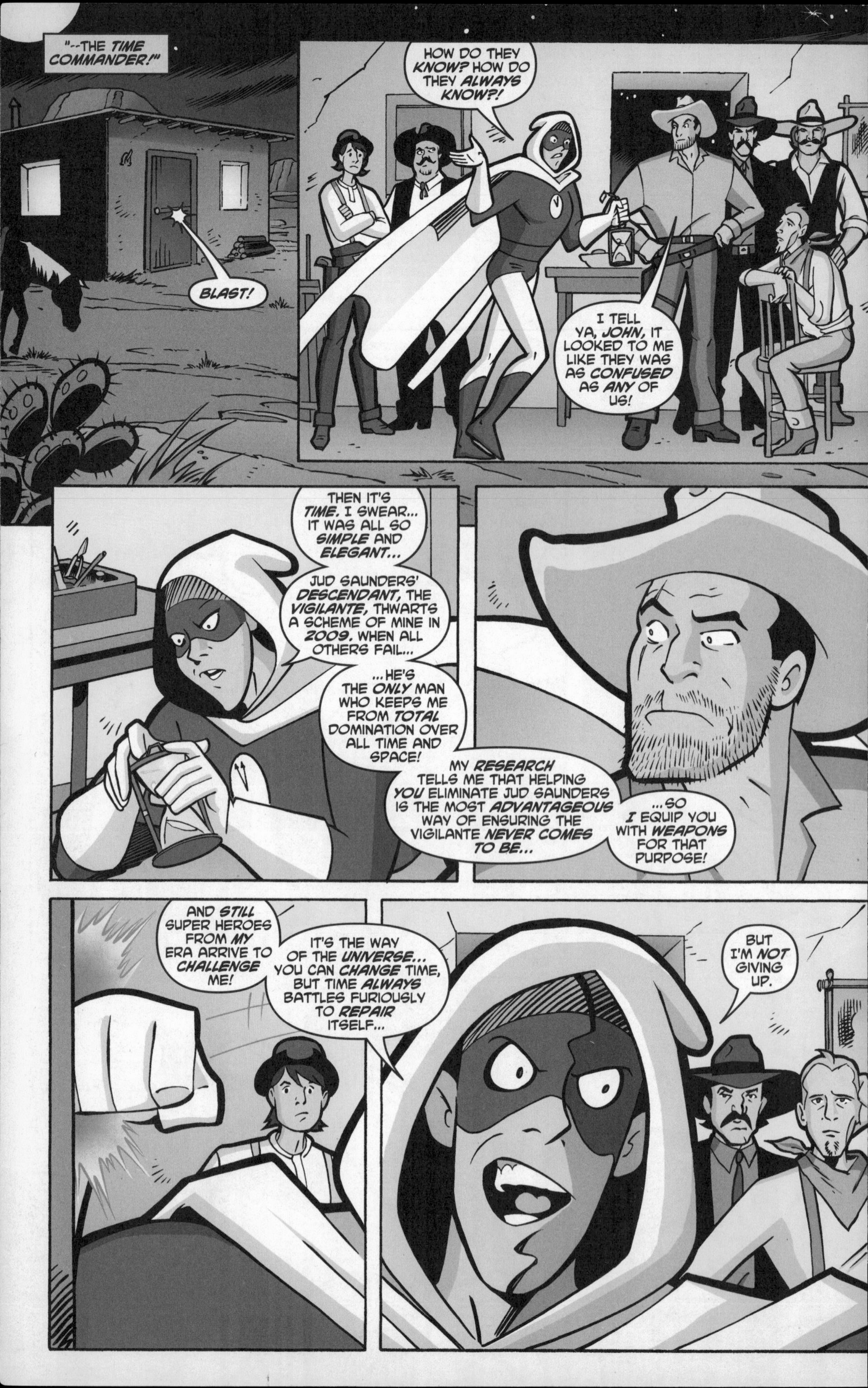
"--THE TIME COMMANDER!"
BLAST!
HOW DO THEY KNOW? HOW DO THEY ALWAYS KNOW?!
I TELL YA, JOHN, IT LOOKED TO ME LIKE THEY WAS AS CONFUSED AS ANY OF US!
THEN IT'S TIME. I SWEAR... IT WAS ALL SO SIMPLE AND ELEGANT...
JUD SAUNDERS' DESCENDANT, THE VIGILANTE, THWARTS A SCHEME OF MINE IN 2009. WHEN ALL OTHERS FAIL...
...HE'S THE ONLY MAN WHO KEEPS ME FROM TOTAL DOMINATION OVER ALL TIME AND SPACE!
MY RESEARCH TELLS ME THAT HELPING YOU ELIMINATE JUD SAUNDERS IS THE MOST ADVANTAGEOUS WAY OF ENSURING THE VIGILANTE NEVER COMES TO BE...
...SO I EQUIP YOU WITH WEAPONS FOR THAT PURPOSE!
AND STILL SUPER HEROES FROM MY ERA ARRIVE TO CHALLENGE ME!
IT'S THE WAY OF THE UNIVERSE... YOU CAN CHANGE TIME, BUT TIME ALWAYS BATTLES FURIOUSLY TO REPAIR ITSELF...
BUT I'M NOT GIVING UP.

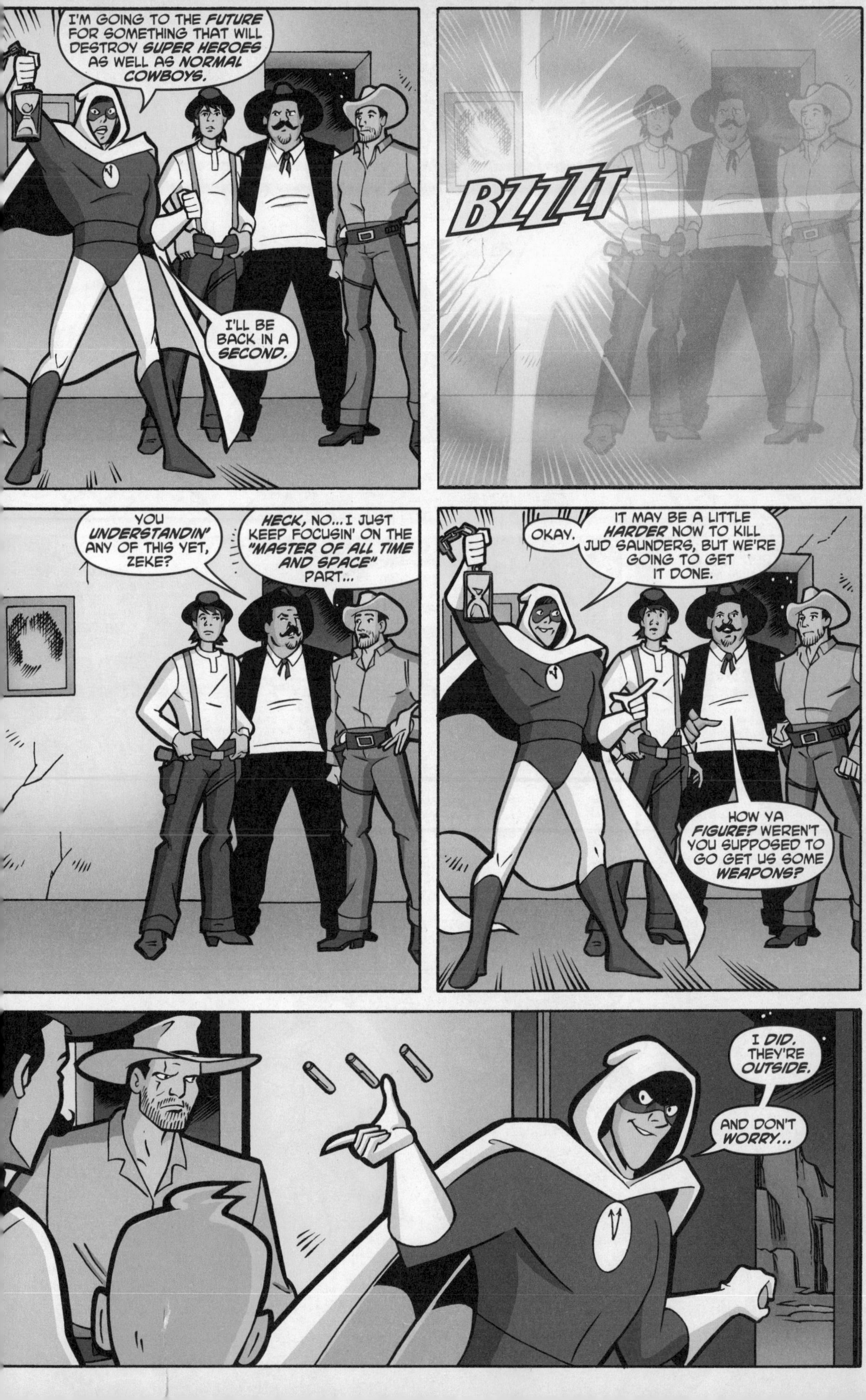
I'M GOING TO THE FUTURE FOR SOMETHING THAT WILL DESTROY SUPER HEROES AS WELL AS NORMAL COWBOYS.
I'LL BE BACK IN A SECOND.
BZZZT
YOU UNDERSTANDIN' ANY OF THIS YET, ZEKE?
HECK, NO... I JUST KEEP FOCUSIN' ON THE "MASTER OF ALL TIME AND SPACE" PART...
OKAY.
IT MAY BE A LITTLE HARDER NOW TO KILL JUD SAUNDERS, BUT WE'RE GOING TO GET IT DONE.
HOW YA FIGURE? WEREN'T YOU SUPPOSED TO GO GET US SOME WEAPONS?
I DID. THEY'RE OUTSIDE.
AND DON'T WORRY...

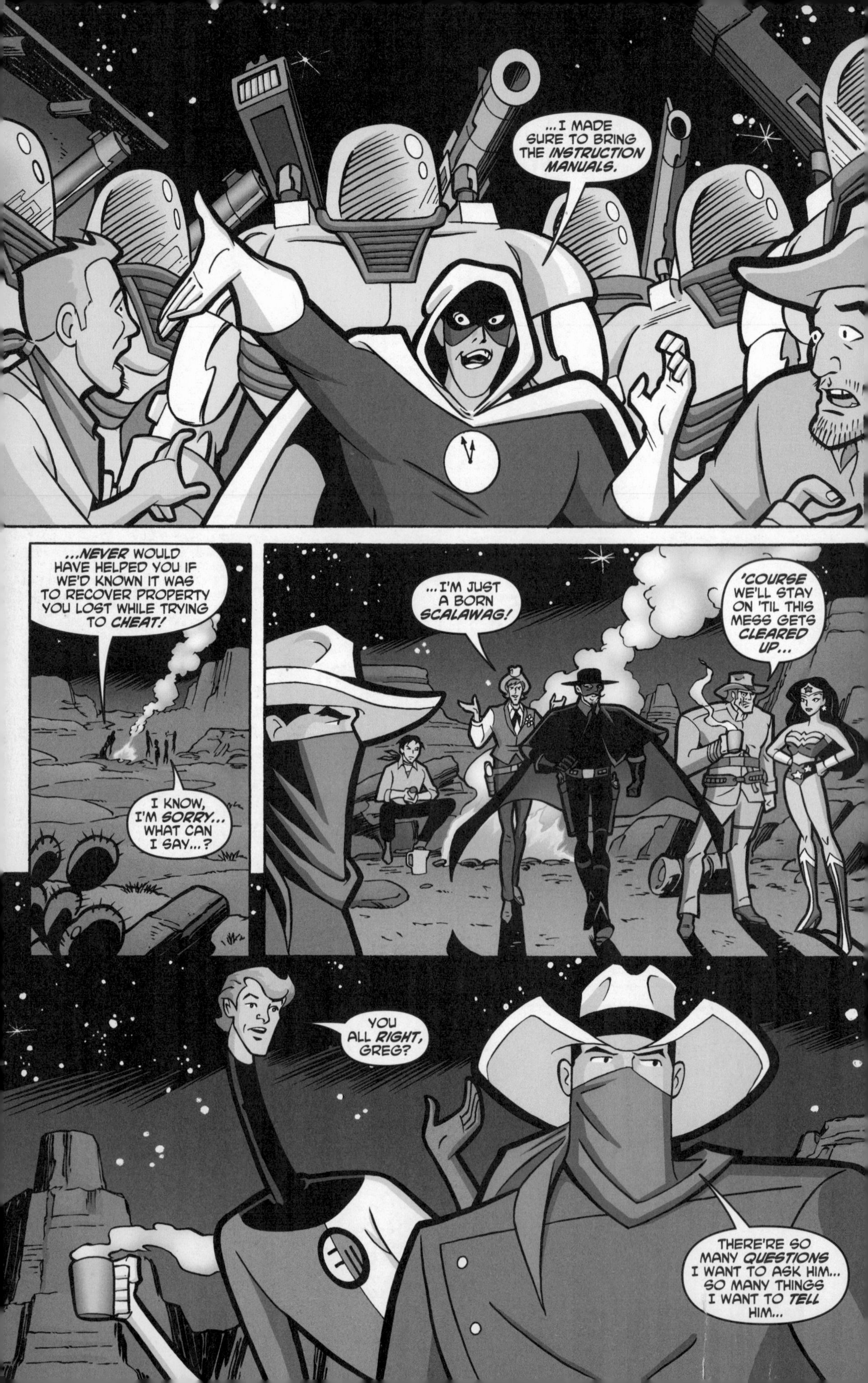
...I MADE SURE TO BRING THE *INSTRUCTION MANUALS.*
...*NEVER* WOULD HAVE HELPED YOU IF WE'D KNOWN IT WAS TO RECOVER PROPERTY YOU LOST WHILE TRYING TO *CHEAT!*
I KNOW, I'M *SORRY*... WHAT CAN I SAY...?
...I'M JUST A BORN *SCALAWAG!*
'COURSE WE'LL STAY ON 'TIL THIS MESS GETS *CLEARED UP*...
YOU ALL *RIGHT,* GREG?
THERE'RE SO MANY *QUESTIONS* I WANT TO ASK HIM... SO MANY THINGS I WANT TO *TELL* HIM...

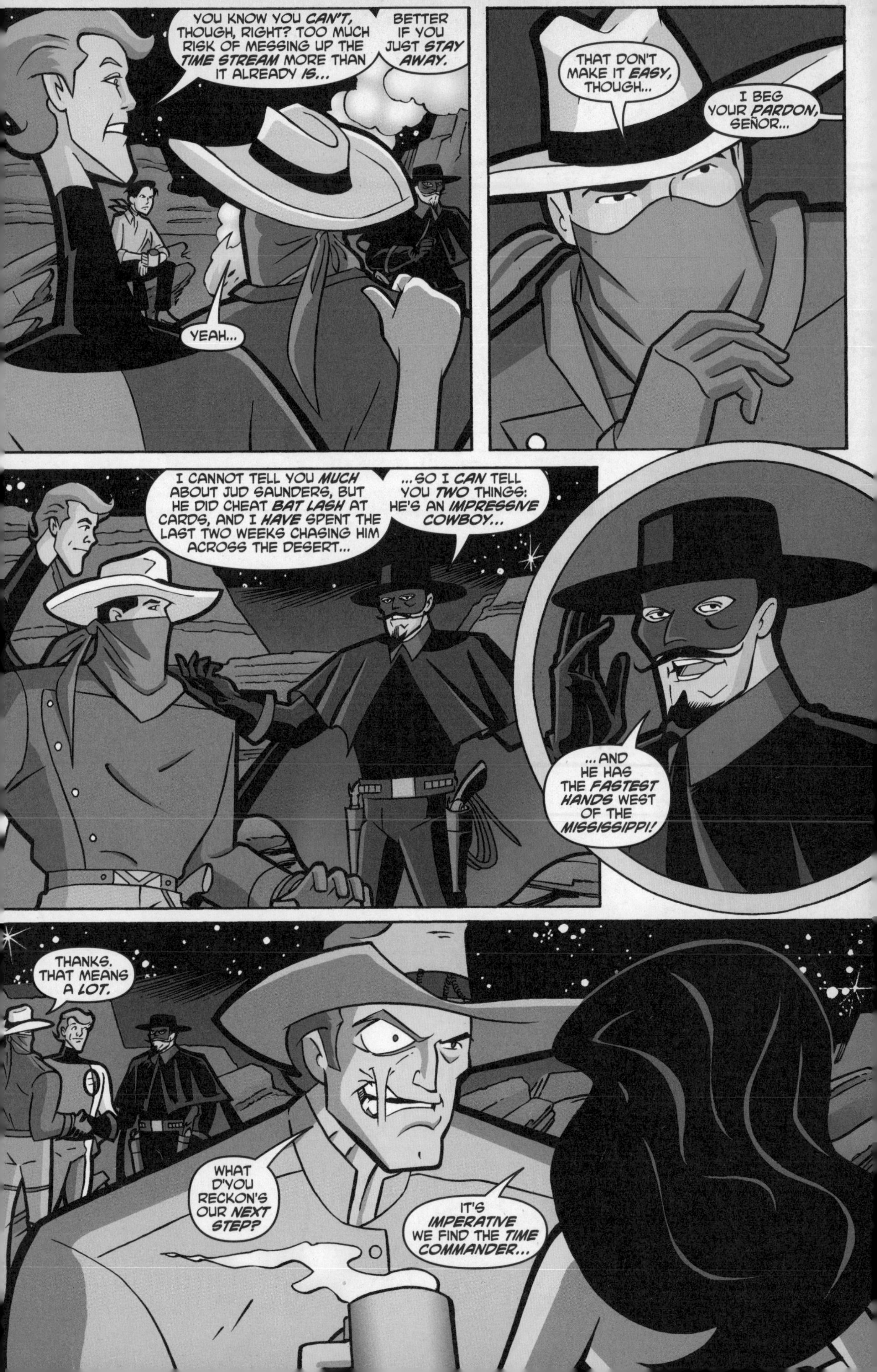
YOU KNOW YOU CAN'T, THOUGH, RIGHT? TOO MUCH RISK OF MESSING UP THE TIME STREAM MORE THAN IT ALREADY IS...
BETTER IF YOU JUST STAY AWAY.
YEAH...
THAT DON'T MAKE IT EASY, THOUGH...
I BEG YOUR PARDON, SEÑOR...
I CANNOT TELL YOU MUCH ABOUT JUD SAUNDERS, BUT HE DID CHEAT BAT LASH AT CARDS, AND I HAVE SPENT THE LAST TWO WEEKS CHASING HIM ACROSS THE DESERT...
...SO I CAN TELL YOU TWO THINGS: HE'S AN IMPRESSIVE COWBOY...
...AND HE HAS THE FASTEST HANDS WEST OF THE MISSISSIPPI!
THANKS. THAT MEANS A LOT.
WHAT D'YOU RECKON'S OUR NEXT STEP?
IT'S IMPERATIVE WE FIND THE TIME COMMANDER...

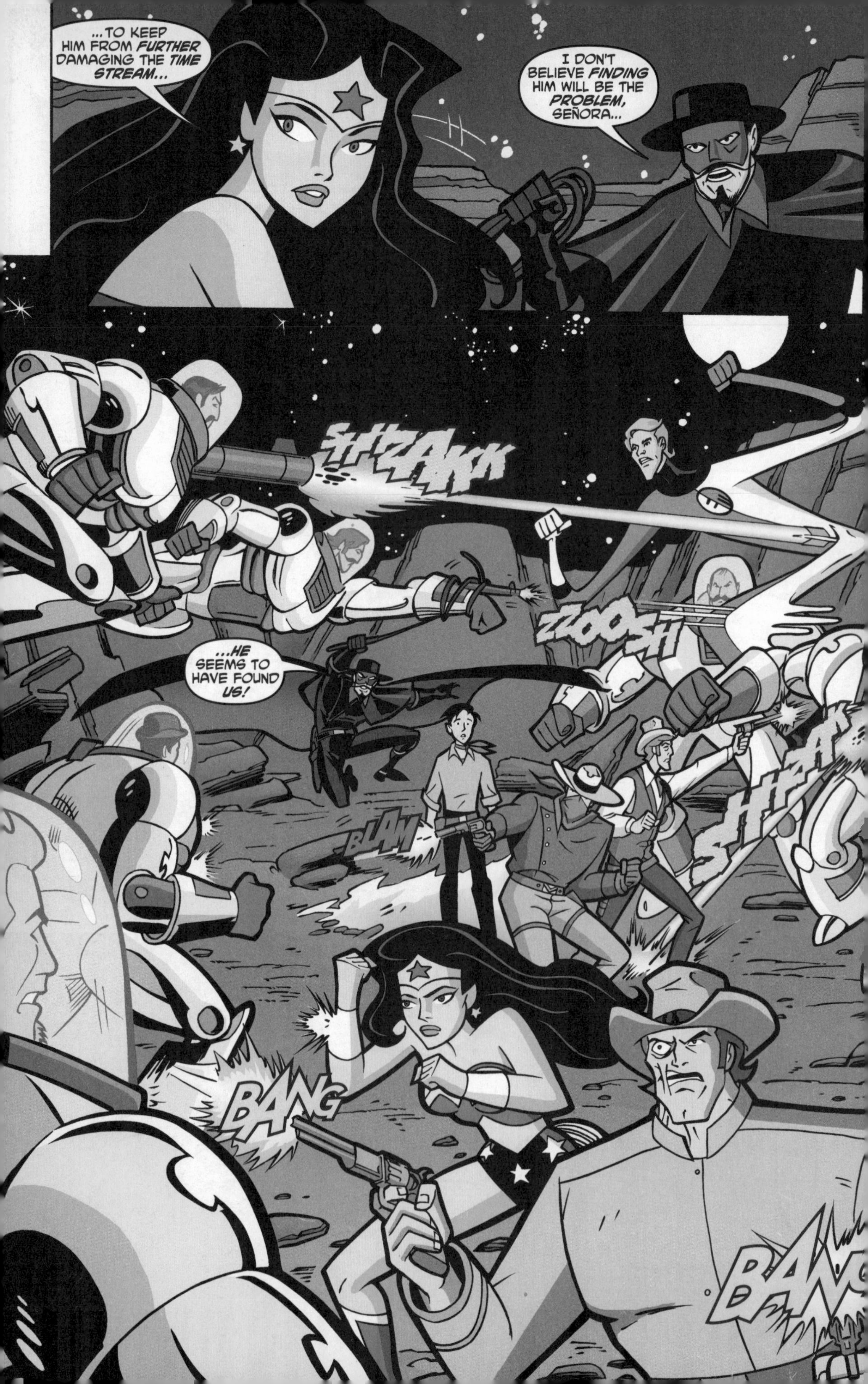
...TO KEEP HIM FROM FURTHER DAMAGING THE TIME STREAM...
I DON'T BELIEVE FINDING HIM WILL BE THE PROBLEM, SEÑORA...
SHZAKK
ZZOOSH
...HE SEEMS TO HAVE FOUND US!
BLAM
BANG
BANG

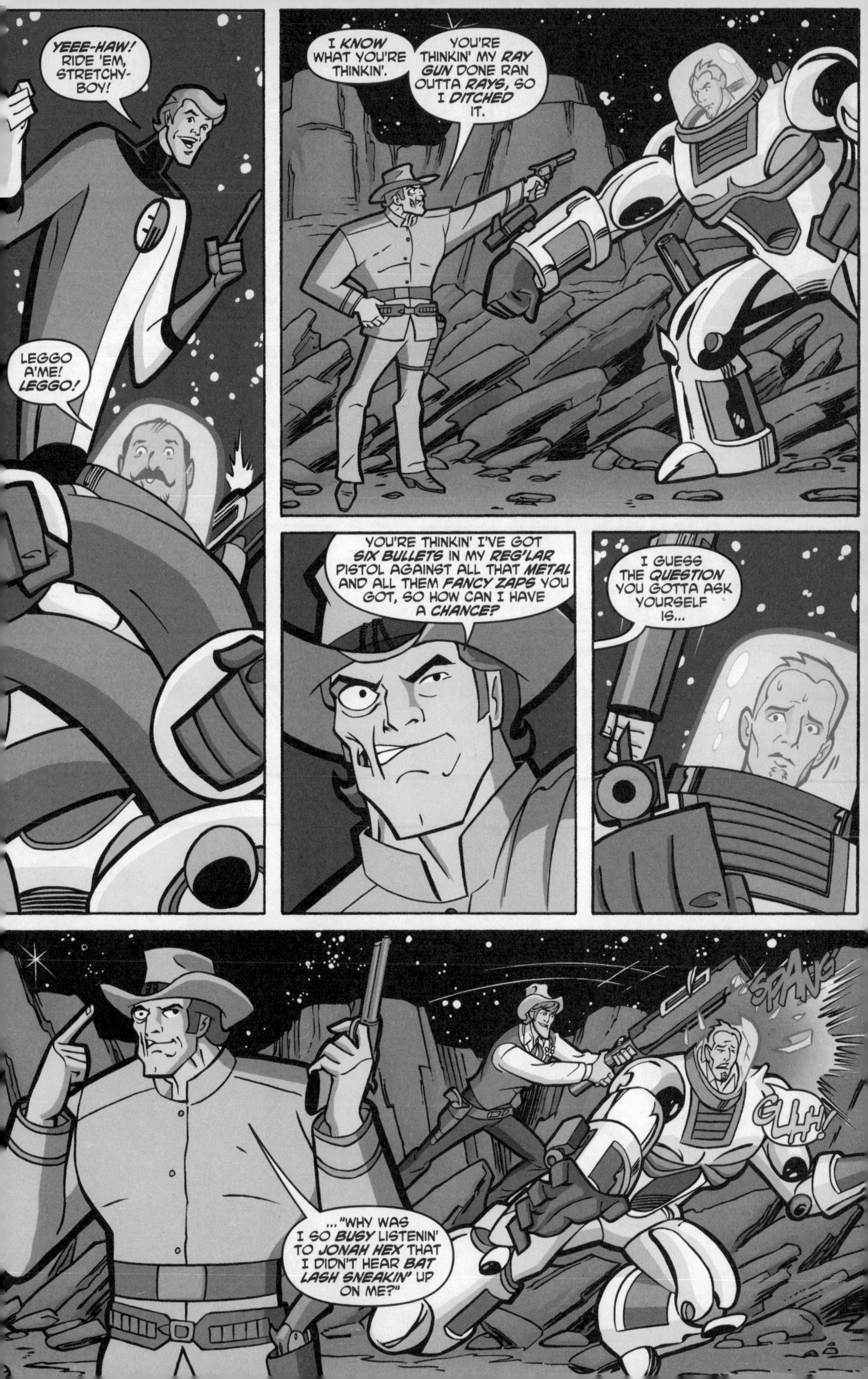
YEEE-HAW! RIDE 'EM, STRETCHY-BOY!
LEGGO A'ME! LEGGO!
I KNOW WHAT YOU'RE THINKIN'.
YOU'RE THINKIN' MY RAY GUN DONE RAN OUTTA RAYS, SO I DITCHED IT.
YOU'RE THINKIN' I'VE GOT SIX BULLETS IN MY REG'LAR PISTOL AGAINST ALL THAT METAL AND ALL THEM FANCY ZAPS YOU GOT, SO HOW CAN I HAVE A CHANCE?
I GUESS THE QUESTION YOU GOTTA ASK YOURSELF IS...
..."WHY WAS I SO BUSY LISTENIN' TO JONAH HEX THAT I DIDN'T HEAR BAT LASH SNEAKIN' UP ON ME?"
SPANG
GLLH!

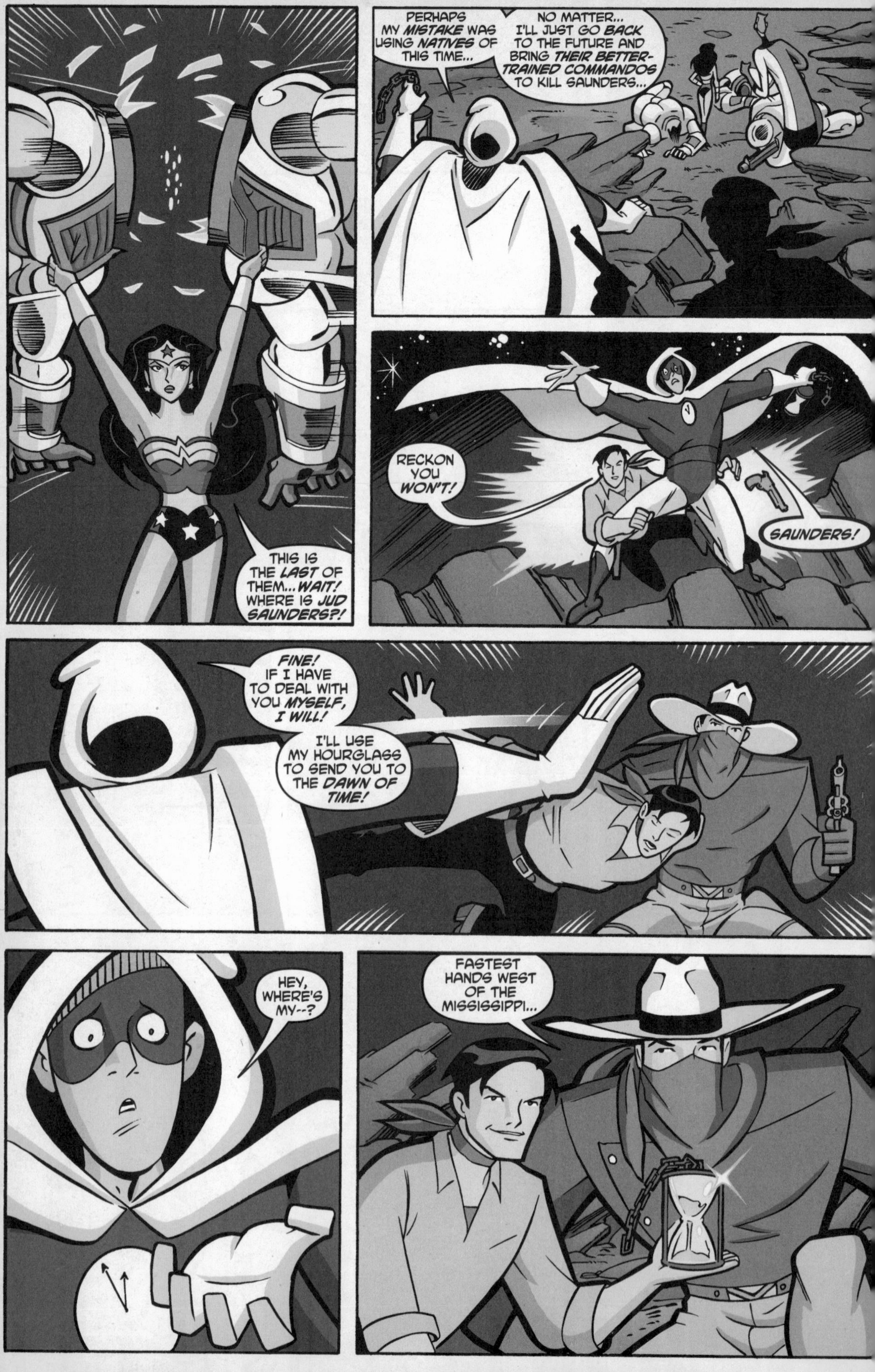
THIS IS THE LAST OF THEM...WAIT! WHERE IS JUD SAUNDERS?!
PERHAPS MY MISTAKE WAS USING NATIVES OF THIS TIME...
NO MATTER... I'LL JUST GO BACK TO THE FUTURE AND BRING THEIR BETTER-TRAINED COMMANDOS TO KILL SAUNDERS...
RECKON YOU WON'T!
SAUNDERS!
FINE! IF I HAVE TO DEAL WITH YOU MYSELF, I WILL!
I'LL USE MY HOURGLASS TO SEND YOU TO THE DAWN OF TIME!
HEY, WHERE'S MY--?
FASTEST HANDS WEST OF THE MISSISSIPPI...

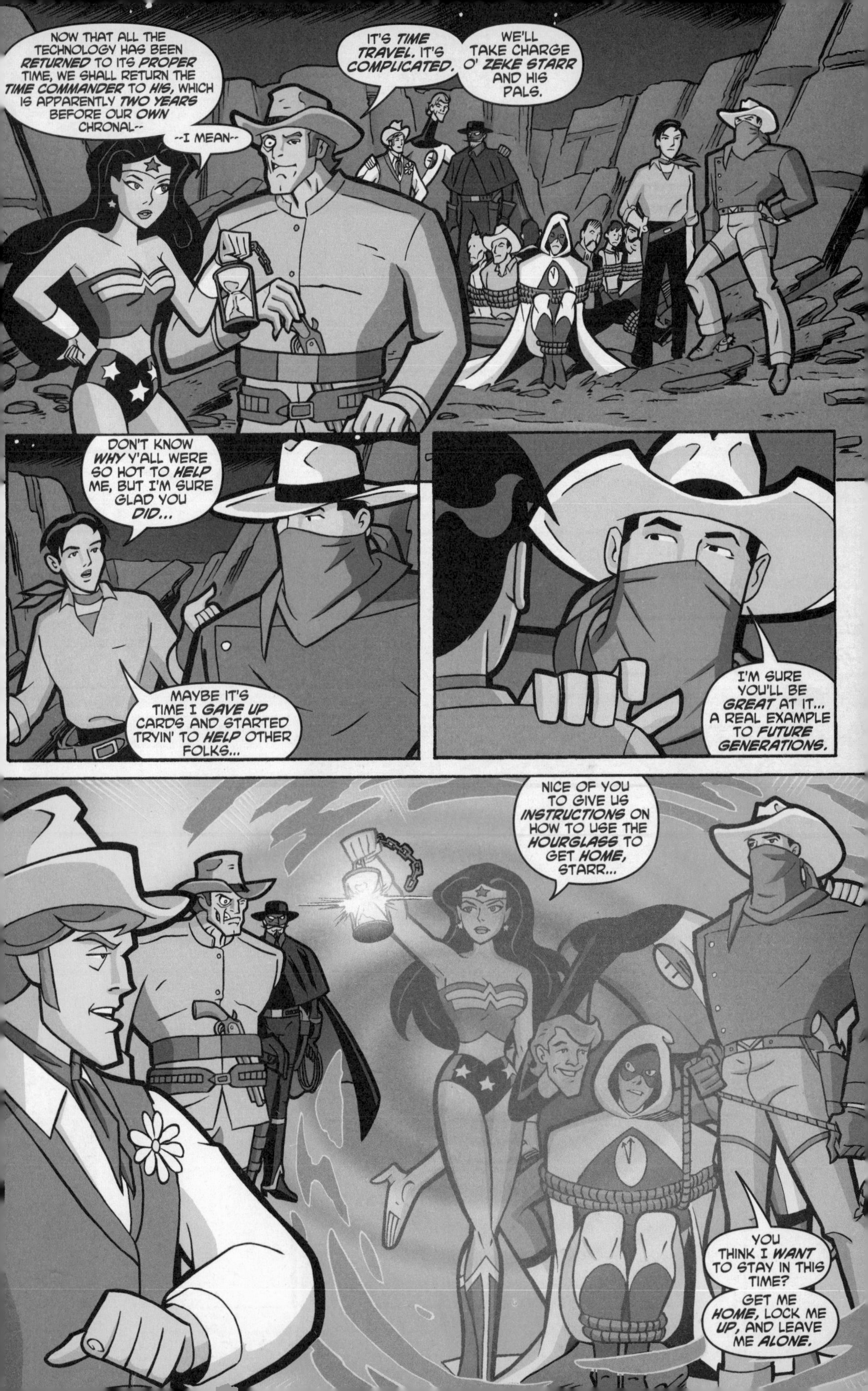
NOW THAT ALL THE TECHNOLOGY HAS BEEN RETURNED TO ITS PROPER TIME, WE SHALL RETURN THE TIME COMMANDER TO HIS, WHICH IS APPARENTLY TWO YEARS BEFORE OUR OWN CHRONAL--
--I MEAN--
IT'S TIME TRAVEL. IT'S COMPLICATED.
WE'LL TAKE CHARGE O' ZEKE STARR AND HIS PALS.
DON'T KNOW WHY Y'ALL WERE SO HOT TO HELP ME, BUT I'M SURE GLAD YOU DID...
MAYBE IT'S TIME I GAVE UP CARDS AND STARTED TRYIN' TO HELP OTHER FOLKS...
I'M SURE YOU'LL BE GREAT AT IT... A REAL EXAMPLE TO FUTURE GENERATIONS.
NICE OF YOU TO GIVE US INSTRUCTIONS ON HOW TO USE THE HOURGLASS TO GET HOME, STARR...
YOU THINK I WANT TO STAY IN THIS TIME?
GET ME HOME, LOCK ME UP, AND LEAVE ME ALONE.

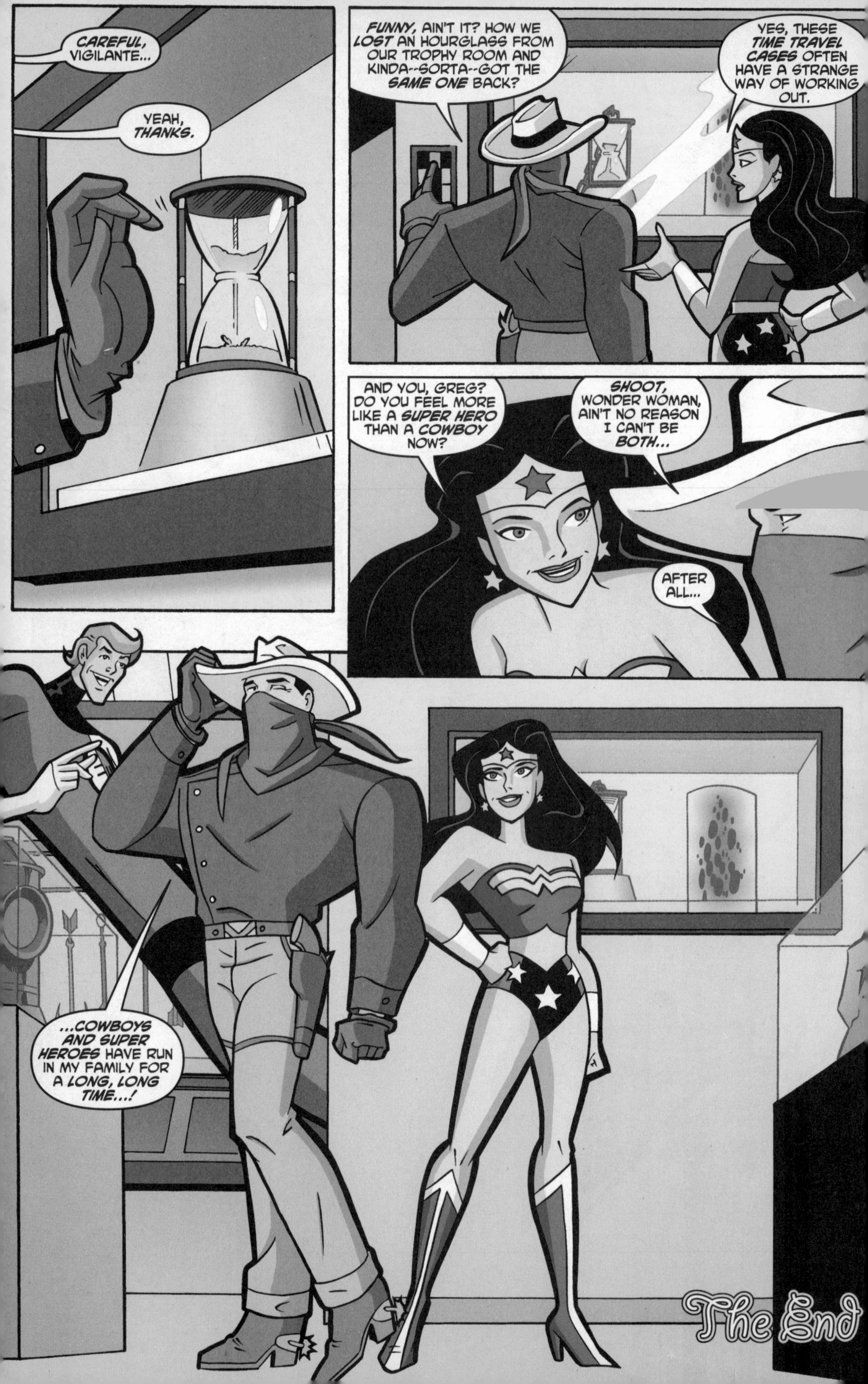
CAREFUL, VIGILANTE...
YEAH, THANKS.
FUNNY, AIN'T IT? HOW WE LOST AN HOURGLASS FROM OUR TROPHY ROOM AND KINDA--SORTA--GOT THE SAME ONE BACK?
YES, THESE TIME TRAVEL CASES OFTEN HAVE A STRANGE WAY OF WORKING OUT.
AND YOU, GREG? DO YOU FEEL MORE LIKE A SUPER HERO THAN A COWBOY NOW?
SHOOT, WONDER WOMAN, AIN'T NO REASON I CAN'T BE BOTH...
AFTER ALL...
...COWBOYS AND SUPER HEROES HAVE RUN IN MY FAMILY FOR A LONG, LONG TIME...!
The End

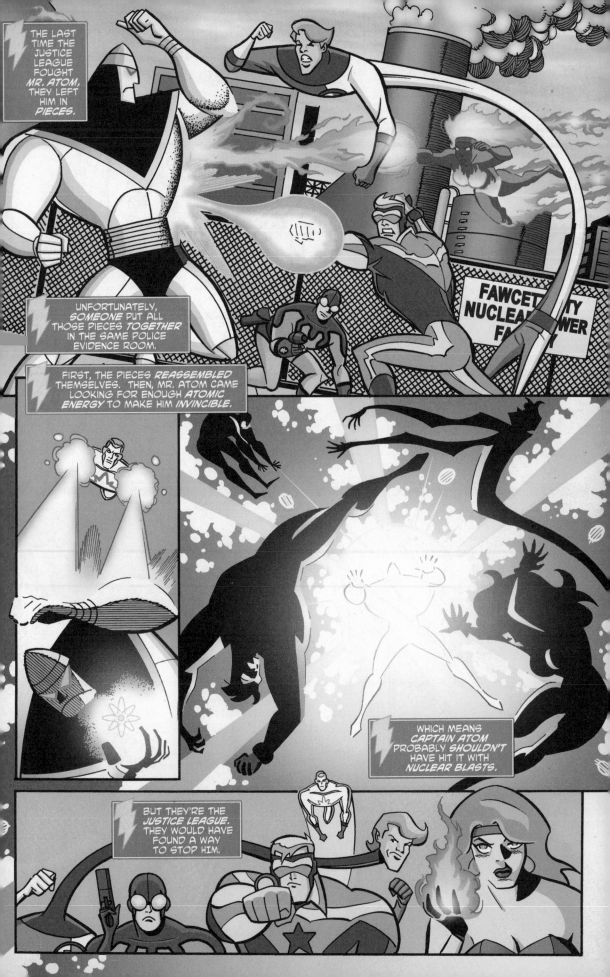

THE LAST TIME THE JUSTICE LEAGUE FOUGHT **MR. ATOM**, THEY LEFT HIM IN **PIECES**.

UNFORTUNATELY, **SOMEONE** PUT ALL THOSE PIECES **TOGETHER** IN THE SAME POLICE EVIDENCE ROOM.

FIRST, THE PIECES **REASSEMBLED** THEMSELVES. THEN, MR. ATOM CAME LOOKING FOR ENOUGH **ATOMIC ENERGY** TO MAKE HIM **INVINCIBLE**.

FAWCETT CITY NUCLEAR POWER FACILITY

WHICH MEANS **CAPTAIN ATOM** PROBABLY **SHOULDN'T** HAVE HIT IT WITH **NUCLEAR BLASTS**.

BUT THEY'RE THE **JUSTICE LEAGUE**. THEY WOULD HAVE FOUND A WAY TO STOP HIM.

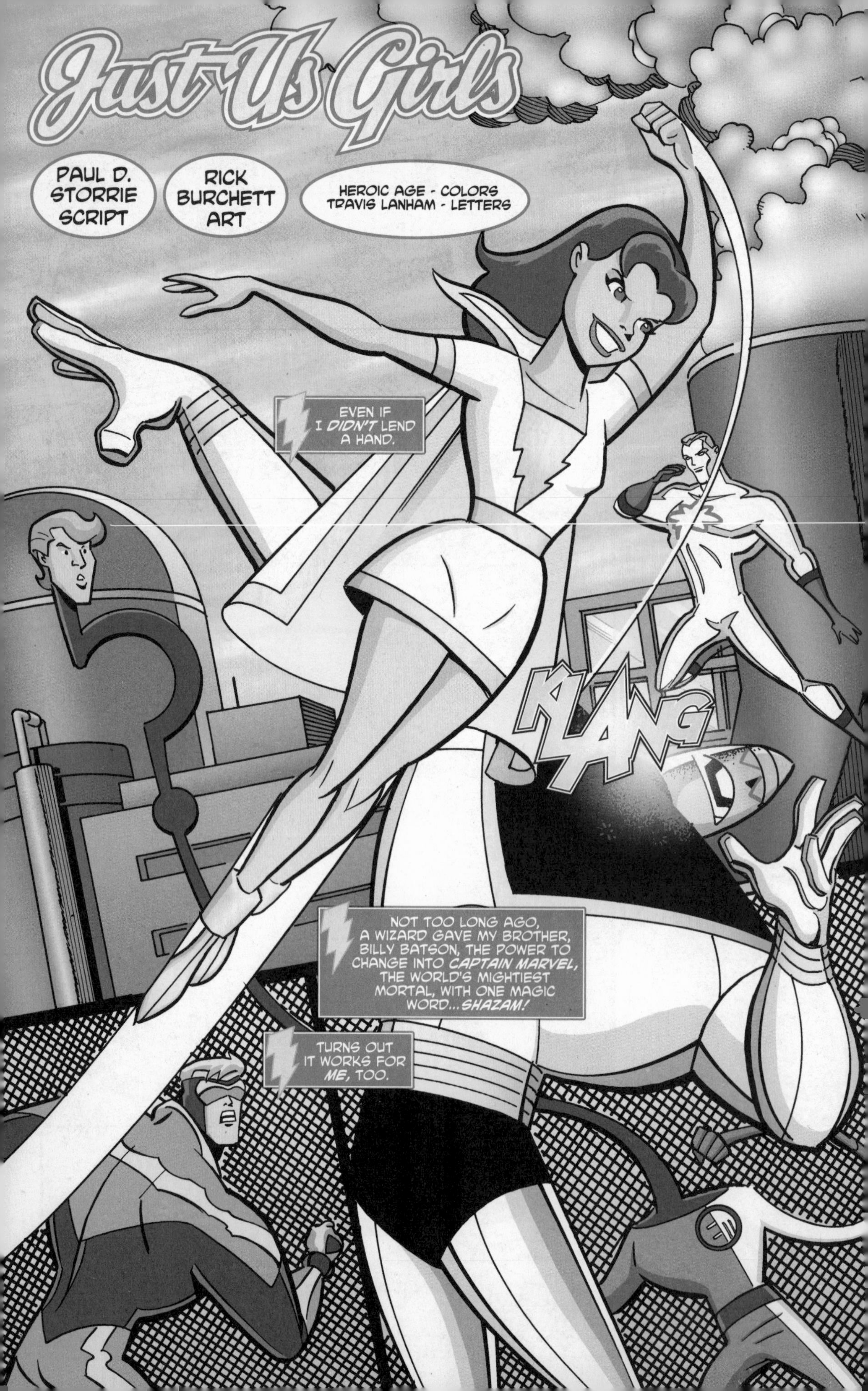

Just Us Girls
PAUL D. STORRIE SCRIPT
RICK BURCHETT ART
HEROIC AGE - COLORS TRAVIS LANHAM - LETTERS
EVEN IF I DIDN'T LEND A HAND.
KLANG
NOT TOO LONG AGO, A WIZARD GAVE MY BROTHER, BILLY BATSON, THE POWER TO CHANGE INTO CAPTAIN MARVEL, THE WORLD'S MIGHTIEST MORTAL, WITH ONE MAGIC WORD... SHAZAM!
TURNS OUT IT WORKS FOR ME, TOO.

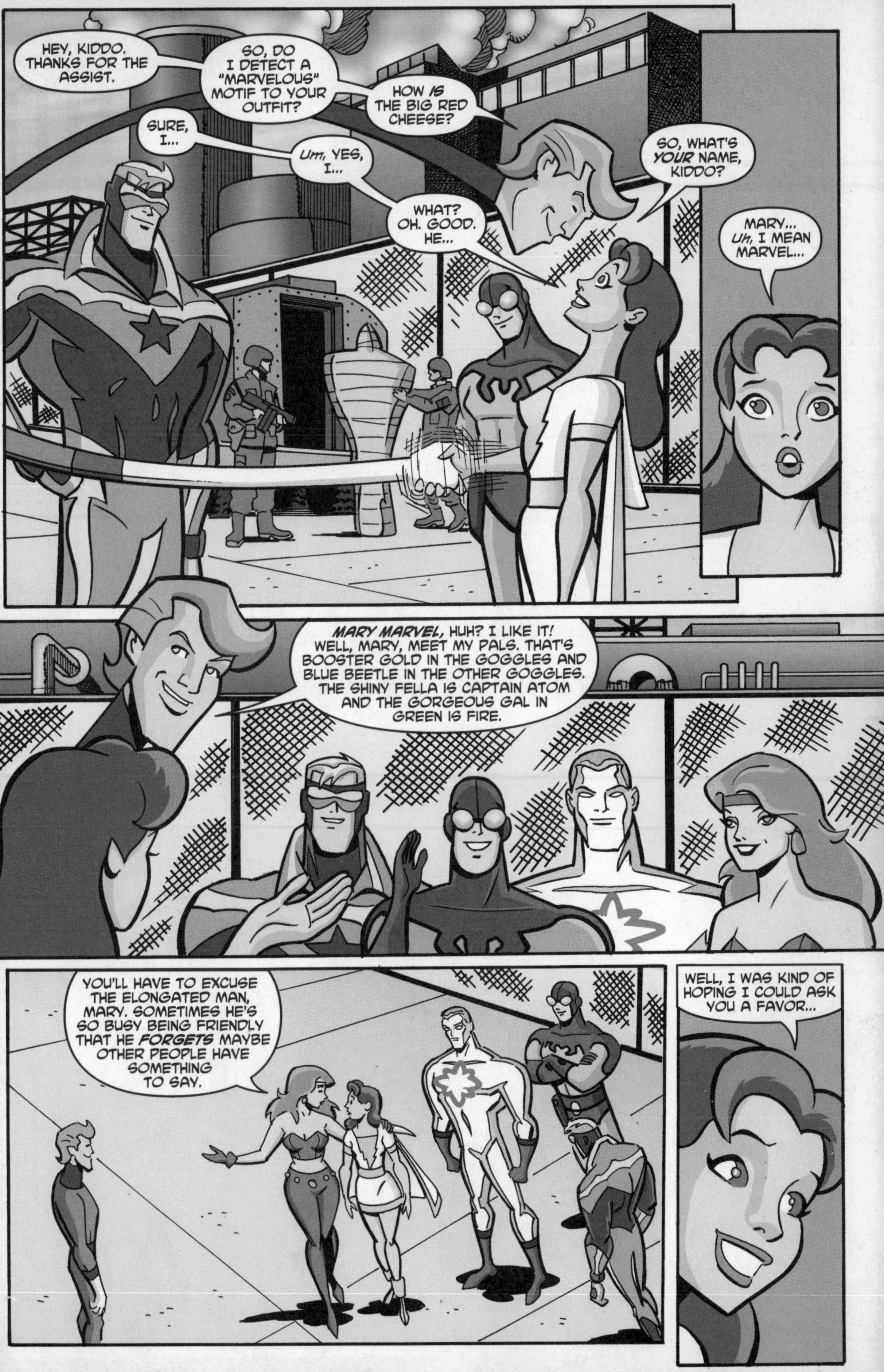
HEY, KIDDO. THANKS FOR THE ASSIST.
SO, DO I DETECT A "MARVELOUS" MOTIF TO YOUR OUTFIT?
HOW *IS* THE BIG RED CHEESE?
SURE, I...
Um, YES, I...
WHAT? OH. GOOD. HE...
SO, WHAT'S *YOUR* NAME, KIDDO?
MARY... *Uh,* I MEAN MARVEL...
MARY MARVEL, HUH? I LIKE IT! WELL, MARY, MEET MY PALS. THAT'S BOOSTER GOLD IN THE GOGGLES AND BLUE BEETLE IN THE OTHER GOGGLES. THE SHINY FELLA IS CAPTAIN ATOM AND THE GORGEOUS GAL IN GREEN IS FIRE.
YOU'LL HAVE TO EXCUSE THE ELONGATED MAN, MARY. SOMETIMES HE'S SO BUSY BEING FRIENDLY THAT HE *FORGETS* MAYBE OTHER PEOPLE HAVE SOMETHING TO SAY.
WELL, I WAS KIND OF HOPING I COULD ASK YOU A FAVOR...

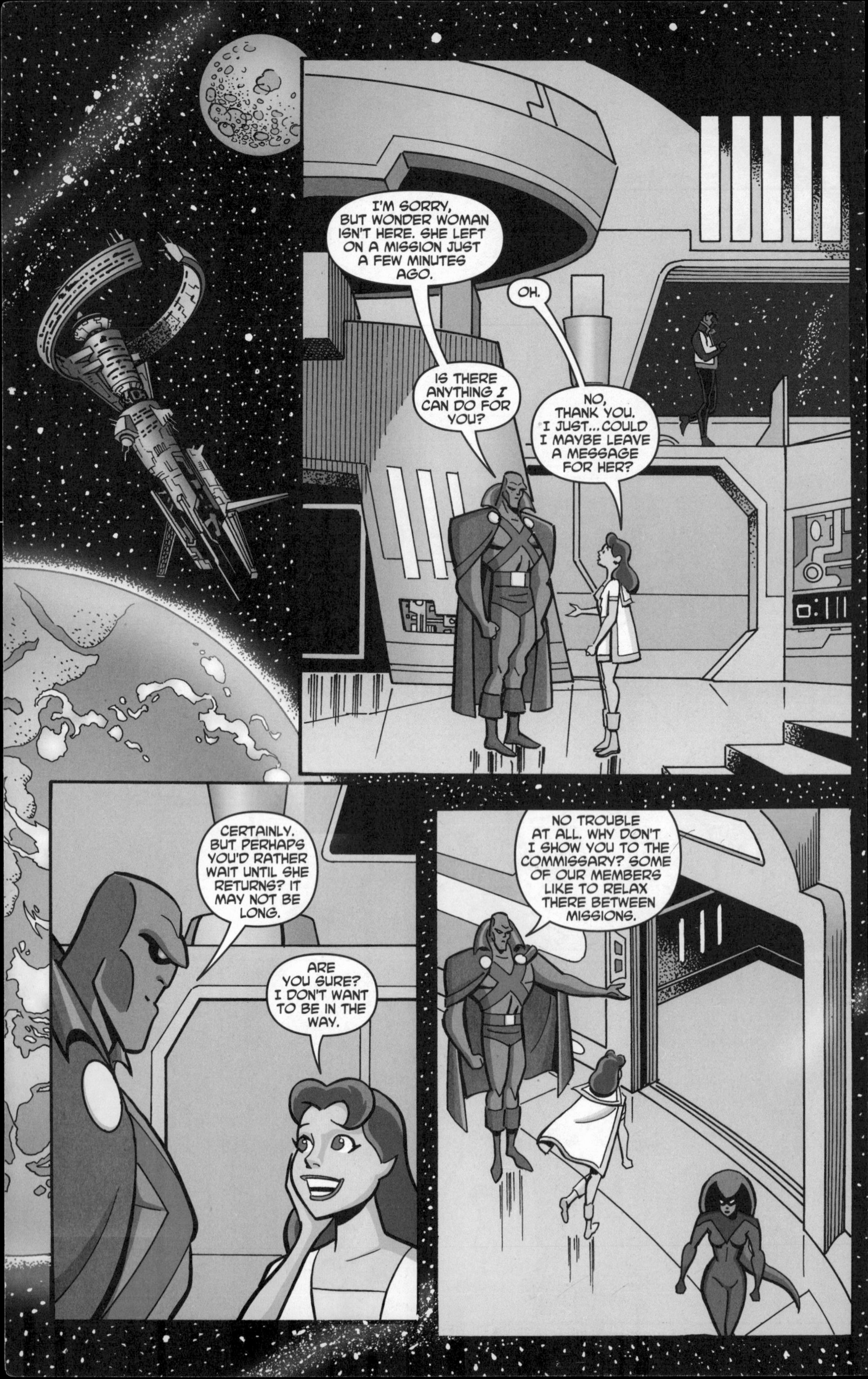
I'M SORRY, BUT WONDER WOMAN ISN'T HERE. SHE LEFT ON A MISSION JUST A FEW MINUTES AGO.
OH.
IS THERE ANYTHING I CAN DO FOR YOU?
NO, THANK YOU. I JUST...COULD I MAYBE LEAVE A MESSAGE FOR HER?
CERTAINLY. BUT PERHAPS YOU'D RATHER WAIT UNTIL SHE RETURNS? IT MAY NOT BE LONG.
ARE YOU SURE? I DON'T WANT TO BE IN THE WAY.
NO TROUBLE AT ALL. WHY DON'T I SHOW YOU TO THE COMMISSARY? SOME OF OUR MEMBERS LIKE TO RELAX THERE BETWEEN MISSIONS.

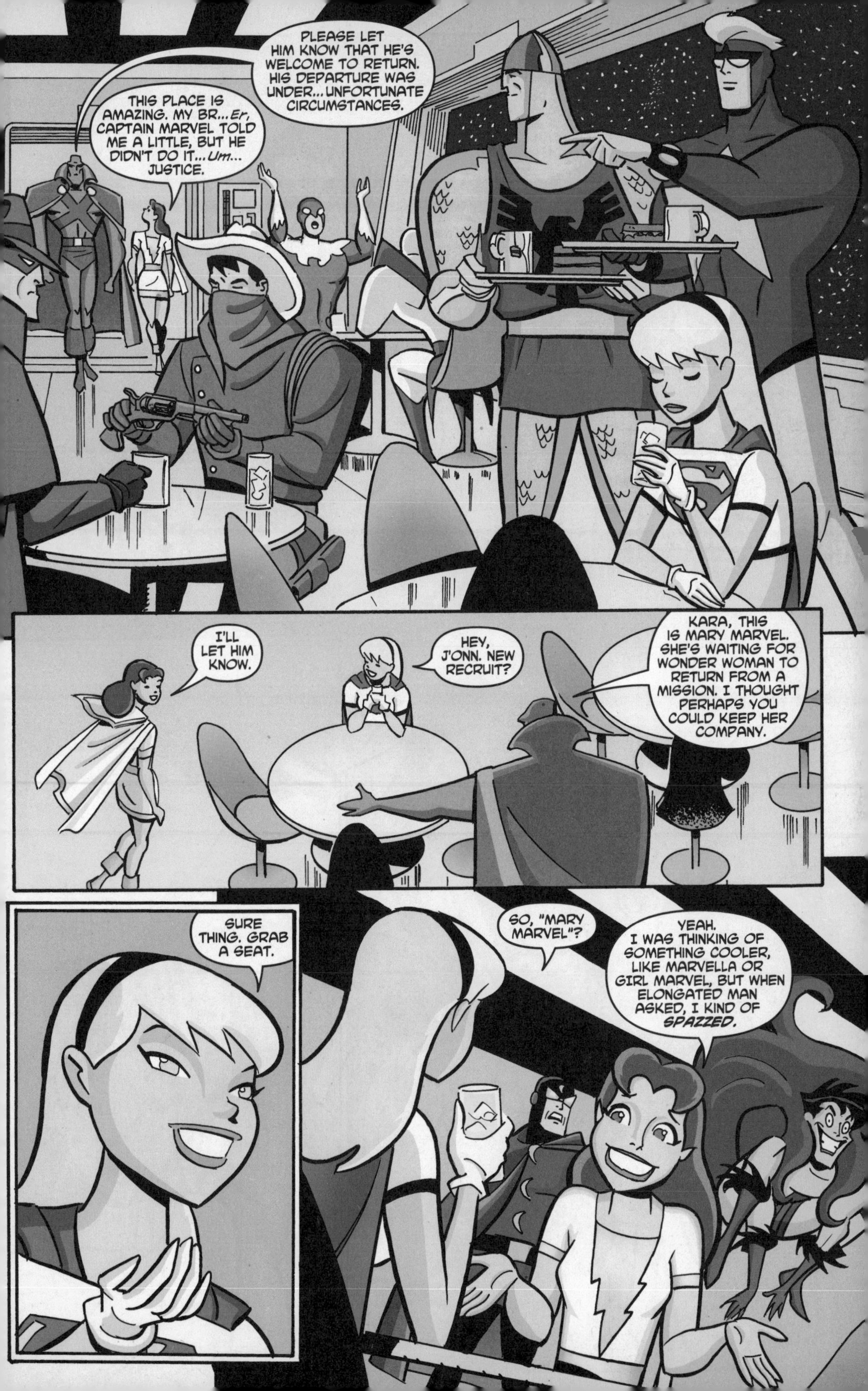
THIS PLACE IS AMAZING. MY BR... *Er,* CAPTAIN MARVEL TOLD ME A LITTLE, BUT HE DIDN'T DO IT... *Um...* JUSTICE.
PLEASE LET HIM KNOW THAT HE'S WELCOME TO RETURN. HIS DEPARTURE WAS UNDER... UNFORTUNATE CIRCUMSTANCES.
I'LL LET HIM KNOW.
HEY, J'ONN. NEW RECRUIT?
KARA, THIS IS MARY MARVEL. SHE'S WAITING FOR WONDER WOMAN TO RETURN FROM A MISSION. I THOUGHT PERHAPS YOU COULD KEEP HER COMPANY.
SURE THING. GRAB A SEAT.
SO, "MARY MARVEL"?
YEAH. I WAS THINKING OF SOMETHING COOLER, LIKE MARVELLA OR GIRL MARVEL, BUT WHEN ELONGATED MAN ASKED, I KIND OF *SPAZZED.*

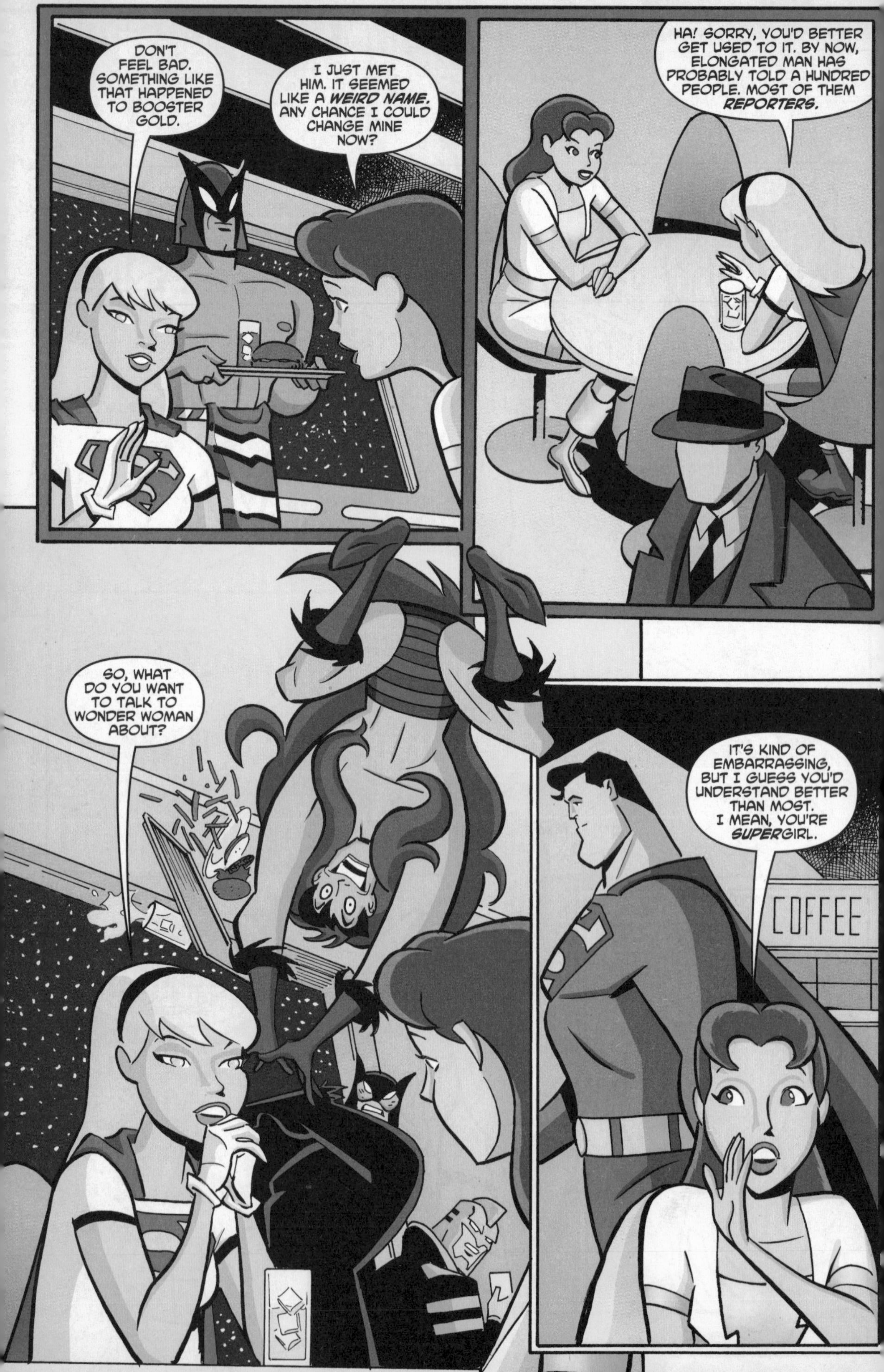
DON'T FEEL BAD. SOMETHING LIKE THAT HAPPENED TO BOOSTER GOLD.
I JUST MET HIM. IT SEEMED LIKE A *WEIRD NAME.* ANY CHANCE I COULD CHANGE MINE NOW?
HA! SORRY, YOU'D BETTER GET USED TO IT. BY NOW, ELONGATED MAN HAS PROBABLY TOLD A HUNDRED PEOPLE. MOST OF THEM *REPORTERS.*
SO, WHAT DO YOU WANT TO TALK TO WONDER WOMAN ABOUT?
IT'S KIND OF EMBARRASSING, BUT I GUESS YOU'D UNDERSTAND BETTER THAN MOST. I MEAN, YOU'RE *SUPER*GIRL.
COFFEE

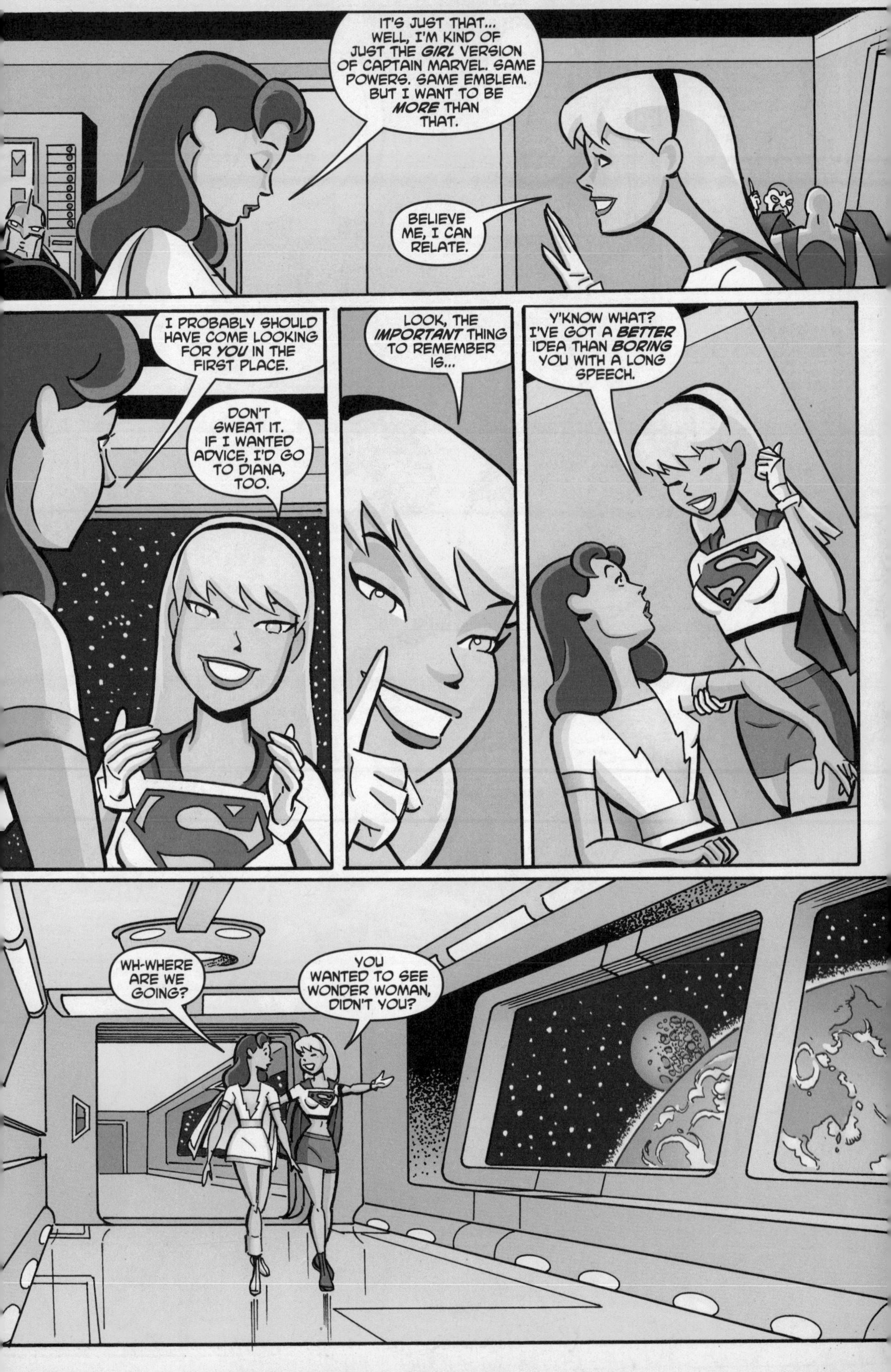
IT'S JUST THAT... WELL, I'M KIND OF JUST THE GIRL VERSION OF CAPTAIN MARVEL. SAME POWERS. SAME EMBLEM. BUT I WANT TO BE MORE THAN THAT.
BELIEVE ME, I CAN RELATE.
I PROBABLY SHOULD HAVE COME LOOKING FOR YOU IN THE FIRST PLACE.
DON'T SWEAT IT. IF I WANTED ADVICE, I'D GO TO DIANA, TOO.
LOOK, THE IMPORTANT THING TO REMEMBER IS...
Y'KNOW WHAT? I'VE GOT A BETTER IDEA THAN BORING YOU WITH A LONG SPEECH.
WH-WHERE ARE WE GOING?
YOU WANTED TO SEE WONDER WOMAN, DIDN'T YOU?

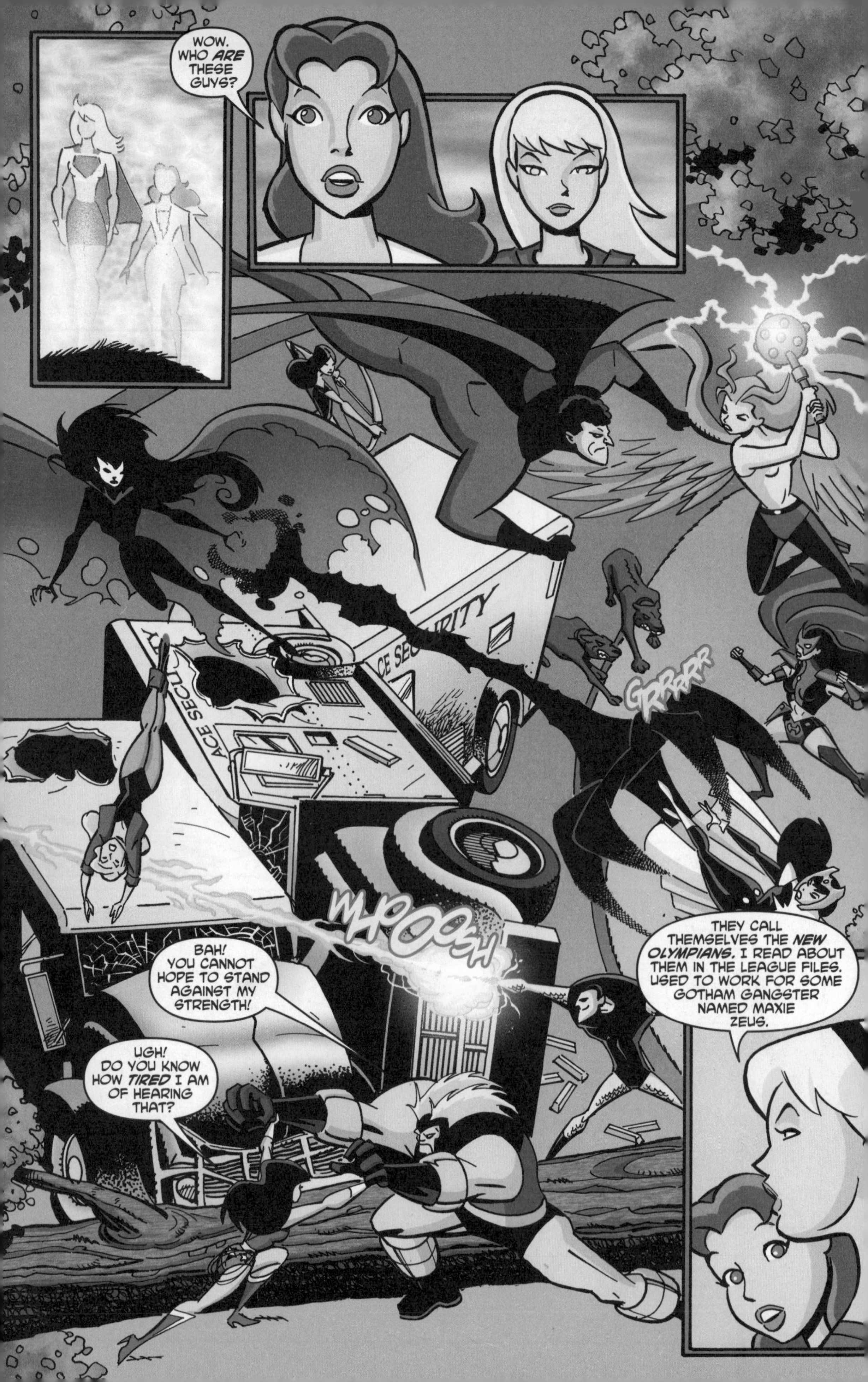
WOW. WHO ARE THESE GUYS?
GRRRRR
WHOOOSH
BAH! YOU CANNOT HOPE TO STAND AGAINST MY STRENGTH!
UGH! DO YOU KNOW HOW TIRED I AM OF HEARING THAT?
THEY CALL THEMSELVES THE NEW OLYMPIANS. I READ ABOUT THEM IN THE LEAGUE FILES. USED TO WORK FOR SOME GOTHAM GANGSTER NAMED MAXIE ZEUS.

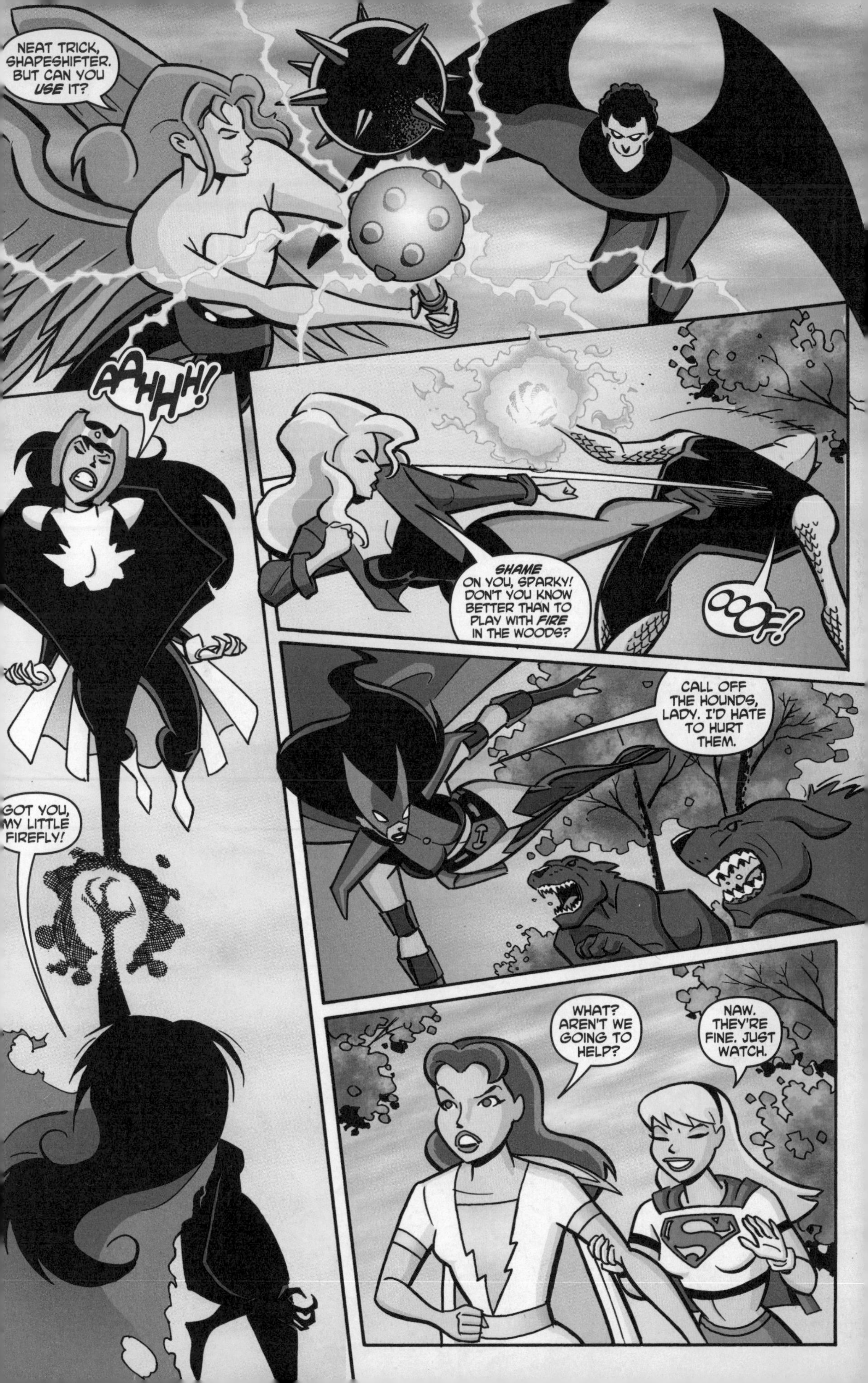
NEAT TRICK, SHAPESHIFTER. BUT CAN YOU USE IT?
AAHHH!
SHAME ON YOU, SPARKY! DON'T YOU KNOW BETTER THAN TO PLAY WITH FIRE IN THE WOODS?
OOOF!
GOT YOU, MY LITTLE FIREFLY!
CALL OFF THE HOUNDS, LADY. I'D HATE TO HURT THEM.
WHAT? AREN'T WE GOING TO HELP?
NAW. THEY'RE FINE. JUST WATCH.

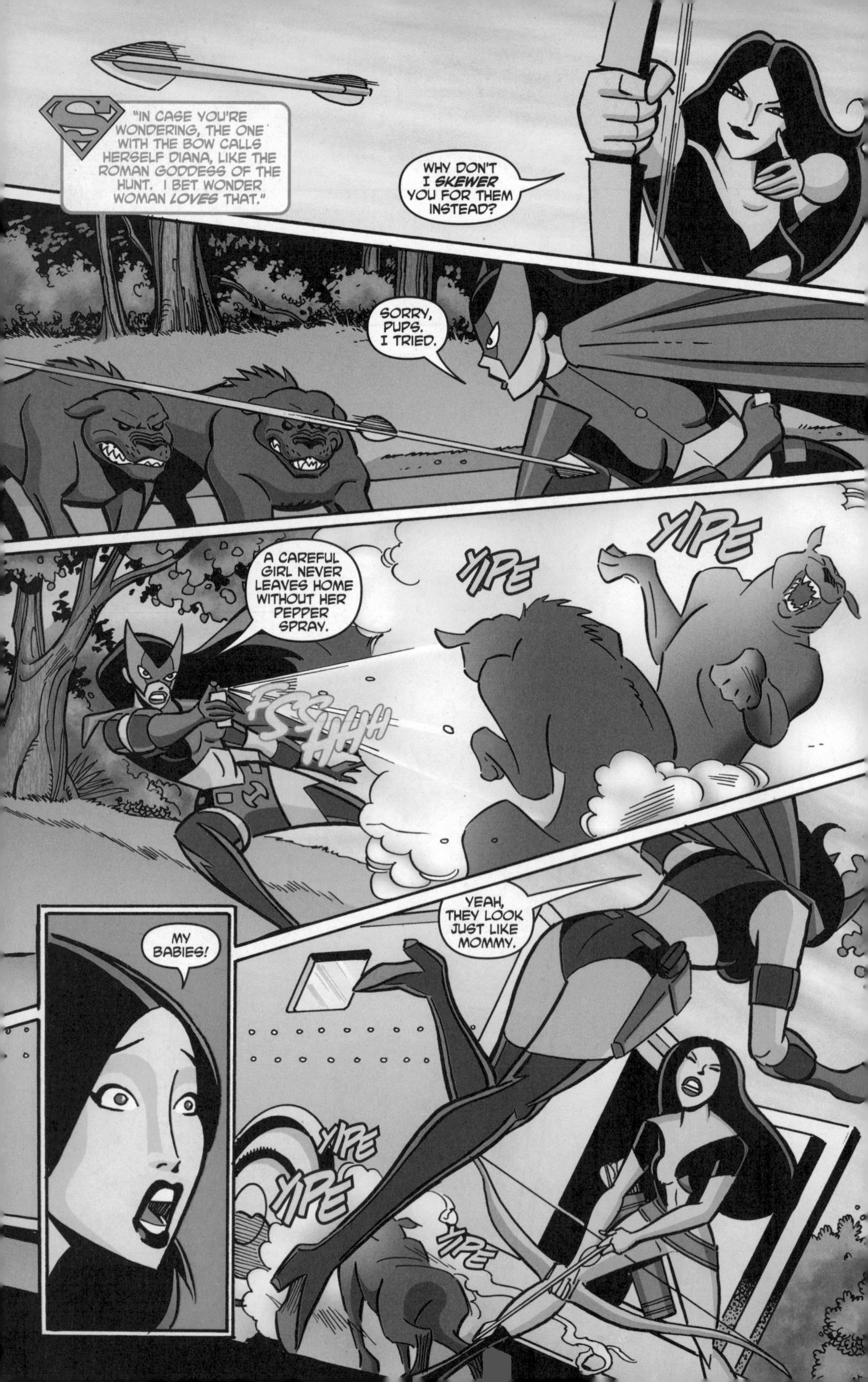
"IN CASE YOU'RE WONDERING, THE ONE WITH THE BOW CALLS HERSELF DIANA, LIKE THE ROMAN GODDESS OF THE HUNT. I BET WONDER WOMAN LOVES THAT."
WHY DON'T I SKEWER YOU FOR THEM INSTEAD?
SORRY, PUPS. I TRIED.
A CAREFUL GIRL NEVER LEAVES HOME WITHOUT HER PEPPER SPRAY.
YIPE
YIPE
FSSHHH
MY BABIES!
YEAH, THEY LOOK JUST LIKE MOMMY.
YIPE
YIPE
YIPE

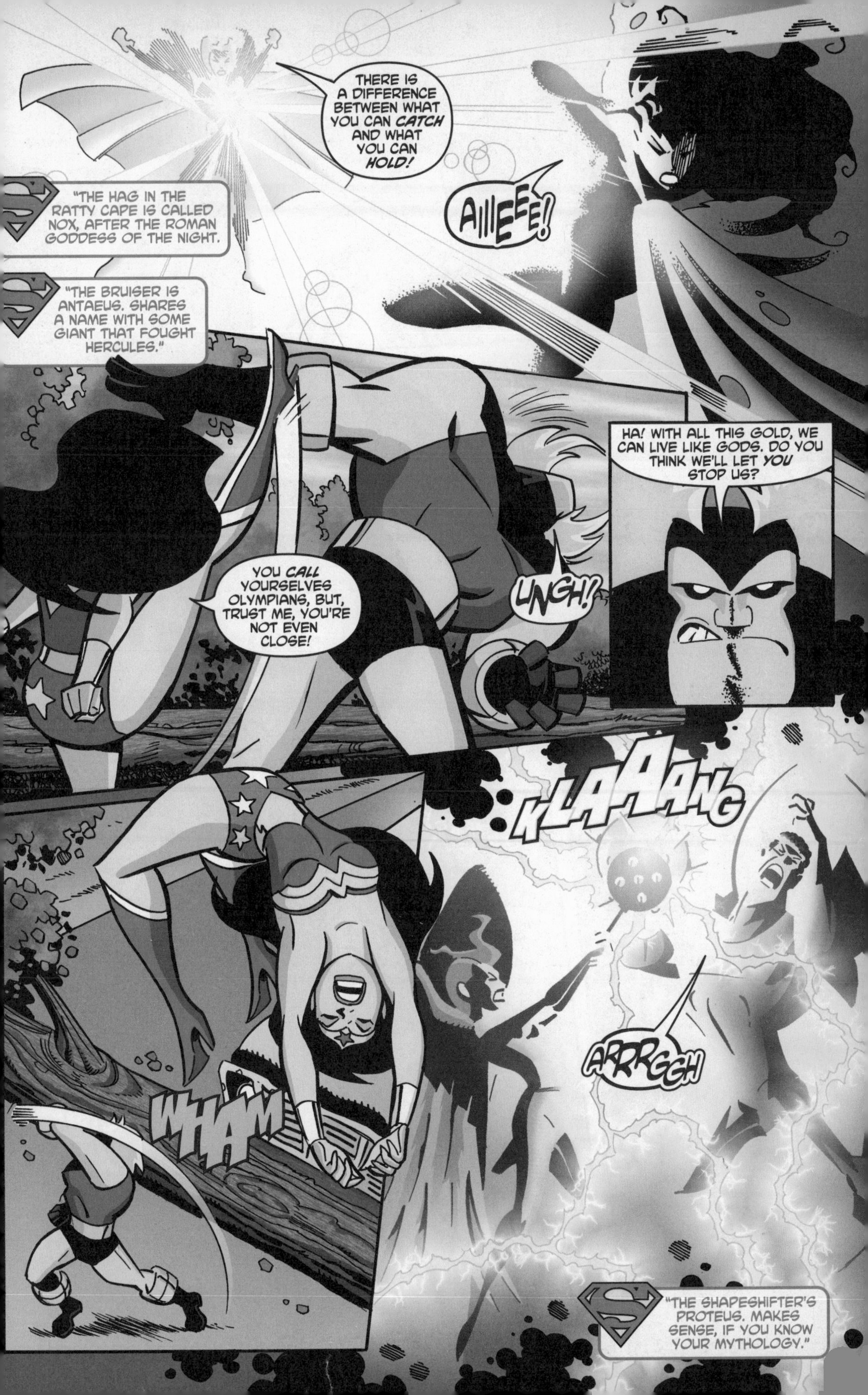

THERE IS A DIFFERENCE BETWEEN WHAT YOU CAN CATCH AND WHAT YOU CAN HOLD!
AIIEEEE!
"THE HAG IN THE RATTY CAPE IS CALLED NOX, AFTER THE ROMAN GODDESS OF THE NIGHT.
"THE BRUISER IS ANTAEUS. SHARES A NAME WITH SOME GIANT THAT FOUGHT HERCULES."
HA! WITH ALL THIS GOLD, WE CAN LIVE LIKE GODS. DO YOU THINK WE'LL LET YOU STOP US?
YOU CALL YOURSELVES OLYMPIANS, BUT, TRUST ME, YOU'RE NOT EVEN CLOSE!
UNGH!
KLAAAANG
WHAM
ARRRGGH
"THE SHAPESHIFTER'S PROTEUS. MAKES SENSE, IF YOU KNOW YOUR MYTHOLOGY."

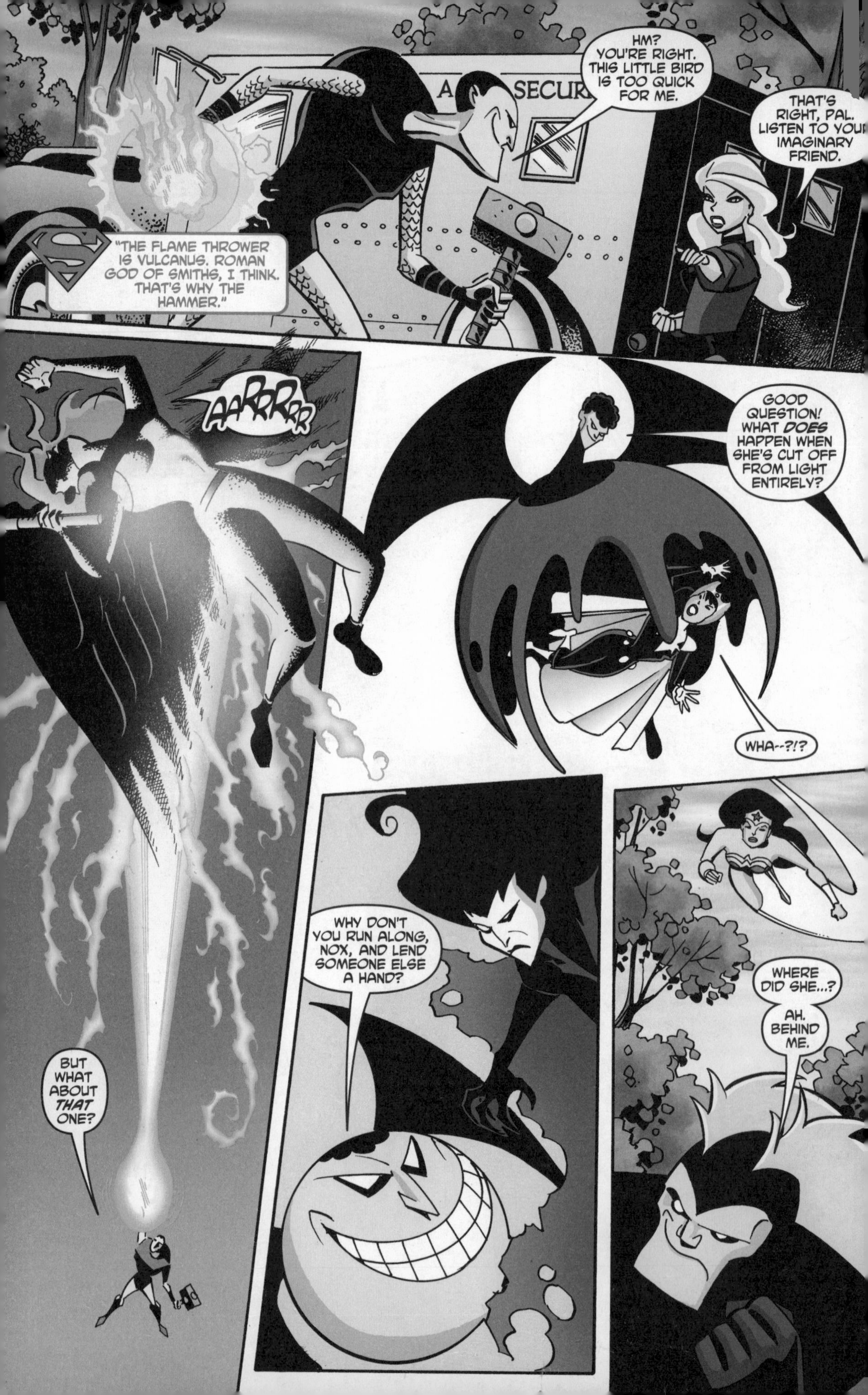
HM? YOU'RE RIGHT. THIS LITTLE BIRD IS TOO QUICK FOR ME.
THAT'S RIGHT, PAL. LISTEN TO YOUR IMAGINARY FRIEND.
"THE FLAME THROWER IS VULCANUS. ROMAN GOD OF SMITHS, I THINK. THAT'S WHY THE HAMMER."
AARRRRR
GOOD QUESTION! WHAT DOES HAPPEN WHEN SHE'S CUT OFF FROM LIGHT ENTIRELY?
WHA--?!?
BUT WHAT ABOUT THAT ONE?
WHY DON'T YOU RUN ALONG, NOX, AND LEND SOMEONE ELSE A HAND?
WHERE DID SHE...?
AH. BEHIND ME.

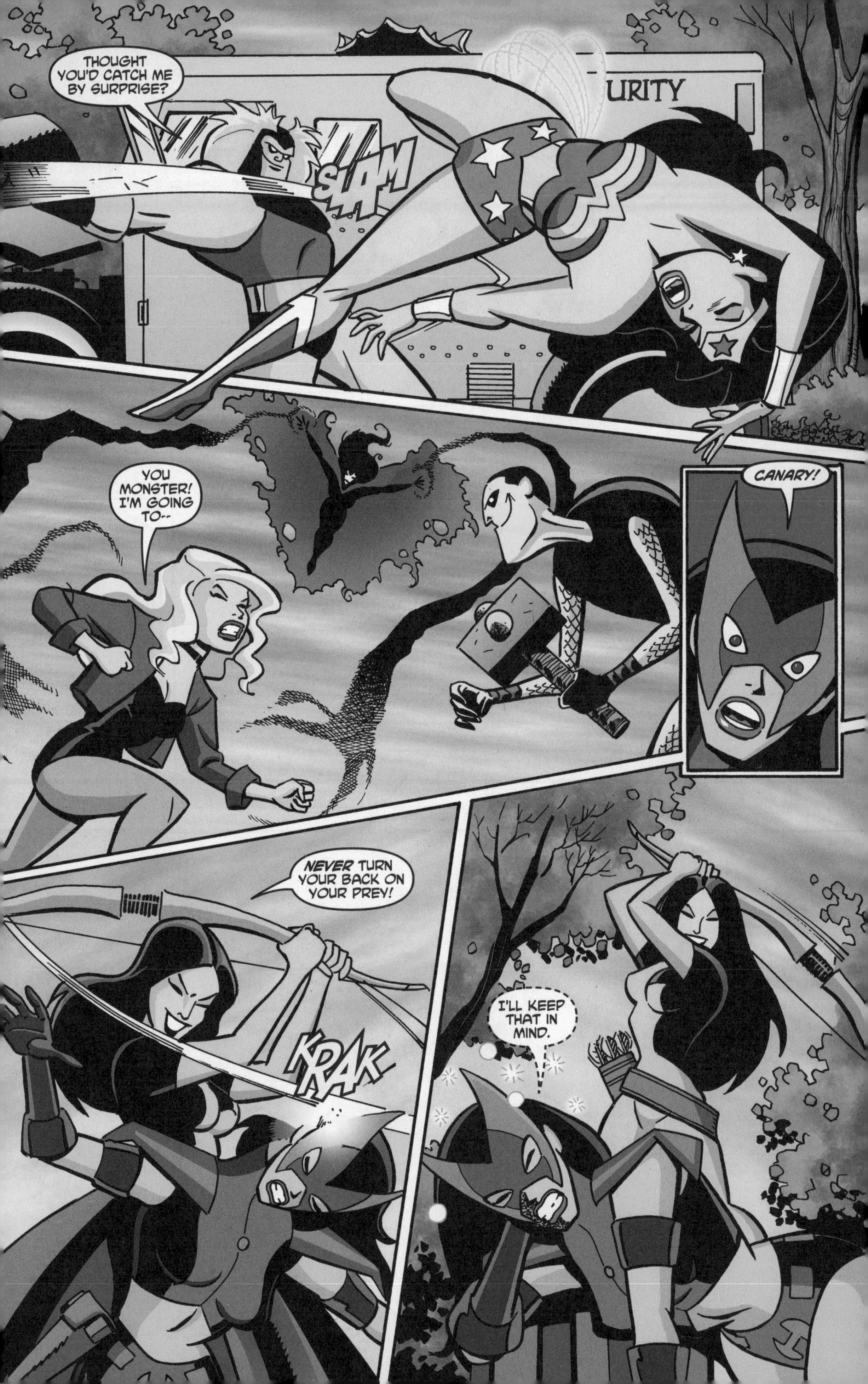

THOUGHT YOU'D CATCH ME BY SURPRISE?
URITY
SLAM
YOU MONSTER! I'M GOING TO--
CANARY!
NEVER TURN YOUR BACK ON YOUR PREY!
KRAK
I'LL KEEP THAT IN MIND.

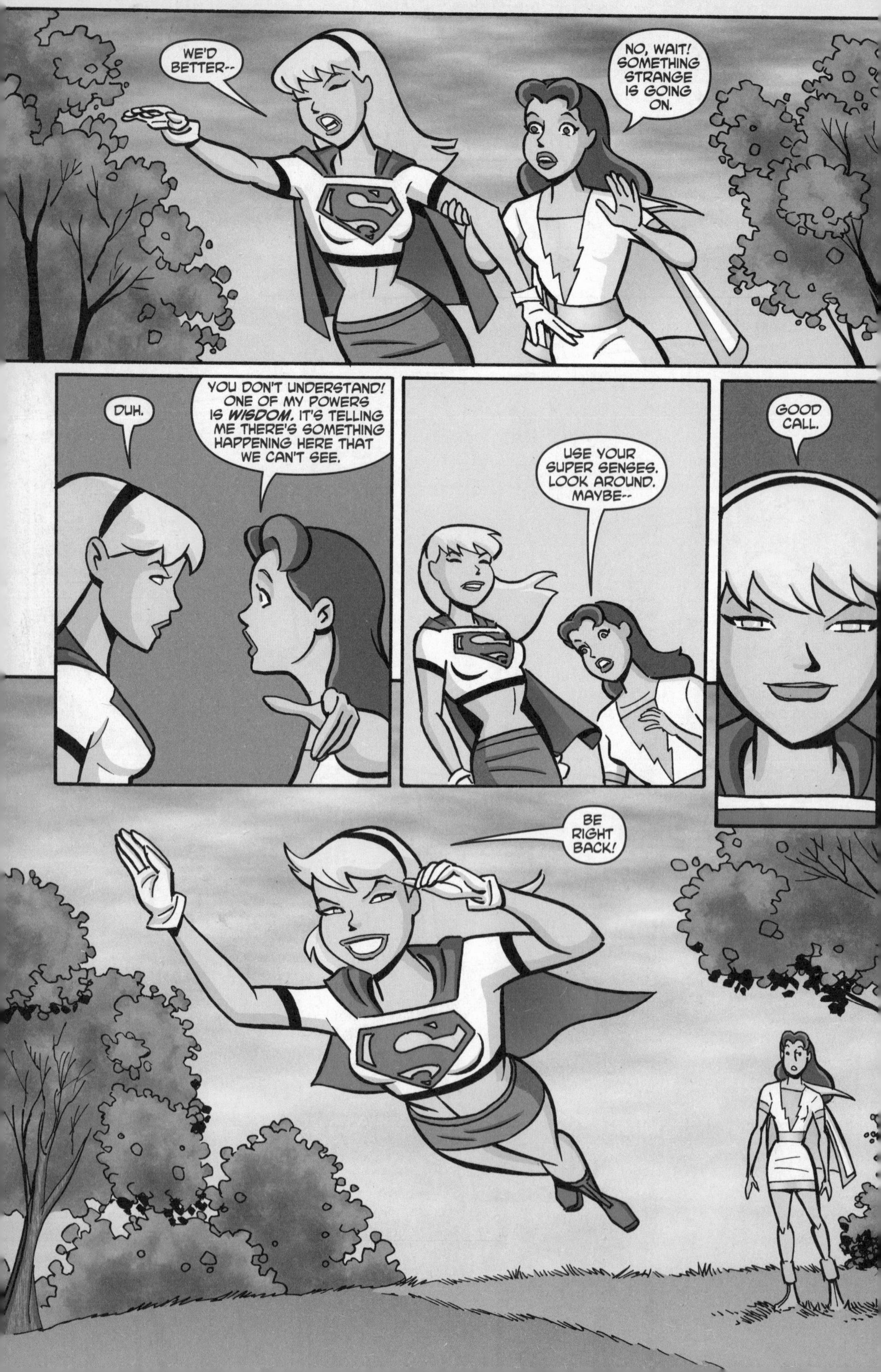
WE'D BETTER--
NO, WAIT! SOMETHING STRANGE IS GOING ON.
DUH.
YOU DON'T UNDERSTAND! ONE OF MY POWERS IS ***WISDOM***. IT'S TELLING ME THERE'S SOMETHING HAPPENING HERE THAT WE CAN'T SEE.
USE YOUR SUPER SENSES. LOOK AROUND. MAYBE--
GOOD CALL.
BE RIGHT BACK!

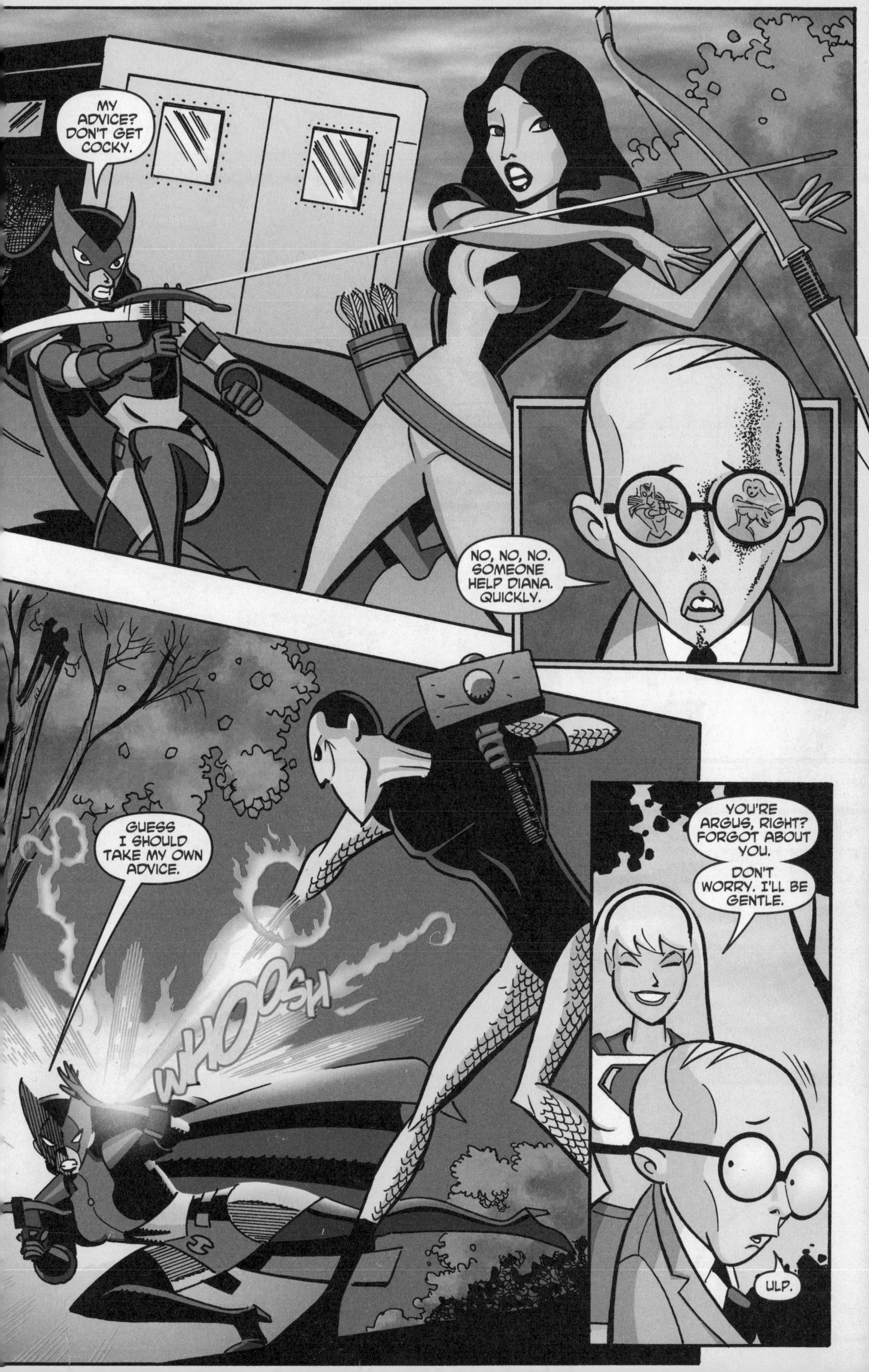
MY ADVICE? DON'T GET COCKY.
NO, NO, NO. SOMEONE HELP DIANA. QUICKLY.
GUESS I SHOULD TAKE MY OWN ADVICE.
WHOOSH
YOU'RE ARGUS, RIGHT? FORGOT ABOUT YOU.
DON'T WORRY. I'LL BE GENTLE.
ULP.

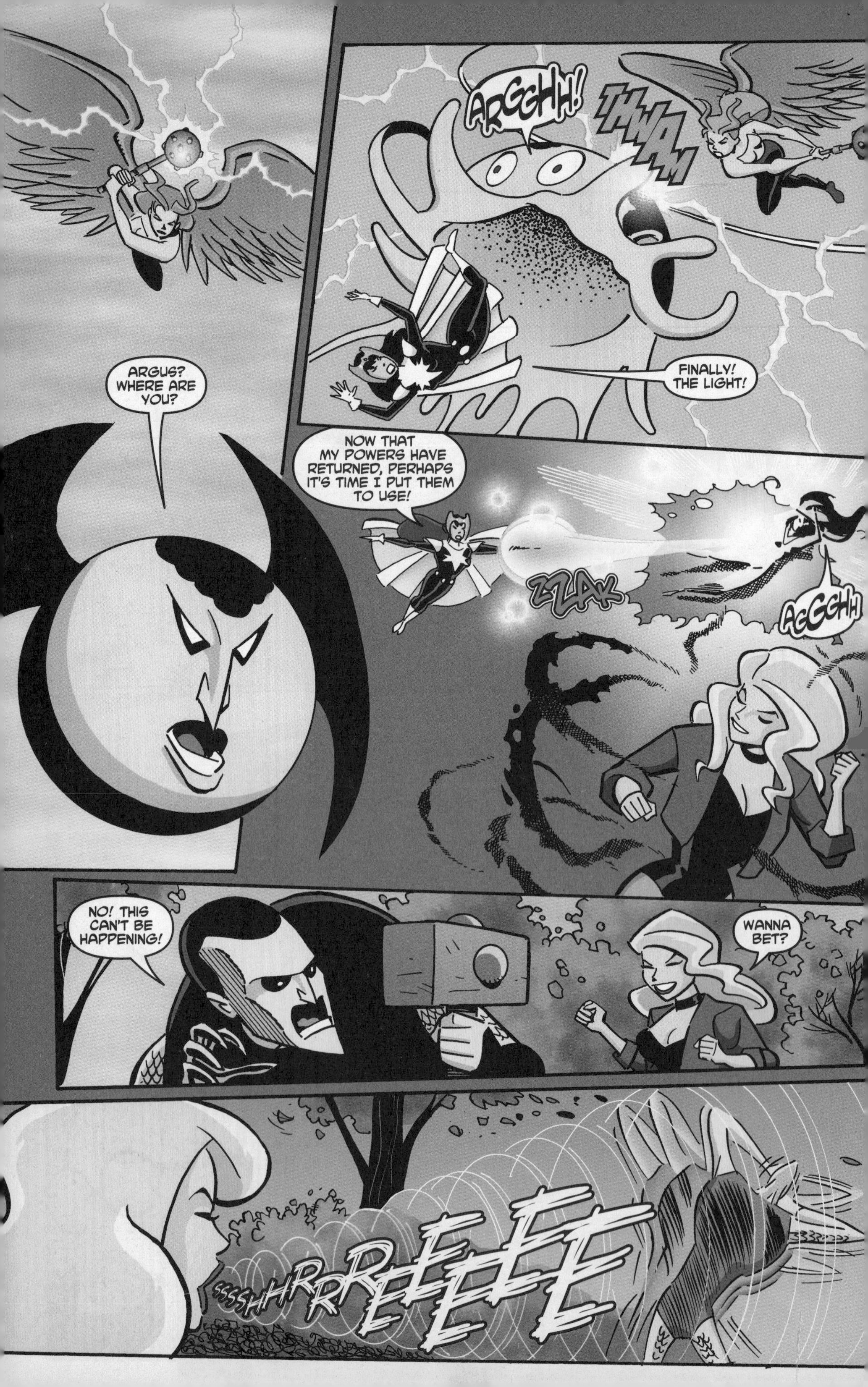
ARGHHH!
THWAM
FINALLY! THE LIGHT!
ARGUS? WHERE ARE YOU?
NOW THAT MY POWERS HAVE RETURNED, PERHAPS IT'S TIME I PUT THEM TO USE!
ZZAK
AGGHH
NO! THIS CAN'T BE HAPPENING!
WANNA BET?
SSSSHHRRRREEEEEE

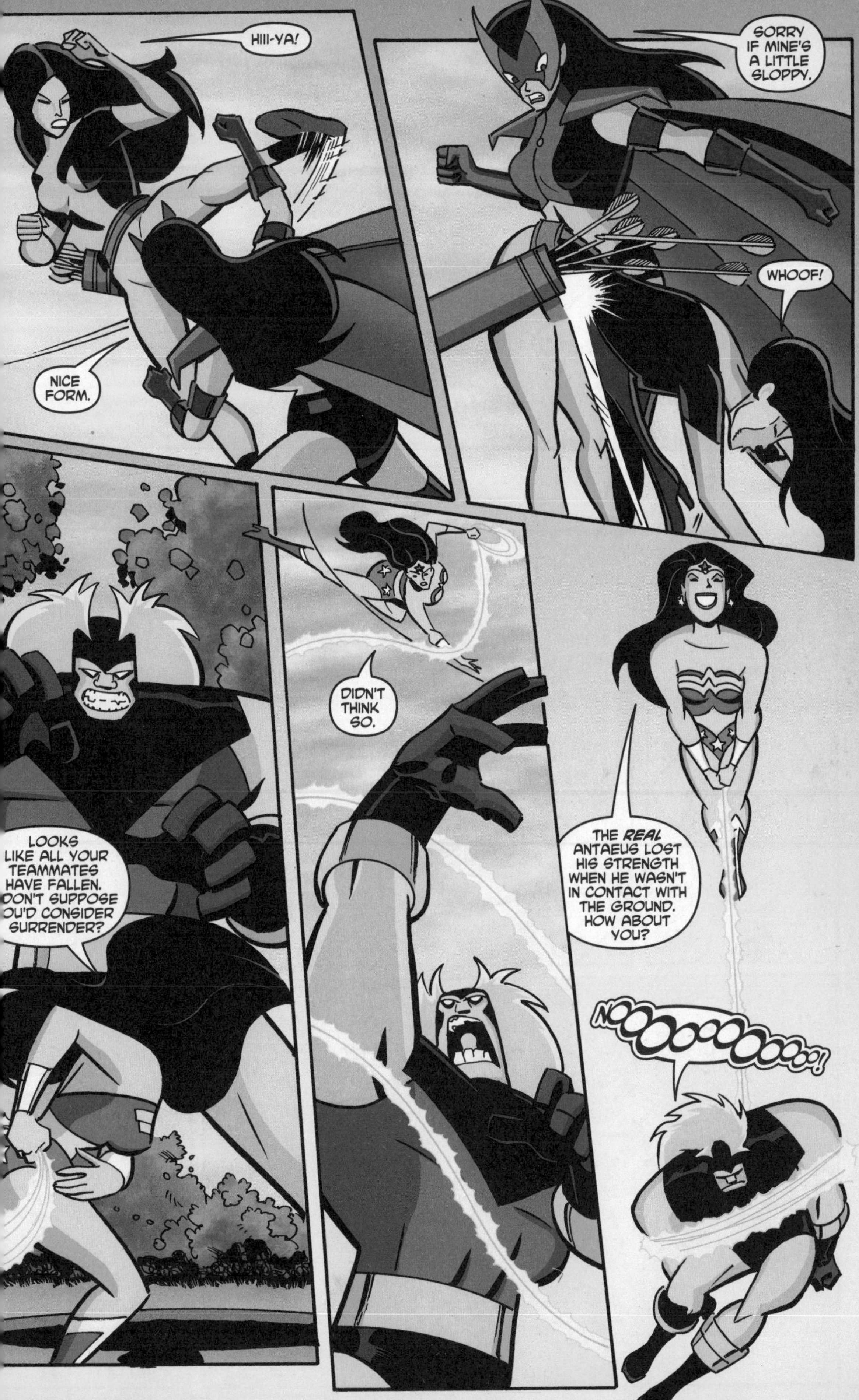
HIII-YA!
NICE FORM.
SORRY IF MINE'S A LITTLE SLOPPY.
WHOOF!
LOOKS LIKE ALL YOUR TEAMMATES HAVE FALLEN. DON'T SUPPOSE YOU'D CONSIDER SURRENDER?
DIDN'T THINK SO.
THE REAL ANTAEUS LOST HIS STRENGTH WHEN HE WASN'T IN CONTACT WITH THE GROUND. HOW ABOUT YOU?
NOOOOOOOOOOOOO!

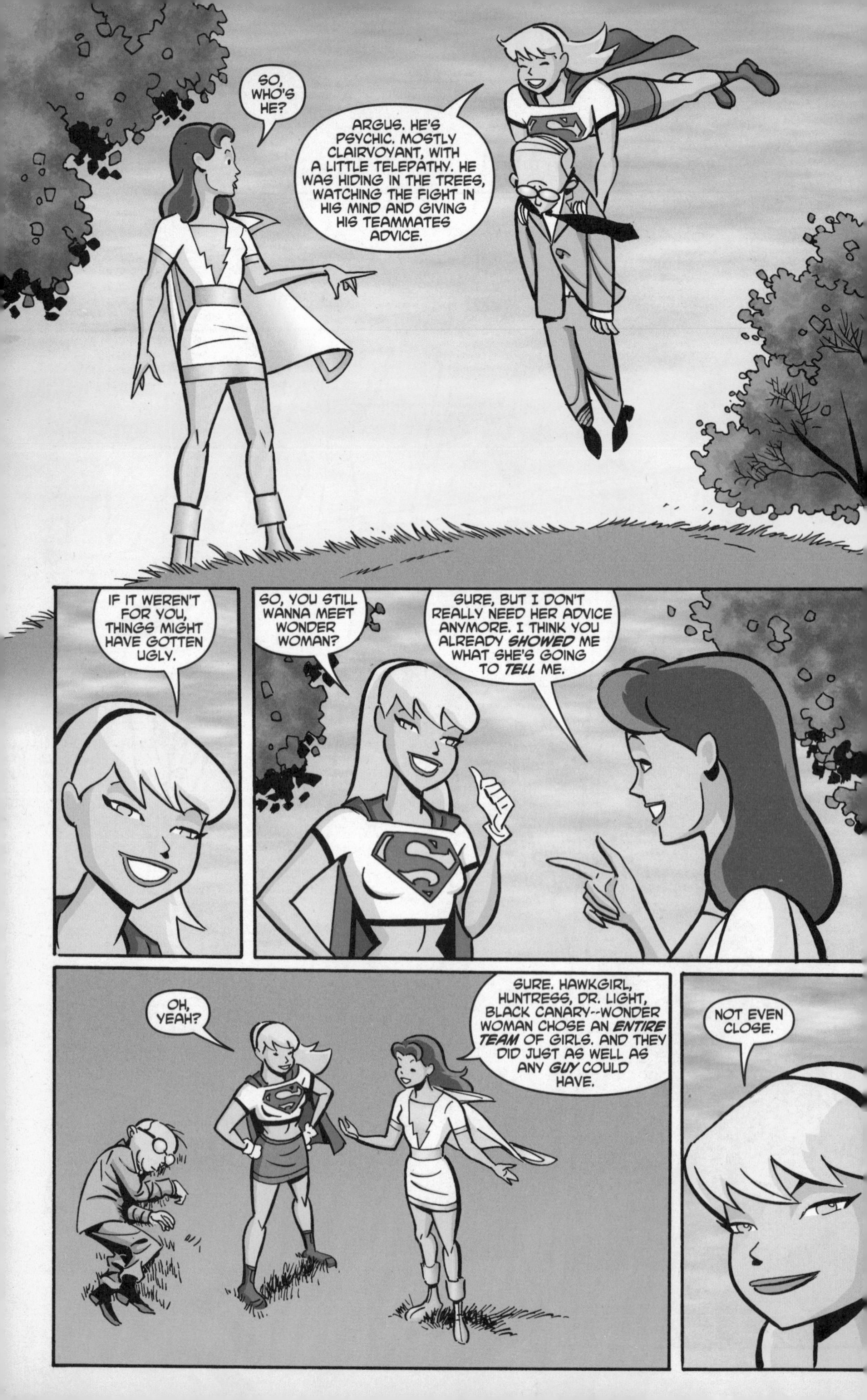
SO, WHO'S HE?
ARGUS. HE'S PSYCHIC. MOSTLY CLAIRVOYANT, WITH A LITTLE TELEPATHY. HE WAS HIDING IN THE TREES, WATCHING THE FIGHT IN HIS MIND AND GIVING HIS TEAMMATES ADVICE.
IF IT WEREN'T FOR YOU, THINGS MIGHT HAVE GOTTEN UGLY.
SO, YOU STILL WANNA MEET WONDER WOMAN?
SURE, BUT I DON'T REALLY NEED HER ADVICE ANYMORE. I THINK YOU ALREADY SHOWED ME WHAT SHE'S GOING TO TELL ME.
OH, YEAH?
SURE. HAWKGIRL, HUNTRESS, DR. LIGHT, BLACK CANARY--WONDER WOMAN CHOSE AN ENTIRE TEAM OF GIRLS. AND THEY DID JUST AS WELL AS ANY GUY COULD HAVE.
NOT EVEN CLOSE.

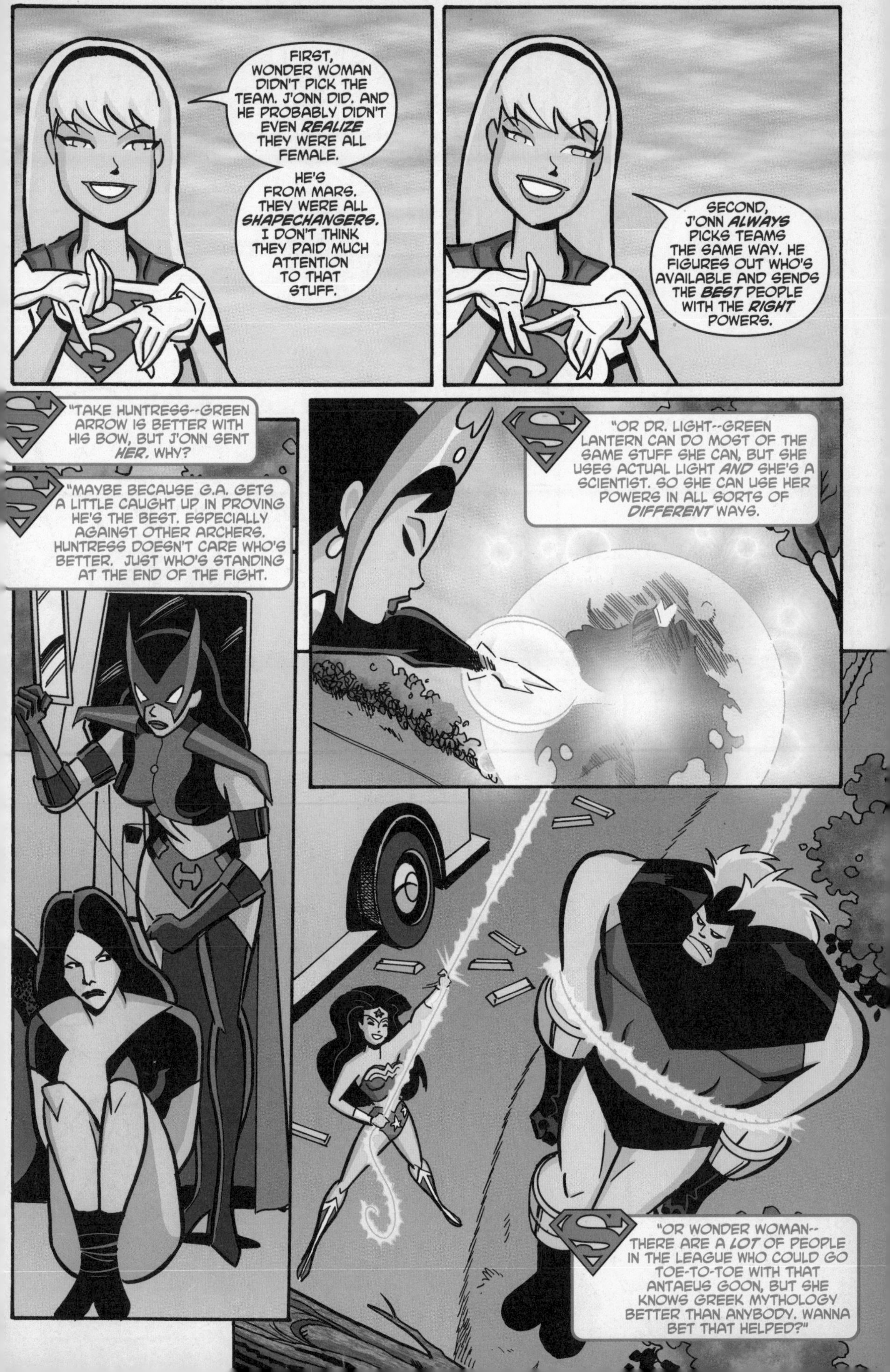
FIRST, WONDER WOMAN DIDN'T PICK THE TEAM. J'ONN DID. AND HE PROBABLY DIDN'T EVEN *REALIZE* THEY WERE ALL FEMALE.
HE'S FROM MARS. THEY WERE ALL *SHAPECHANGERS.* I DON'T THINK THEY PAID MUCH ATTENTION TO THAT STUFF.
SECOND, J'ONN *ALWAYS* PICKS TEAMS THE SAME WAY. HE FIGURES OUT WHO'S AVAILABLE AND SENDS THE *BEST* PEOPLE WITH THE *RIGHT* POWERS.
"TAKE HUNTRESS--GREEN ARROW IS BETTER WITH HIS BOW, BUT J'ONN SENT *HER.* WHY?
"MAYBE BECAUSE G.A. GETS A LITTLE CAUGHT UP IN PROVING HE'S THE BEST. ESPECIALLY AGAINST OTHER ARCHERS. HUNTRESS DOESN'T CARE WHO'S BETTER. JUST WHO'S STANDING AT THE END OF THE FIGHT.
"OR DR. LIGHT--GREEN LANTERN CAN DO MOST OF THE SAME STUFF SHE CAN, BUT SHE USES ACTUAL LIGHT *AND* SHE'S A SCIENTIST. SO SHE CAN USE HER POWERS IN ALL SORTS OF *DIFFERENT* WAYS.
"OR WONDER WOMAN-- THERE ARE A *LOT* OF PEOPLE IN THE LEAGUE WHO COULD GO TOE-TO-TOE WITH THAT ANTAEUS GOON, BUT SHE KNOWS GREEK MYTHOLOGY BETTER THAN ANYBODY. WANNA BET THAT HELPED?"

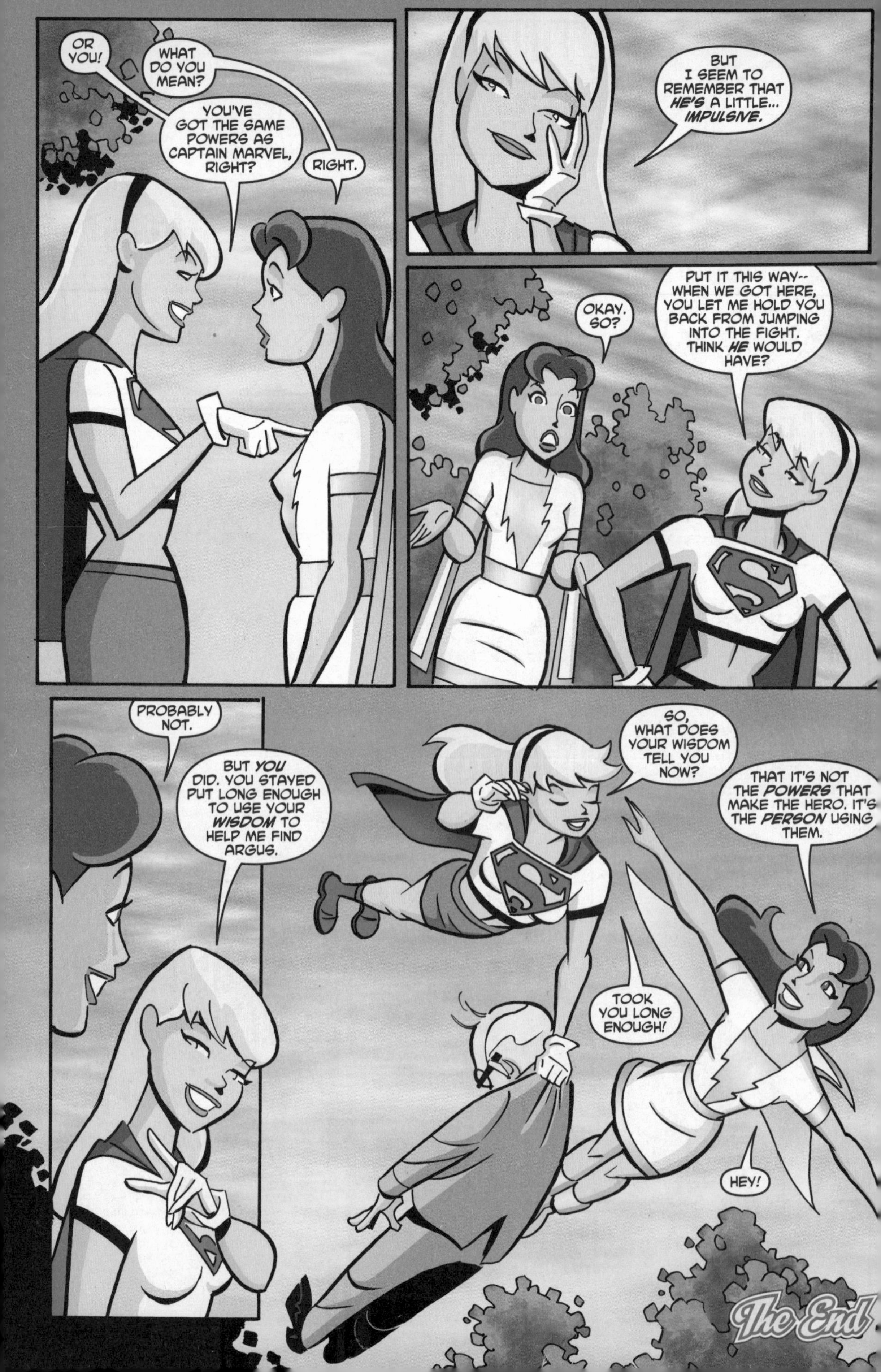
OR YOU!
WHAT DO YOU MEAN?
YOU'VE GOT THE SAME POWERS AS CAPTAIN MARVEL, RIGHT?
RIGHT.
BUT I SEEM TO REMEMBER THAT HE'S A LITTLE... IMPULSIVE.
PUT IT THIS WAY-- WHEN WE GOT HERE, YOU LET ME HOLD YOU BACK FROM JUMPING INTO THE FIGHT. THINK HE WOULD HAVE?
OKAY. SO?
PROBABLY NOT.
BUT YOU DID. YOU STAYED PUT LONG ENOUGH TO USE YOUR WISDOM TO HELP ME FIND ARGUS.
SO, WHAT DOES YOUR WISDOM TELL YOU NOW?
THAT IT'S NOT THE POWERS THAT MAKE THE HERO. IT'S THE PERSON USING THEM.
TOOK YOU LONG ENOUGH!
HEY!
The End

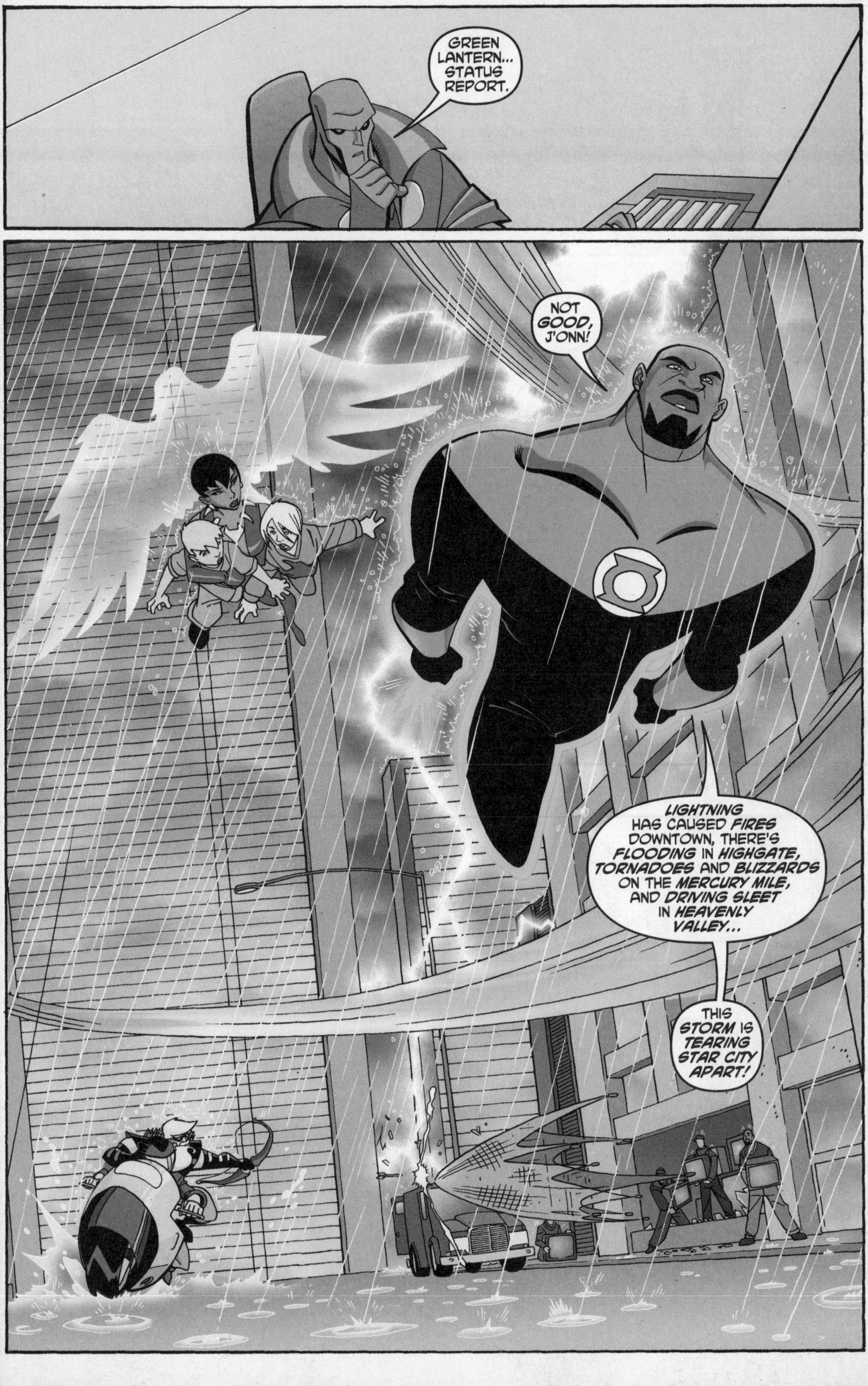
GREEN LANTERN... STATUS REPORT.
NOT GOOD, J'ONN!
LIGHTNING HAS CAUSED FIRES DOWNTOWN, THERE'S FLOODING IN HIGHGATE, TORNADOES AND BLIZZARDS ON THE MERCURY MILE, AND DRIVING SLEET IN HEAVENLY VALLEY...
THIS STORM IS TEARING STAR CITY APART!

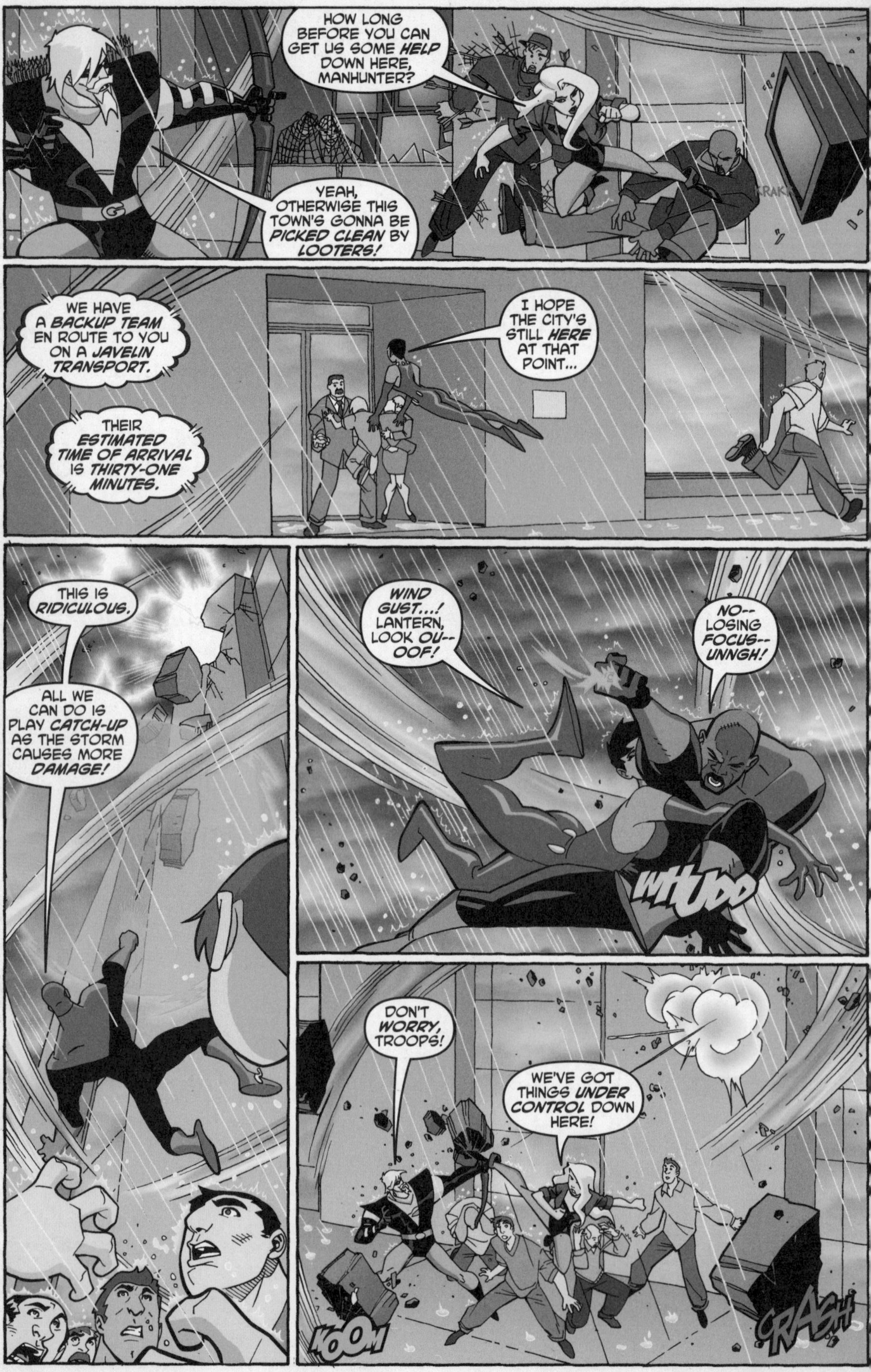
HOW LONG BEFORE YOU CAN GET US SOME *HELP* DOWN HERE, MANHUNTER?
YEAH, OTHERWISE THIS TOWN'S GONNA BE *PICKED CLEAN* BY *LOOTERS!*
KRAKK
WE HAVE A *BACKUP TEAM* EN ROUTE TO YOU ON A *JAVELIN TRANSPORT.*
THEIR *ESTIMATED TIME OF ARRIVAL* IS *THIRTY-ONE MINUTES.*
I HOPE THE CITY'S STILL *HERE* AT THAT POINT...
THIS IS *RIDICULOUS.*
ALL WE CAN DO IS PLAY *CATCH-UP* AS THE STORM CAUSES MORE *DAMAGE!*
WIND GUST...! LANTERN, LOOK *OU-- OOF!*
NO-- LOSING FOCUS-- UNNGH!
WHUDD
DON'T *WORRY,* TROOPS!
WE'VE GOT THINGS *UNDER CONTROL* DOWN HERE!
KOOM
CRASH

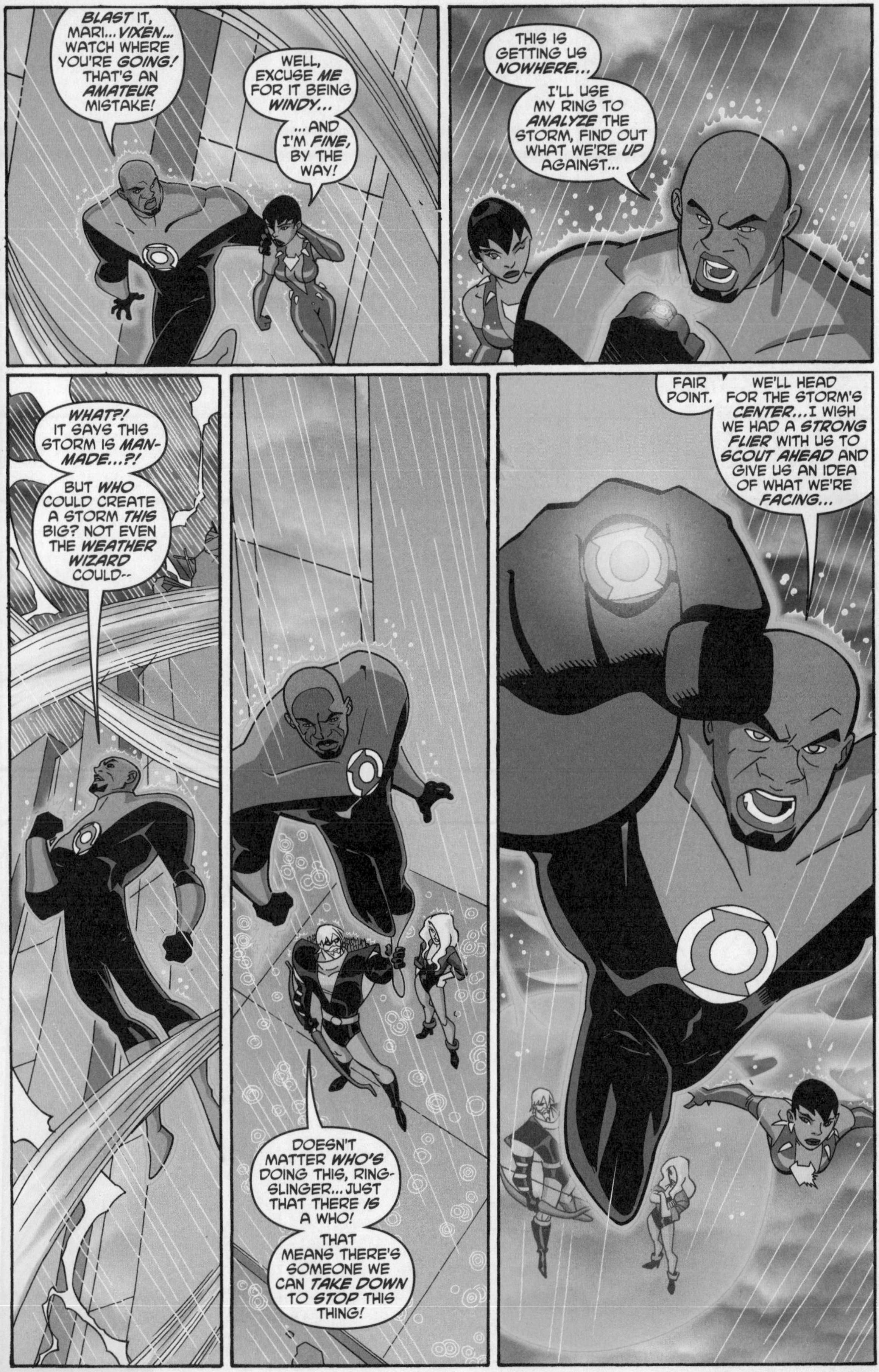
BLAST IT, MARI... VIXEN... WATCH WHERE YOU'RE GOING! THAT'S AN AMATEUR MISTAKE!
WELL, EXCUSE ME FOR IT BEING WINDY...
...AND I'M FINE, BY THE WAY!
THIS IS GETTING US NOWHERE...
I'LL USE MY RING TO ANALYZE THE STORM, FIND OUT WHAT WE'RE UP AGAINST...
WHAT?! IT SAYS THIS STORM IS MAN-MADE...?!
BUT WHO COULD CREATE A STORM THIS BIG? NOT EVEN THE WEATHER WIZARD COULD--
DOESN'T MATTER WHO'S DOING THIS, RING-SLINGER... JUST THAT THERE IS A WHO!
THAT MEANS THERE'S SOMEONE WE CAN TAKE DOWN TO STOP THIS THING!
FAIR POINT.
WE'LL HEAD FOR THE STORM'S CENTER... I WISH WE HAD A STRONG FLIER WITH US TO SCOUT AHEAD AND GIVE US AN IDEA OF WHAT WE'RE FACING...

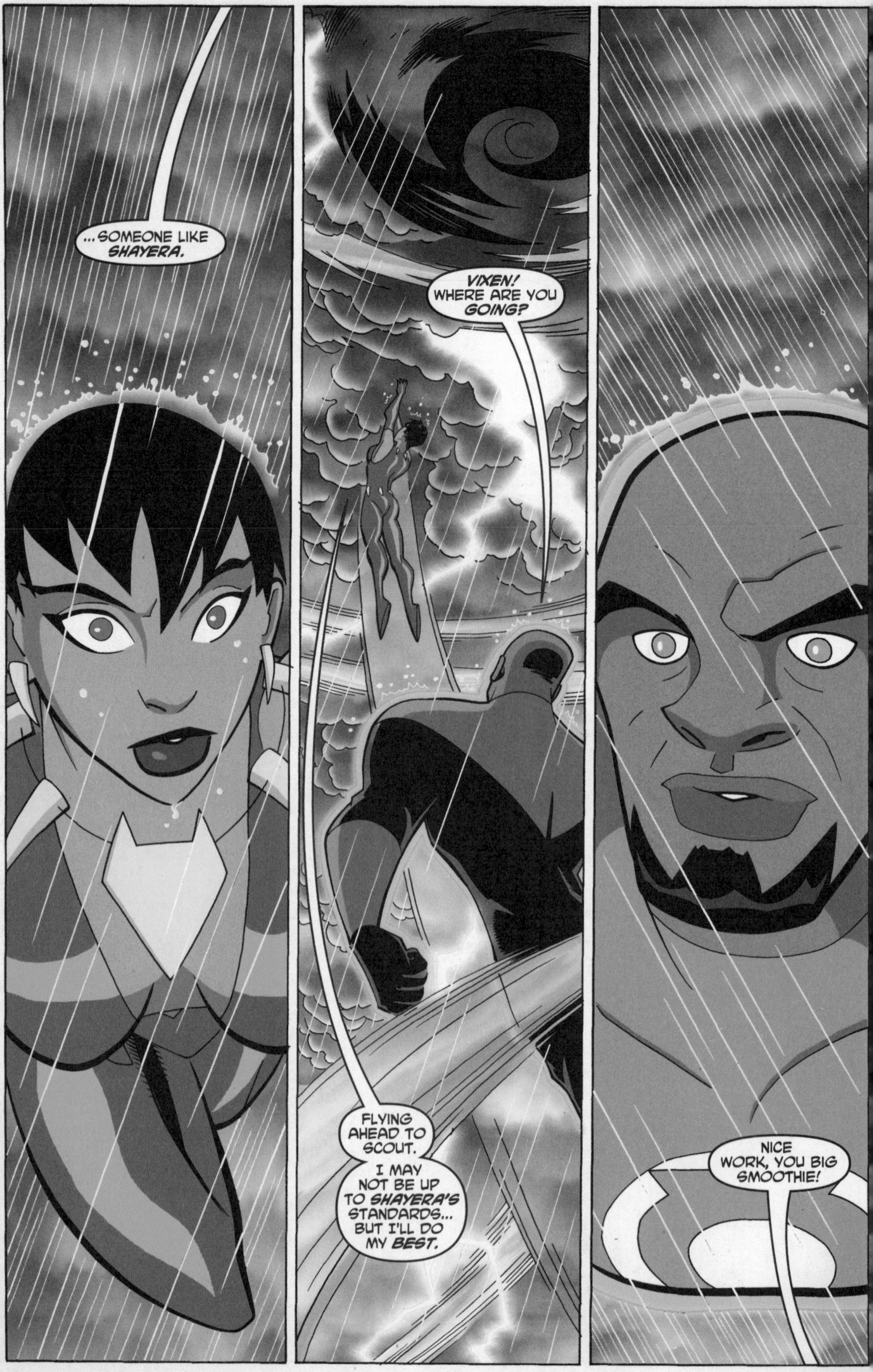
...SOMEONE LIKE SHAYERA.
VIXEN! WHERE ARE YOU GOING?
FLYING AHEAD TO SCOUT.
I MAY NOT BE UP TO SHAYERA'S STANDARDS... BUT I'LL DO MY BEST.
NICE WORK, YOU BIG SMOOTHIE!

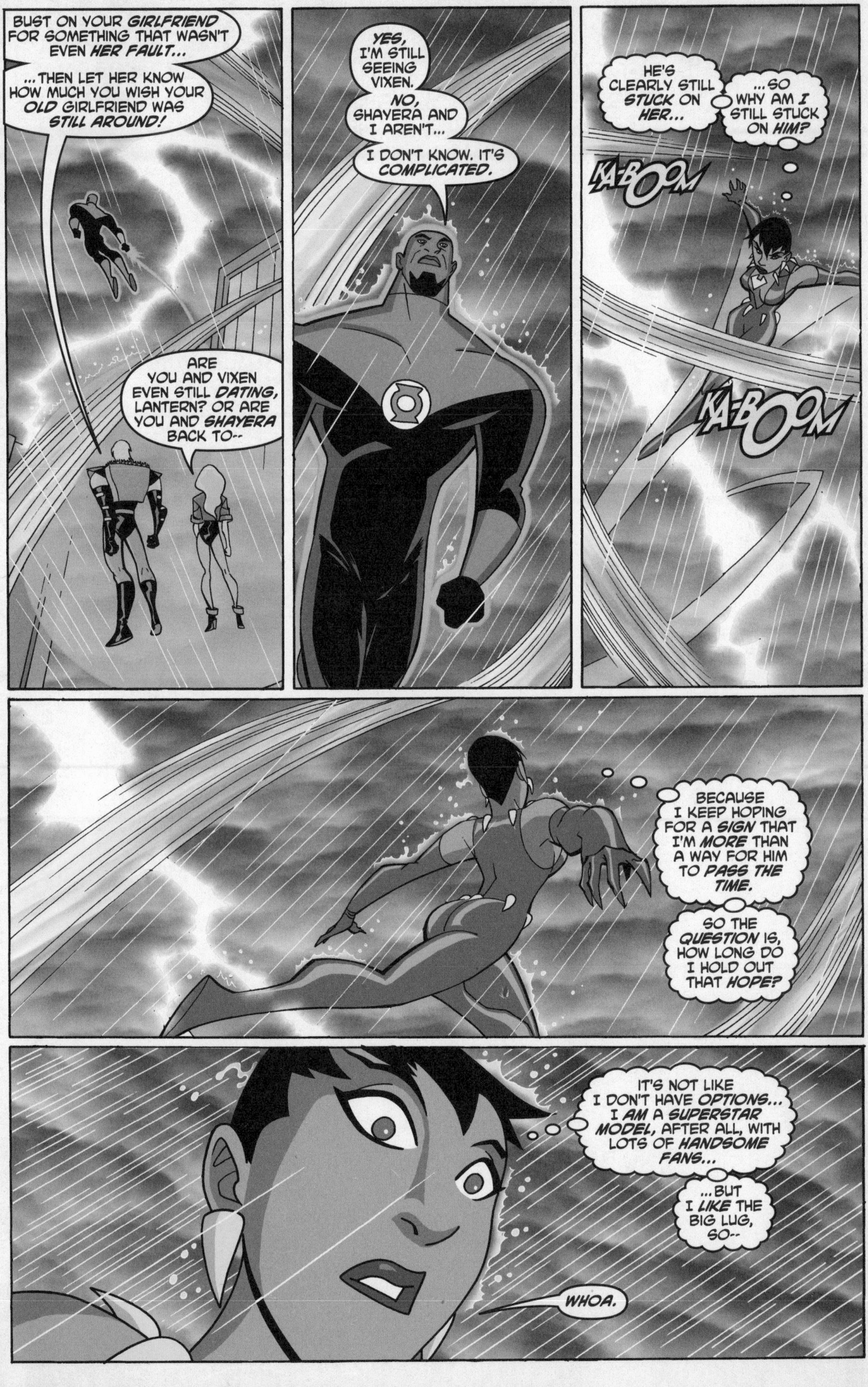
BUST ON YOUR GIRLFRIEND FOR SOMETHING THAT WASN'T EVEN HER FAULT...
...THEN LET HER KNOW HOW MUCH YOU WISH YOUR OLD GIRLFRIEND WAS STILL AROUND!
ARE YOU AND VIXEN EVEN STILL DATING, LANTERN? OR ARE YOU AND SHAYERA BACK TO--
YES, I'M STILL SEEING VIXEN.
NO, SHAYERA AND I AREN'T...
I DON'T KNOW. IT'S COMPLICATED.
HE'S CLEARLY STILL STUCK ON HER...
...SO WHY AM I STILL STUCK ON HIM?
KA-BOOM
KA-BOOM
BECAUSE I KEEP HOPING FOR A SIGN THAT I'M MORE THAN A WAY FOR HIM TO PASS THE TIME.
SO THE QUESTION IS, HOW LONG DO I HOLD OUT THAT HOPE?
IT'S NOT LIKE I DON'T HAVE OPTIONS... I AM A SUPERSTAR MODEL, AFTER ALL, WITH LOTS OF HANDSOME FANS...
...BUT I LIKE THE BIG LUG, SO--
WHOA.

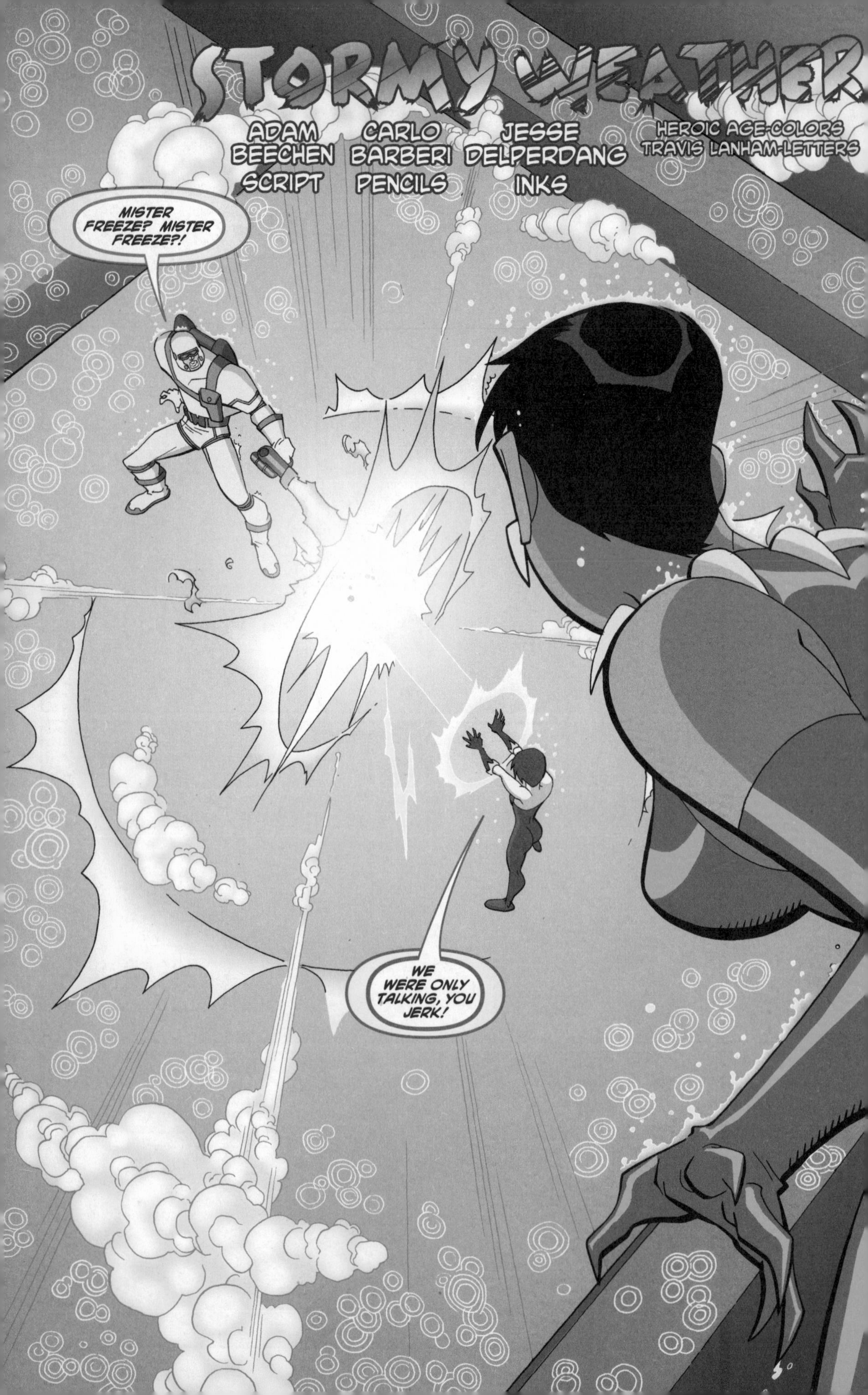
STORMY WEATHER
ADAM BEECHEN SCRIPT
CARLO BARBERI PENCILS
JESSE DELPERDANG INKS
HEROIC AGE-COLORS
TRAVIS LANHAM-LETTERS
MISTER FREEZE? MISTER FREEZE?!
WE WERE ONLY TALKING, YOU JERK!

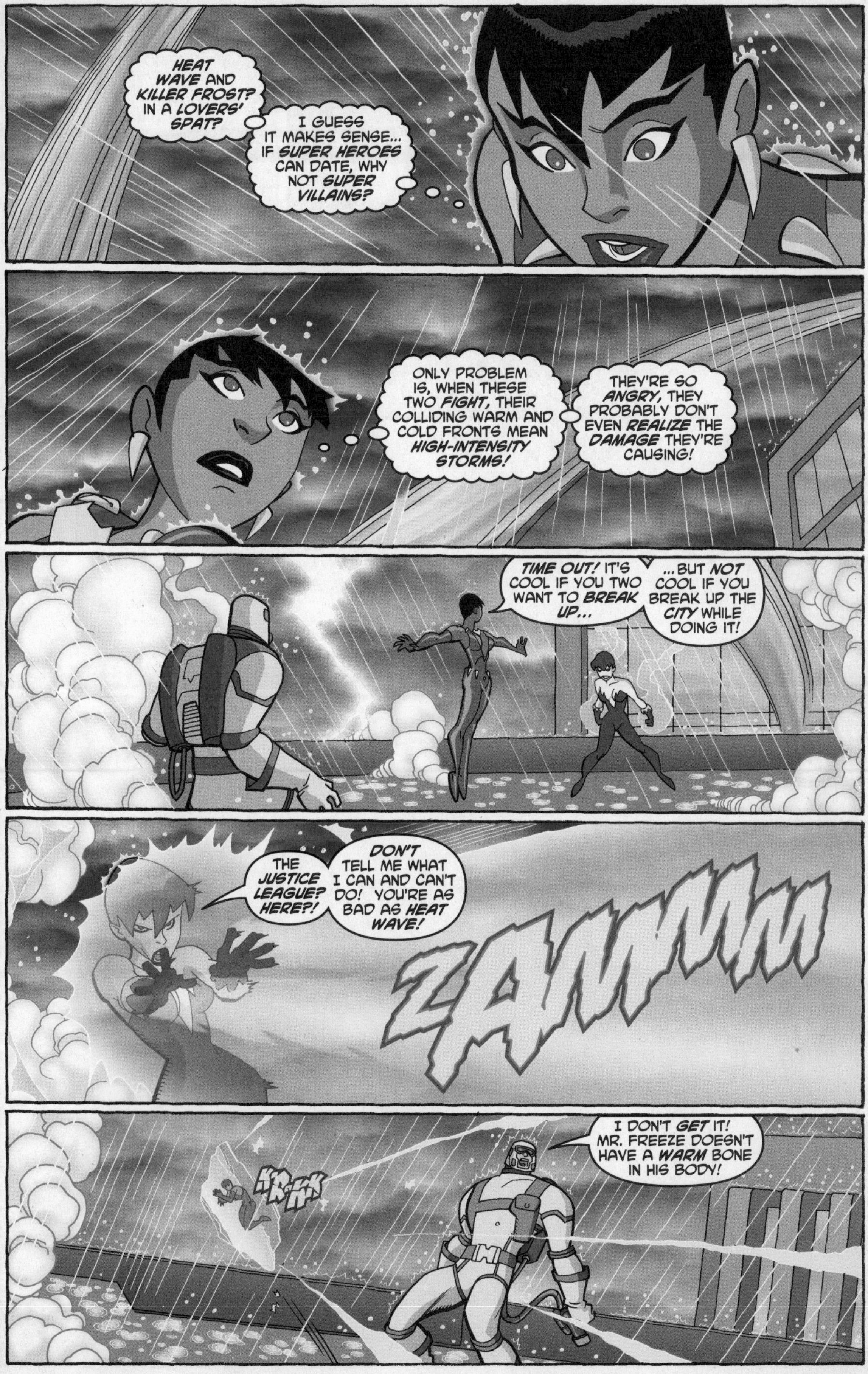
HEAT WAVE AND KILLER FROST? IN A LOVERS' SPAT?
I GUESS IT MAKES SENSE... IF SUPER HEROES CAN DATE, WHY NOT SUPER VILLAINS?
ONLY PROBLEM IS, WHEN THESE TWO FIGHT, THEIR COLLIDING WARM AND COLD FRONTS MEAN HIGH-INTENSITY STORMS!
THEY'RE SO ANGRY, THEY PROBABLY DON'T EVEN REALIZE THE DAMAGE THEY'RE CAUSING!
TIME OUT! IT'S COOL IF YOU TWO WANT TO BREAK UP...
...BUT NOT COOL IF YOU BREAK UP THE CITY WHILE DOING IT!
THE JUSTICE LEAGUE? HERE?!
DON'T TELL ME WHAT I CAN AND CAN'T DO! YOU'RE AS BAD AS HEAT WAVE!
ZAMMM
KRAKK
I DON'T GET IT! MR. FREEZE DOESN'T HAVE A WARM BONE IN HIS BODY!

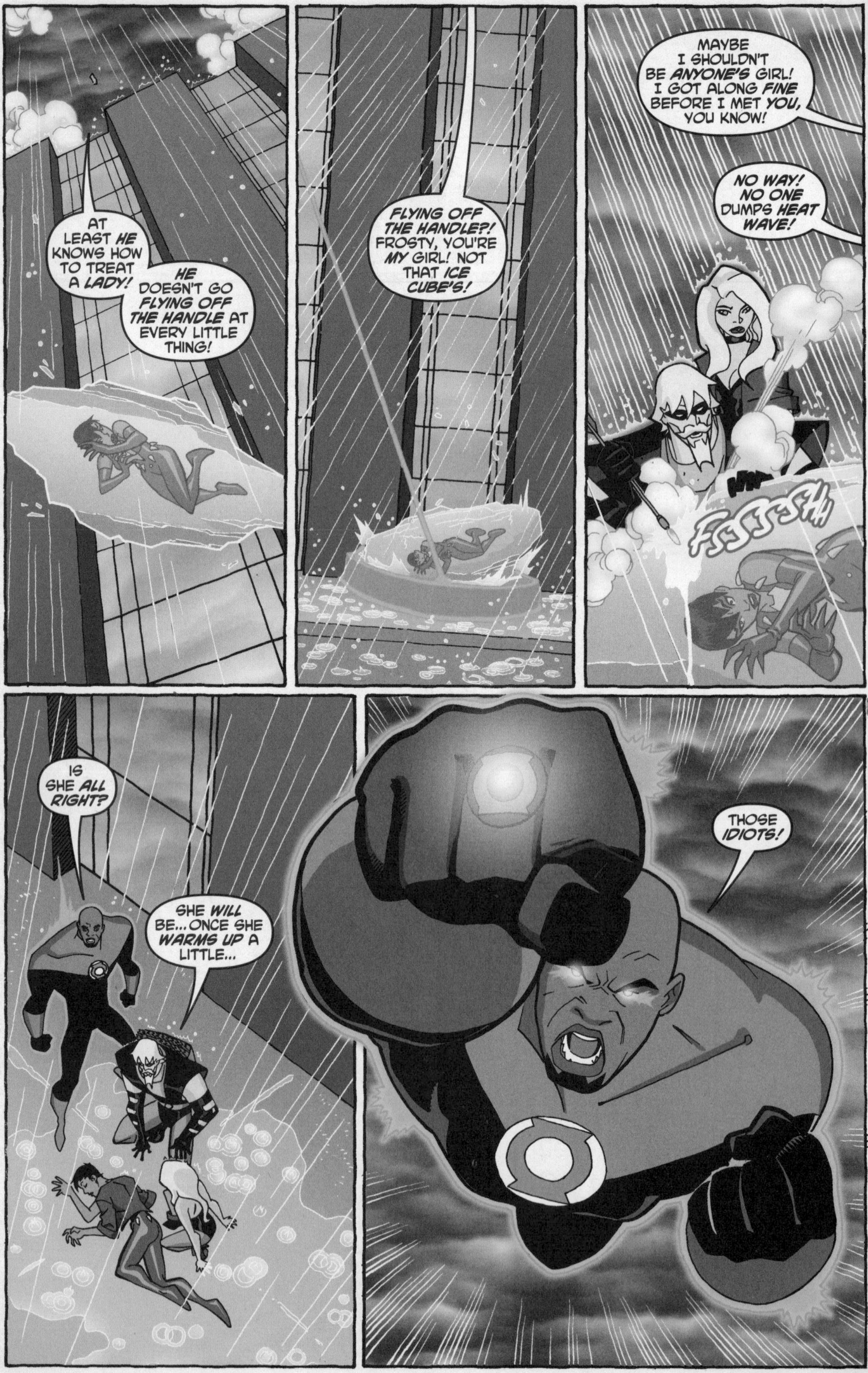
AT LEAST HE KNOWS HOW TO TREAT A LADY!
HE DOESN'T GO FLYING OFF THE HANDLE AT EVERY LITTLE THING!
FLYING OFF THE HANDLE?! FROSTY, YOU'RE MY GIRL! NOT THAT ICE CUBE'S!
MAYBE I SHOULDN'T BE ANYONE'S GIRL! I GOT ALONG FINE BEFORE I MET YOU, YOU KNOW!
NO WAY! NO ONE DUMPS HEAT WAVE!
FSSSSHH
IS SHE ALL RIGHT?
SHE WILL BE...ONCE SHE WARMS UP A LITTLE...
THOSE IDIOTS!

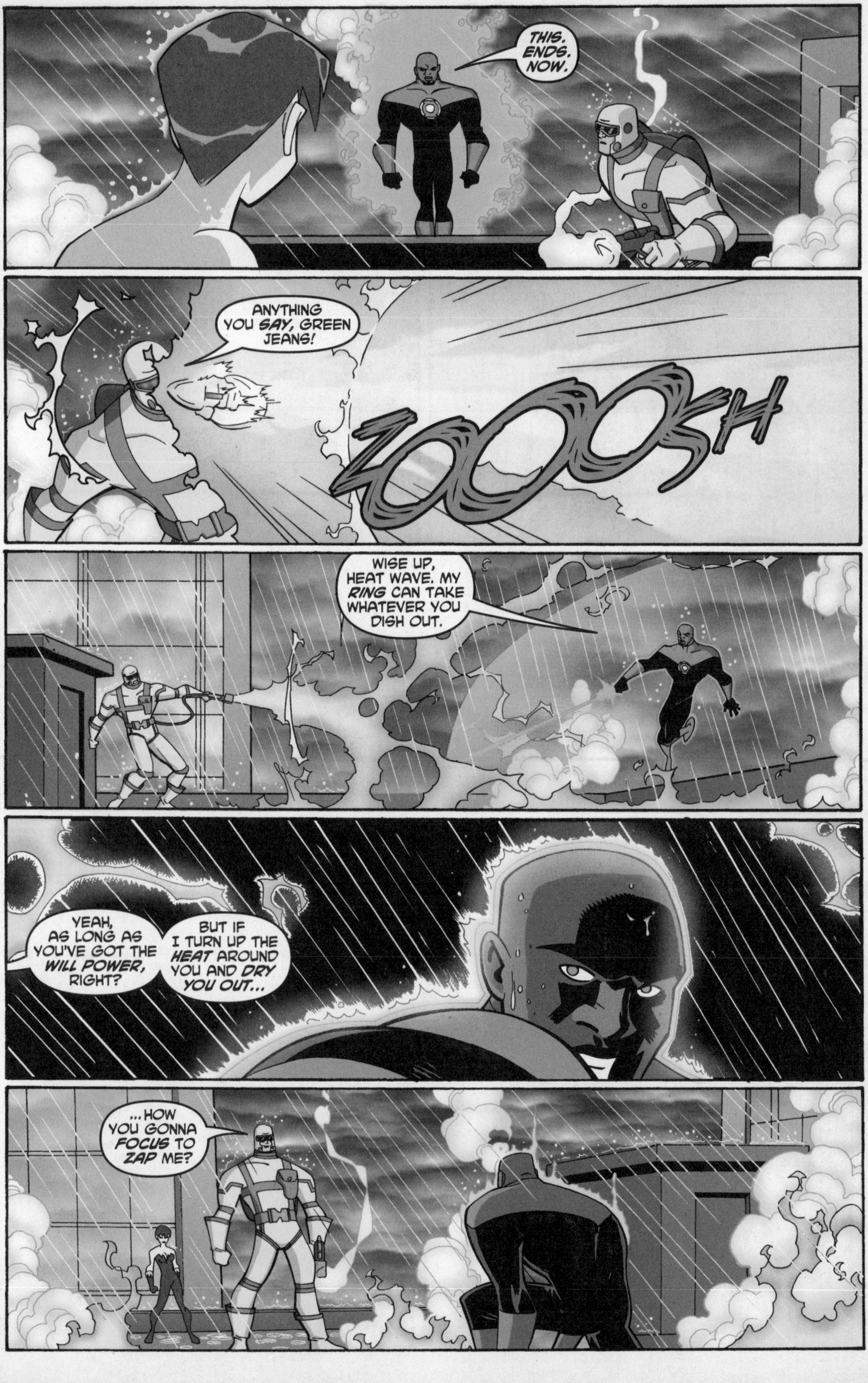
THIS. ENDS. NOW.
ANYTHING YOU SAY, GREEN JEANS!
ZOOOOSH
WISE UP, HEAT WAVE. MY RING CAN TAKE WHATEVER YOU DISH OUT.
YEAH, AS LONG AS YOU'VE GOT THE WILL POWER, RIGHT?
BUT IF I TURN UP THE HEAT AROUND YOU AND DRY YOU OUT...
...HOW YOU GONNA FOCUS TO ZAP ME?

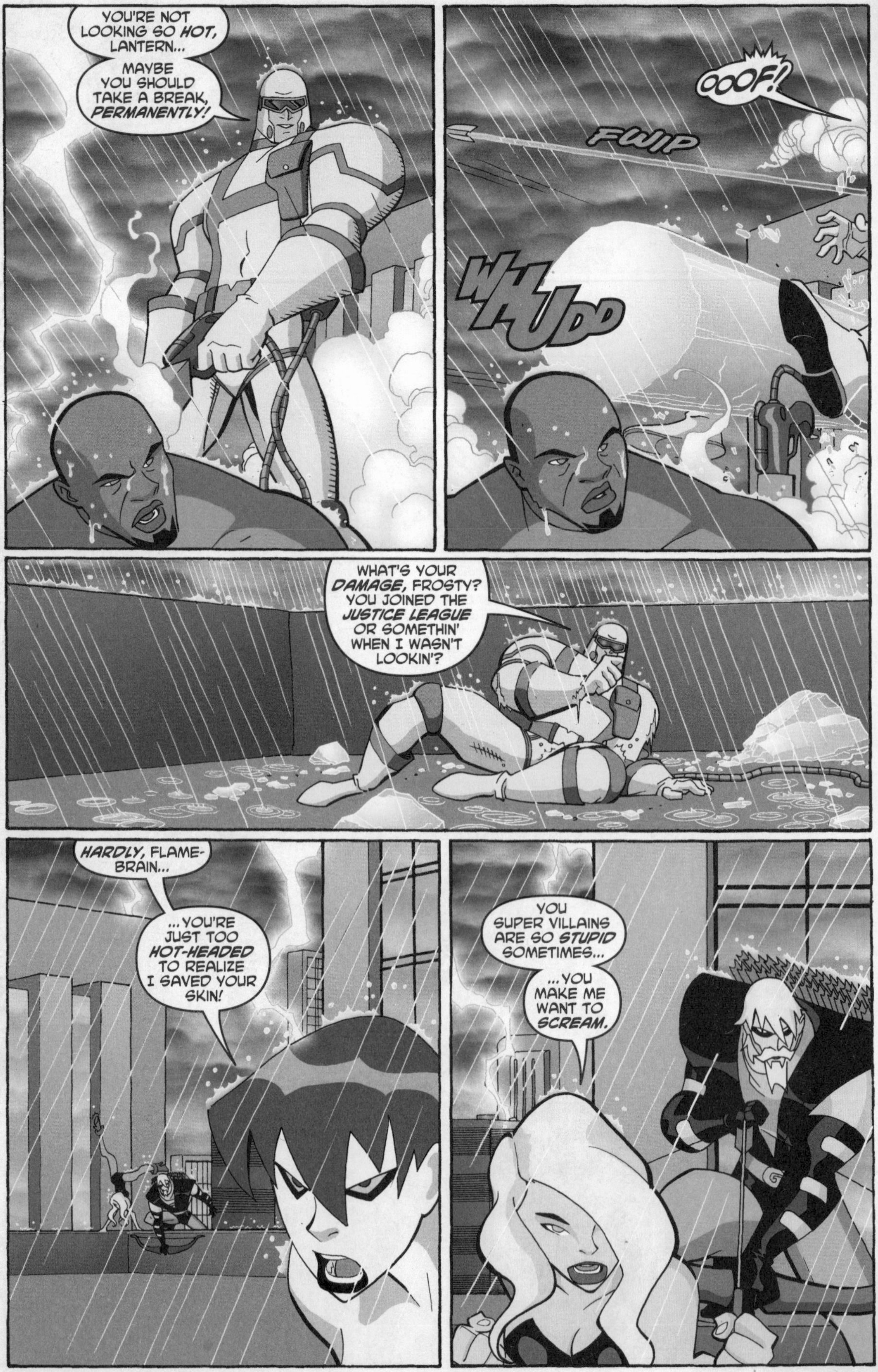
YOU'RE NOT LOOKING SO HOT, LANTERN...
MAYBE YOU SHOULD TAKE A BREAK, PERMANENTLY!
OOOF!
FWIP
WHUDD
WHAT'S YOUR DAMAGE, FROSTY? YOU JOINED THE JUSTICE LEAGUE OR SOMETHIN' WHEN I WASN'T LOOKIN'?
HARDLY, FLAME-BRAIN...
...YOU'RE JUST TOO HOT-HEADED TO REALIZE I SAVED YOUR SKIN!
YOU SUPER VILLAINS ARE SO STUPID SOMETIMES...
...YOU MAKE ME WANT TO SCREAM.

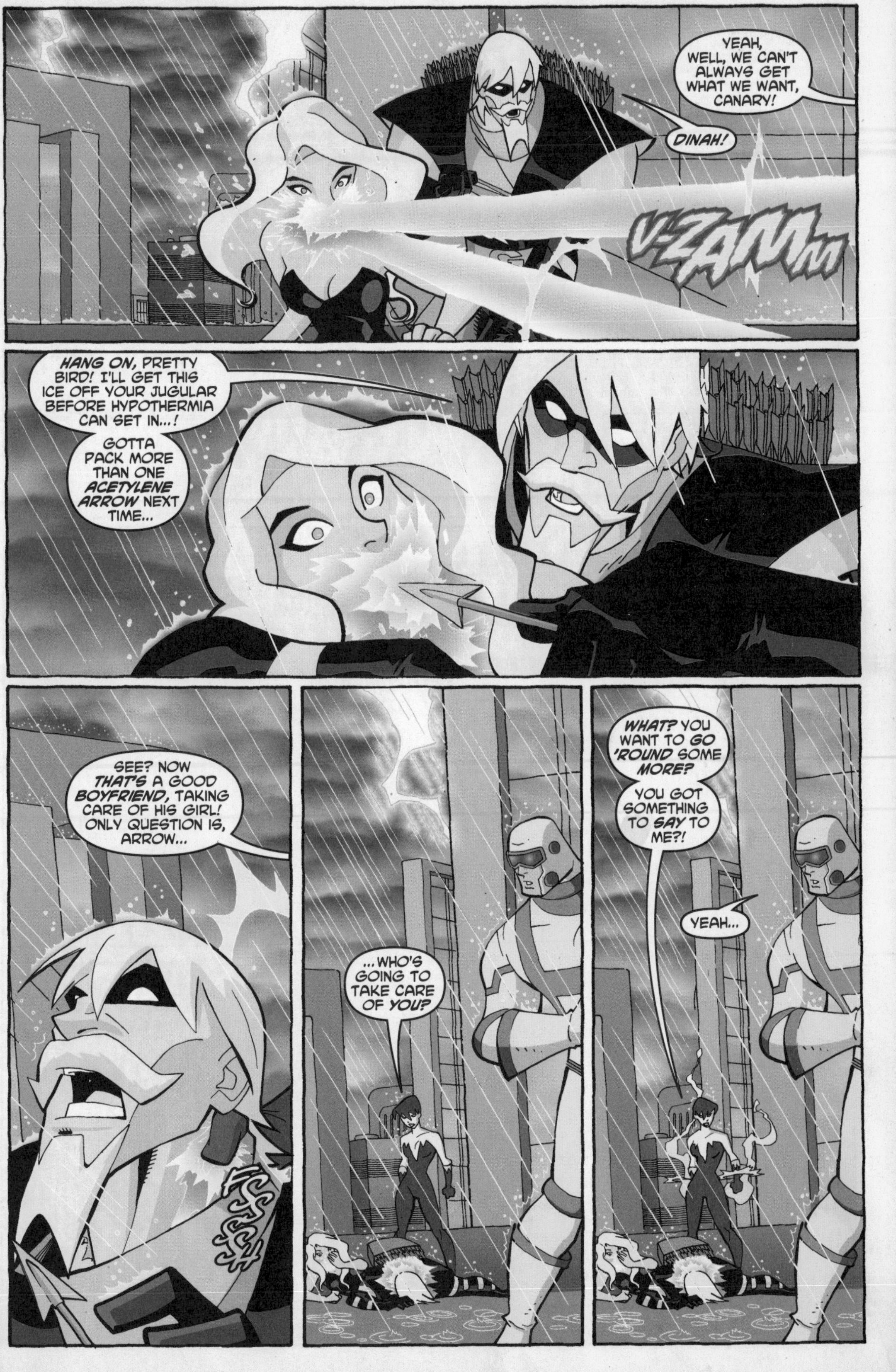
YEAH, WELL, WE CAN'T ALWAYS GET WHAT WE WANT, CANARY!
DINAH!
V-ZAM
HANG ON, PRETTY BIRD! I'LL GET THIS ICE OFF YOUR JUGULAR BEFORE HYPOTHERMIA CAN SET IN...!
GOTTA PACK MORE THAN ONE ACETYLENE ARROW NEXT TIME...
SEE? NOW THAT'S A GOOD BOYFRIEND, TAKING CARE OF HIS GIRL! ONLY QUESTION IS, ARROW...
...WHO'S GOING TO TAKE CARE OF YOU?
WHAT? YOU WANT TO GO 'ROUND SOME MORE?
YOU GOT SOMETHING TO SAY TO ME?!
YEAH...

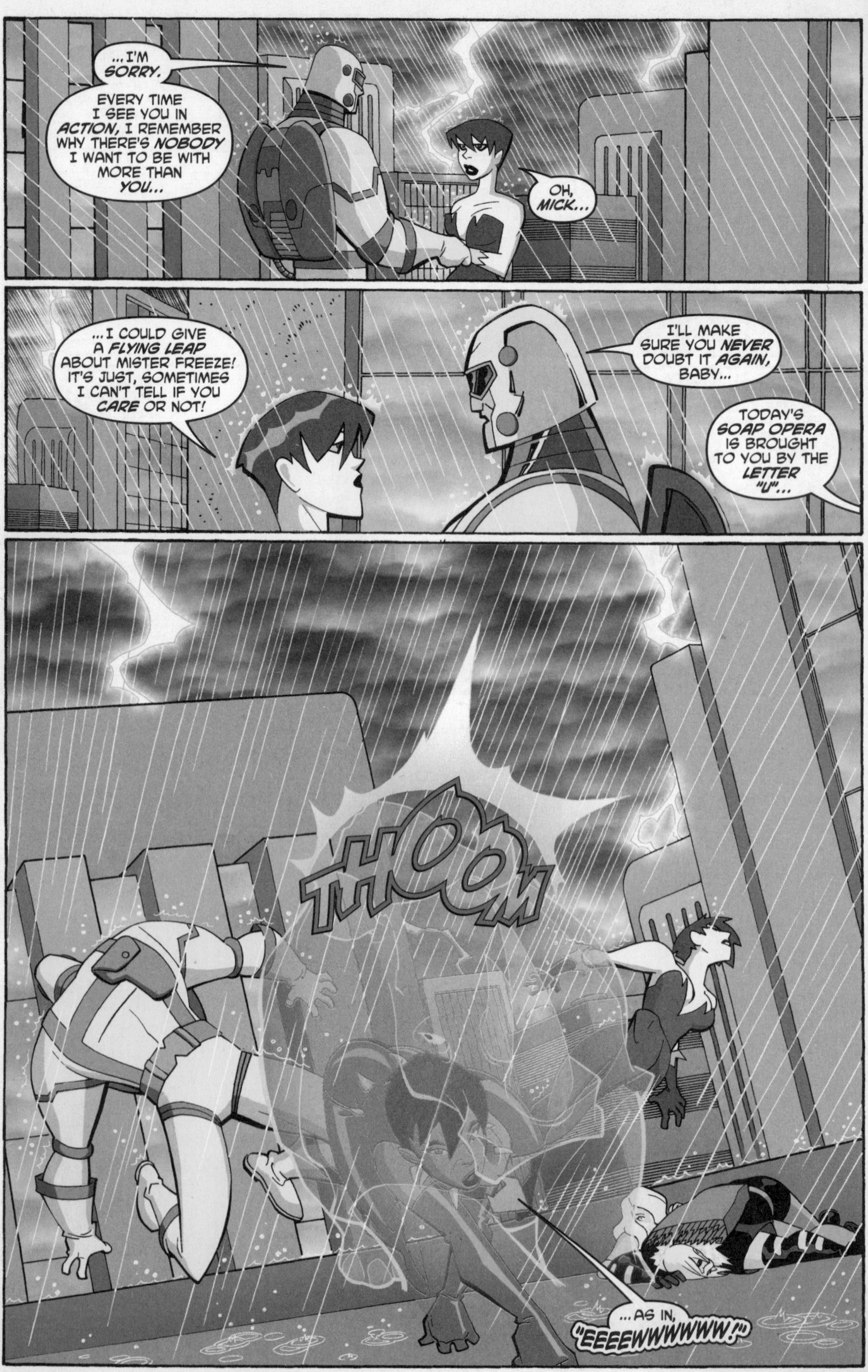
...I'M SORRY.
EVERY TIME I SEE YOU IN ACTION, I REMEMBER WHY THERE'S NOBODY I WANT TO BE WITH MORE THAN YOU...
OH, MICK...
...I COULD GIVE A FLYING LEAP ABOUT MISTER FREEZE! IT'S JUST, SOMETIMES I CAN'T TELL IF YOU CARE OR NOT!
I'LL MAKE SURE YOU NEVER DOUBT IT AGAIN, BABY...
TODAY'S SOAP OPERA IS BROUGHT TO YOU BY THE LETTER "U"...
THOOM
...AS IN, "EEEEWWWWWW!"

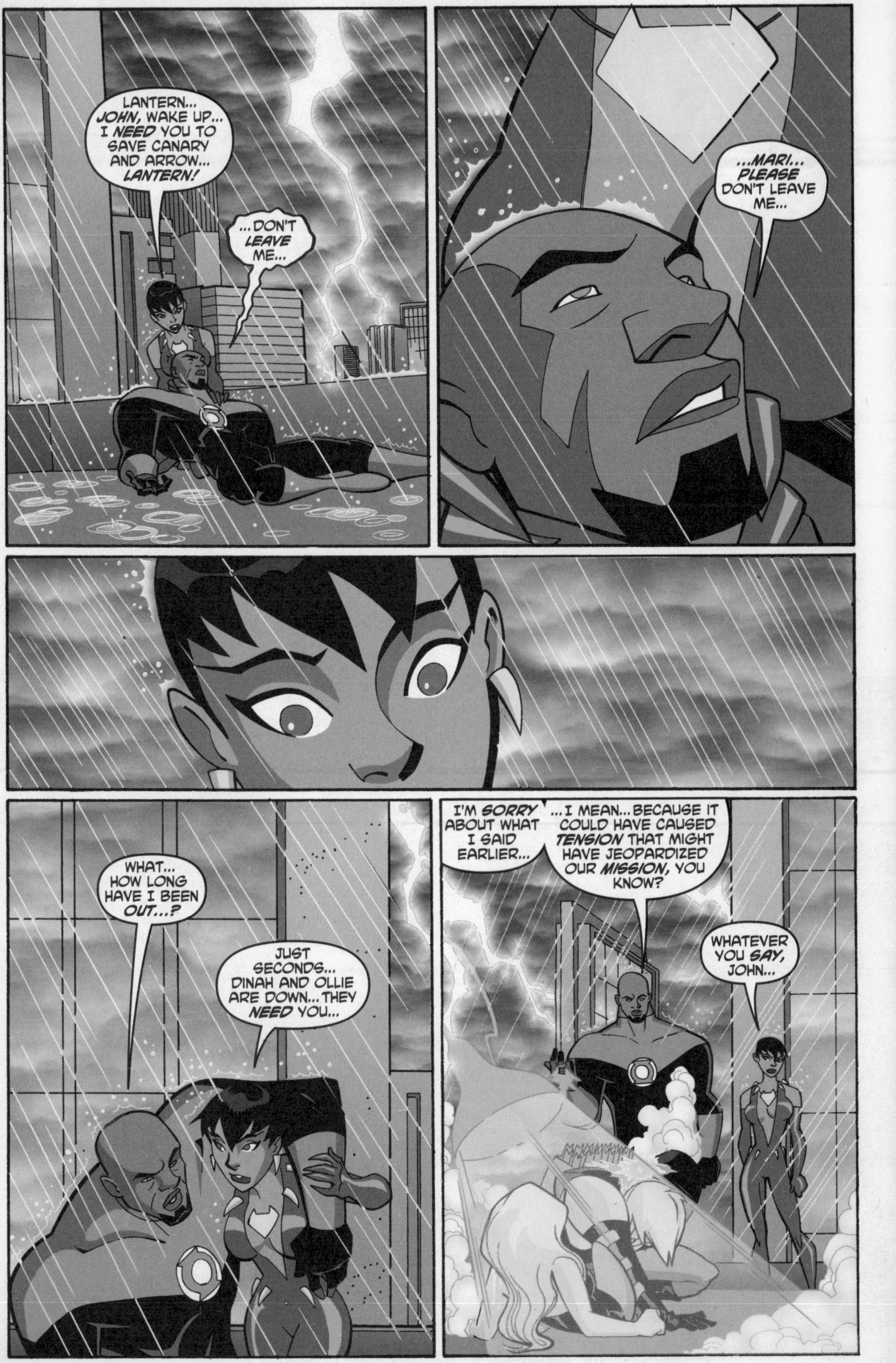
LANTERN... JOHN, WAKE UP... I NEED YOU TO SAVE CANARY AND ARROW... LANTERN!
...DON'T LEAVE ME...
...MARI... PLEASE DON'T LEAVE ME...
WHAT... HOW LONG HAVE I BEEN OUT...?
JUST SECONDS... DINAH AND OLLIE ARE DOWN... THEY NEED YOU...
I'M SORRY ABOUT WHAT I SAID EARLIER...
...I MEAN... BECAUSE IT COULD HAVE CAUSED TENSION THAT MIGHT HAVE JEOPARDIZED OUR MISSION, YOU KNOW?
WHATEVER YOU SAY, JOHN...

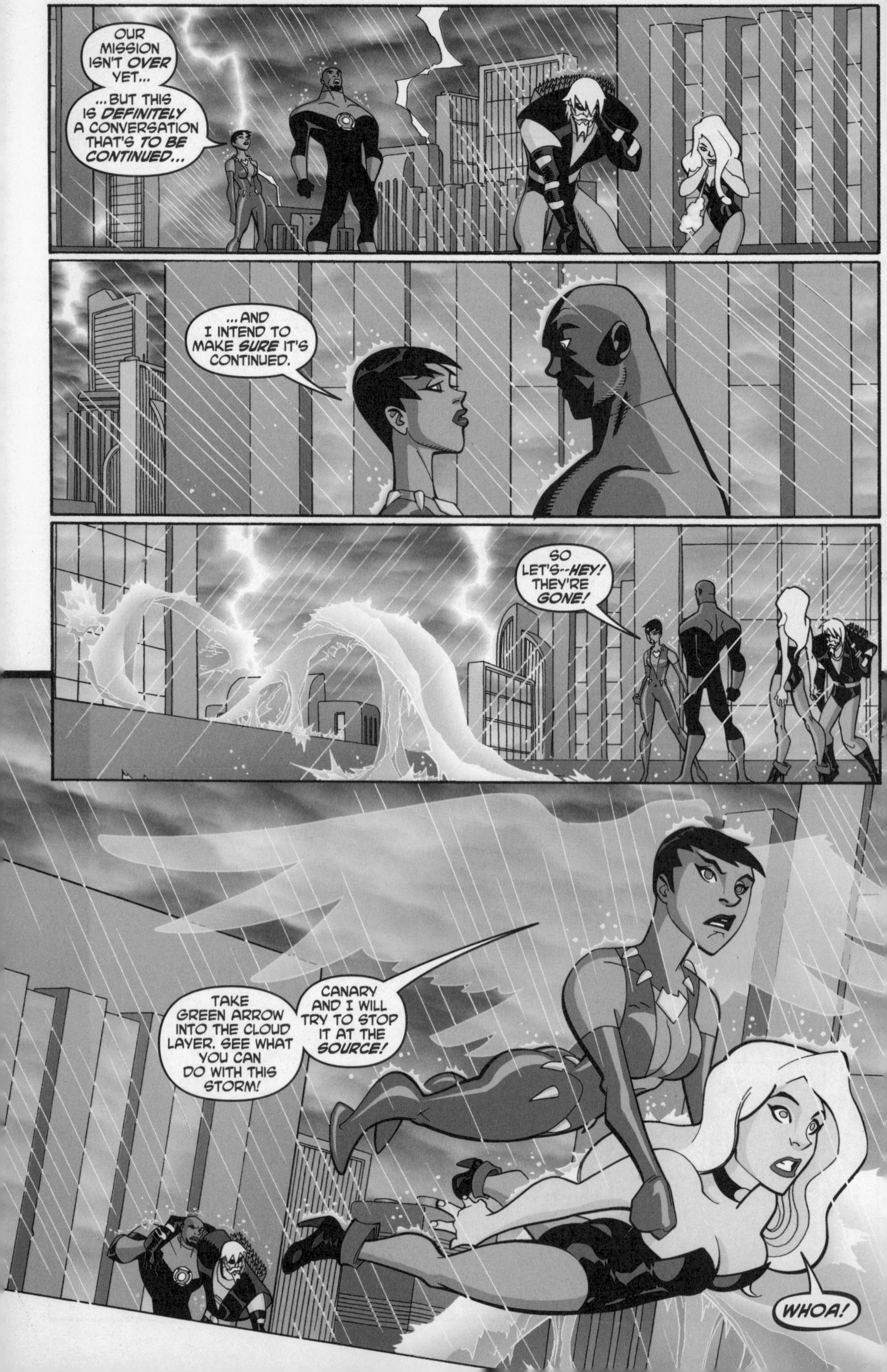

OUR MISSION ISN'T OVER YET...
...BUT THIS IS DEFINITELY A CONVERSATION THAT'S TO BE CONTINUED...
...AND I INTEND TO MAKE SURE IT'S CONTINUED.
SO LET'S--HEY! THEY'RE GONE!
CANARY AND I WILL TRY TO STOP IT AT THE SOURCE!
TAKE GREEN ARROW INTO THE CLOUD LAYER. SEE WHAT YOU CAN DO WITH THIS STORM!
WHOA!

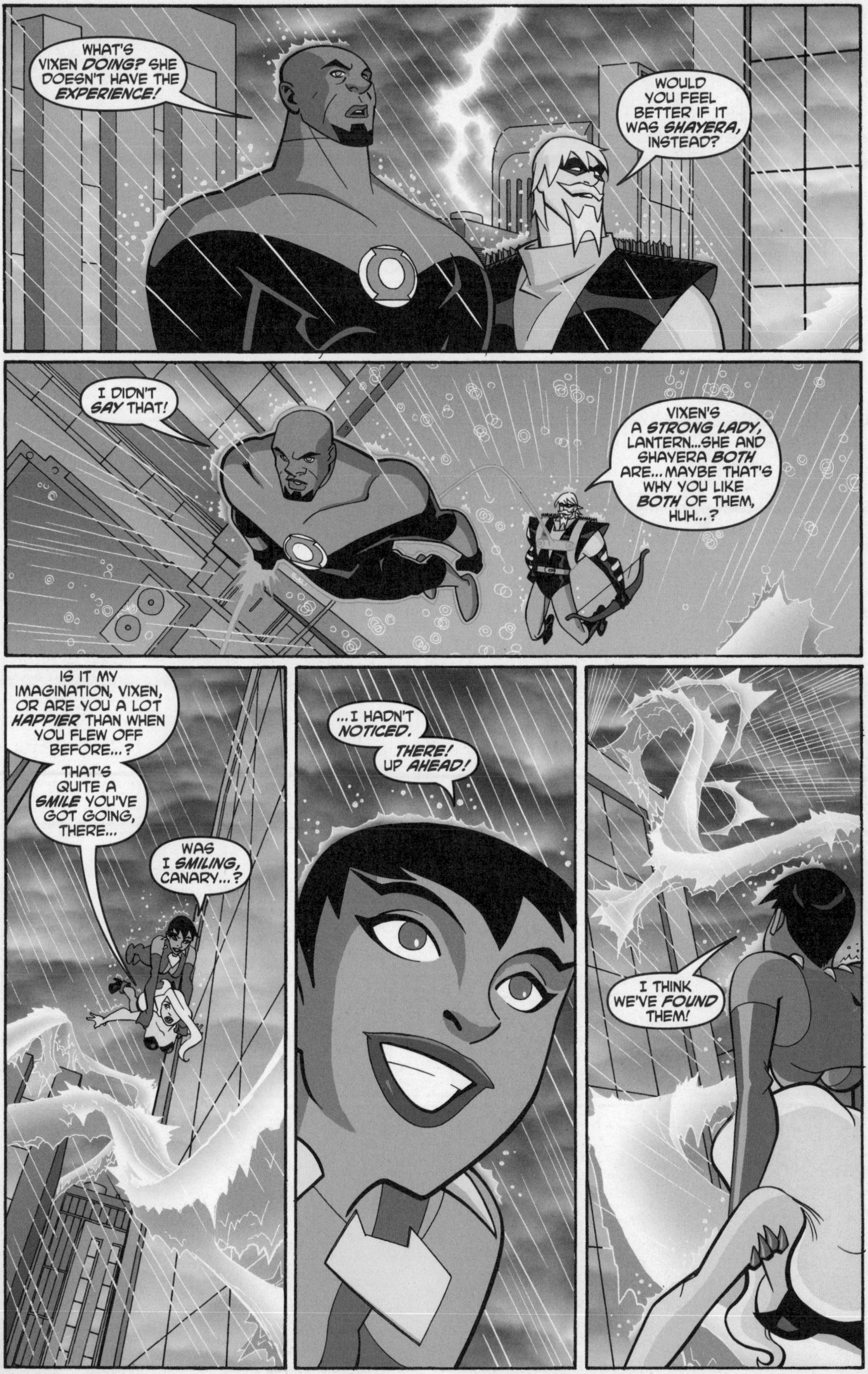
WHAT'S VIXEN DOING? SHE DOESN'T HAVE THE EXPERIENCE!
WOULD YOU FEEL BETTER IF IT WAS SHAYERA, INSTEAD?
I DIDN'T SAY THAT!
VIXEN'S A STRONG LADY, LANTERN...SHE AND SHAYERA BOTH ARE... MAYBE THAT'S WHY YOU LIKE BOTH OF THEM, HUH...?
IS IT MY IMAGINATION, VIXEN, OR ARE YOU A LOT HAPPIER THAN WHEN YOU FLEW OFF BEFORE...?
THAT'S QUITE A SMILE YOU'VE GOT GOING, THERE...
WAS I SMILING, CANARY...?
...I HADN'T NOTICED.
THERE! UP AHEAD!
I THINK WE'VE FOUND THEM!

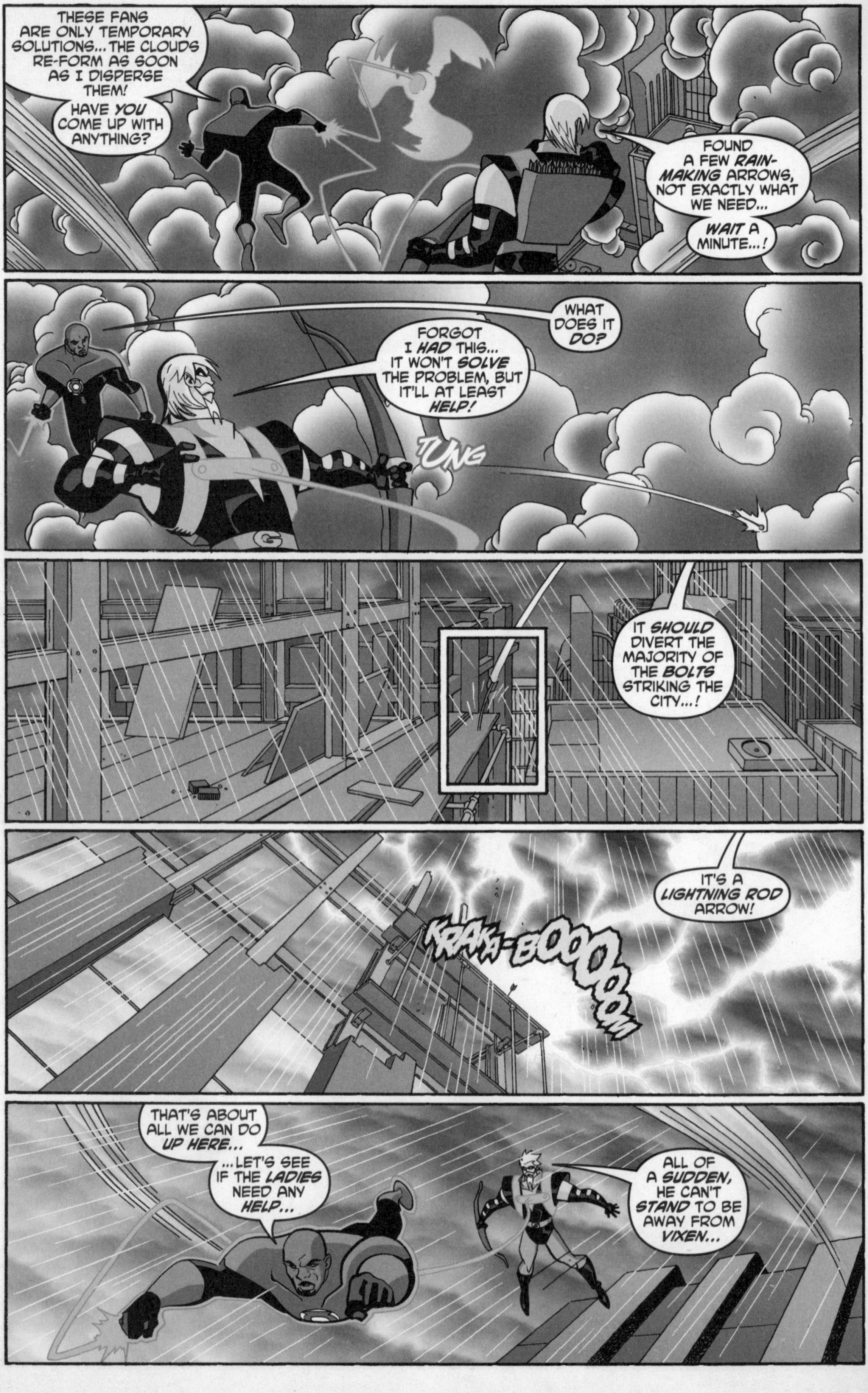
THESE FANS ARE ONLY TEMPORARY SOLUTIONS... THE CLOUDS RE-FORM AS SOON AS I DISPERSE THEM!
HAVE YOU COME UP WITH ANYTHING?
FOUND A FEW RAIN-MAKING ARROWS, NOT EXACTLY WHAT WE NEED...
WAIT A MINUTE...!
FORGOT I HAD THIS... IT WON'T SOLVE THE PROBLEM, BUT IT'LL AT LEAST HELP!
WHAT DOES IT DO?
TUNG
IT SHOULD DIVERT THE MAJORITY OF THE BOLTS STRIKING THE CITY...!
IT'S A LIGHTNING ROD ARROW!
KRAKA-BOOOOOOM
THAT'S ABOUT ALL WE CAN DO UP HERE...
...LET'S SEE IF THE LADIES NEED ANY HELP...
ALL OF A SUDDEN, HE CAN'T STAND TO BE AWAY FROM VIXEN...

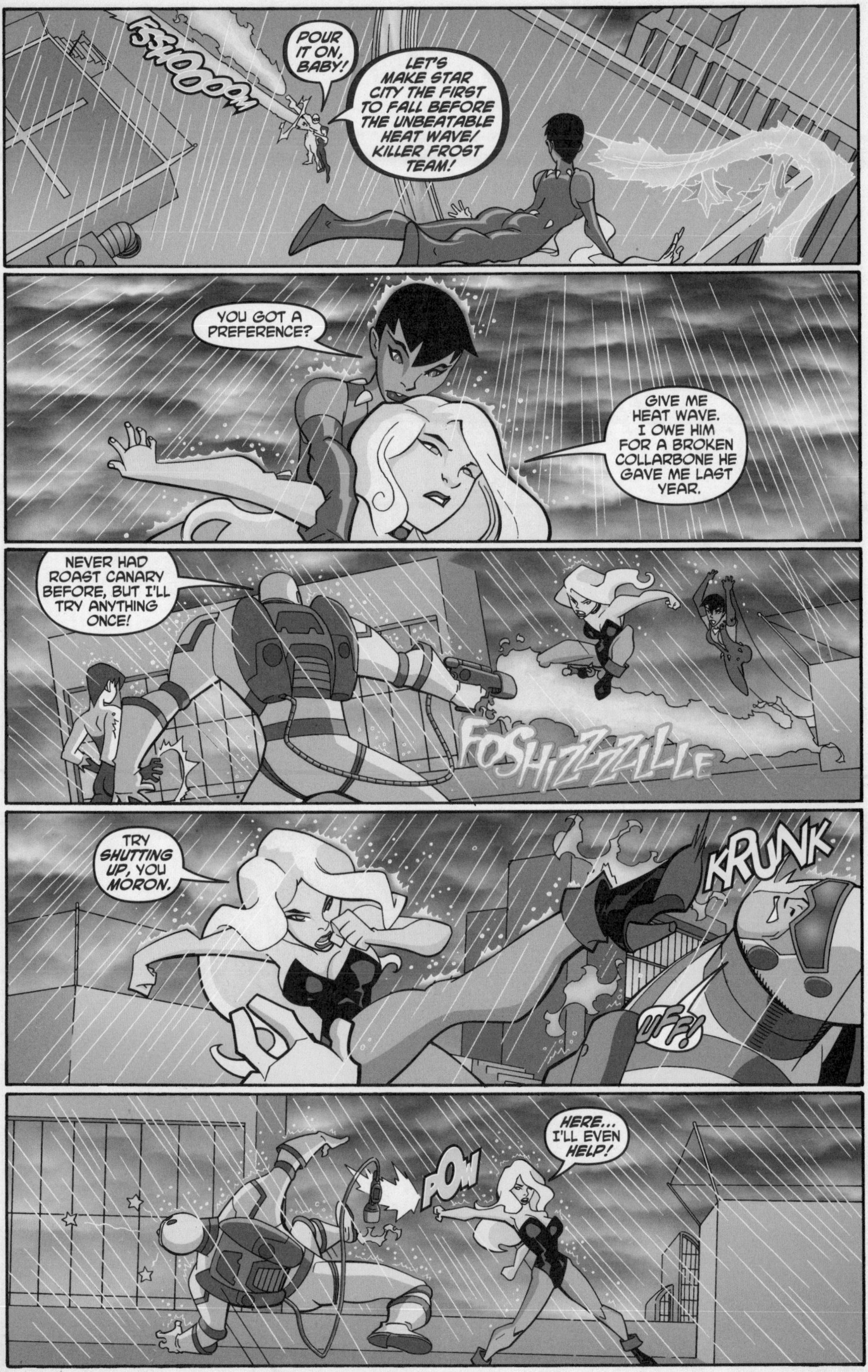
FSHOOOOM
POUR IT ON, BABY!
LET'S MAKE STAR CITY THE FIRST TO FALL BEFORE THE UNBEATABLE HEAT WAVE/KILLER FROST TEAM!
YOU GOT A PREFERENCE?
GIVE ME HEAT WAVE. I OWE HIM FOR A BROKEN COLLARBONE HE GAVE ME LAST YEAR.
NEVER HAD ROAST CANARY BEFORE, BUT I'LL TRY ANYTHING ONCE!
FOSHIZZZZILLE
TRY SHUTTING UP, YOU MORON.
KRUNK
UFF!
HERE... I'LL EVEN HELP!
POW

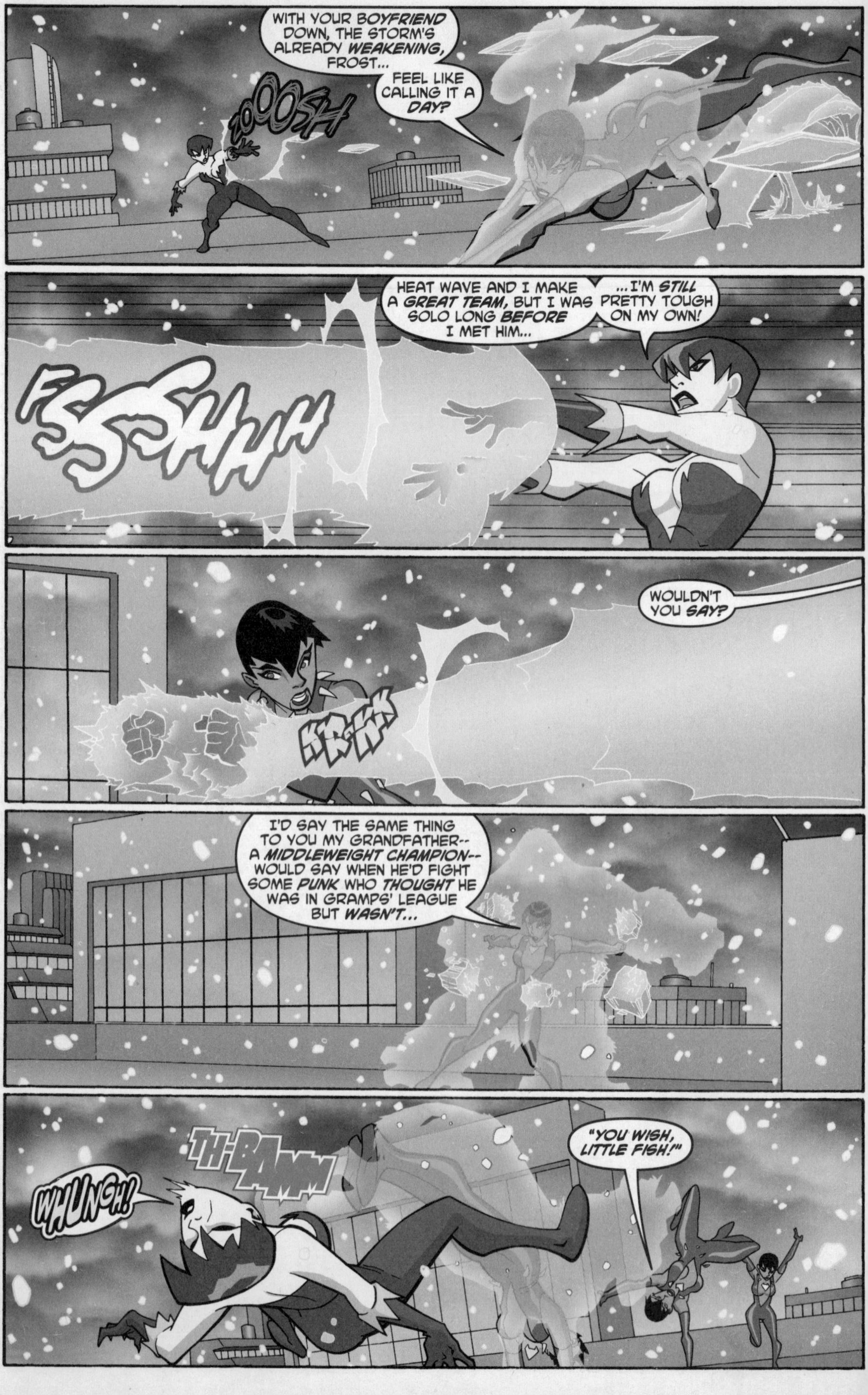
WITH YOUR BOYFRIEND DOWN, THE STORM'S ALREADY WEAKENING, FROST...
FEEL LIKE CALLING IT A DAY?
ZOOOOSH
HEAT WAVE AND I MAKE A GREAT TEAM, BUT I WAS SOLO LONG BEFORE I MET HIM...
...I'M STILL PRETTY TOUGH ON MY OWN!
FSSHHH
WOULDN'T YOU SAY?
K-R-K
I'D SAY THE SAME THING TO YOU MY GRANDFATHER-- A MIDDLEWEIGHT CHAMPION-- WOULD SAY WHEN HE'D FIGHT SOME PUNK WHO THOUGHT HE WAS IN GRAMPS' LEAGUE BUT WASN'T...
TH-BAMM
WHUNGH!
"YOU WISH, LITTLE FISH!"

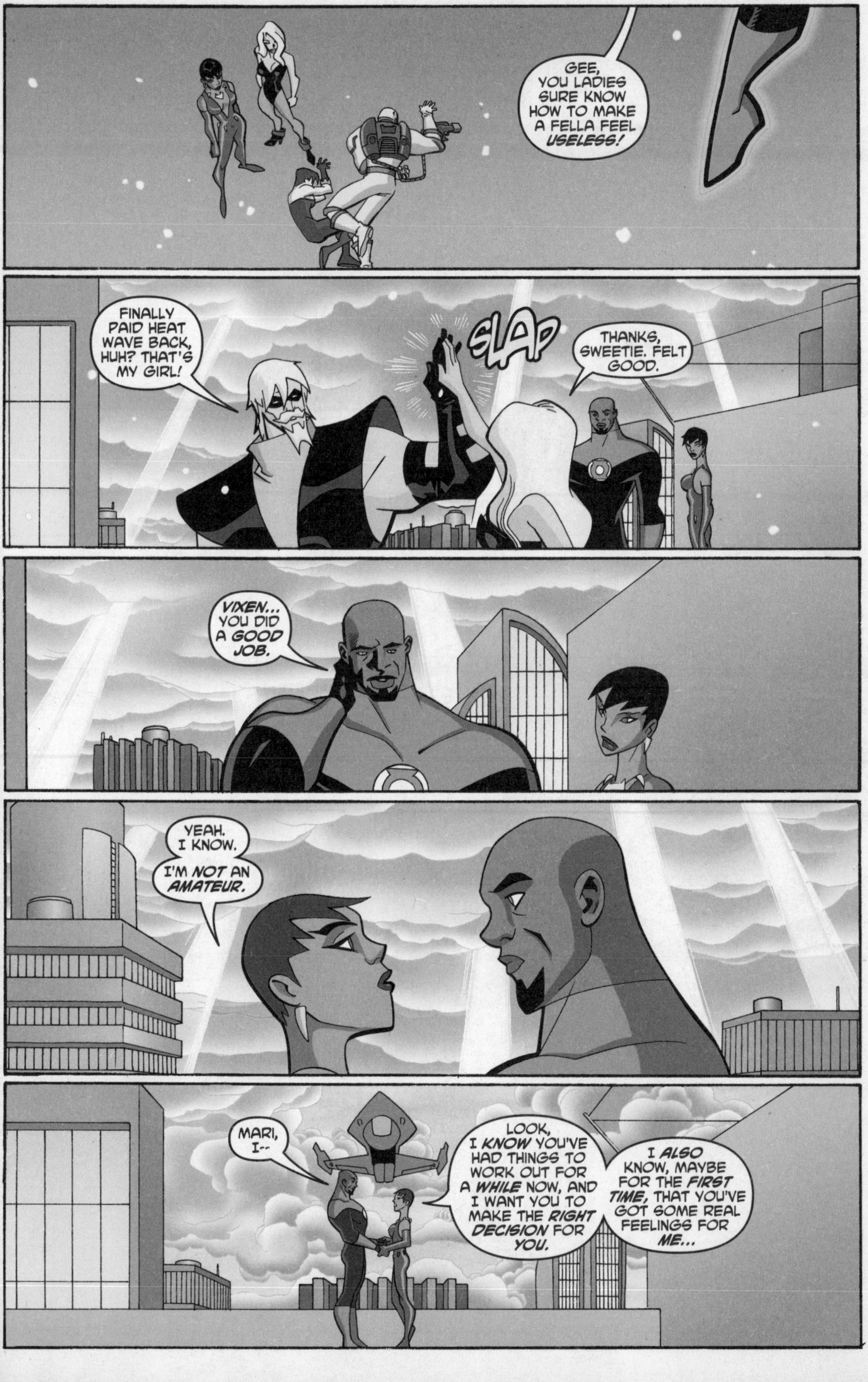
GEE, YOU LADIES SURE KNOW HOW TO MAKE A FELLA FEEL *USELESS!*
FINALLY PAID HEAT WAVE BACK, HUH? THAT'S MY GIRL!
SLAP
THANKS, SWEETIE. FELT GOOD.
VIXEN... YOU DID A *GOOD JOB.*
YEAH. I KNOW.
I'M *NOT* AN *AMATEUR.*
MARI, I--
LOOK, I *KNOW* YOU'VE HAD THINGS TO WORK OUT FOR A *WHILE* NOW, AND I WANT YOU TO MAKE THE *RIGHT DECISION* FOR *YOU.*
I *ALSO* KNOW, MAYBE FOR THE *FIRST TIME,* THAT YOU'VE GOT SOME REAL FEELINGS FOR *ME...*

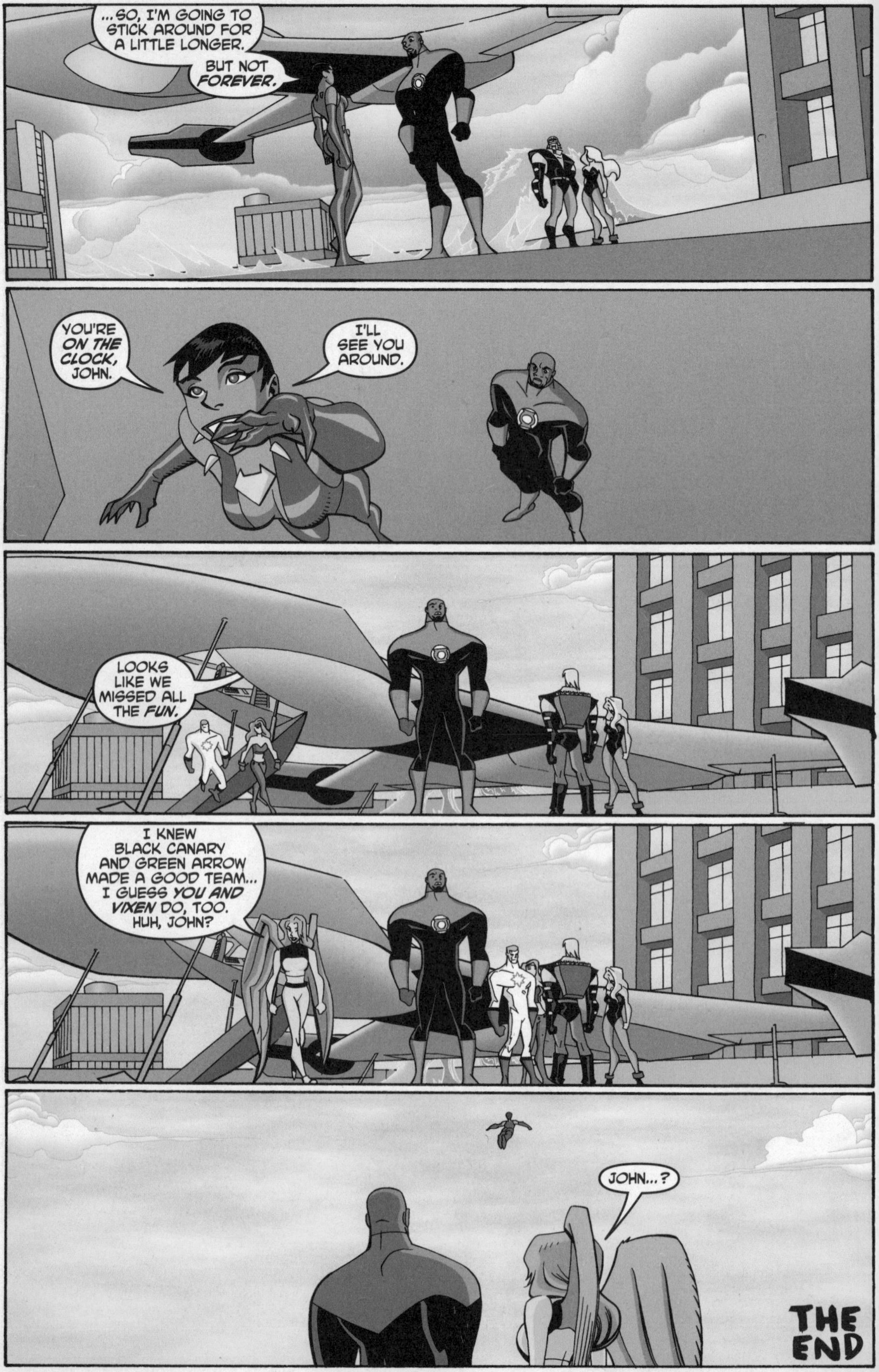
...SO, I'M GOING TO STICK AROUND FOR A LITTLE LONGER.
BUT NOT *FOREVER*.
YOU'RE *ON THE CLOCK*, JOHN.
I'LL SEE YOU AROUND.
LOOKS LIKE WE MISSED ALL THE *FUN*.
I KNEW BLACK CANARY AND GREEN ARROW MADE A GOOD TEAM... I GUESS *YOU AND VIXEN* DO, TOO. HUH, JOHN?
JOHN...?
THE END

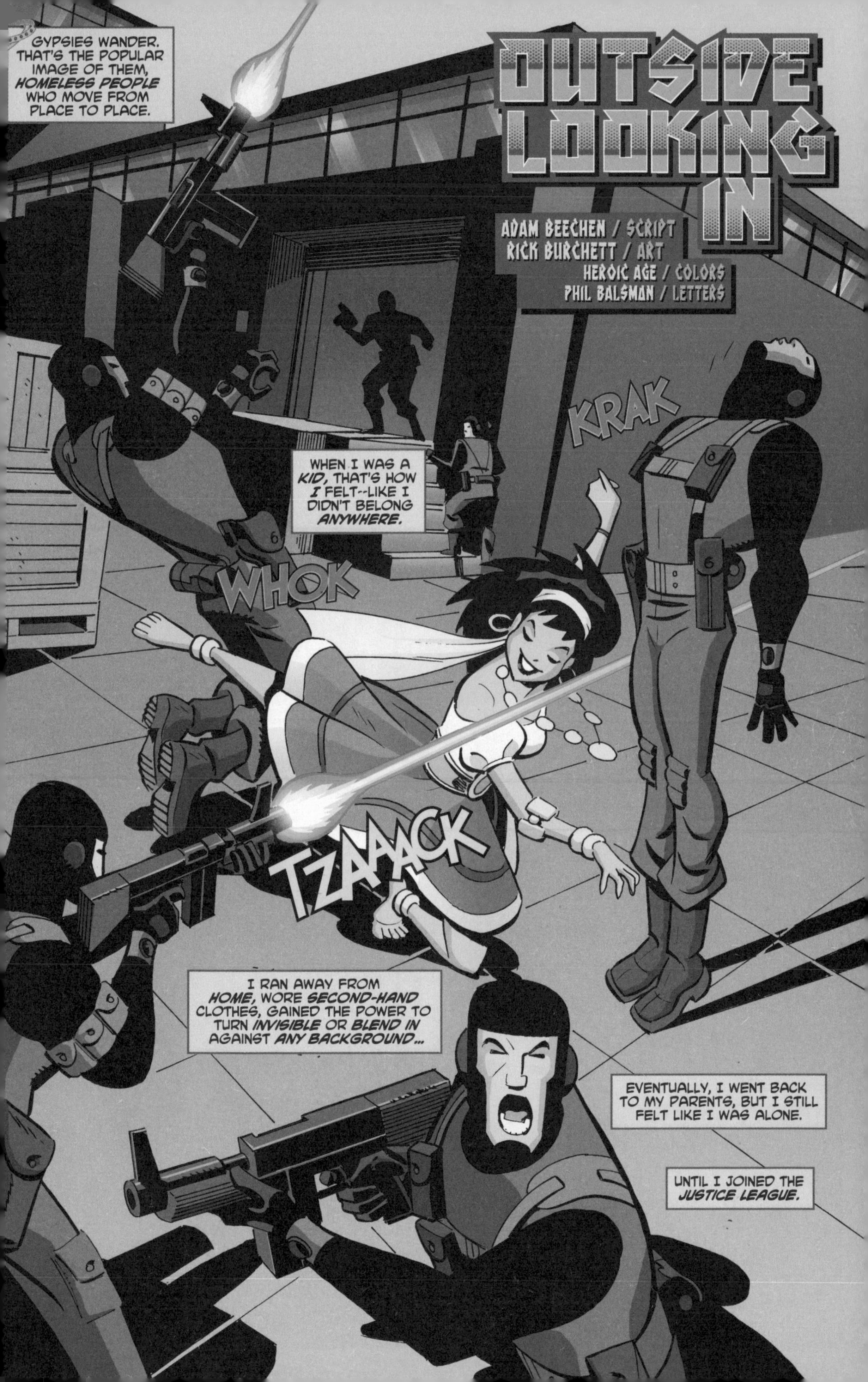
GYPSIES WANDER. THAT'S THE POPULAR IMAGE OF THEM, *HOMELESS PEOPLE* WHO MOVE FROM PLACE TO PLACE.
OUTSIDE LOOKING IN
ADAM BEECHEN / SCRIPT
RICK BURCHETT / ART
HEROIC AGE / COLORS
PHIL BALSMAN / LETTERS
WHEN I WAS A *KID*, THAT'S HOW *I* FELT--LIKE I DIDN'T BELONG *ANYWHERE*.
KRAK
WHOK
TZAAACK
I RAN AWAY FROM *HOME*, WORE *SECOND-HAND* CLOTHES, GAINED THE POWER TO TURN *INVISIBLE* OR *BLEND IN* AGAINST *ANY BACKGROUND*...
EVENTUALLY, I WENT BACK TO MY PARENTS, BUT I STILL FELT LIKE I WAS ALONE.
UNTIL I JOINED THE *JUSTICE LEAGUE*.

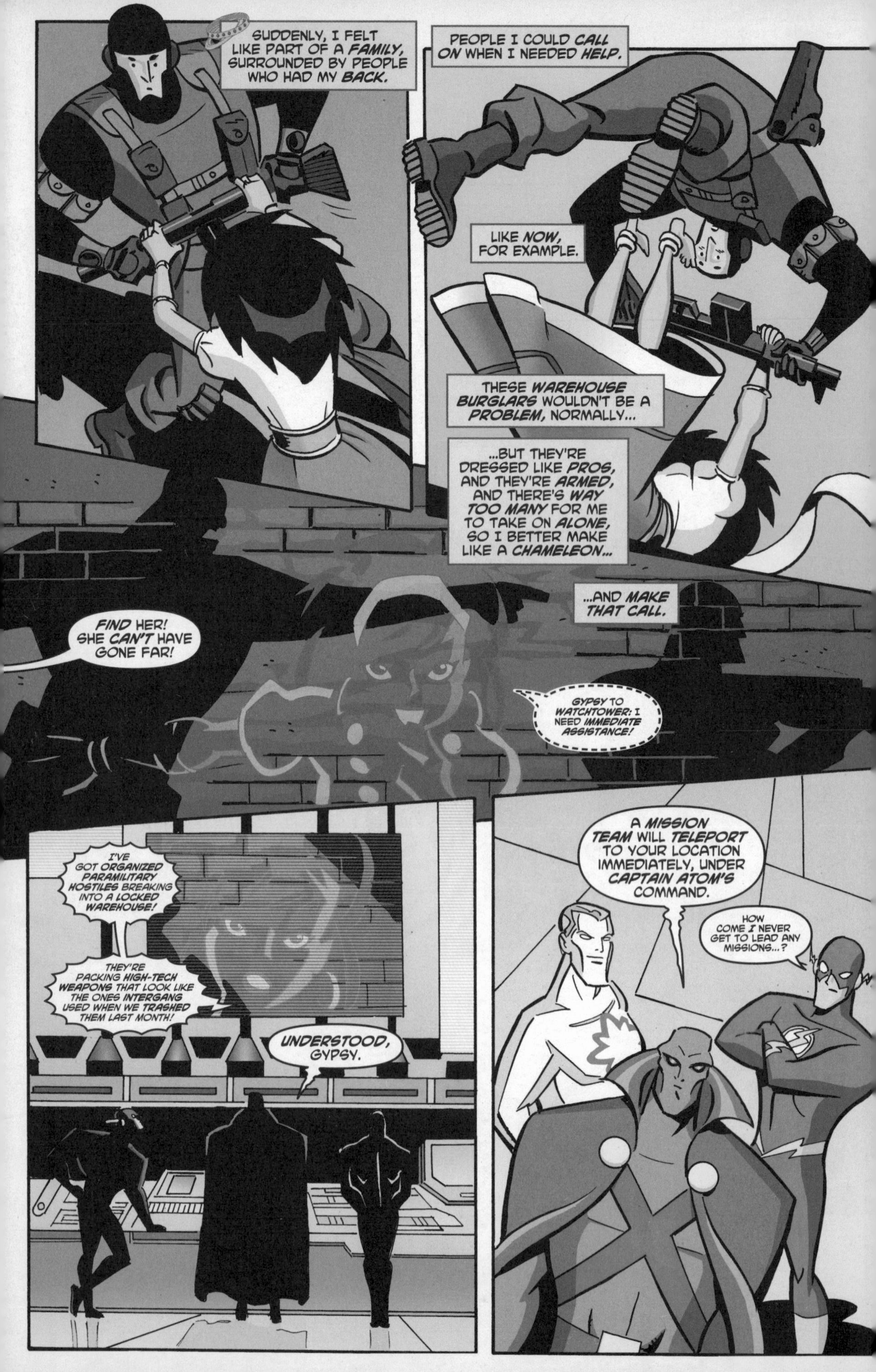
SUDDENLY, I FELT LIKE PART OF A FAMILY, SURROUNDED BY PEOPLE WHO HAD MY BACK.
PEOPLE I COULD CALL ON WHEN I NEEDED HELP.
LIKE NOW, FOR EXAMPLE.
THESE WAREHOUSE BURGLARS WOULDN'T BE A PROBLEM, NORMALLY...
...BUT THEY'RE DRESSED LIKE PROS, AND THEY'RE ARMED, AND THERE'S WAY TOO MANY FOR ME TO TAKE ON ALONE, SO I BETTER MAKE LIKE A CHAMELEON...
...AND MAKE THAT CALL.
FIND HER! SHE CAN'T HAVE GONE FAR!
GYPSY TO WATCHTOWER: I NEED IMMEDIATE ASSISTANCE!
I'VE GOT ORGANIZED PARAMILITARY HOSTILES BREAKING INTO A LOCKED WAREHOUSE!
THEY'RE PACKING HIGH-TECH WEAPONS THAT LOOK LIKE THE ONES INTERGANG USED WHEN WE TRASHED THEM LAST MONTH!
UNDERSTOOD, GYPSY.
A MISSION TEAM WILL TELEPORT TO YOUR LOCATION IMMEDIATELY, UNDER CAPTAIN ATOM'S COMMAND.
HOW COME I NEVER GET TO LEAD ANY MISSIONS...?

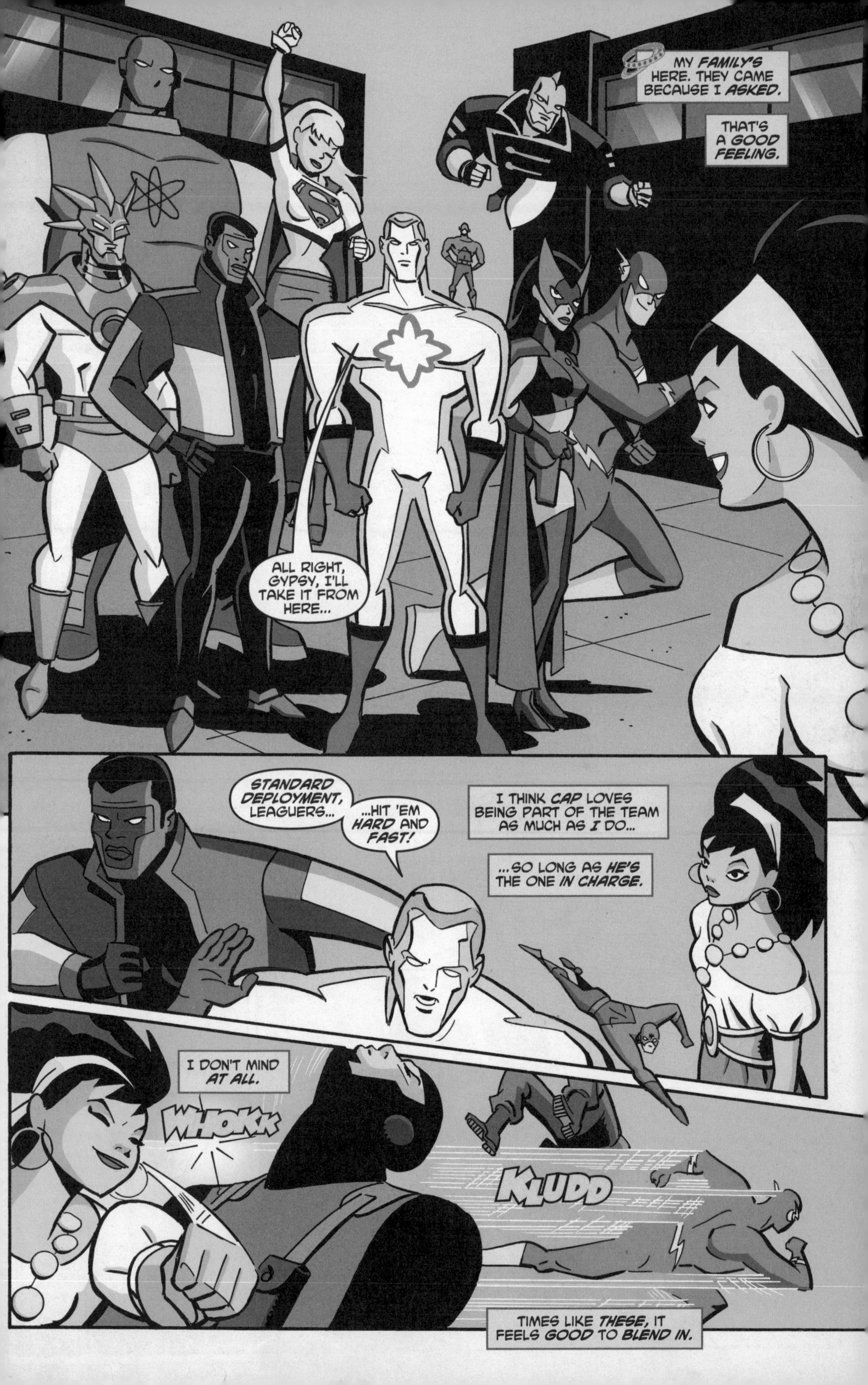
MY FAMILY'S HERE. THEY CAME BECAUSE I ASKED.
THAT'S A GOOD FEELING.
ALL RIGHT, GYPSY, I'LL TAKE IT FROM HERE...
STANDARD DEPLOYMENT, LEAGUERS...
...HIT 'EM HARD AND FAST!
I THINK CAP LOVES BEING PART OF THE TEAM AS MUCH AS I DO...
...SO LONG AS HE'S THE ONE IN CHARGE.
I DON'T MIND AT ALL.
WHOKK
KLUDD
TIMES LIKE THESE, IT FEELS GOOD TO BLEND IN.

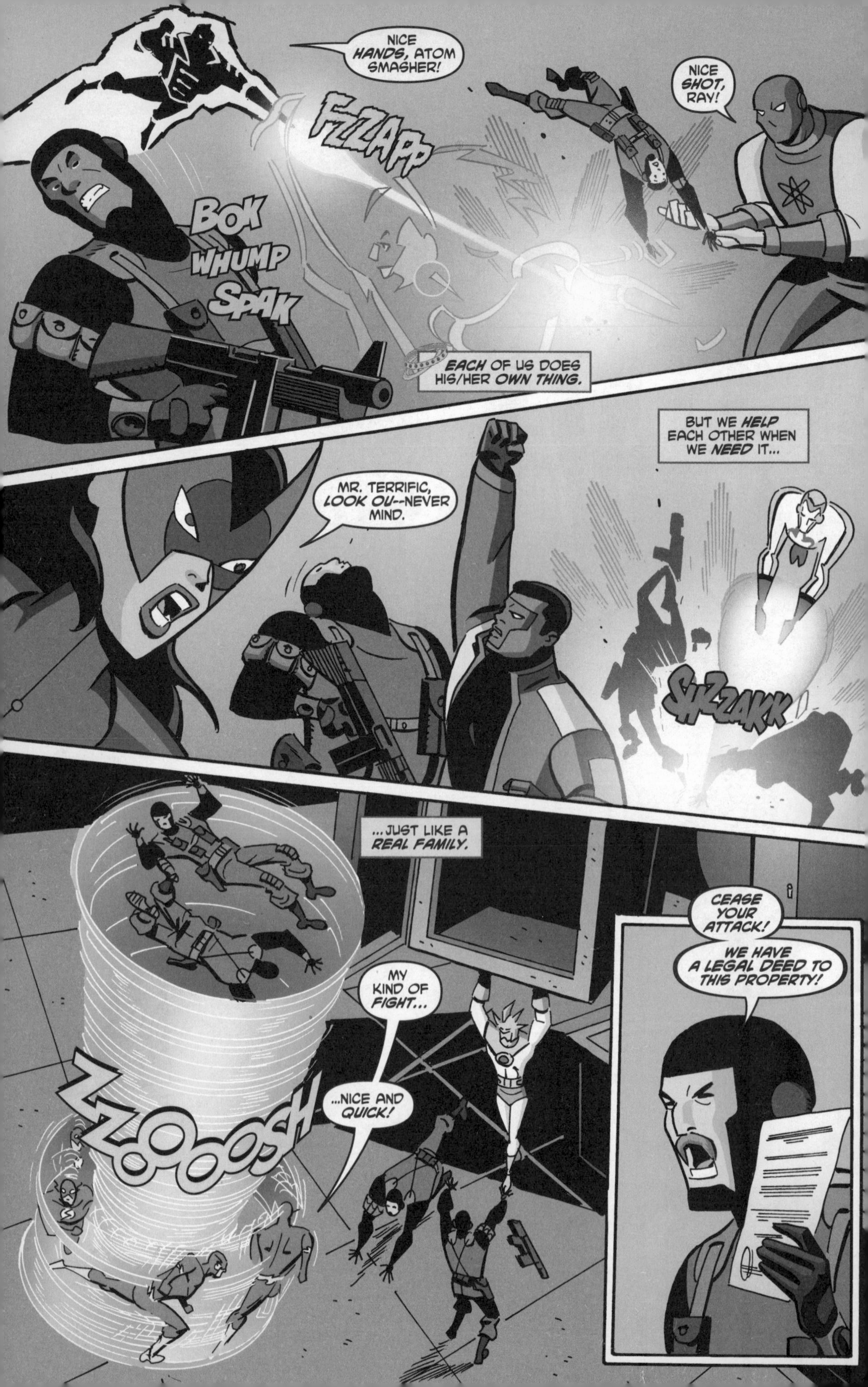
NICE HANDS, ATOM SMASHER!
FZZAPP
NICE SHOT, RAY!
BOK
WHUMP
SPAK
EACH OF US DOES HIS/HER OWN THING.
BUT WE HELP EACH OTHER WHEN WE NEED IT...
MR. TERRIFIC, LOOK OU--NEVER MIND.
SHZZAKK
...JUST LIKE A REAL FAMILY.
CEASE YOUR ATTACK!
WE HAVE A LEGAL DEED TO THIS PROPERTY!
MY KIND OF FIGHT...
...NICE AND QUICK!
ZZOOOOSH

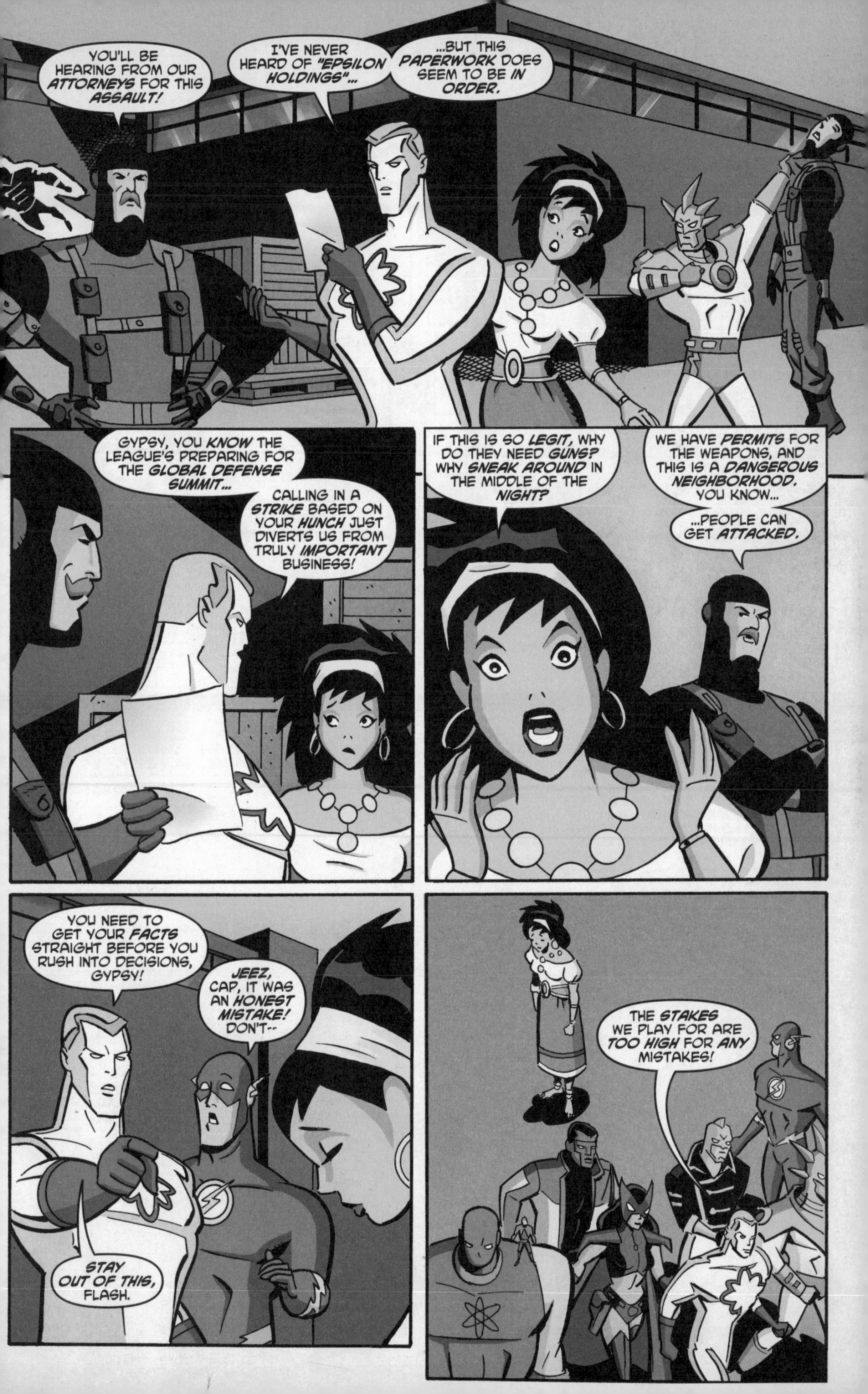
YOU'LL BE HEARING FROM OUR ATTORNEYS FOR THIS ASSAULT!
I'VE NEVER HEARD OF "EPSILON HOLDINGS"...
...BUT THIS PAPERWORK DOES SEEM TO BE IN ORDER.
GYPSY, YOU KNOW THE LEAGUE'S PREPARING FOR THE GLOBAL DEFENSE SUMMIT...
CALLING IN A STRIKE BASED ON YOUR HUNCH JUST DIVERTS US FROM TRULY IMPORTANT BUSINESS!
IF THIS IS SO LEGIT, WHY DO THEY NEED GUNS? WHY SNEAK AROUND IN THE MIDDLE OF THE NIGHT?
WE HAVE PERMITS FOR THE WEAPONS, AND THIS IS A DANGEROUS NEIGHBORHOOD. YOU KNOW...
...PEOPLE CAN GET ATTACKED.
YOU NEED TO GET YOUR FACTS STRAIGHT BEFORE YOU RUSH INTO DECISIONS, GYPSY!
JEEZ, CAP, IT WAS AN HONEST MISTAKE! DON'T--
STAY OUT OF THIS, FLASH.
THE STAKES WE PLAY FOR ARE TOO HIGH FOR ANY MISTAKES!

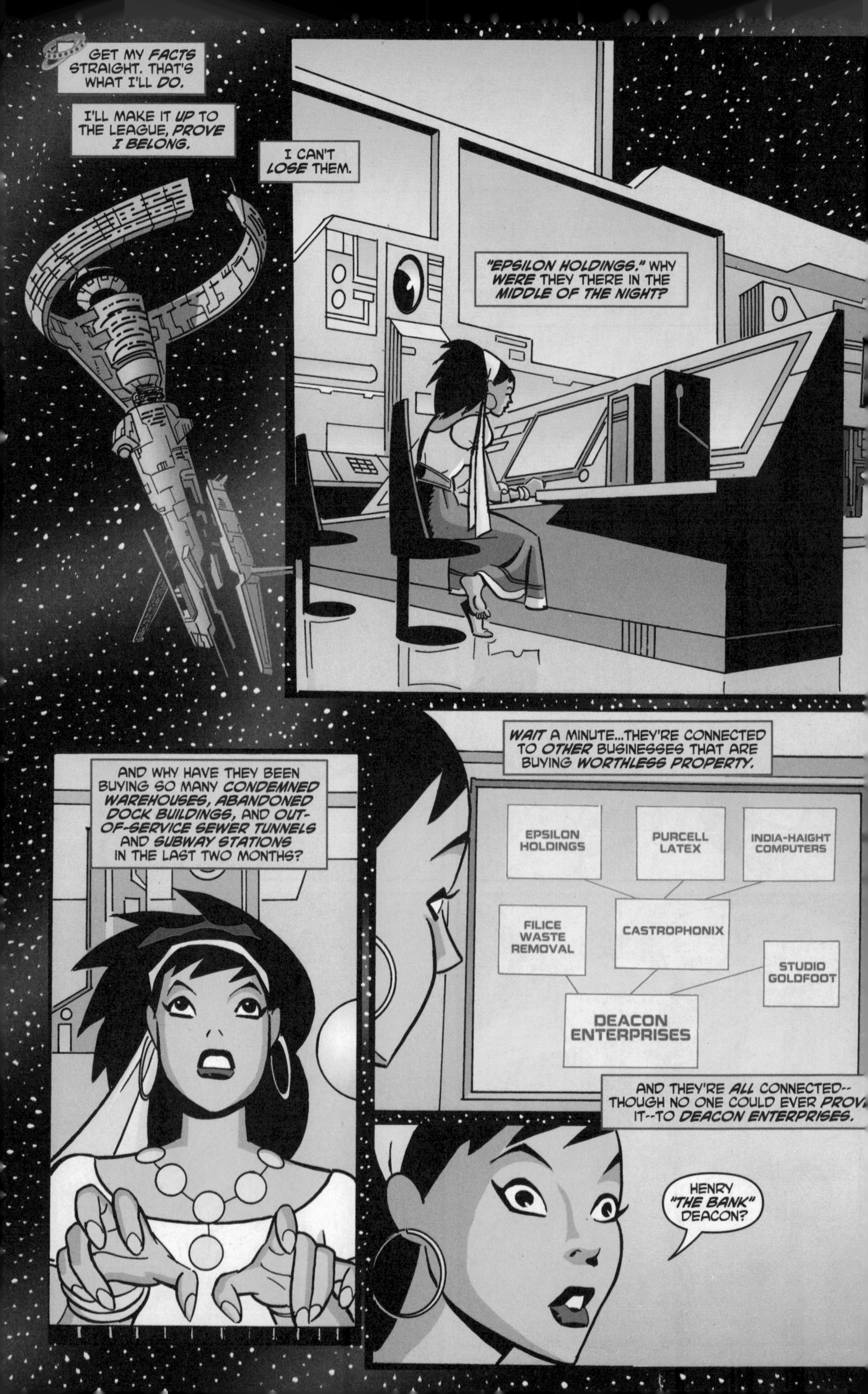

GET MY FACTS STRAIGHT. THAT'S WHAT I'LL DO.
I'LL MAKE IT UP TO THE LEAGUE, PROVE I BELONG.
I CAN'T LOSE THEM.
"EPSILON HOLDINGS." WHY WERE THEY THERE IN THE MIDDLE OF THE NIGHT?
AND WHY HAVE THEY BEEN BUYING SO MANY CONDEMNED WAREHOUSES, ABANDONED DOCK BUILDINGS, AND OUT-OF-SERVICE SEWER TUNNELS AND SUBWAY STATIONS IN THE LAST TWO MONTHS?
WAIT A MINUTE...THEY'RE CONNECTED TO OTHER BUSINESSES THAT ARE BUYING WORTHLESS PROPERTY.
EPSILON HOLDINGS
PURCELL LATEX
INDIA-HAIGHT COMPUTERS
FILICE WASTE REMOVAL
CASTROPHONIX
STUDIO GOLDFOOT
DEACON ENTERPRISES
AND THEY'RE ALL CONNECTED--THOUGH NO ONE COULD EVER PROV IT--TO DEACON ENTERPRISES.
HENRY "THE BANK" DEACON?

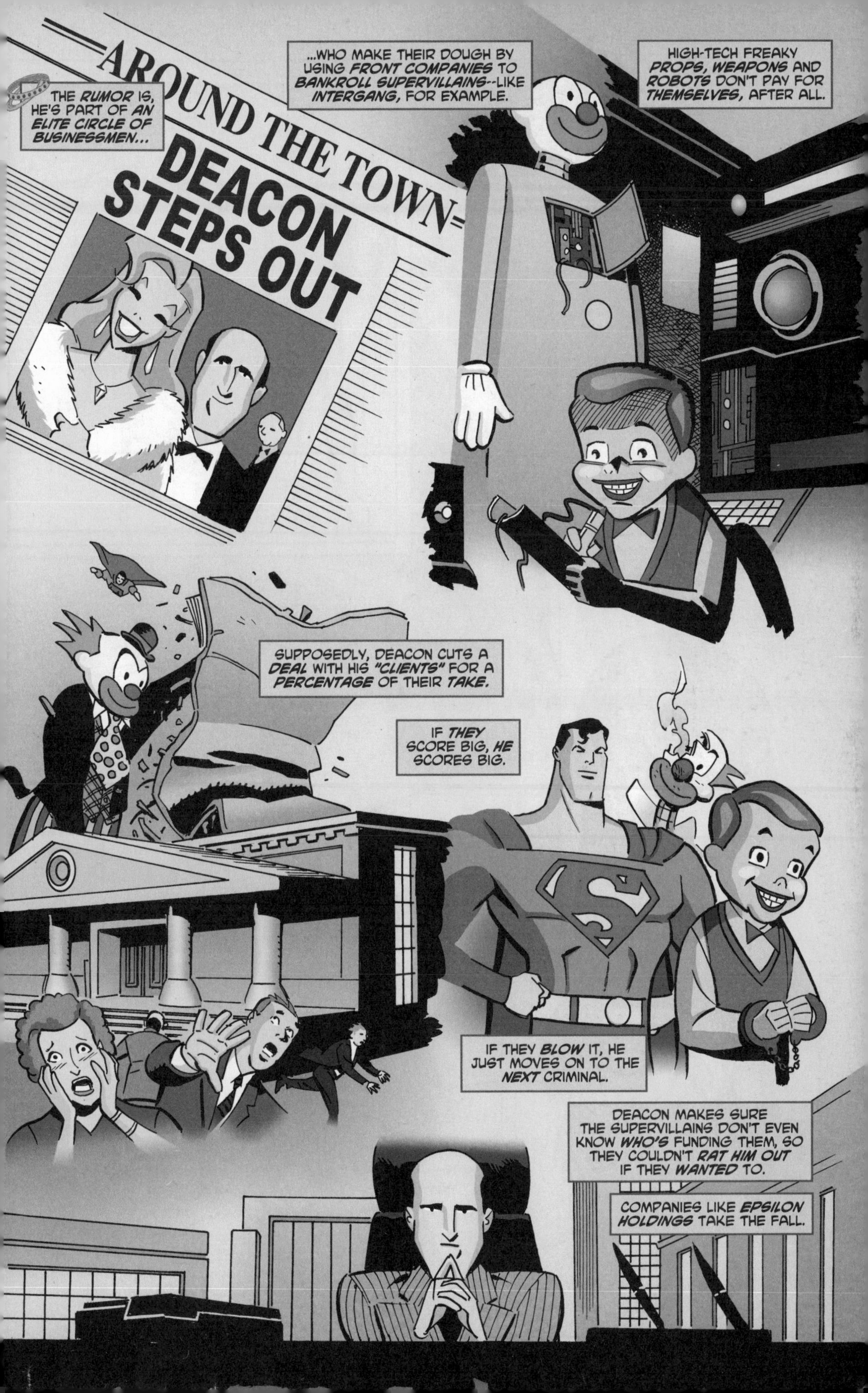
AROUND THE TOWN
THE RUMOR IS, HE'S PART OF AN ELITE CIRCLE OF BUSINESSMEN...
...WHO MAKE THEIR DOUGH BY USING FRONT COMPANIES TO BANKROLL SUPERVILLAINS--LIKE INTERGANG, FOR EXAMPLE.
HIGH-TECH FREAKY PROPS, WEAPONS AND ROBOTS DON'T PAY FOR THEMSELVES, AFTER ALL.
DEACON STEPS OUT
SUPPOSEDLY, DEACON CUTS A DEAL WITH HIS "CLIENTS" FOR A PERCENTAGE OF THEIR TAKE.
IF THEY SCORE BIG, HE SCORES BIG.
IF THEY BLOW IT, HE JUST MOVES ON TO THE NEXT CRIMINAL.
DEACON MAKES SURE THE SUPERVILLAINS DON'T EVEN KNOW WHO'S FUNDING THEM, SO THEY COULDN'T RAT HIM OUT IF THEY WANTED TO.
COMPANIES LIKE EPSILON HOLDINGS TAKE THE FALL.

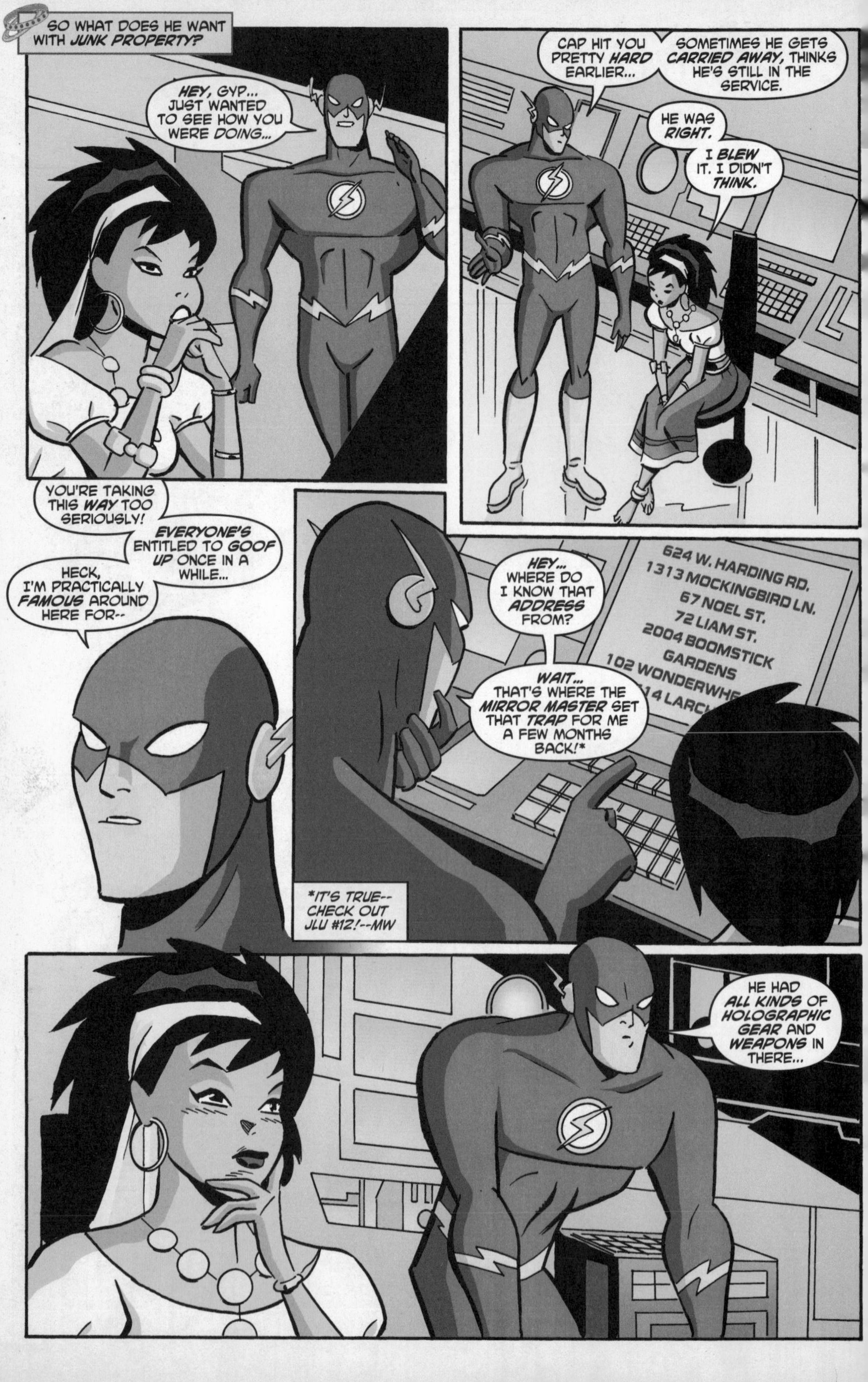
SO WHAT DOES HE WANT WITH JUNK PROPERTY?
HEY, GYP... JUST WANTED TO SEE HOW YOU WERE DOING...
CAP HIT YOU PRETTY HARD EARLIER...
SOMETIMES HE GETS CARRIED AWAY, THINKS HE'S STILL IN THE SERVICE.
HE WAS RIGHT.
I BLEW IT. I DIDN'T THINK.
YOU'RE TAKING THIS WAY TOO SERIOUSLY!
EVERYONE'S ENTITLED TO GOOF UP ONCE IN A WHILE...
HECK, I'M PRACTICALLY FAMOUS AROUND HERE FOR--
624 W. HARDING RD.
1313 MOCKINGBIRD LN.
67 NOEL ST.
72 LIAM ST.
2004 BOOMSTICK GARDENS
102 WONDERWHE
HEY... WHERE DO I KNOW THAT ADDRESS FROM?
WAIT... THAT'S WHERE THE MIRROR MASTER SET THAT TRAP FOR ME A FEW MONTHS BACK!*
*IT'S TRUE-- CHECK OUT JLU #12!--MW
HE HAD ALL KINDS OF HOLOGRAPHIC GEAR AND WEAPONS IN THERE...

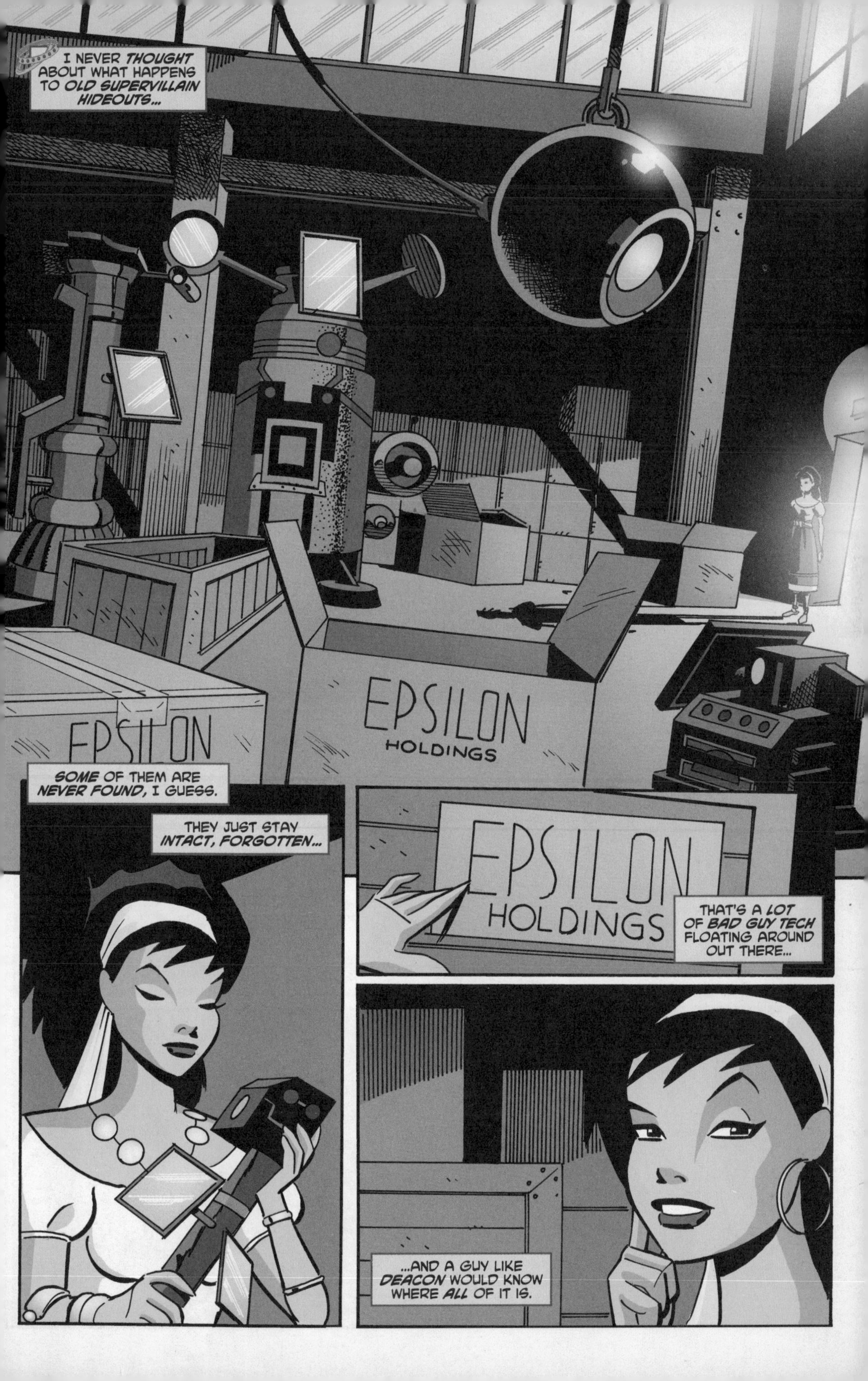

I NEVER THOUGHT ABOUT WHAT HAPPENS TO OLD SUPERVILLAIN HIDEOUTS...
EPSILON
EPSILON HOLDINGS
SOME OF THEM ARE NEVER FOUND, I GUESS.
THEY JUST STAY INTACT, FORGOTTEN...
EPSILON HOLDINGS
THAT'S A LOT OF BAD GUY TECH FLOATING AROUND OUT THERE...
...AND A GUY LIKE DEACON WOULD KNOW WHERE ALL OF IT IS.

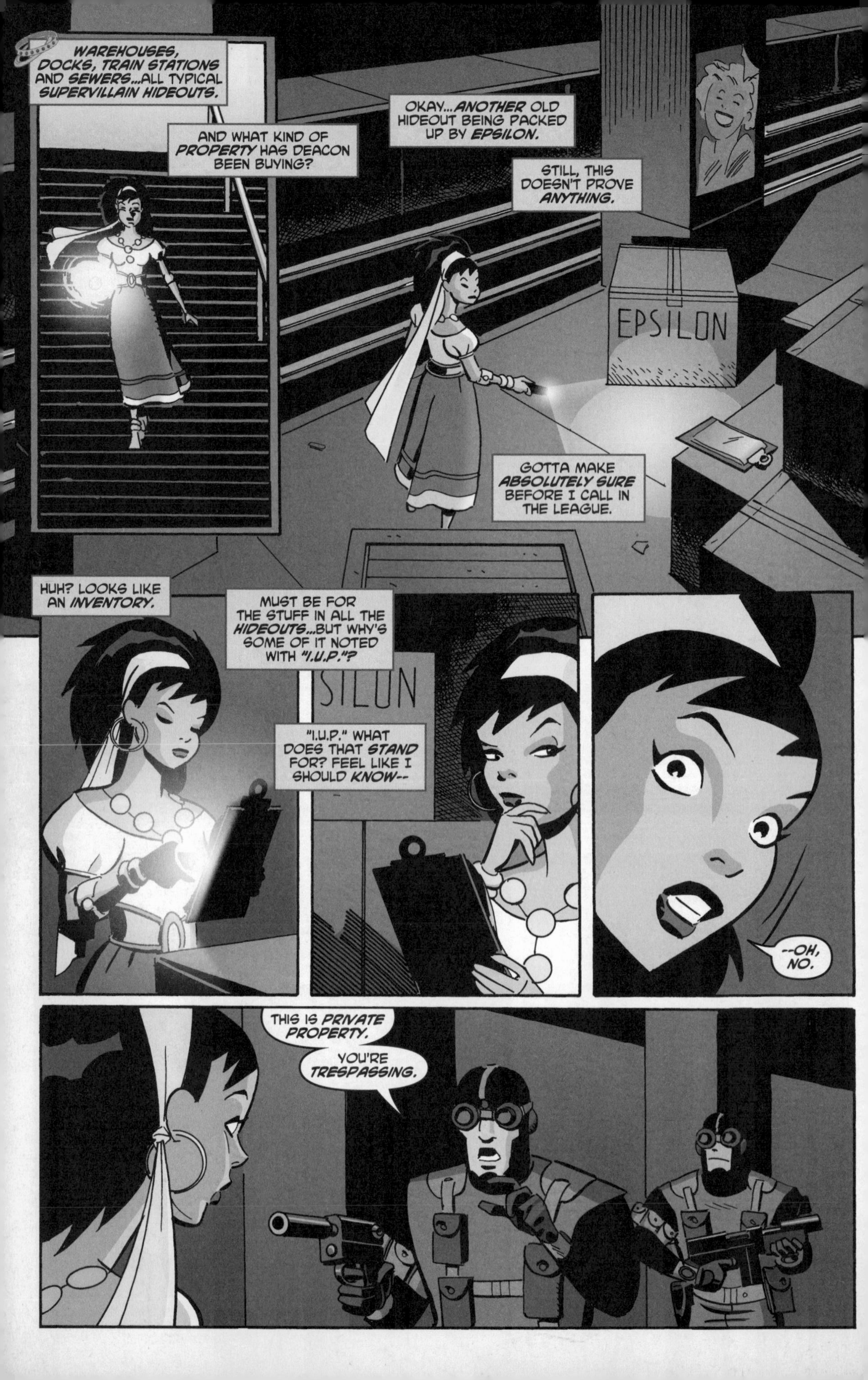
WAREHOUSES, DOCKS, TRAIN STATIONS AND SEWERS...ALL TYPICAL SUPERVILLAIN HIDEOUTS.
AND WHAT KIND OF PROPERTY HAS DEACON BEEN BUYING?
OKAY...ANOTHER OLD HIDEOUT BEING PACKED UP BY EPSILON.
STILL, THIS DOESN'T PROVE ANYTHING.
EPSILON
GOTTA MAKE ABSOLUTELY SURE BEFORE I CALL IN THE LEAGUE.
HUH? LOOKS LIKE AN INVENTORY.
MUST BE FOR THE STUFF IN ALL THE HIDEOUTS...BUT WHY'S SOME OF IT NOTED WITH "I.U.P."?
"I.U.P." WHAT DOES THAT STAND FOR? FEEL LIKE I SHOULD KNOW--
--OH, NO.
THIS IS PRIVATE PROPERTY.
YOU'RE TRESPASSING.

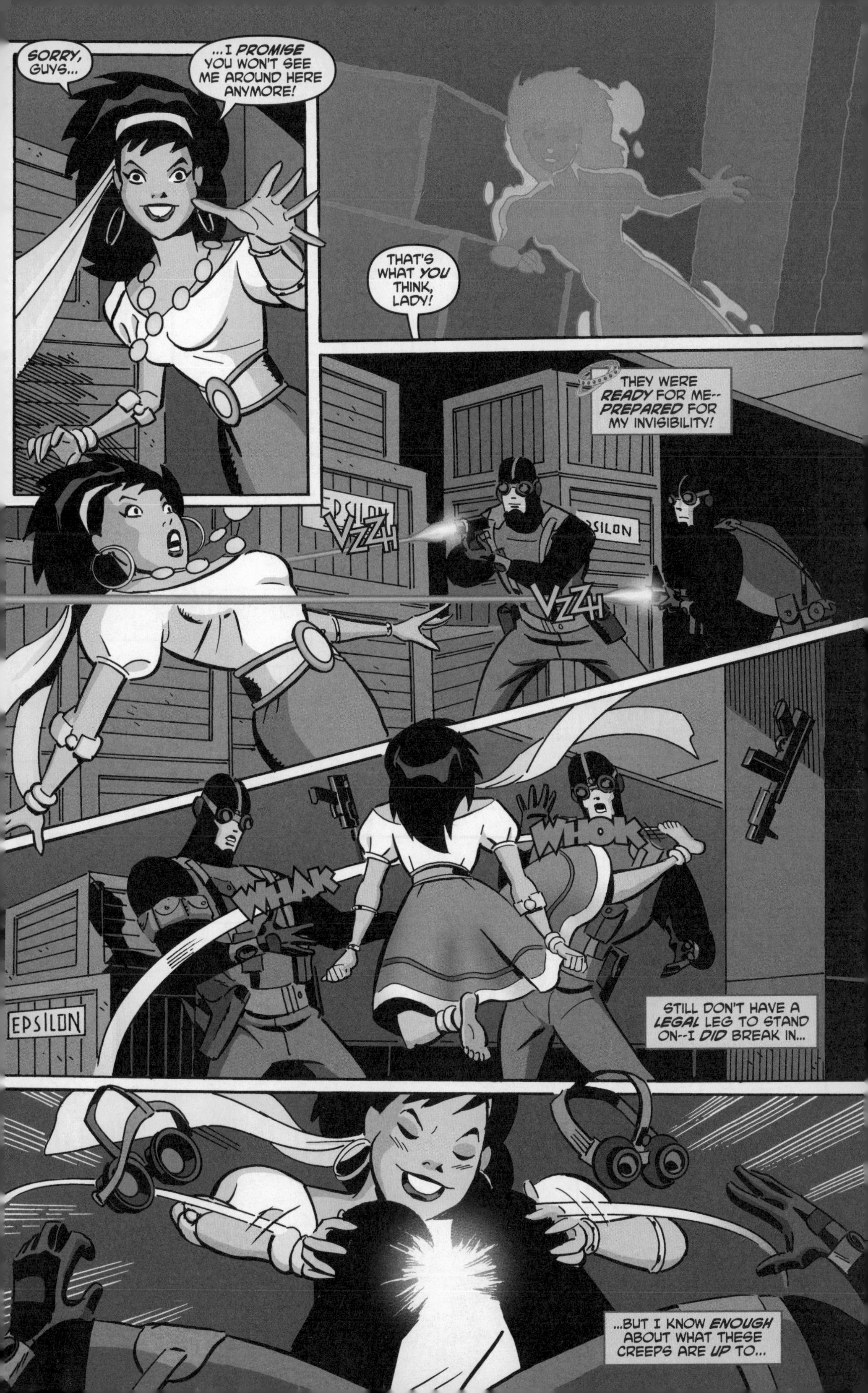
SORRY, GUYS...
...I PROMISE YOU WON'T SEE ME AROUND HERE ANYMORE!
THAT'S WHAT YOU THINK, LADY!
THEY WERE READY FOR ME-- PREPARED FOR MY INVISIBILITY!
EPSILON
VZZH
EPSILON
VZZH
WHOK
WHAK
EPSILON
STILL DON'T HAVE A LEGAL LEG TO STAND ON--I DID BREAK IN...
...BUT I KNOW ENOUGH ABOUT WHAT THESE CREEPS ARE UP TO...

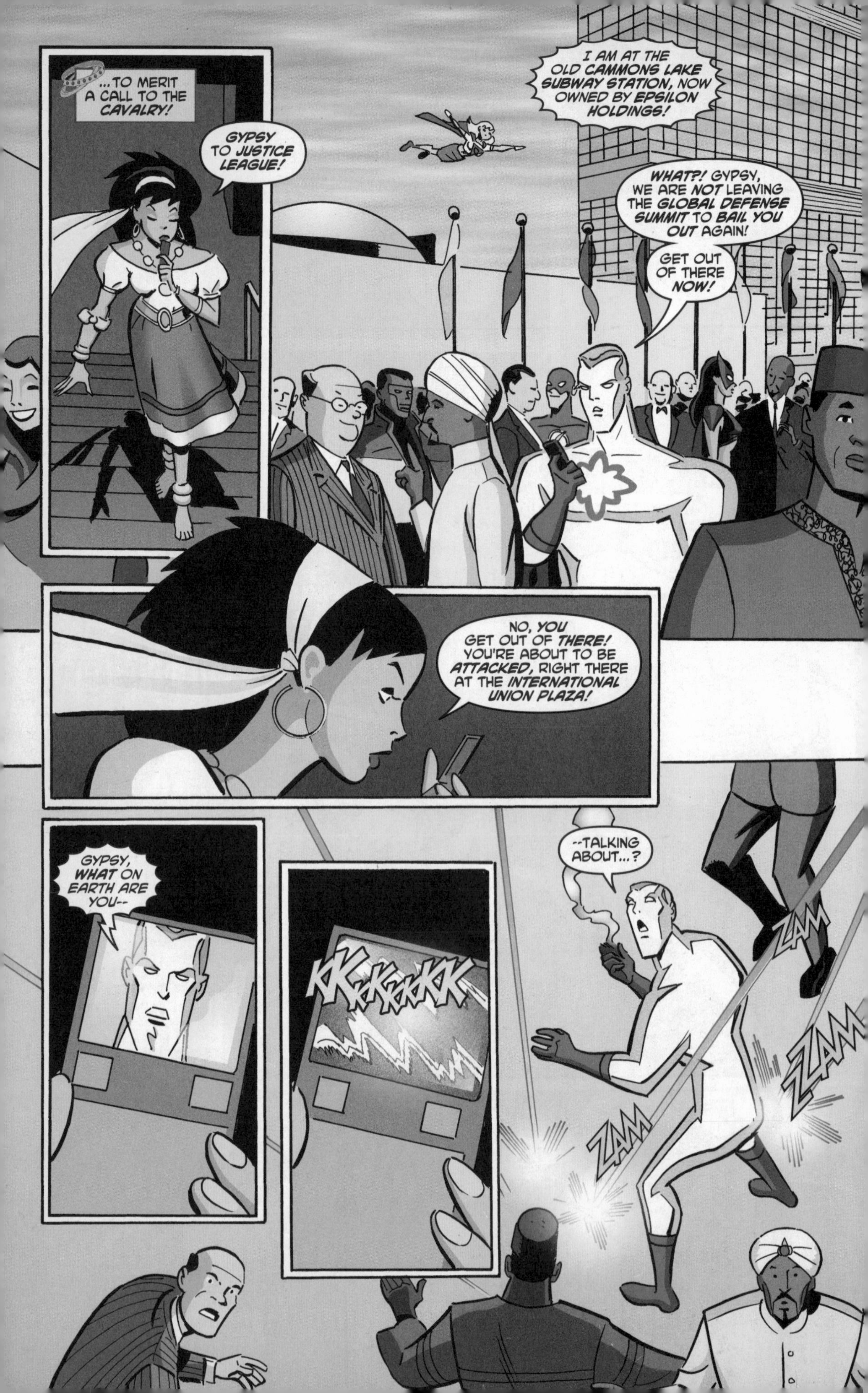
...TO MERIT A CALL TO THE CAVALRY!
GYPSY TO JUSTICE LEAGUE!
I AM AT THE OLD CAMMONS LAKE SUBWAY STATION, NOW OWNED BY EPSILON HOLDINGS!
WHAT?! GYPSY, WE ARE NOT LEAVING THE GLOBAL DEFENSE SUMMIT TO BAIL YOU OUT AGAIN!
GET OUT OF THERE NOW!
NO, YOU GET OUT OF THERE! YOU'RE ABOUT TO BE ATTACKED, RIGHT THERE AT THE INTERNATIONAL UNION PLAZA!
GYPSY, WHAT ON EARTH ARE YOU--
KKKKKKKK
--TALKING ABOUT...?
ZAM
ZAM
ZAM

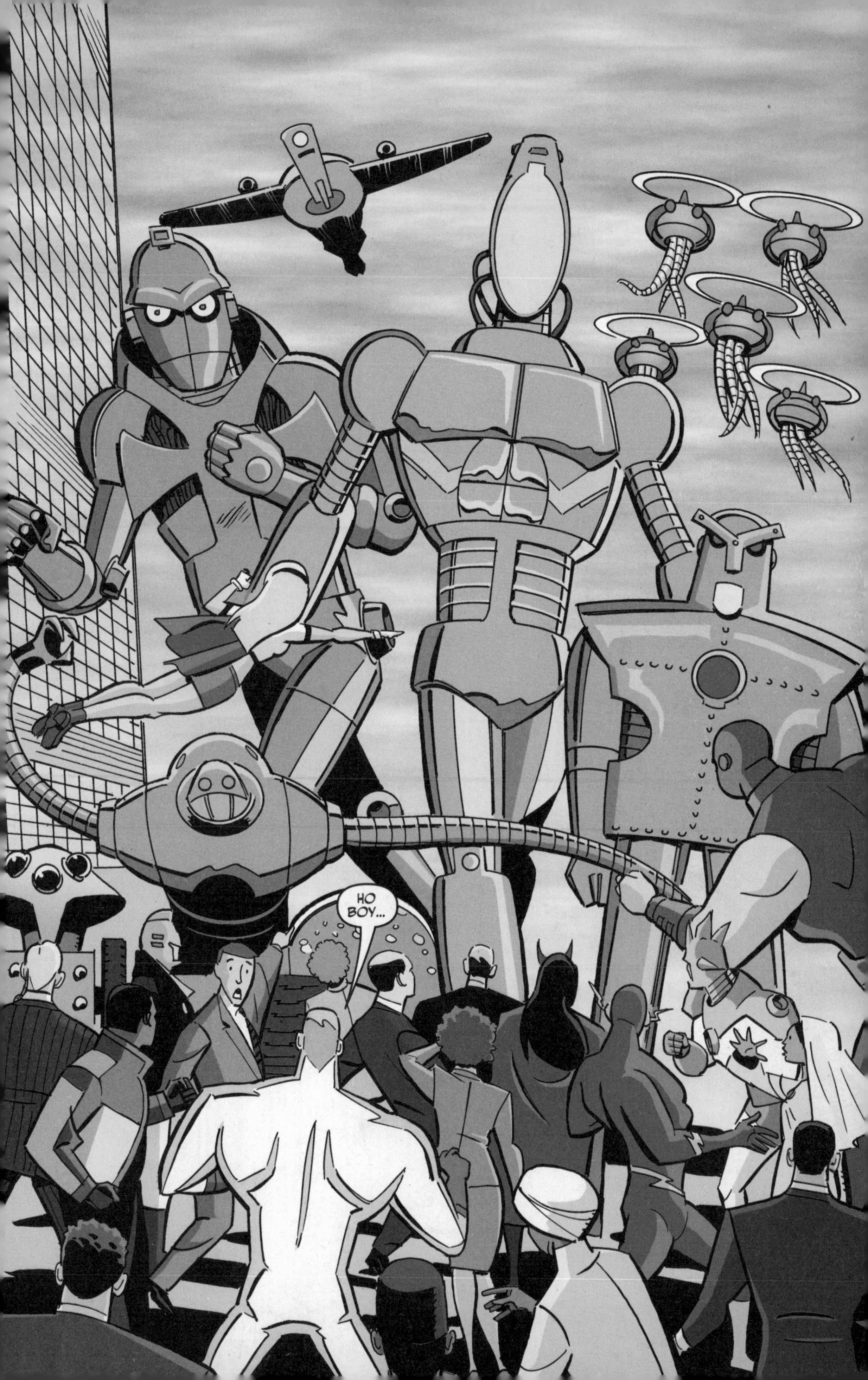
HO BOY...

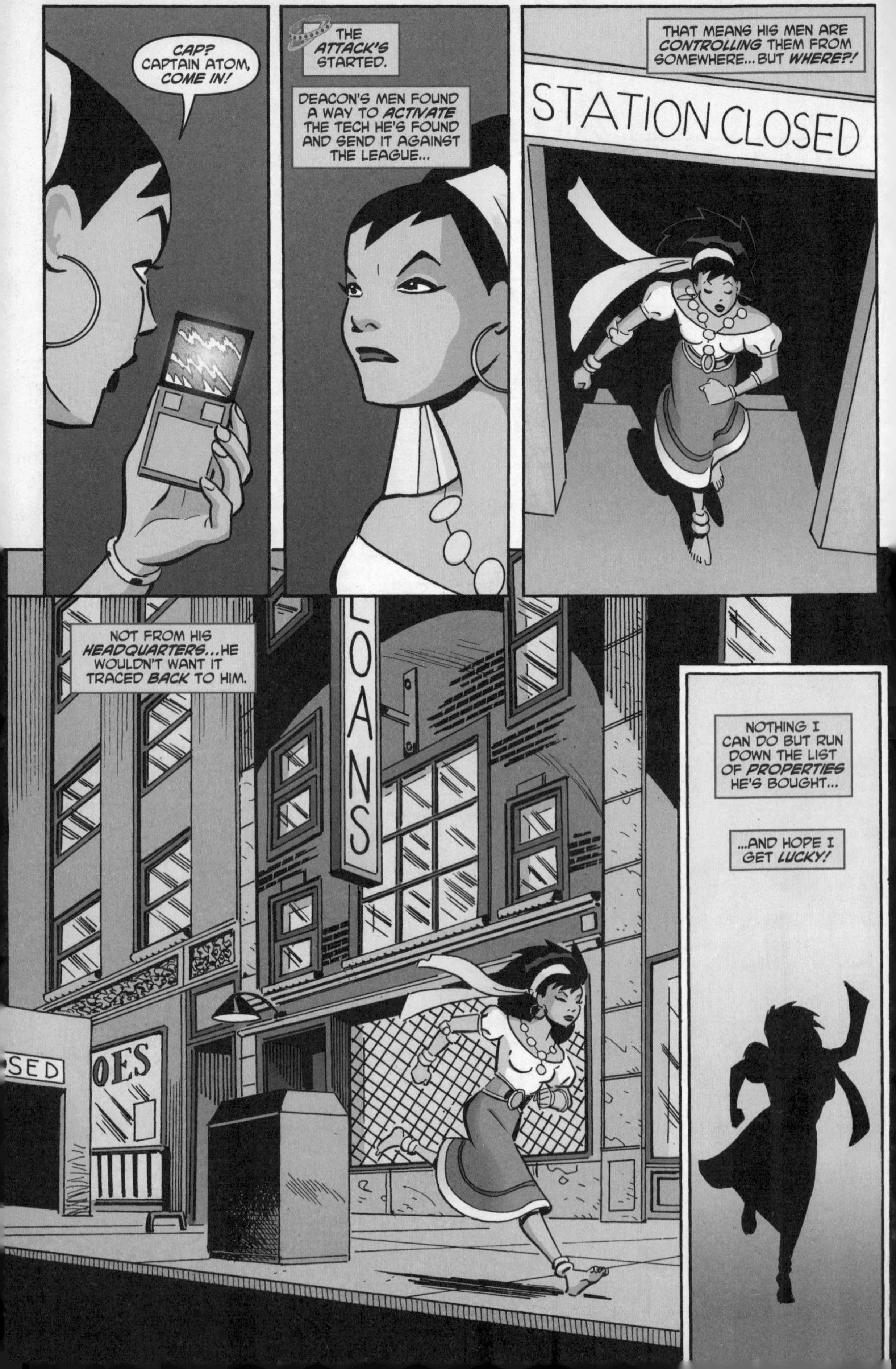
CAP? CAPTAIN ATOM, COME IN!
THE ATTACK'S STARTED.
DEACON'S MEN FOUND A WAY TO ACTIVATE THE TECH HE'S FOUND AND SEND IT AGAINST THE LEAGUE...
THAT MEANS HIS MEN ARE CONTROLLING THEM FROM SOMEWHERE... BUT WHERE?!
STATION CLOSED
NOT FROM HIS HEADQUARTERS...HE WOULDN'T WANT IT TRACED BACK TO HIM.
LOANS
SED
OES
NOTHING I CAN DO BUT RUN DOWN THE LIST OF PROPERTIES HE'S BOUGHT...
...AND HOPE I GET LUCKY!

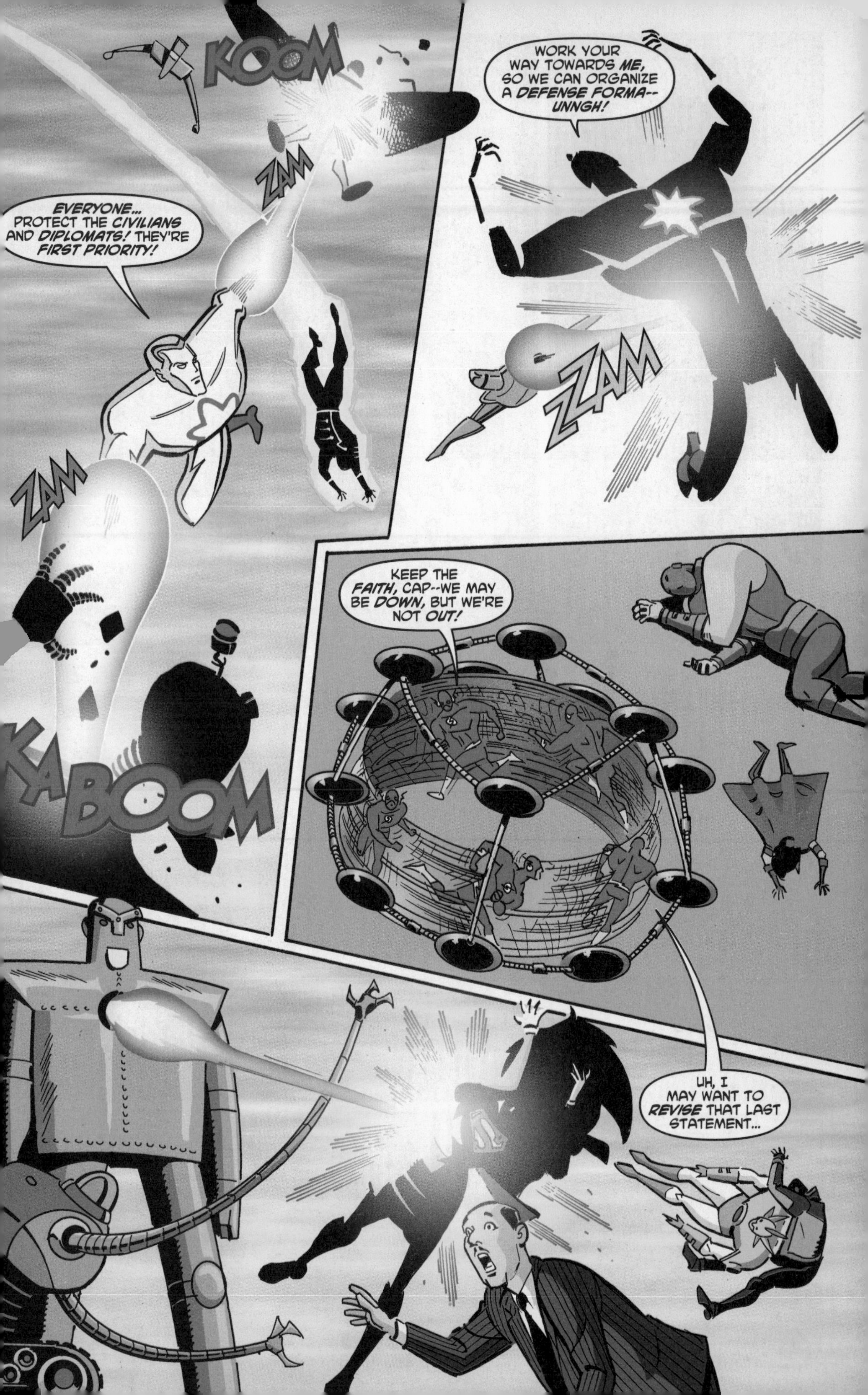
KOOM
ZAM
EVERYONE... PROTECT THE CIVILIANS AND DIPLOMATS! THEY'RE FIRST PRIORITY!
WORK YOUR WAY TOWARDS ME, SO WE CAN ORGANIZE A DEFENSE FORMA-- UNNGH!
ZAM
ZAM
KABOOM
KEEP THE FAITH, CAP--WE MAY BE DOWN, BUT WE'RE NOT OUT!
UH, I MAY WANT TO REVISE THAT LAST STATEMENT...

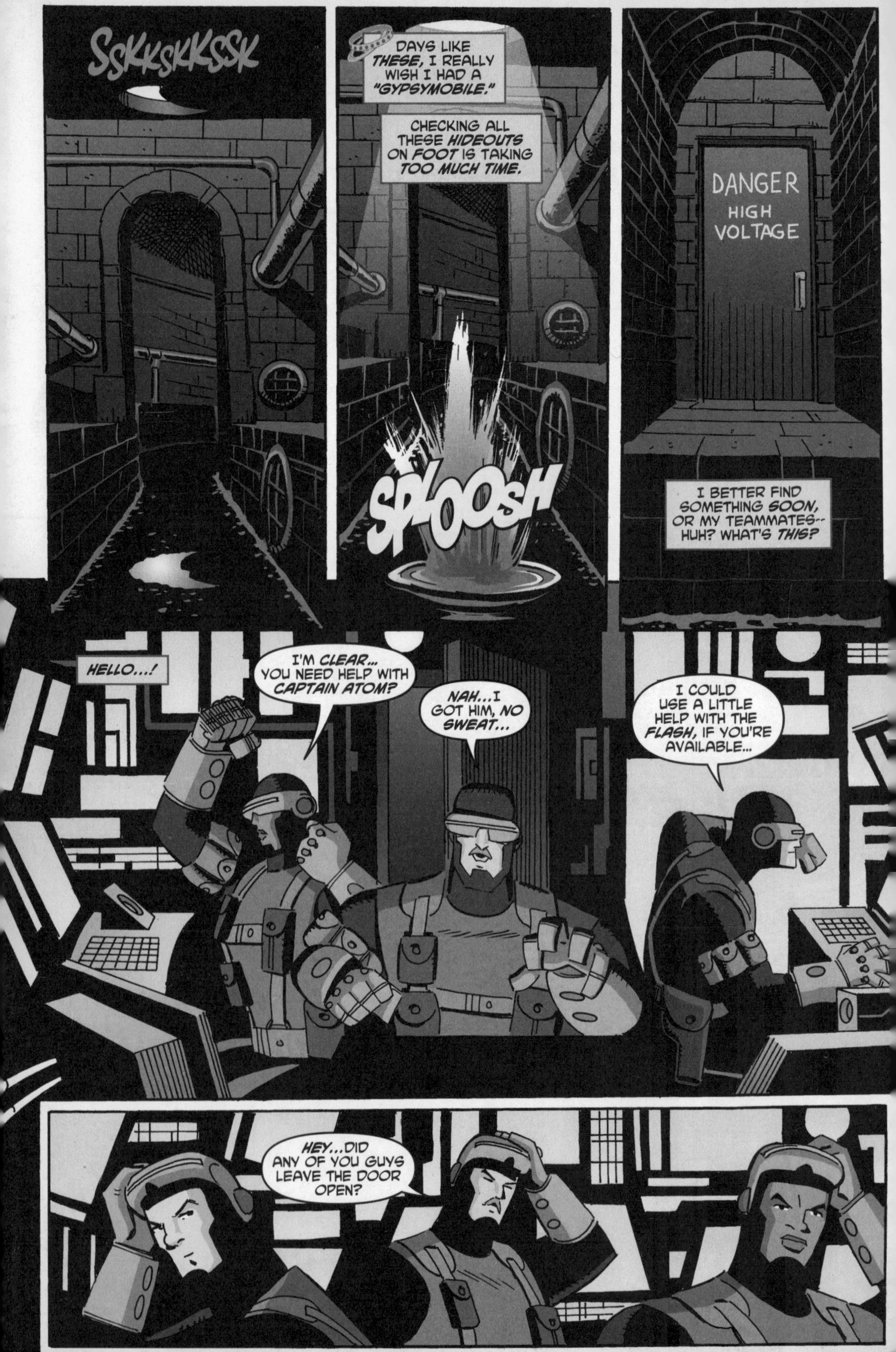
SSKKSKKSSK
DAYS LIKE *THESE*, I REALLY WISH I HAD A *"GYPSYMOBILE."*
CHECKING ALL THESE *HIDEOUTS* ON *FOOT* IS TAKING *TOO MUCH TIME.*
SPLOOSH
DANGER HIGH VOLTAGE
I BETTER FIND SOMETHING *SOON*, OR MY TEAMMATES-- HUH? WHAT'S *THIS?*
HELLO...!
I'M *CLEAR*... YOU NEED HELP WITH *CAPTAIN ATOM?*
NAH...I GOT HIM, *NO SWEAT*...
I COULD USE A LITTLE HELP WITH THE *FLASH*, IF YOU'RE AVAILABLE...
HEY...DID ANY OF YOU GUYS LEAVE THE DOOR OPEN?

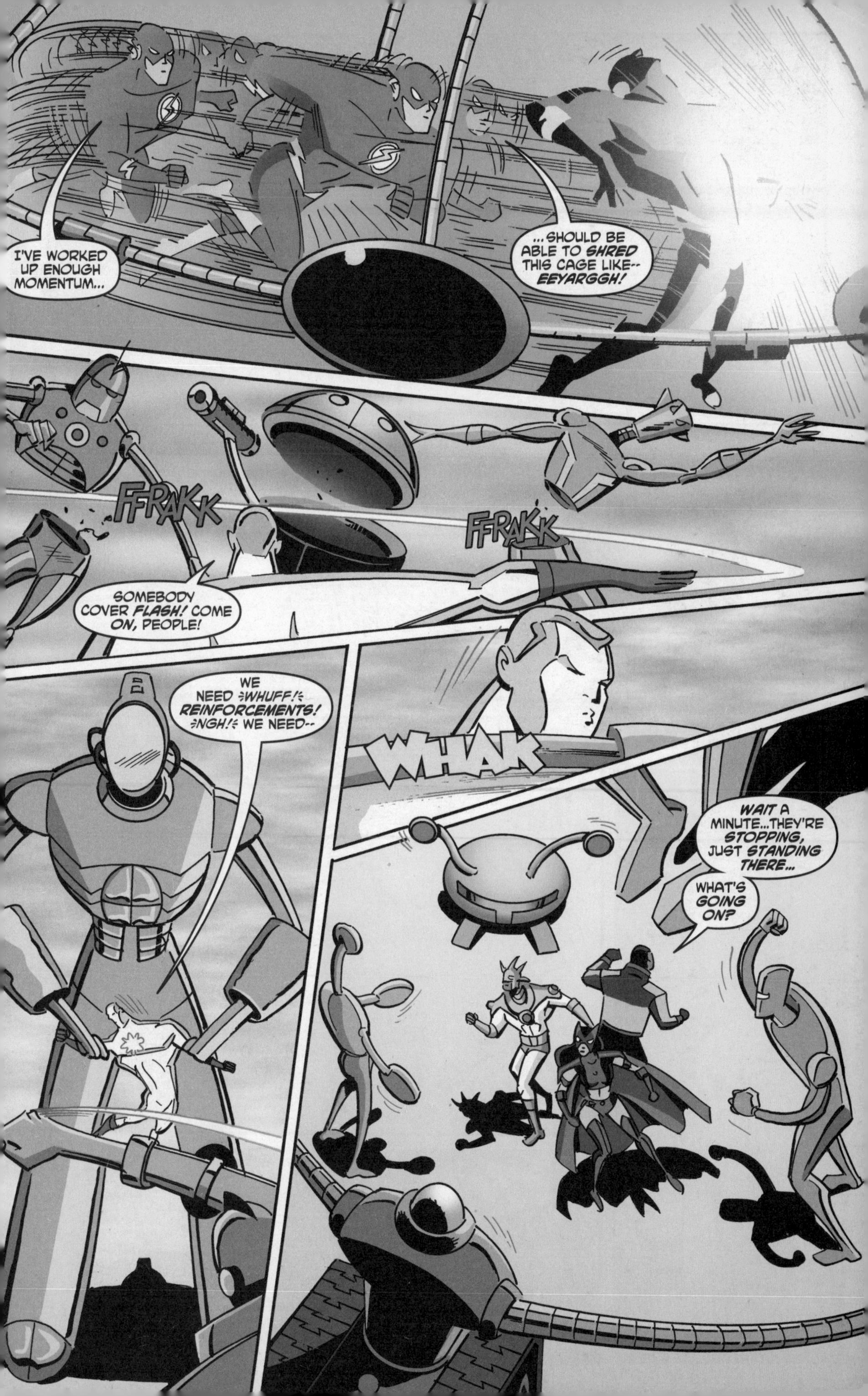
I'VE WORKED UP ENOUGH MOMENTUM...
...SHOULD BE ABLE TO SHRED THIS CAGE LIKE-- EEYARGGH!
FFRAKK
FFRAKK
SOMEBODY COVER FLASH! COME ON, PEOPLE!
WE NEED *WHUFF!* REINFORCEMENTS! *NGH!* WE NEED--
WHAK
WAIT A MINUTE...THEY'RE STOPPING, JUST STANDING THERE...
WHAT'S GOING ON?

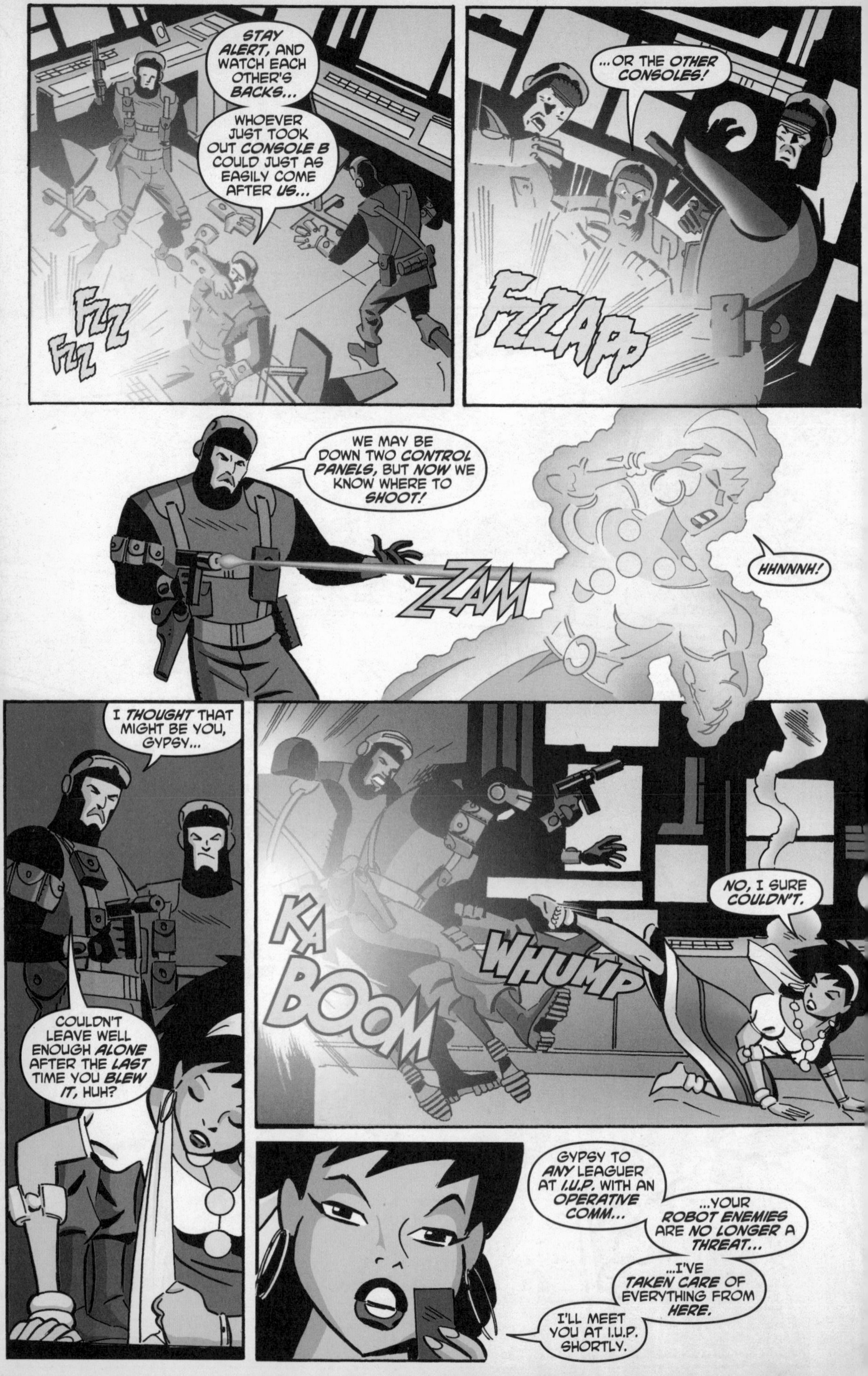
STAY ALERT, AND WATCH EACH OTHER'S BACKS...
WHOEVER JUST TOOK OUT CONSOLE B COULD JUST AS EASILY COME AFTER US...
FZZ FZZ
...OR THE OTHER CONSOLES!
FZZZAPP
WE MAY BE DOWN TWO CONTROL PANELS, BUT NOW WE KNOW WHERE TO SHOOT!
ZZAM
HHNNNH!
I THOUGHT THAT MIGHT BE YOU, GYPSY...
COULDN'T LEAVE WELL ENOUGH ALONE AFTER THE LAST TIME YOU BLEW IT, HUH?
KA BOOM
WHUMP
NO, I SURE COULDN'T.
GYPSY TO ANY LEAGUER AT I.U.P. WITH AN OPERATIVE COMM...
...YOUR ROBOT ENEMIES ARE NO LONGER A THREAT...
...I'VE TAKEN CARE OF EVERYTHING FROM HERE.
I'LL MEET YOU AT I.U.P. SHORTLY.

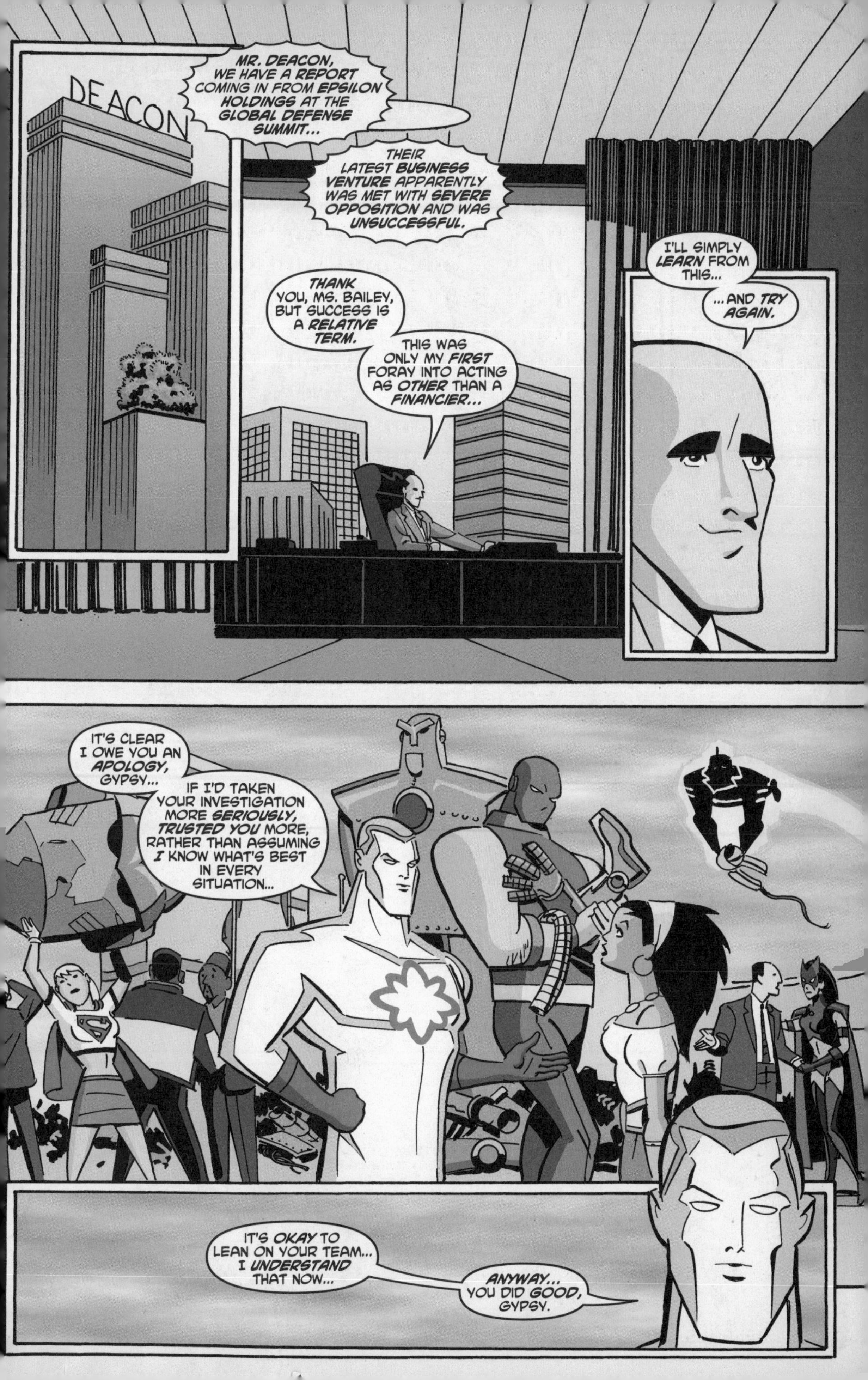
MR. DEACON, WE HAVE A REPORT COMING IN FROM EPSILON HOLDINGS AT THE GLOBAL DEFENSE SUMMIT...
THEIR LATEST BUSINESS VENTURE APPARENTLY WAS MET WITH SEVERE OPPOSITION AND WAS UNSUCCESSFUL.
THANK YOU, MS. BAILEY, BUT SUCCESS IS A RELATIVE TERM.
THIS WAS ONLY MY FIRST FORAY INTO ACTING AS OTHER THAN A FINANCIER...
I'LL SIMPLY LEARN FROM THIS...
...AND TRY AGAIN.
IT'S CLEAR I OWE YOU AN APOLOGY, GYPSY...
IF I'D TAKEN YOUR INVESTIGATION MORE SERIOUSLY, TRUSTED YOU MORE, RATHER THAN ASSUMING I KNOW WHAT'S BEST IN EVERY SITUATION...
IT'S OKAY TO LEAN ON YOUR TEAM... I UNDERSTAND THAT NOW...
ANYWAY... YOU DID GOOD, GYPSY.

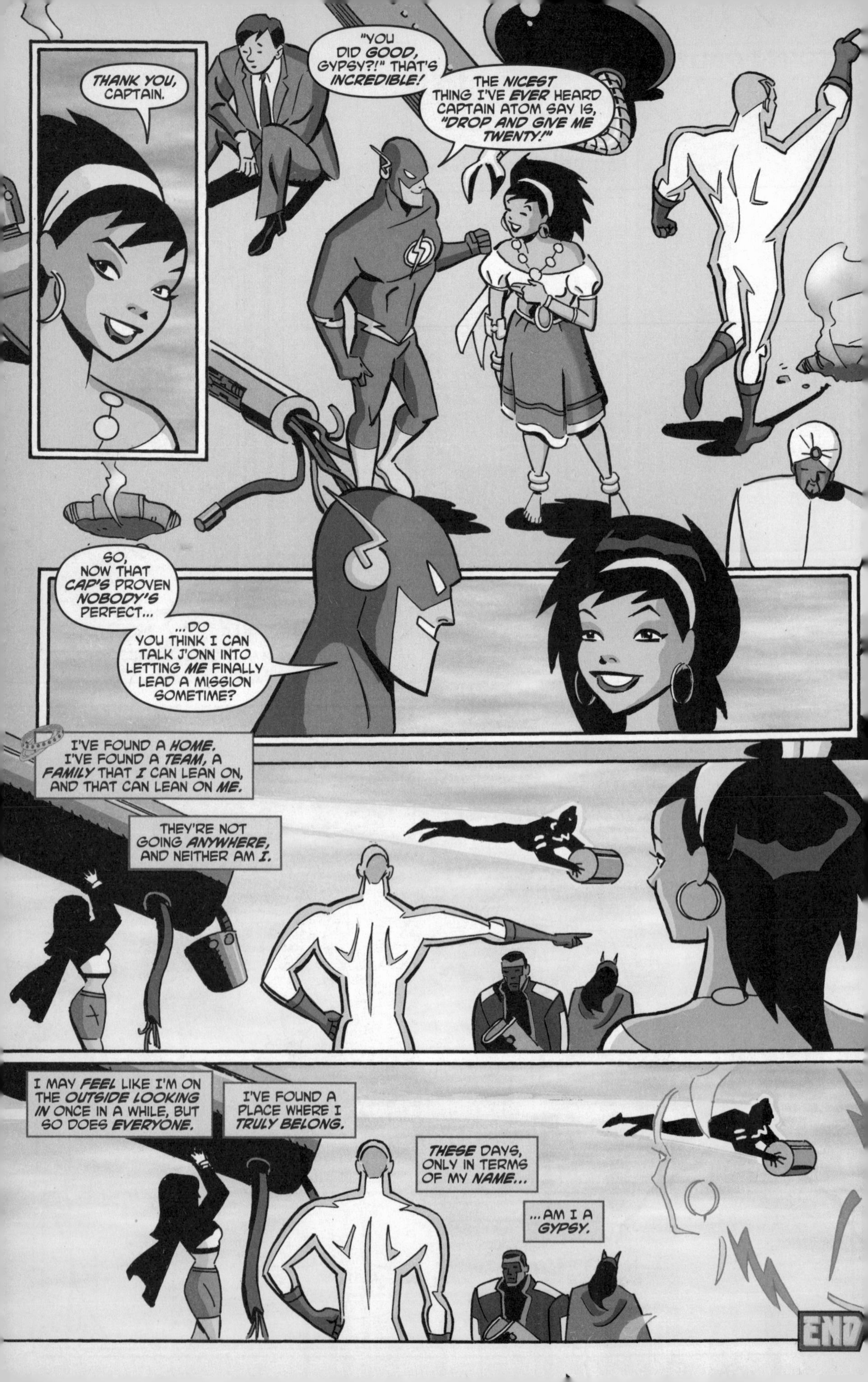
THANK YOU, CAPTAIN.
"YOU DID GOOD, GYPSY?!" THAT'S INCREDIBLE!
THE NICEST THING I'VE EVER HEARD CAPTAIN ATOM SAY IS, "DROP AND GIVE ME TWENTY!"
SO, NOW THAT CAP'S PROVEN NOBODY'S PERFECT...
...DO YOU THINK I CAN TALK J'ONN INTO LETTING ME FINALLY LEAD A MISSION SOMETIME?
I'VE FOUND A HOME. I'VE FOUND A TEAM, A FAMILY THAT I CAN LEAN ON, AND THAT CAN LEAN ON ME.
THEY'RE NOT GOING ANYWHERE, AND NEITHER AM I.
I MAY FEEL LIKE I'M ON THE OUTSIDE LOOKING IN ONCE IN A WHILE, BUT SO DOES EVERYONE.
I'VE FOUND A PLACE WHERE I TRULY BELONG.
THESE DAYS, ONLY IN TERMS OF MY NAME...
...AM I A GYPSY.
END

COVER GALLERY

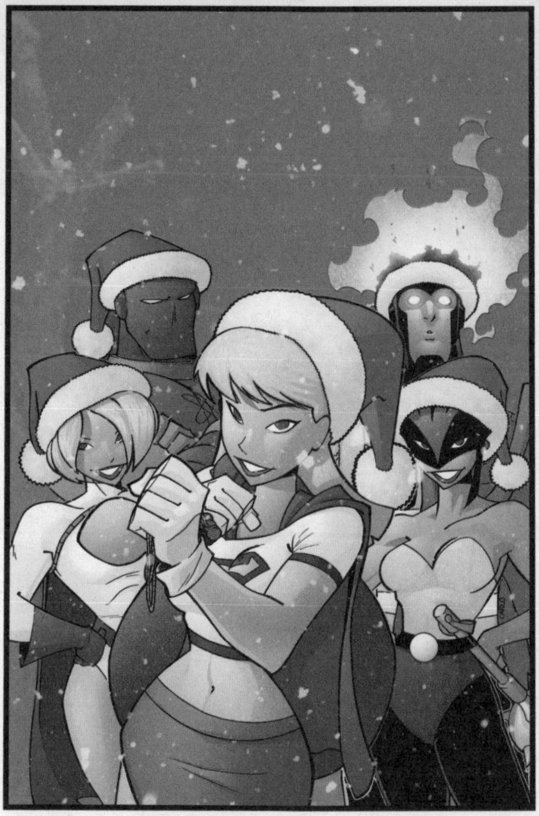

#16 ART BY **CARLO BARBERI** • COLOR BY **KANILA TRIPP**

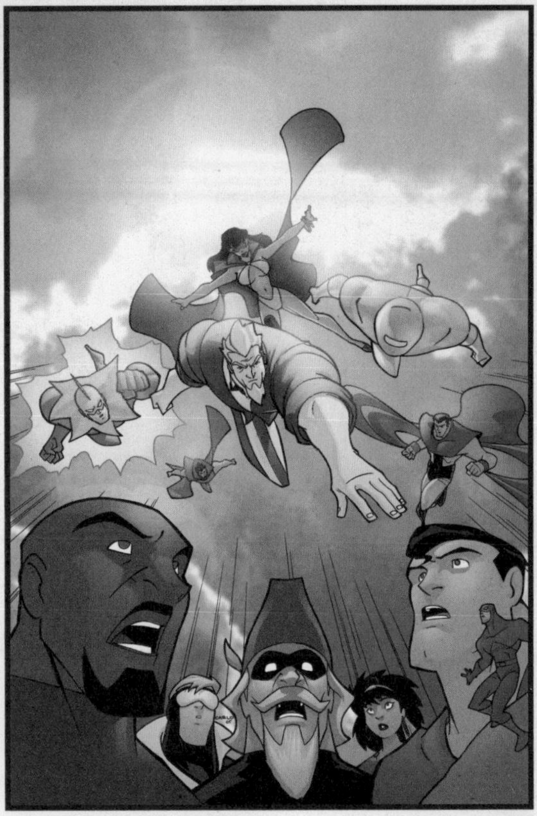

#17 ART BY **CARLO BARBERI** • COLOR BY **KANILA TRIPP**

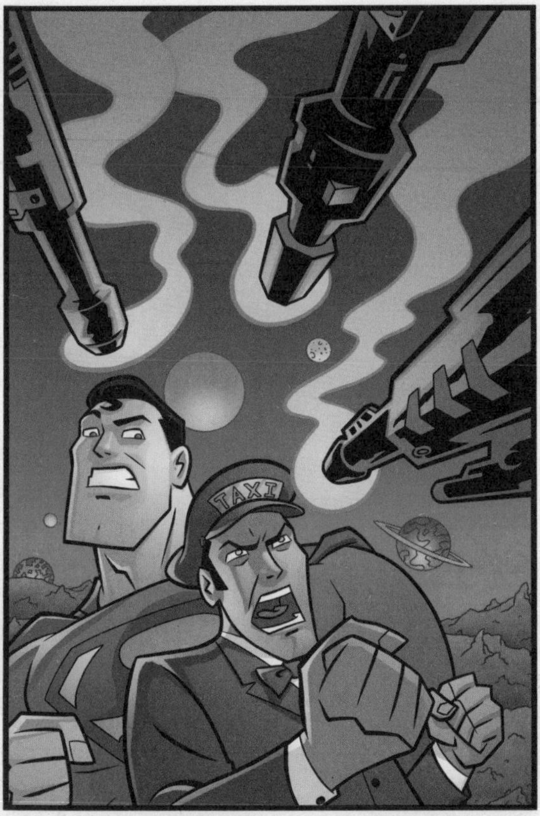
TAXI

#18 ART BY **ETHEN BEAVERS** • COLOR BY **KANILA TRIPP**

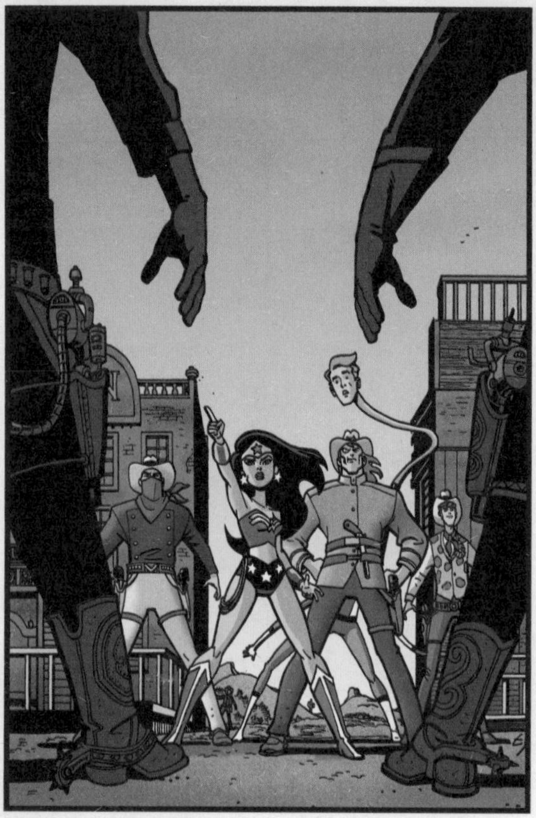

#19 ART BY **TY TEMPLETON** • COLOR BY **HEROIC AGE**

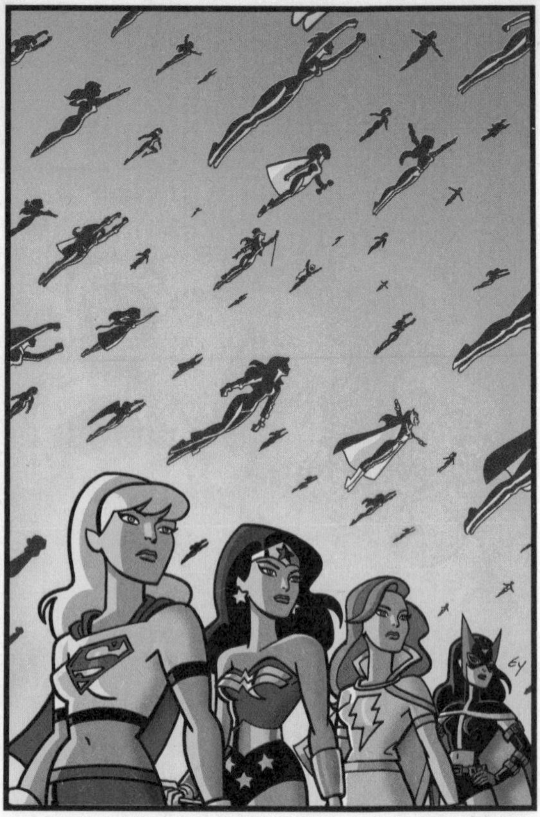

#20 ART BY **TY TEMPLETON** • COLOR BY **HEROIC AGE**

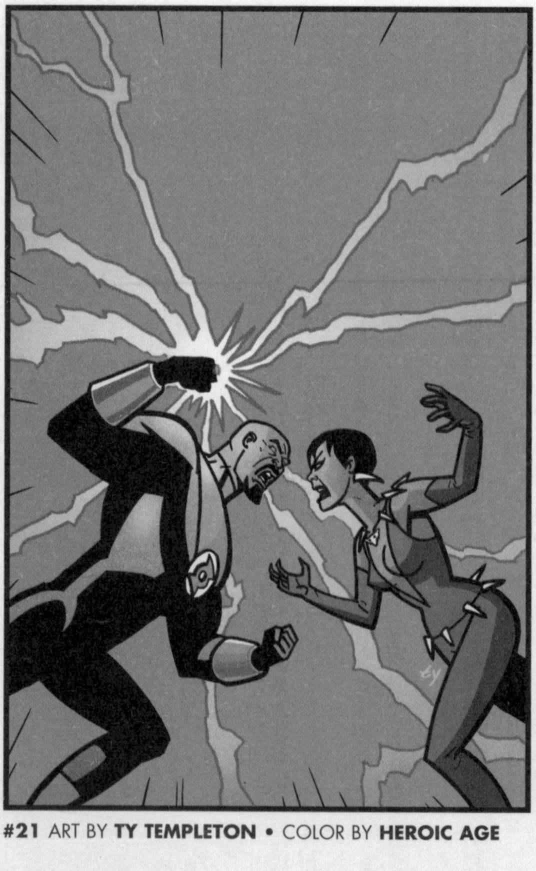

#21 ART BY **TY TEMPLETON** • COLOR BY **HEROIC AGE**

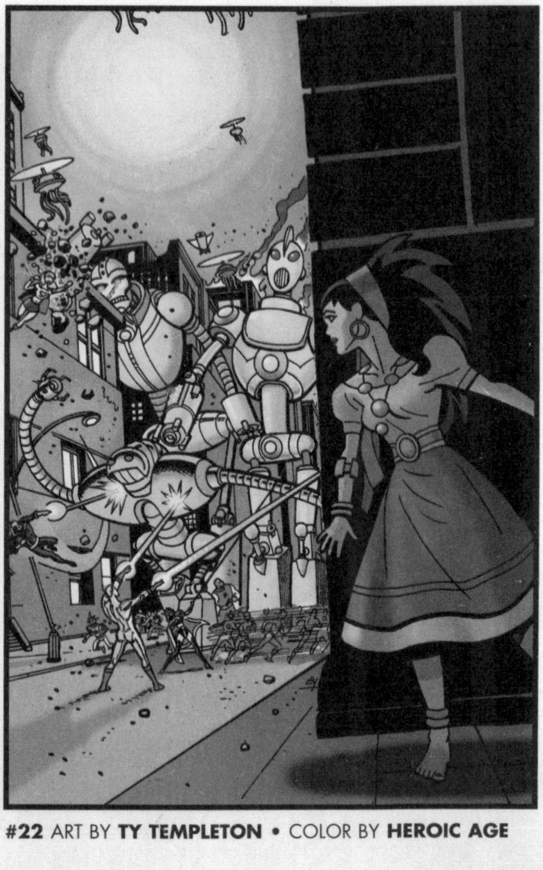

#22 ART BY **TY TEMPLETON** • COLOR BY **HEROIC AGE**